MINOR EPISODES
MAJOR RUCKUS

Also by Garry Thomas Morse

*After Jack**
*Death in Vancouver**
*Discovery Passages**
Streams
Transversals for Orpheus

*Available from Talonbooks

MINOR EPISODES MAJOR RUCKUS

EPISODES

GARRY THOMAS MORSE

TALONBOOKS

Talonbooks
P.O. BOX 2076
Vancouver, British Columbia, Canada V6B 3S3
www.talonbooks.com

Typeset in Garamond (and many more) and printed and bound in Canada
Printed on 50% post-consumer recycled paper
First printing: 2012

Cover figurines by Parastone
The Garden of Earthly Delights by Hieronymus Bosch
Cover design & typeset by Typesmith

The publisher gratefully acknowledges the financial support of the Canada Council
for the Arts; the Government of Canada through the Canada Book Fund; and the
Province of British Columbia through the British Columbia Arts Council and the
Book Publishing Tax Credit for our publishing activities.

LIBRARY AND ARCHIVES CANADA CATALOGUING IN PUBLICATION

Morse, Garry Thomas
    Minor episodes ; Major ruckus / Garry Thomas Morse.

(The chaos! Quincunx.)
Book contains Minor Episodes and Major Ruckus, two novels
    of five in the series The chaos! Quincunx.
Also issued in electronic format.
ISBN 978-0-88922-697-5

    I. Title. II. Title: Major ruckus. III. Series: Morse, Garry
Thomas. Chaos! Quincunx.

PS8626.O774M55 2012   C813'.6   C2012-903917-9

What reason I ask, a reason much vaster than the other, makes dreams seem so natural and allows me to welcome unreservedly a welter of episodes so strange that they would confound me now as I write? And yet I can believe my eyes, my ears; this great day has arrived, this beast has spoken.

— ANDRÉ BRETON

MINOR
EPISODES

I – A Billboard Wonder

Signor Minor throws on his dusky black coat and assumes all manner of diurnal potencies. The elevator senses an inception outside, and each of its round, numbered buttons lights up. He breathes through an arrangement of bare branches, and several cherry blossoms burst into bloom. A stately, bleary-eyed lady on her way to work faints at this spontaneous demonstration of halitosis in a frantic bluster of primavera. She has read nothing of this novelty (a new agent of growth) and upon the sweating pavement unconsciously ixnays her subscription to *Spore Monthly*. Erect and bedazzling upon triumphant volleys of cement, our hero hacks up a silk kerchief of finely wrought corpuscles. With her last gasp at the calendar, she admires this object and claws herself toward it while mulling over the wine material.

"O to waste away like that!"

Well past the gallantry of a lascivious wink, he bids her prone frame the most casual of farewell waves that germinates into a milling chorale of red-winged blackbirds – a warbling of two-fingered whistles at once shrill and sweet. Signor Minor is tickled by this oral performance, however beaky in nature, and conjures up a monotonous lineage of aquiline noses to fall in love with and casts them away in the same breath, scarcely halting to inhale the magnitude of his handiwork. An old country proverb upon the public lavatory wall instructs him to keep on the move and not to reflect more than necessary. As if he could! Meanwhile, he cuts a rather cutting figure, with an elevated degree of ostentation that grounds under every pebble that has fashioned the gravel diagonal across the square of green space where in the distant future, just after five in the afternoon, large dogs with full bladders will find release and condiment the grass or path with perfectly charming turds.

O remember that day in February what we found in the frozen hedge …

No, it is best to forget her shivering wrist and look of dismay. Signor Minor pauses in the middle of a dirty thought to doff his imaginary hat in accordance with a distant custom. A wizened man with wild teases of white hair is so absorbed scratching his scalp that he is caught off guard and succumbs to this passing display of invisible gentility, a thing that penetrates his chest and develops into a malignant case. The man slips from the bench and sprawls upon a green mound, inviting play and lying in wait for those inevitable hounds. A bold stripling slouches up to our lordly stroller and reveals a tear-soaked missive tucked into the front of his drawstring athletics. His request for a subsidy is met with a box to the lobes and a slap to the backside. Minor tears the letter open. The hospital of his birth and the street that has recorded his entire life are scheduled for annihilation in an unforgettable beam of positivism to be held next Wednesday.

"Ah, where am I to sign, my slippery little urchin?"

That is the reply of our noble. Let it be said it is best to dip every trace, even the very heel of our existence, into the deepest waters of oblivion.

"They once saved your life," backdrop the birds.

Signor Minor shrugs and laughs until a number of inert bodies rise and begin to dance, their hollow flesh full of chortling breath. Then they drop again. After all, what is to be done? Minor has sworn not to over-exercise his fabulous connexions.

"After all, there's my membership to consider. What's a few more bodies?"

Yet overcome by an instant of grandeur, he yearns to wear a yellow sash of warning and curl up into a fetal wrecking ball to achieve the utter destruction that is promised to him, before unfurling directly into a bran new development. He starts off in singsong talky talk, intending to express the difficulty of demolishing one's most vague memories but begins to giggle before he can complete a single note.

At that moment, a striking, oleaginous woman ambles out on a pair of crutches and prepares to do battle. Outraged, the cleaning union opens fire. Minor leaps to her rescue and deflects each rubber bullet with his coat of the finest tallest giraffe. She is overwhelmed by the suggestiveness of that waxy acacia smell and the promise of more graphic violence, and he carries her down to the basement on his back, where they toss aside a freshly baked tray of cafeteria loaves and start to copulate on a hard slab with an insatiable groan as the building tumbles down around them.

Afterward, she covers herself on the sickly green tiles in the same pose she observed an hour ago upon a copy of *Trampstamp* in the waiting room. Minor makes obscene gestures with his eyebrows and sets about sucking out a stray rubber bullet beneath the flickering lampreys and repairs her broken hip bones with the abundant dexterity of his airbrush, a trick he picked up on a demobilized submarine. And what flair he exhibits! Around the ruins of that demolished hospital, a bloodthirsty crowd is moved by his sheer celebrity and begins to weep and applaud.

"Yes, that *is* him. Yes, he plays one on the tube. See how he fills our blank faces with meaning! Tell us what to do! Should we rebuild?"

Yet the dust begins to settle and these scraps of remembrance scatter with seasonal gusts and blow chunks of brilliance that form a sunset. Minor gazes on while a Glaucous-winged gull abandons its flap and dives beak-first into a metaphorical sea of what have you. In imitation, a flame-ridden personally assistive mobility device beeps at this musical ruckus and a *V* of migratory feathers honks in a crowd-pleasing medley of acknowledgement and derision.

"What's this? Have you ever seen such a throaty hullaballoo?"

O at an opportune time, Minor wants to reach down deep to regurgitate the solitary name that still causes him to bristle and even shrivel up, but some rarely visited attic of his brain with erratically nailed plywood over the gables and windows is becoming self-aware and acting in a manner most contrary to this fizzing impulse. The name of what? This street this hospice this woman. Who so presumptively crosses me right in the middle of ripping open my plush costume? The singing birds flap in agitation and feed him a reminder in the form of an itch at the back of his neck. He scratches at the welt of the implant under his high collar.

"No wonder I can't remember anything. What was that again? And what is this itch that so bewitches me?"

Minor slaps his palm against the nape of his neck, and after a high-pitched squelching, he feels far better. His blood is now up. He curses vilely over the cacophony of gravel underfoot, mostly for the joy of hearing himself, scrunching out that grey music of imperfect spheres with gin-soak complaints for this city of medium size, a clumsy thing of stumbling right into, lacking the pedestrian ballet he craves – amorphous bodies moving to and fro in anticipatory awareness, led on by a lively choreography of no known origin. Here, without intervention, the elbow to head and knee and groin is required to remember we are alive.

"Are we merely a streaming sequence of cardboard cut-outs in distressed clothing?"

"Hey ... speak for yourself!"

Without warning, Signor Minor unclamps a giant canker sore of philosophy, an airborne bubble of astonishment. A buxom billboard features Bébé Lala smiling down from her position over the speeding intersection of Z-lines. She is content with her most recent incarnation because all of her carnality has been stripped away for the sake of those synthetic frailties draped about her pearish gems. Minor wants to scream up at her tanned, almost visible treasures about the secret of the ages and so on, but he knows so little of her true story, simply guessing those polished fingers have never known the monotony that went into trying to obtain a single chicken to feed a family for a week.

The urban ambassadors loom, fresh from turning over mothy blankets and gunnies on the gravel, with pockets full of the pawned, and hand Minor a ticket for playwalking, which is a form of not parking. And who can deny something roguish is in his step, a hint of merriment and mirth that could lead to mischief? It would only take a reading of the toxicity level to produce a fine mist that would tarnish the most beautiful yet vulnerable skin cells of Bébé. Minor fills his cheeks with Labour Party atmosphere. The ambassadors nod smugly.

"We're all the same, you and us in the end."

One of the urban ambassadors gives Minor a complimentary cuddle. The other lifts a boot to his bottom and sends him on his way. That ambassador is drinking something that spurts out of his nose as he kicks and snorts. Signor Minor glances back and takes down the man's number.

"When the revolution at last arrives, we shall see who is snorting what out of their nose. Adieu. And as for you, Bébé Lala, our business is unfinished."

In response, her tangled hair gives life to chirping black-capped chickadees, which contend for crumbs of chemical bread from another billboard and are thus enriched.

Minor concentrates, sprouting nostril hairs to such an extent that an entire subway of fingerless orchestral beggary sprouts up on the spot. Satisfied with his bluster, he storms off with a flap of black coat and finds an automatic photo booth, a heritage item in fact. Signor Minor closes the aquamarine curtain behind him and reaches for a sovereign with strange markings upon it. He deposits it in the slot and immediately comes face to face with a frowsy-maned lady who mostly furrows her brow and frowns, offering him continual ethical challenges. She is none other than the Automatic Muse. Her hypnotic voice tells him to quit his freelancing work and to do nothing rather than something. Already, within the presence of this perpetually flashing Muse, Minor feels dizzy.

"Breathe clear breathe pure breathe breathy ..."

Minor also feels dirty. He harbours secret caverns of lust inspired by each one of her old-fashioned whims and she senses even those. The Automatic Muse is sensible to everything and speaks in an enchanting runaround. Minor kneels and prays ardently in the tradition of ancient tympana and very drippy candelabra.

"O discongealment, wolf me down for I have been naughty among the ink blots. O come forth my comely and brute denizens and spermatize into this unforgettable event in the company of your fructifying offspring and fetal gleams to appease our lady, the Automatic Muse!"

Minor hears hollow laughter, followed by the dispensing of a fatal punch card. He fondles one of the holes in the wan yellow card and at last receives an intimate whisper.

"Please deposit another deposit ..."
"Mmm ... yes."
"There is an additional service charge."
"Oooooh ... there you go."
"Proceed, you man of many devices you!"
"Am I to consult and gentrify and provide a framework for the unfranchised?"
"Yes, but of course."

Minor exits the booth, imbued with renewed purpose and revived by a nip of homemade thinner. He sings into a peak of frenetic activity until bridge traffic halts before a barely imperceptible rise in obsolescence. A greeter on a leash faints and collapses in front of a dying company. Signor Minor nods his lone dreadlock in assent and the sun drops into the sea. He is agitated and could not have waited another minute for eventide, the hour of crazed yet tasteful congress. He walks along the shore, nurturing a sorrow too callous to comprehend.

"I have the latchkey to perception and the incalculable code to her flat."

He wonders at length, negotiating a shoal of rocks about the black water, where local rats nose the air. They have had more than a nibble at that memory. He hears the human voice at last, an object he admires in spite of his general distaste for those who carry it around with them, and is immediately moved into another transubstantiation. The rocks are moving and all buttocks are rutting with the monotony of the tide, rife with the smell of Spurious, the personal flesh spray of Bébé Lala. Minor listens to the *cabaletta* of echoes for a moment before clapping his hands. One of his handlers materializes and with white gloves gingerly tugs down his fly and parts the loose tails of his shirt. While he is relieving himself, orgiastic rocks lift up their variegated orifices and accept this sacrament. Alone as stones, they declare him a civic statue of a god they were manufactured to worship.

"If not Minor, who or what else? Rock on, rocks!"
"Well said, friend. You are my rock!"

With Vacancy signs in his eyes, Minor kicks up his heels and sends sand flying over every liquid crystal memory of her. She wore gangrene neon in a time when cruel was the new cool. Yet she only subsists as he subsists, upon this rather popular brand of memory-loss products. And the affair with Mémoire, or Mémé, had ended long ago, or so she had told him.

II – On the Bottom

Where is he in the days of slavery and vehicular soft service? Diving to the floor of a polluted coast, looking for takeout with a tri-pronged spork. Deciding resolutely upon an altered ego, he swipes the corporate entity of his domestic and then dives through fecal cries, taking on the solemnity of a coliform sect and all its obligatory rites in an exquisite dinner jacket composed entirely of wet dreams. To @tlantisity™ for the weekend.

"*¡Pronto!* Wipe your feet upon the very red carpet! Glosh glosh!"

The atmospherical release is enervating and the décor is a tasteful gazpacho. Toxic tiling to die for. The Automatic Muse gymnasts forth with waterbirthing thighs and lands upon the face of a calendrical hunk like no mortal could.

"Mistress," he ejaculates, sputters.

Cinemanically, she slaps him. He is hysterical. There are hordes of carrion birds winging in circles, wrathful portents, while she parades him about on the lead of his pocket protection. She decides to tie his tongue with her elegant sea rose. The fruits of the sea are ripe this season and discreetly tucked into wobbly still lifes. Meanwhile, our guest, in his most dapper and gelatinous ensemble to date, treads over lingering cuttlebones of beauty and shudders to feel old corsets of whalebone underfoot being ground into cosmetic ash with an unheard-of crumble.

"What do the bones represent?" gills a merchick after consulting her phrase book.

Our guest avoids her eelish advances and pushes a warm button repeatedly. She drops through the floor of the sea, unspeakably. In all the excitement, his slacks erode and disperse with the ebb tide. Only a snug pair of gazelle briefs remains, a mild surprise for Hortenzia. The old urban war-hero, in far dodgier days, even a few ticks earlier, might have convulsed even to consider such a predicament. But this is the illustrated man of means with no more than a visible twinkle of influence. Carnivorous starcod float out of his eyes and pursue the trapdoored merchick to the bitter end. There is nothing left but a lactiferous skeleton. He lifts his left wrist and the price of cufflinks plummets. Before the yawning double doors of the resort, a pair of cabana boys swoon and clunk heads together. Unluckily for them, the starcod are still ravenous. The newest incarnation of the Concierge snaps polished boots to attention, sending adrift a dozen climbers still in mid-lick. The jacket lacks epaulettes, yet the image of a waterlogged tattoo is more than enough. This can be none other than Special Operations Brigadier Minor in the guise of a suave doppelgängerbanger.

"Please enter your pinword."

"What, you can't identify my swagger of satisfaction, my personal catwalk? *Lebensmittelgeschaft*!"

He enunciates this secret nothing into the ear of the Concierge, who promptly bends over and reaches into the seabed, waggling furiously. A brazen sexaphone starts to tendril into their waxy ears.

"What unguent undulations! And would you look at that view!"

Two old biddies are crushed by a sinking atomic sunset, although S.O.B. Minor shrugs it off with such delicacy that the entire room prostrates itself. The inexperienced hold themselves. A pair of pink cleaning gloves starts to plunk keys dissonantly while a few visiting serpents retire to their suites in disgust.

"You must remember this / a hiss is just a hiss / a lie is just a lie / the fundamental poor apply / as crime goes by ..."

A wily plant posing as the hydrophobic tycoon Delt Milton takes this tune as his cue to dog-paddle through a plate of glass. The Concierge gives the incessantly plunking gloves a swift kick.

"Best not to let on about our little protectionist racket. Another song like that and you are out on your ear!"

He returns to a series of meditative bows. The S.O.B. laughs gallantly.

"The gloves are new, you must pardon them. And how are you keeping? Still in black market groceries?"

S.O.B. Minor stares into the face of the Concierge for a full moment of untold and ambiguous longing. He did not hear what he thought he did. A gaffer adjusts his collar and an exceptional best boy applauds with reservation, an obvious sign of breeding. In the sequel, he will be messaged that Minor is his bloodfather, a rumour he already senses within the wild unicorn of his loins. At last, Minor breaks off his stare and eases back against a moist tunnel and titters. The Concierge is reminded of encounters with trolling bureaucrats on the pull a little behind Saucy Street. The closest prompter points to a card and silently mouths the felt writing upon it. Minor waves off another plug for hot sauce enumerating its usages.

"The third this week, muchas gracias. ¡No!"

A production assistant swallows the entire bottle and spontaneously combusts. There is a brief huzzah, although the rise in ratings calms the staff and placates the audience as they are rewarded by a ringing bell and lengthy strings of trout and tripe and sheep intestine that tumble from the ceiling.

"I caught an eye," screams a plucky little urchin.

In fact, the boy drops his emergency pistol, overpowered by his zeal for constant attention. There is a shared gasp before he is smothered by falling balloons.

"And are you ready to order?" coughs the Concierge.
"I want this ... no, *that* one."
"An excellent selection, sir."

Minor reaches for a choice rump of a stellar colour and rapidly squeezes three times for luck and takes a more than perfunctory whiff. A fiddler with a missing glass eye and yolky fangs from a new drugstore novel has been shadowing these happenstances, waiting for his opportunity to bite into wherever the action is. The way he moves his arm and the crook of his neck, there is a hint of romance, a musky undercurrent. Minor stares, indubitably thrilled by the furtive promise of that ossified socket. He signals for the fiddler to be sent a glass of the finest acid on hand. There is a suspenseful instance as a new girl delays, uncertain whether to pour in the kahlua or brandy or free-trade coffee first. She had a drink of her own, didn't she? But her übergregarious cohort gives her a sensitive fondle before downing the works. As he evaporates, the fiddler grins and the new girl smiles inwardly.

"If tonight goes well, I'll be promoted. More pay, more flexibility, more laughs. I am the perfect product!"

Meanwhile, the chosen ass pulsates steadily in tempo with the throb of the feed. It is so beautiful to behold that everyone is overwhelmed by a desire to taste its sublime flesh, for the sake of reputation alone. Some visitors have journeyed umpteen thousand leagues just to elbow through and get a peek. Something to scribble home about. They are dying of it in fact, even those older than the sea. One of the dry-goods carriers nearly drops his tray.

"Magnifique! Ce sont de belles fesses!"

Fresh rumours circulate after the arrival of more aquawheels. Piles of the latest rag called *Feuilleton* are launched, positively bulbous with this sighting of the bulging ass and Minor together (at last!).

"Say, wasn't that the stand-in ass in *The Watermelon Roller*? Or am I thinking of the shower scene in *Afterschool Species*?"
"That is a naked bottom," confirms another choirboy, breaking his voice into a thrillion pieces.
"And let it be considered that an ass is, after all, no more than an ass."

"Hah, the bard could not have penned it better himself, my precious young scalawag. Now go and goose the butcher in the next block and this mint-condition farting is yours."

But a once well-matched widow among a number of who's who ladies-who-lunch limply raises her socialite finger.

"Sold! To the philanthropish scene-stealer in the front row, the widow of the late Derrick Derrick, crude magnate of the Plateaus, for a pretty penny I must say, the bid for the last item in our auction, the delectable ass is 99 and 44/100ths hers for one night. The house keeps the rest. And remember, what happens in @tlantisity™ never happened!"

The humanoid face attached to the ass emerges and glowers at the auctioneer. The entire room doubles over laughing at the pair of moving lips.

"Hey man, I have rights!"
"Too bad they all make a wrong!"
"O talking head, you are too much. You spoil everything. Methinks you protest too much."

Hermione Derrick reaches into her horny rhinoceros handbag and resource-fully produces a strap-on dill of reinforced ivory for the room to observe.

"Heh heh, ream that punk ass to death," hisses the Concierge, betraying his less than savoury past.

The ass is led away by Lady Derrick's entourage and tossed upon the seedy pulp of a solitary confinement cell within a pumpkin limuck. Her reputation precedes her, regarding her activities in her Flexnaster interrogation chamber. Rumours persist that the ghost had got the hell out of old Derrick after a fifteen-minute seizure induced by a very rare obsidian vegetable in her collection, one she had inherited from the Freud estate through a previous marriage. Those were spotty, crazy days of raw experimentation. As for black masses and uninhibited orgies, one was positively tripping over them.

But she had long ago entered her far quieter middle period. Aside from the occasional pinch of snuff, she likes a bit of flesh now and again, as her personal physician Dr. F advises. Why, it does wonders for the blood work. He was one of the few Sanitators with enough biochemical knowledge to distill the raw elements of pure enema and whip together a few hemogoblin restoratives and home remedies. He had long ago assumed complete control over her finances in his capacity as a Registered Finagler with the Association of Earnest Fiddlers, who were beyond investigation, questions or reproach. His laboratories took up most of the Derrick estate, although she rarely saw him. On occasion, she was visited by strange incubi before daybreak that seemed at first guess a group of torrid zeitgeists. She had learned about such practices in a giant grocery chain warehouse in Frankfurt. But most denizens had been compelled to sign a psychical restraining order. Once, she couldn't help prodding him over tea.

"Pray tell, was that you last night, good doctor?"

He had merely bit into a spicy sausage of Latinate extract and pooh-poohed the whole notion.

"Hermione, what do you take me for, a common backdoor remote? I have my reputation to consider. Now about your portfolio, isn't it time to get out of pleasure dome DIY and into global grocery transmatting?"

All of this, Minor telemorses out of her electrical impulses as she godivas off. The Concierge watches him, knowing in his marrow that Minor (whoever really knows what such a man is capable of) is going to keep raising the stakes, especially after flubbing the auction. He can read him like a book, although he was never one for books, except for the incomparable education he had acquired directly from a vintage collection of dime-store potboilers. His pious Uncle Seltzer had a weakness for ancient erotica, as well as a heap of jacketed noirs he believed would set his good-for-nothing nephew on the straight and narrow. His purposes were crystalline at the seance.

"Don't die in the embrace of some goddamned statutory gold digger like I did! I left you the lot, boy, no need to thank me, but cast your sights no farther than these dusty primers."

The Concierge has studied each book, his impatience quelled only by those screaming faces in glamorous demi-shadow on the cover. They ate up all his youthful vim and vinegar, but when he came of age, his dominating stepmother disappeared. He received a weighty trust and the key to @tlantisity™. However, following after his uncle, the Concierge had gotten himself into a right fix with the first woman who cottoned onto him. The only difference was the wretched introduction of legality. Yet the potboilers had ill-prepared him for the series of unimaginable encounters and double-crosses that had transpired in less than a fortnight.

Now, it was common gossip that Minor was a silent partner in this sunken flotilla of racy games. However, their silent agreement permitted the Concierge to have his pick of all the gills and brackles who vied to run the gaming tables. Minor himself was given a great deal of leeway and often forgiven a number of whopping debts he accumulated. For he was the greatest shill there ever was, in other words, *the real thing*. On the other hand, his uncanny winnings more often than not went back into @tlantisity™ instead of his other holdings. The Concierge put up with every one of his charades in order to derive this singular pleasure in his life, to be able to lend him a faded shirt and a pair of torn slacks, along with a pair of sandals that read @tlantisity™, marking the mark, as it were, who was too proud to backstroke home barefoot. This moment of petty triumph gave incomparable meaning to the life of the Concierge.

With this mismatched couple of lads, it was hard to tell exactly who was feeding on whom, because in spite of the exhilaration of winning twelve hundred Tritons, Minor craved this moment of tipping the scales and returning the favour with a single word from his nasty mountain dialect, a mirthful curse that made the Concierge shiver. Each man would snark it off and humbly accept, but inwardly he steeled against his partner and was only waiting for the next opportunity to see the tide turn against him. This vicious cycle ratified their mutual addiction. But in spite of Minor's intimacy with his investments in *subterra enterstrata*, the Concierge suspected him of being a brilliant double agent, perhaps one familiar with his past life.

This suspicion hearkened back to a brief excursion the Concierge had taken to Venice, where everything has to be shifted by gondola. He had met up with a peerless, fearless gal with moxie and legs furry enough he could not say he had remained entirely disinterested. In fact, he had been in the process of kissing and biting those divine follicles in their shared gondola upon a makeshift bed of limited edition Algers when she had first begun to speak of other machinations. Uncle Seltzer, mostly on account of his planned release of a hair-removal product, had downplayed the magnitude of the brittle split ends of his own plans.

"It doesn't hurt," she had stressed, plucking out a choice leg hair with her fingertips.

Seltzer had blown his top. But the Concierge was enamoured with this bold and intriguing girl, and he was positively itching for some kind of collusion. All the same, throughout the cloistered canals of Venice, through the unhealthy stink, he felt he could sniff the punchy cologne of none other than S.O.B. Minor in several places. He had also heard eerie hummings beneath open windows. Grim serenatas. Then, at a masquerade, one particular figure had thrown a monkey wrench into his whole sex holiday. And who had pried Hortenzia out of his hands and stolen away with her and her budding schemes? That cloaked figure in a harlequin mask, Histrionicus Histrionicus! But that laugh he would never forget! He had felt Minor up and down the streets, much as he felt him now, real close.

For this reason, he had consented one night, when he was down on his own luck, to let Minor into this oceanic enterprise. Something would come of it. O yes! Now they glint deeply into one another, each dealing a hand and playing off the other at the same time. There is no other game of Fuhbang in the world like this one. In the background, there is a healthy smack as a pyramid of @tlantisity™ balls are broken across an emerald table. One of them floats off with an orange anemone.

"Pick your number, Monsieur Minor! Don't be a prick now. Just pick a number, heh heh!"

"333, no other!"

"333 it is!"

The wheel begins to spin in a great whirlpool of fortune before a crowd of washed-out onlookers. And the stakes before the vortex comes to a groaning halt.

"Your bizarre briefs are safe tonight, Monsieur. And the dinner jacket of bursting dreams is yours to flipper home with ... tonight."

"And Hortenzia, has she kept well?" enquires Minor.

His double entendre confirms the worst nightmares of the Concierge and nearly cannonballs a neuron through a purple vein in his sweating forehead. He cannot hedge bets now, nor advise the odds. They both know that trick too well. The eyes of the Concierge are wet. Hypertension. But Minor is full of spunk and conservatively letting it ride. Suddenly, the Concierge notices the fishbowled face in the quickly consulted fob of Minor's and explodes into gnarled asides and twisted soliloquies.

"Yes I knew it. He is here on S.O.B. purposes only. This could be a bust. How can I cave in to him? That man is a walking conflict of interests."

The wheel continues to starfish. The organs of the ballooned boy are now available for universal bidding. Slinky tentacles from the Pleasurety Room are starting to wrap around the writing on his thighs.

"But what if I did him a good turn? A real service on the up and up? What if I gave him a hand? O the blackguard!"

The rather lubricious tentacles relax, and the Concierge wriggles free and hisses frantically into a medical bracelet, all without being detected.

"And the number is 333! Indeed, 333 again! Monsieur is the winner, yet again. That brings a close to this session of games. We will resume indefinitely. Please retire to the execution suites if you are in fact a guest, and if not, good night gentlemen good night ladies, see you again soon, and please surf and scuttle home safely."

III – Get Widget

In the concurrent dovetailing editions of *Caliente* and *Junk*, Minor is the featured chief execution officer of countless sign-offs. A glossing spreadout includes a series of popular poses – Minor stepping out of the shower, Minor leaning forward and puffing up his chest, Minor draped in a facsimile of his hardcore logo, the sizzling (**m**) so many aficionados have had branded into ankle and tuchus flesh.

"Aaaaaaaahhhhh," cries Kundalina in unbridled testimonial.

At her behest, the marking parlour is renovated into a writhing mass of eroticized body art. But that's just something for the kids. Minor has other kippers to smoke. He has innumerable holdings in Biofare Properties and AutomateX. Once in a while, if he is bored, he plants a handful of holy relics in a quarrelsome quarry and triggers the establishment of more than one puppet government around them. Occupants of the surrounding territories invest one hundred and ten percent of their content in Omnivirous wares. Cults and bogs sprout and flower. The young, the volatile, malnourished waifs, and the chemically dieted, are all excellent candidates for the movement. There is nothing left to hope for, other than to explode in a massive))) **m** (((upon the prattlefield.

The featurette continues. Minor is renowned for his motivational talks. In the private stall of a corporate *¡¡¡help!!!* blog, an insider has disclosed that the Interactive Chief enjoys swinging a lacrosse stick at his underlings before any crucial deal is made. Although Minor is of unknown extract, it is very difficult to deny this kind of patriotism. Stepping gingerly over a breathtaking collection of concussed skulls, the one-on-one foreign correspondent strides challengingly into the fall collection of the Bellatio department and starts to squeeze merchandise.

"Were these Bellatios modelled together abroad?"

Minor offers assurances through a *buon fresco* of a couple going out of their mind-blown minds.

"We will not outsource this exploding industry. What are we, Sucks.crap? Just what you are implying with your quizzical glare?"

The weathered tattler has no response. The relays he just received reflected nothing of this, although it is obvious that Minor is manipulating the values of Sucks.crap through five or six other congloms. And this exclusive media parrot cannot deny that *Bellatio for None-Too-Bright Bumpkins* has been a bestseller. He lifts his craggy face and admits he is an ardent subscriber to (**b**). Then, in a drunk-on-sales-margins display of exuberance, he reveals a tiny (m) burned into a none-too-savoury place. And it is easy as whipped cream on a pie to get the old coot to try out the new Organomic Duchesse Brisée. Then Bébé Lala returns from her dip and offers him a sublime chaser. By the time she is tenderly licking his wrinkled logo, he is considering accepting the position at MediaX.

In the face of borderline retirement, here was a way to go out with a real bang! And just think of those Old Boys' Network benefits! He already knows their inalterable policy and credo. At MediaX there are no dreams, only hyper-masculine fantasies. His wattles are wavering. He is completely unaware that a leggy adolescent Bébé signed away both her essence and assorted simulacra in a scrotum-bursting sensorium agreement for the corporate dental plan alone. Few of her followers know about her earlier struggles with Walrus Syndrome (WS). Now she positively titters about the whole thing.

"Well, those upper canines weren't going to whiten themselves!"

However, even she is unaware a serf war has developed over a broken wish-bone, and that Minor has developed various prototypes of Hotbutton, an entertaining self-harm device for ages seven and up whose sales are through the roof (and off of it). There is also a new mutation of nausea known as *nautea* that arises from the accelerated blits per nano and quivering vacillations that inundate anyone with a hardcore connexion. The recent tragedy involving a football hero mysteriously autoeroticized to death in the presence of abusive cheerleaders is still under investigation and has led to petitions for a hot action lawsuit.

This weekend, Minor has taken the company pod with Bébé to an interna-tional conference about rampant boxiness in our contemporary epoch. The box is an ever-expanding epidemic, and yet, there is perpetual rhetoric about getting out of that racket. The ameliorative visual aids and sonic retrieval cues will appreciate no limit that depreciates. And there is a hopping multitude waiting to be on the make behind these outlines of burgundy curtain.

"Curses! I asked for wanish periwinkle!"

These fiery-eyed souls spend more time in these squares of sales than they do in their leased cubbies. Mercifully, *gratis benedictus*, the company, *nomine beate*, covers both expenditures. Everyone pauses in mid-unpack. The guest speaker, a popular national humorist, is telling a ticklish anecdote for the thousand and third time about being handcuffed to a radiator on the way to the conference.

"So I'm looking at my watch with my only free hand if you know what I mean, and then suddenly I hear this hissing sound … and I think to myself the pâté is sure outta tha goose now! I mean the dung heap has really struck up a dialogue with the fan, if ya follow ..."

Gaggles of mesmerized listeners cannot resist. They snort out their blow and crap their company attire. There is a huge queue for the middle ages dirty laundry service and associated dirty schmutter services. Minor scans the territory. There are different species of salesaurs, some Slipperies and some Smoothies. They lived on our planet long before us, but now they live among us in oily harmony.

The Slipperies are the extremely slick and moussey and eelish creatures in smoking jackets and slippers. They have the advantage of high-speed access to the reptilian brain beneath their material, which assists them in oozing raw airborne product. But Smoothies are almost invisible, barely known for their subtlety and strawberry shake–like tact. Their gift is a talent for translation, a low-flow backless saccharine and flattering touch-free touch that does not leave a single physical mark. Their loose grey liveries are disarming, to say the least. Many passersby have been given the business behind the burgundy drapery without even realizing it – that is how smoooooth they are! Thus, their population exponentially quadruples throughout suburban identicals.

As for the Slipperies, they prefer a continental approach that allures inner city cliques and claques in equal proportions. They haunt safe infusion sites and virtual playgrounds and ply their wicked trade. Once, one of the urban ambassadors thought he saw one of the Slipperies by the swings, but then the Slippery dematerialized behind one of the monkey bars. That is how sliiiiiippery they are. And no matter the methodology, each species drags out a pile of colourful luminations and waggles them in the waft of stale buns and burnt coffee. A moonish gleam in the hawker's glare. And then the looky loos shuffle along, hooting inanely.

"Looky looooo loooky loo loo looooo!"

And Minor has seen it all. That lingering cloud of uncertainty before the inevitable plummet into debt. Still, there is no other plunge to match this one. Of course, in response to extensive litigation against a fistful of entities alone, Minor has invented the first in-house DebtMaster program.

"Tired of being a corporate slave in a never-ending fantasy camp? Sign up with DebtMaster and earn valuable debt points! Sign up before it's too late!"

Each member of DebtMaster is encouraged to join the exceptional From a Turnip program and have their lifetime earnings in cold hard cash (in some cases in offshore swear-jar currency) covered in a light garnish. And through this form of atonement, they can attain higher and higher levels upon the

DebtPharoah Pyramid. While biting a burning ear, Bébé lets slip that she is already a level ninety-eight. The Queen Spree, the other drones call her. Now she assumes control readily.

At some point, the incessant cycle of such conferences loses its regimental cohesion and all that is left is the box. These diverse exchanges of sensuous genius must come to a sticky end and must be repackaged and effected elsewhere, in the bowels of another radiating centre that looks exactly the same. That is why so many faces and facts blur into the same thing. Memory becomes no more than mud at another Infomercial Inn. There is so much frustration that builds within the viewing frustum of any soul with an ounce of perception. There is nothing but a particle of dust flitting by, a floating little mote, and that tremulous uncertainty before a single object comes into focus. Just before desire becomes manifest. Just before the answer to everything at hand.

"Read the literature. Free stuff!"

The solution was elementary to a man like Minor. After the initial liquidation, he briskly arranged for a putrefaction. Merely precautionary. Then he set round to work. It took a few hours for the prototype, but everyone agreed his intelligent design was the realization of *Sandselig Genialitet*, popularized by the Danish graphic novel of the same name. Not only had Minor managed to tempura out every existing trademark for an immeasurably hotter widget with unspeakable properties of the unspoken verboten, but he had also supplied a catchphrase that summed up the most intimate intricacies of its subroutines and confounded its hearers into dumbfoundedness:

Widget is the gadget don't fidget

At the moment of release, Widget™ was the only string of encoded characters blogging up olfactory messaging systems to the point of crapulous overload, reverbing on and on with such an insistent and fricative force of unnaturalness that the resultant vectors of heat began to break the ice of the world earlier than projections shone. And this audible buzz made several phyla of parasites extinct, and engendered an overpopulation of choral frogs that sounded vaguely like tropical birds and burst the eardrums of snoozing tourists with each performance of a dulcet centet.

Totally lagged and bloody of lobes, they went mad for more. There had never been such a concerto of unifying dissonance. No flood, no volcano, no quake, no tornado, no duster could compare to this mass hysteria of communicative bliss and horror. *Widget*™ was the word to text. *Widget*™ was the verbal to enter. Widget™ was the one to buy. Widget™ was the one to simply die for.

The ceiling was so immense on the stock that anyone who had missed the proverbial looks-good-on-paper boat leapt out of their respective thinking tanks and looming towers without a thought, leaving no memory behind, only a single careening cry –

"WwwiiiiiiiiiiiiiiiiiiiiiiiiiiiiiiiiiiiiiiiiidgeT!!!"

And even that final tribute from the jaws of oblivion only made the stock climb higher and higher and only induced its holders to jump from higher and higher a height. Why??? Because Widget™ lends our lives meaning. And at the conferences themselves, Minor insisted on promoting Widget™ himself.

"This is a limited time offer! Getcha Widget™ or you'll just die!"

Lineups were intolerable. Many perished when they were sooooo close. They were the lucky ones. Passions were illimitable. When some souls finally reached the front, unkempt and unwashed and excruciatingly stained, and they at long last touched a peekaboo edge of Widget™, they burst into flame on the spot. At least that is what witnesses claim, of those who survived. But Widget™ contained such a refined objectification of free-form particles its resultant desire fructified a built-in deity complex that killed most avidists in seconds. The realization and embodiment of exactly what they wanted was too horrible to comprehend, and a mess to behold. Only Minor could have shortcut the circuitous milk run we so tentatively refer to as existence, i.e., *life*.

"Got life?"

It was a secondary buzz phrase and my my my how they lined up to get some! And Minor had known this from the get-go! But who was prepared for self-fulfillment, for honesty and love and total user-friendly actualization? Minor had without compunction created a plague for the bran new dawn of civilization. Mass suffering and torments would occur, if Widget™ continued to process itself unchecked and untaxed. Widget™, the box of every want, a menace! Minor went further. He was optimistic that an unprecedented age of Art would rise anew from these ashes of commerce. But what that want let out of the closet and glove compartment was emptiness, a continuous lack, a holocaust of need and avarice. Desires ran amok among exploding individuals.

The surface of mortality stirred and bubbled like unattended soup upon the element. And dreary things seethed out, not of imagination, but rather of stale monotonous copyism. Giant apes and dragons. Ogres, gnomes and elves. Wizards and pithy bards. Goth and vampire culture, hurrah. Utter submission and admissions and mortifications and ravishment. Collars abounded. The rather frilly and frivolous underworld of the world turned inside out. Everyone got exactly what they wanted and grew nauseous in the lack of attempt, and died from smugness alone. The nervous system is sorely equipped to handle a complete lack of adversity. From complete luxury stemmed utter strangeness. Cross-town fertilizations arose. Fresh tediums sprouted and were picked as chivalrous gifts for special buddies upon the bestiary grounds. People rode in desperate circles of evolution around their lack of inventions. Most of them, after literally burning out and burning up, met their maker in a convulsion of self-actualization, a dopey grin plastered *a secco* across their scorched faces. An inordinate number soared into the sun, based on some ultraviolet programming.

There was not one drug that could lick the potency of Widget™. It *simplified* matters. It was bound to be. Once the rutting herd was thinned out, the remainders in post-traumatic coitus threw over their religions and even centuries-deep sects for the sake of more Widget™. Eventually, a dreamless huddle of dullards formed and reinitiated a proud tradition of bureaucracy that had lain dormant for several short attention spans. They brought about sanctions and a new impasse to molecular trade. They voted at once to shut the globule shield and lock out the majority of Widget™ addicts. Withdrawal programs were set up. In the end, the entire populace learned to despise these desires that had robbed them of once upstanding and even priggish normalcy. After they returned to substandard oxysmog, canisters of fruity antifart helped them remember.

"Widget™ ... why, Minor, my god! What have we done? What happened to our sound rearing?"

They had gotten sidetracked, had forgotten the pure joys of profit and loss, and the promise of extended vacations to troubled places. People at the conference began to toss their little drinks with umbrellas in them, leaving behind piles of occidental merchandise. Minor made soteriological protestations. He had suffered for their sake. He was an Artist working in the medium of volcanic glass. He had some more ceramic idols in the limuck. But they chased him more madly than ever.

"Minor is to blame! Let's tear him a new one and have a natural gas barbecue!!!"

But he had dissolved, leaving behind only a frying egg on the velvety carpet (additional charge, not included with booth or burgundy hangings) and a half-eaten hunk of tabloid, crammed with cardiac-arresting murmurs that he and Bébé were no longer an item, save physically. In their last project together, she has blue-bodied the essence of his obsession in order to develop the newest promotion for his personal fragrance. The old campaign for Minor toiletries with the Chernobylean übermodel scantily plunking a dominant with her sixth toe while surrendering to a leading actor of the day was a tad passé. It was time to get back to basics. He stayed with the same director, Linus Schlock, and changed the name of the fleshwash and companion lust elixir from Mmminor to À Trois, following recent trends.

And as history has shown, these two spots known in the business as floaters are currently running non-stop within eyes rolling upward of more than a thrillion conference attendees in a perpetual display of woo and assuage and marginally priced massage.

IV – A Close Shave

Miss Sharp looks about tentatively and awaits the last clink of coins in the karma jar to diminuendo off ... A long half-day to be sure. Hell on the ankles. I've been here too long. She glares at a loitering regular, scratching his red pate and adjusting his hard bridge pince-nez, purple of face. The indomitable cabaret chanteuse and foxy voxian, for she has all mode of voice for all manner of occasion, props up her portfolio-shot profile with her strumming elbow. You start to hate, you really do. She checks her hair in the reflection of a glass cabinet.

"Well, bottles. Time to buzz off!"

The glass crashes down. Closing, we are closing ... Her emerald eyes melt into the years on the labels. I must get my ducks in a row, really. And for a while, I thought the mortuary broker loved me, when I was still waiting to meet that special oddsbody. A mercenary lot, they are. All sharks, circling your dreams. Meanwhile, stuck in here, with people needing to get well past potted to tell a word of truth. And this hunch of a stump here, what was he saying the other day, about his wet dream in the tip jar of the world? Some truth you can just keep.

Her eyes widen, equipped with the power of cats to absorb the energy of pigment and the electricity of passing stimuli, although lately she has felt too fagged to attenuate herself. The psychic cabaret was just another fad, milked once or twice, and now she is stuck with the sour-smelling bucket of that flunky enterprise. Just couldn't make a go of it. Now she longs for physicality, for bawdy clowns, for mad acrocrats again. Something carnal. Men gathering from the burning corners of the earth and hounding her being, transfixed. Once, she had hoped to be a household name. Maybe even a VM, an honest-to-goodness, tell-it-like-it-is Virtual Monologist on the fibreless. Then a vert here and there, before last plunging into liquivision.

For this reason, she dips her not-so-everyday existence in celebrity bathwater. The lives and lifestylings of the swollen stars. Only on select evenings does she deign to appear and stare into the stare of dark strangers, and they are *hers* for the duration of the performance. Sometimes longer. And that man down the road who thought I was the cat's whiskers with his automatic writing? Who has the bloody time for that? Could you really meet someone with the personal fortitude to peer into your private universe and take a seat upon the furniture you imagine? Nothing. The same old story. The wanted and their wanting ... Better off to live with Corkscrew in mutt years and become a fantastic spinster, the talk of the neighbourhood!

The red-pated purple face gets up off his duff and staggers over to the bar. He snickers at the sight of the near-depleted karma jar.

"Was the wet dream about your wife, sir?"

"Cheeky mare."

A rainbow of bills and coins offers redemption. Now alone, Miss Sharp eyes the newspaper. **STROPPER LOPS AGAIN!!! Nothing to fear, offer police.** She reaches for her things with a twinge of anxiety. They say he's a charmer and has his wicked way beforehand. What is that like, when you're that freaked? Known only by the octave of his eight blades in the throat of his victims, he lashes out at anyone who doesn't strike his fancy, mostly those who won't be missed. Walkers of the night and sometimes clubbers looking to get lucky. Pawnbrokers, addicts, transients, democrats. Still, not really a lopper, more of a slicer, not even a dicer. I should write in.

Earlier the same day, the Stropper whistles his way into the adjacent barbershop. He picks up the paper and taps the front page into a spectacular crinkle with his knuckles.

"What do you think of that, eh? All these mutilations! What is the world coming to, I say!"

"You want a mullet or just a plain shearing?"

"A light trim and a shave, if you please."

He leaps into the closest chair with a great swivel. The barber grumbles to himself, draping the Stropper in a protective layer of paisley.

"These little snots today with their diplomas and their clippers! Arrhhh. I used to go to an old feller in Chinatown for less than a buck. Came home with scissor holes in my neck. Do you think I cried wolf every time? The old man wouldn't stand for no nonsense. Off with the belt if I said boo."

The barber spoke to the mirror, rubbing a scar along his neck.

"What, sir, don't tell me you admire this cold-blooded killer?"

"Not on your life. All I says is the man sure knows his instruments. And somebody has to stand up against the pinkolefty agenda. You want our kids growing up in some tinseltown without an effing job? He uses a strop for one thing and that tickles my fancy just fine."

"Actually, he uses an eight-bladed innovation of his own design. And this pet name, the Stropper, is a mistake on behalf of the media, bless their black-and-white hearts!"

The barber steadies his hand and applies an exquisite lather (enriched by a locally brewed lager) to the grisly afternoon shadow of the Stropper.

"Yes, take care, my good man. My skin is rather sensitive, and I want it smooth as a newborn heinie."

"Shut the heck up. I gots to keep my hand steady. Since my little squaw passed, I find a helpin' of cologne and brandy with a dash of turpentine is the only thing to do me any goddamn good."

The Stropper falls silent. He feels a whelm of respect for this man and his fading trade and vanishing clientele. There is a sublime quietude as the barber runs the edge of the razor along one cheek and then another. The radio station has reached its obligatory hour of classical content. An aria begins.

"Yes, that bit from *Die Zauberflöte*. Thinking Tamino is gone for good, Pamina is singing that she also wants to die. The saddest part of the whole opera."

While the barber continues to shave the local snuffer-outer of lives, neither man can hide his sensitivity any longer. Both men redden with a free range of running tears. And neither can admit he had never felt such exquisite release.

"Just thinkin' of the squaw an' all, how she loved that little tune."
"Her time was up."
"An' I never got the chance to say what was on my mind –"
"Life is cheap, sir. Life is sure goddamned cheap, you son of a gun!"

The men exchange a bleary-eyed glance in the mirror, followed by a lingering kiss. The barber rolls up his sleeves and closes his eyes and bends over the counter. He knows the drill.

"Easy there, big felluh."

The Stropper pats him gently, straightening the man's shirt pocket before tucking a large bill inside, taking his time to rub his chest through the material.

"I'd rather not take that road and say we did. It might end badly."

The barber stiffens, bristles.

"You just remind me of the little woman is all. And that song was tootin' on and on ..."
"At least it wasn't *The Barber of Seville*!"

Laughter. The barber pole swirls in striped enthusiasm. The Stropper enjoys his smooth face outside, musing over what could have been. Trimmed and brushed and powdered, who could stop him? A passing beauty on her way to a fang-whitening modelling shoot lets it slip. She cruises by slowly in her bran new Cougar XL, admiring the baby's bottom of his cheeks. She steps out of the car in a low-cut top and swanky pants, giving him an eyeful before instinctively kissing his cheek. In a swift flap of coat, she is enveloped.

Hours later, they find her LeatheX clobber poking out of an alley bin.

"Nothing to see here."

"She was on her way to a shaving spot, yeah."

"No, we sent that serial profiler packing. He was never one of us."

They tug off her leopard jacket with TouchyTouchy gloves and drop it into a largegantic bag.

"Nothing to see here, folks ..."

A shivering binner, their only eyewitness, is pointing with a fingerless glove toward the sky.

"T'was the Stropper, I tells ya, the Stropper, the STROPPER!!!"

But the Stropper is already three blocks away, lovingly washing off his multi-strop in the lane and putting on his razor-blade costume. Last week he was dressed as a beef dog and giving free auditions for prospective buns in an abandoned office. He has stayed one step ahead of the authorities by occasionally posing as a franchise donut. Over coffee and maple bacon bettybits, they speak openly about everything he needs to know. In addition, he is the solitary owner of a less than kosher processing plant downtown. His business cards read White Veal Deal in a number of tongues. However, megamarket shoppers have begun to whisper about personal articles and medical bracelets cropping up in their gross cases of Luncheonettes. And there are definitely murmurs about the exact contents of the Everymeats establishment on the Downtown Lower Side.

Miss Sharp is ready to lock up. Her scarf is wrapped tightly around her neck. She hears a step across the cobbles near the bars of the old gaol. Maybe the wind, another upchucking addict, just a loose bit of macadam, that's all. The heel of her new right boot is already a little worn. She shutters and seals the green door with a shove. Takes a step. A figure in a long, flapping coat appears out of an alcove of the historic gaol. She cannot see his eyes or nose or mouth.

"Where are you headed, Mademoiselle? Some house of pleasure, some after-hours den of iniquity?"

"Sir, you are barking up the wrong arbutus! I have just finished a long day of work and would like to go home. And my sister is in labour and taking to it rather poorly. She is not well at all. No no no, I must go at once."

The shadow menaces closer for a moment, and then disappears in a great flap of coat.

"On your way, child, on your way," echoes the disembodied voice.

The next morning, over an egg and bacon butte, she unfolds the paper only to read about another stropping, to this day unsolved.

V – Renovation of the Soul (Just Newly Repossessed)

Spring. A cold, long weekend. Minor lowers the dark wings of his parasol and adjusts his turquoise tam, which matches his blue patent PleatheX loafers. He has just returned from one of his notorious excursions to the lower islands of the dead as a revolutionary hero and a minor deity. He did a little spin just before the marauders opened fire and for all intents and purposes he appeared to die.

"But my doppelgänger is still there – and the intellectual property of my soul."

Minor rises from a steamy jungle heap of bodies and bids one of the villagers suck out the offending shells while another slathers him in tribal warming liquid.

"Haysus," they chant. "Haysus!!!"

Ammo and organs and blood jewelry make for a finicky business. Minor got in on the ground floor for the perks but the global industrial dendrite complex is not everything it is cracked up to be. And the turnovers are often terrible. Hazard of the trade. Also, the discovery of alien skulls is a continual distraction. Minor is becoming very concerned about numerous full-frontal articles that are eating into his slop-running trade along the border, and the undeniable fact that his holdings in Murderware have peaked.

"Gone soft," snorts the competition.

And yet, after administering a massage beyond question, the villagers instruct him in the elusive practices of the Incubasti, an ancient and vigorous people. And during the tribal challenge that devastates acres of habitat, Minor is able to pay Miss Sharp a short call, while her sweetheart Saran is touring the Neo-Demilitarized Zone with the irresistible Una Loca. And today is delightful, with a humid veil of coastal drizzle and mist to nourish the flora and fauna and every little creature. Meanwhile, a drop of acid rain burns a hole in his tam.

A rainy day. Miss Sharp holds two fingers to her temple. She pouts beautifully. She has a glam-shot sex headache. Or else she feels like just pulling the covers over her head for a few more hours, maybe all day. Nearby, a clock chimes. Miss Sharp remembers that Saran is off plying her trade with Una Loca. She waits in bed, staring at the ceiling. She is holding her head with both hands now.

Don't think of him, she thinks.

Then through the light hush of rain, she hears the mocking cry of a passing flicker. Her lips remember his. Her cool thighs are warmed by invisible hands. He is ubiquitous. He hears her step in the middle of the night and listens to her breathing. He eavesdrops on her dreams. She stirs and stretches her arms, staring through her bedroom window into grey sky. There is not much passion or heat, only wrath. She hums to herself, as if to ward off his apparition with her ancestral charms. She is born of a long line of fiddlers and songstresses, and he can sniff the music off her. It is like something locked away in an old flask that he has unstopped. She can hear the buzzer, incessant as ever. She need not get up. Her consent is enough. She stares up, feeling repressed by the grey that fills her window and her blinking green eyes.

The lift drones to life. The touch is now tender as the introduction of a pair of hands into a piano concerto. But there is a brutal knock at the door, followed by a joke melody of knuckles. The door flings itself open, admitting one visitor, and then slams itself shut. He strides into the bedroom and the flaming small print upon a contract is brought to her attention. But she has no regrets. He throws off his overcoat, leaving nothing to the imagination. Soaked through. He has been walking barefoot all night, perhaps in his sleep. He also holds his head in agony. He climbs into bed and she fevers in his grasp. Ever since that night she tendered her resignation to utter materiality and signed the waiver for ethereality, she has felt languid, sluggish, powerless. And caught in the thrall of this monster.

"Once you covered my neck with kisses."
"Once you beat me into next week."
"Once you drenched a broken stall."

They cannot resist such repartee any longer. This time, her visiting wraith has come to her in a limited time offer of the local rainmaker Minoris Pluvius. He recalls to her mind a particular resort during her experimental years. It was raining then too. Amid a hundred dripping candelabra, an unattended iron sinks right through the middle of Saran's favourite shirt. The gulls are flying low underneath the grey and moaning unhappily. The rain god continues to wriggle in the wake of her glaucous stare.

"I am the rare rhinoceros that purifies our drink. Perform the ritual mistress. Ride me to Glistendom!"

She delicately covers his pulsating body with shrink wrap.

"You can never be too careful, Pluvius."

Miss Sharp holds her head between her palms. What manner of dream was this? The bedroom is warm. She is sweating. Moist. Time to run a nice warm bath. She listens to the filling tub and studies a grey hair in the bathroom mirror. Then she runs her hand through the hot of her reflection before tightening each faucet and stepping inside. The water is still. Her mind begins to drift. She thinks of Saran, packing that thick book for the plane.

"Why that one?"

"It's about libertinage."

Saran is glued to Una Loca in the Nether-Regions where they are celebrating the crumbling of yet another oppressive regime. The grimly smiling statue of Hegemony (Heggy to her followers) blows apart into bits. Some of the onlookers are struck by molten shards of her sublime countenance. Saran is chanting for destruction in the name of liberation, completely caught up in the energy of the crowd. And Una impulsively seizes her head and kisses her. Then they walk hand in hand back to their accommodation, bidding the strict keeper of the hostel a pithy greeting before retiring to the common area and curling up with a complimentary copy of *Juliette* in front of the roaring fire. An axe swings and they shiver. Señora Litupa tosses a split log into the fire, before fetching a tray loaded with glasses of cognac and smelly cheese. Saran reclines upon the sofa with her head upon Una's lap, and they underline their favourite passages of de Sade, reading them aloud to one another.

> *Have at it, Euphrosine, frig me, my love, lay on, I want to die drunk on her fuck! Quick now, we'll change about, let's vary what we're doing.*

Señora Litupa takes a moment to adjust the ears of the Gandar. The image materializes of a man being whipped in a slate-grey dungeon by an anonymous woman. He is blindfolded and dangling from a coat hanger.

"Is this the new administration or the old one? Maybe that new reality program ..."

"Poor Hegemony. I understand she was a fine painter. And undeniably, there was a touch of the artist to all her official actions."

"In some countries, you are free to do as you please, and in others, you are free to think as you please. But I doubt you can do both at the same time."

"Heggy was not afraid to wear the pants. And it was too intimidating for the unwashed."

"Well, tomorrow, we have to get up in time to vote."

Una picks up the book and smiles at Señora Litupa. Together, they peruse one of the underlined parts.

> *"You, my pigeon," she went on, kissing me with inordinate feeling, "you'll not leave my clitoris unattended, will you? 'Tis there the true seat of woman's pleasure: rub it, worry it, I say, use your nails if you like – never fear ..."*

Una begins to play with Saran's dreads. The revolution is now reality, a bran new world of black bean quesadillas. Señora Litupa opens up Saran's fatigues and reaches for her aroused *flower*. For that is what she called it, and she had seen many *flowers* over the years, just as she had seen the start and end of innumerable administrations. The man on the Gandar is whipped with increasing enthusiasm, and he moans and groans accordingly. As Señora Litupa hikes up the most frivolous aspect of her official domestic costume, Una traces another smattering of underlined type.

Once again we fell to frigging one another – and immediately were all three plunged back into the wildest excesses of lubricity. We struck a thousand different poses; continually altering our roles, we were sometimes wives to fuckers whom the next instant we dealt with as husbands . . .

Miss Sharp stirs securely in the tepid bathwater, surprised by her own passion. She is rubbing her aroused sex and burning up with the kind of pleasure that only arises from the most terrible case of jealousy, mingled with an ounce of focused humiliation.

"Hot hot hot –"

An hour later, Miss Sharp makes her way along the thoroughfare, somewhat satisfied for having *gotten off*, although she is also wounded by Saran's disappearance. The sketch artist has lengthened her hair and softened her looks for the evening paper.

"We'd just like her to look a little more *victimy* for the late edition."

Miss Sharp thinks she notices the hauntingly familiar, however low-key Minor. She is clad in a smart new jacket, brown in shade, with a sensible dark skirt and white stockings dropping into worn black boots. Already, she can feel her consciousness shifting again ... She crosses the rushing street to avoid his eyes and thoughts, imploring or accusative. She hides under her umbrella and hurries along. Minor rubs his eyelids with his knuckles, still a bit bloody with kidneys and fish guts, and stinky with a sideline in picklemongering. Blood and gherkin trails down his gnarled knuckles and lands in an unrepaired pothole, where a flagging bouquet of irises spontaneously rises. But it is too late. She does not see them in the slightest.

"Pschaw! Caring is truly for chumps! Don't you know who I am?"

The entire boulevard erupts into bloom. This coming is foretold. He steps out of the bus shelter, for his local troika has arrived. No express service on a holiday. The whole resurrection thing will have to wait. How about some water into wine into clean water first? Minor strides aboard the kneeling bus and presents his universal pass. The driver holds himself. The day has come. Everyone bows before his turquoise tam. One young lady (who swears she is eighteen) melts on the spot, leaving little more than skin and bone. Minor curtsies ineffably and bundles up the remains for later. Everyone produces an ornate handkerchief or snotty rag and dots their field of vision.

"Ahhh Minor ... is there no end to his compassion?"
"Minor, this milk run is the thrill of our lives!"

This outstanding reception cheers his barren soul and almost makes him forget his lack of a specific heir to his ten hundred and three catastrophes. Since Catalina of Aragon had *dropped the ball*, giving life to several daughters, Minor had set his hopes on Miss Sharp being the mother of the incredibly prodigious Cromwell Minor. He makes this declaration as his stop approaches, and the driver and everyone else has a splendid cry. They each get a fondle in as Minor makes his way to the front and bends over and waggles his goods to an uproarious gaggle of applause. Minor floats off down the invigorated boulevard, giving high fives, already thinking about stopping for a garlic schmeer. The people on the bus cluster together and drool in anticipation of the lordly one eating his traditional fare. Minor stops to admire a sign being finished in screeching chalk:

HAPPY PASSOVER!

Minor makes a mental note to pick up a fresh shipment of goat's blood. A screaming ambulance passes, and is noticeably unnoticed.

"We've just seen Minor. We can tell our greatgrankids! We met the man in the flesh. Now we can freakin' die –"

The Stropper passes and stops, hands in pockets, resisting a sensation to stroke his own smooth cheek. He smiles at the agitated crowd.

"What a fine day for a holiday!"

VI – The Man Without Qualities

Terence Cockerel lets off a big one and looks around furtively. Had anyone heard? He pulls his brown lapels tighter.

"Too much cabbage. Less fibre, more bran."

He swings his aluminum walking stick about gaily. But someone had heard. A grim and severely sober Agent Minor is casually shadowing every step. He had observed Mr. Cockerel earlier that morning in Lacey's, the last dying monolith of a department store, coughing up its last cash transaction. Minor, in his guise as a store dick, had allowed Cockerel to walk out of the store with a hideous and deliberately unalarmed angling hat. True, he had also bought a mesh camisole with matching accessories, but he had adamantly refused to pay for the hat. It was the principle of the matter. Perhaps he had been a boy milliner in a period when bouncy striplings had to wade through hats just to get to the hat factory. But it is precisely such a characteristic by which we betray ourselves.

"I'm a pensioner and your cheap perfumes got me all mixed up!"

Cockerel would supply a dozen and one stories, if the situation demanded it, for the love of a hat that struck his fancy. And they would scratch their pates and let him off, never suspecting he had taken the hat simply because he could. But Minor had digested the man's entire edible file and knew that he was an admitted cupolamaniac. That was just an hors d'oeuvre to begin with. As for the entrée and dessert menu portion of his file, Cockerel had whipped up the most lavish of poisonous appetizers and parasitic main courses, and if there were room, an absolutely killer soufflé and puff-scream pastries to make your mouth water. Literally. He took pride in his carrot-ginger gypsy moth broth and his risqué shellfish bisque, each untraceably containing that *je ne sais quoi*, only one of the newest toxins to grace the last page of *Dining Squad Monthly*. After all, he was a man of taste. He never served quickie dishes. It was beneath him to prepare anything that would not result in a slow and agonizing loss of life.

Minor, during his early years of scouting and infiltration, had written a short article for the newsletters of many a conspiratorial organization pointing out the folly of resolving a global problem with a sniper, when a dish would serve just as well, if not even more sumptuously. Hell, a sniper couldn't measure up to the threat of a thoughtfully prepared gazpacho or a thinner consommé. Just then, a hair trigger above Minor's carefully combed part, a shot fires. Cockerel reels around, scratching his ankle blade, and resumes his stroll. Cabbage again? Minor launches an official apology and dispatches a contract for future assignments in the general direction of the sniper union. Another shot fires from the roof across the boulevard, and a rose bursts into bloom over Minor's heart.

"Another invitation to the Sniper Ball, I assume! What to wear?"

Just around the corner in Café Amaricano, the Concierge is flirting with a buff barista and feigning the reception of a wound from the sex god's dismissive rebuff. In fact, the Concierge is quite nervous. He has agreed to follow Minor through all the world (in a small-print clause for a term not exceeding eternity). However, living with the überagent in his cavernous den behind a vulture's nest smacks of living in an off-road Thrummer commercial. This mountainous fortress is also the home of the TerraGiggle, the most phallic quantum computer available to man. The Concierge is considering his next move when an adorable little monster dumps his caffeinated sundae all over him. At once, the parents begin to lick and clean off the Concierge, who struggles in the immobility of their familial grip. Their gifted progeny had made an adorable mess. They would clear it up. Forever.

Minor glares back in unbelievable annoyance. Meanwhile, Cockerel pushes open the door of his favourite second-hand bookshop, The Counter-Stall, seemingly unaware of the intrigue outside. Why, his salad days are well behind him. Even his soup and trifle days are well behind him. Not that he has any appetite for it these days. No more yummy fixings for generals and presidents. Now, Cockerel desires nothing more than a quiet life. He enjoys a stroll in the afternoon or evening, especially to invigorate his poor circulation. Sometimes a concert matinee on Sunday. And another guilty pleasure is perusing the subversive shelves of The Counter-Stall.

Taking out a democratically elected despot or insufferable windbag was one thing. At leisure, he has time to consider the mistakes of the *condottieri* and how far they were out of their depth when consulting the Ancient Greek annals of long-departed generals. For his own soft hours, he loves to handpick an item or two from the Kounter Kultur section and curl up in a lawn chair, hidden among amiable faces of hawthorn. There is nothing finer than freedom of mind, to sip some ginger beer in the backyard with a camisole in one hand and a good read in the other, and to find yourself infinitely transported. He cherished the intricate and terrifying and hallucinatory universe of, say, a Burroughs, although some of those well-fondled volumes heightened his fear of the insectile. However, these books dragged him outside of himself. And now with this allergic twitch in one eye, there is no longer the preparation, the readiness, the execution he once had.

"Why, I can barely wake up for the sake of this damned tray of horse pills. I once toppled entire global networks, and now I worry about smelling the flowers in the sunshine. And when you dole out death like rebate coupons, you come to learn that being in the moment means nothing. Everything is the passage of time and happy hours well spent."

And this discovery is the reason Cockerel so enjoyed his retirement, because he had learned the precious secret of sameness. It is of course no secret, but often the most overlooked philosophy of being in the world. That is, the sweetness of routine. But Cockerel, if he could, and he always could, loved to do the very same thing every day. For him, a thin slice of hot veg pizza and the scent of dust in second-hand shops became synonymous. Why, the entire street is a musical phrase for his senses. He had mastered the art of living ever so low-key a life. The familiar characters he observed every day, whether he knew them or not, made his life into an incomparable opera. Those industrious grocers, those endearing bagel and babka pushers, those megamarket cashiers with a touch of carpal tunnel, those yawning theatre tenders making fresh popcorn, those cell- and coffee-juggling moms with their jaws firmly locked around a perambulator handle – this lovely microcosm of life was the only one Cockerel would require until his dying day, full of souls he would never need to assassinate.

"Play what you want while you shelve."

"Brahms?"

"Especially not Brahms."

"Not even the clarinet quintet?"

"Like it gets me all romanticky and makes me want to go into the mountains."

"Fine. O, watch out. This dude talks to himself. Grain of salt."

Cockerel flips to a long hand-job scene in a banned tetralogy. But it hadn't always been this way. He was a descendent of the illustrious Cockerel clan. Why, the entire ginger beer empire could have been his!

"Were it not for that wretched brother of mine! Well, I *was* having it off with Fizz. All that chatter of adventure in foreign climes, it went straight to her head. But who could blame me? We were in Bengal, I remember. And the sun had done something peculiar to that cask. We mopped our brows and bodies with the stuff, and the next thing we knew, we were smooching madly. O Fizz! I'd give my eye teeth for you and this street!"

But Cockerel had turned his back on those effervescent royalties forever, which included use of the trademarked adjective *effervescent*™. Afterward, his years of hired killing simply seemed to fly by. He had been so busily employed in the change of world governments, he had missed out on the big buyout of his namesake ginger beer by a huge and mysterious megaconglom that he refused to speak of. And it killed Cockerel to see his family crest on every golden can in the sunshine of a sultry afternoon, occluded by the storm cloud of this monster's corporate logo.

"Where was the tradition, the proud legacy of civilizing? Stomping out the Noble Savage and so on?"

And what is more, this organization had had the gall to ask him to be their promotional mascot and sell his likeness, so they could have a kindly old Cockerel on street corners and outside strip malls, offering free samples. Maybe it hurts more when you're a remittance man, living from cheque to cheque in the oddest locales. Assassination was far more practical than these bitter carbonation wars. Far more direct. Cockerel sneezes.

"Joy Division, isn't it?"

One chap with an immature Van Dyke leers over the counter, and his cohort pops out of the back of the shop, alarmed and attempting to muscle up. Cockerel grins weakly. They are paranoids in the neoclassical sense. Cockerel rubs his bristling nostrils emphatically. Van Dyke rubs his nose in response.

"You doin' okay, Terry?"

"Yes, just the dust, the dust."

"*The Man Without Qualities*. Excellent choice!"

"But this one is missing the posthumous papers –"

At that moment, Minor kicks open the door with one muckraker. Everyone spins around. He does not hesitate. He lifts a .22 out of his flapping coat and levels it at the crinkling face of Mr. Terence Cockerel, if that is even his real name. Van Dyke ducks behind the counter in a cloud of cartoonish dust and Muscles races into the back. Out of a box of YA classic *Minor Love* leaps a shelver with the reddest, most bloodshot look the store has ever seen. Minor wavers with both barrels, targeting the clerk.

"And I want *both* volumes of *Orlando Furioso*, my good fellow."

The clerk somersaults haphazardly backward and dives behind a duck blind of unshelved pulp. A stray bullet nicks *A Dance to the Music of Time*. Cockerel stares at the menacing face through the dust and sighs. Thought bubbles emerge ...

"Agent Minor! Yes, I've been expecting you since our Mensa days."

He taps the floorboards with his foot in an inquisitive manner, wondering whether to bite into the poison-dart bendy straw he is so casually chewing. Minor turns and takes aim. Behind the counter, Van Dyke overturns a box of Hammett and searches blindly for an old literary Luger.

"I have soooo been waiting for this day."

The Concierge screams. A shot rings out ...

VII – Low Noon (Redux in 3-D)

An echo of thunder. A Cold War interpretation of the sky affects the mood of the entire township. Minor is back in town and everyone can smell it. The younger Mr. Growlewicz can barely dole out imported smokes and gherkins in the back room, the way his hands keep shaking. Hortenzia can barely turn a trick, she is so very nervous. Among many black market industries, there are murmurs. The embryo dealers are certainly perturbed.

"I'm just an old fart, if you want the truth. Too long in the tooth to start afresh. And what to do with all this extra stock? And just look at that steaming clock! Time is a'gainin' ..."

And as for Terence Lauren Cockerel, he is a reluctant participant in the Civic Watch program and the chief target this week. He is wearing an adhesive name tag that says as much to Señorita Sharp, who hootchy-kootchies through the trendy boutique double doors. She gives Civilizer Cockerel a playful squeeze, followed by an agonizing yank. As his blood pressure accelerates, she stares his pancake makeup down with grim admonition.

"You think I don't know that man. I know him through and through. He run me through and through. I am no way afraid to fink. He could not get it up in time, hee hee, and you laugh, but that just make him angrier. I hear he's settled down in Hillock Springs. Good luck I wish him and his little woman! I hear those springs have the power to revive the most flaccid of aspirations."

Her *fusilli lunghi bucati* laughter is interrupted by the swinging of double doors. Minor strides in with a huge two-seater papoose around his neck.

"These colicky screamers must be proof of something!"
"Sorry to say, but those twins have your limp and cowardly eyes. Where did you buy them? At the global general store?"

They slap each other for a full five minutes until they are raw with melodrama.

"Why don't you whap me again?"
"Why, you are the one who is whipped now, or so I hear down the vine."
"Why, I could reach the end of the celluloid throwing you about. But I got business in this township. You seen anything of Cockerel?"

Señorita Sharp turns her head and pretends not to notice a shivering figure with his pants down and a lampshade on his head.

"I haven't seen nothing. ¡And even if I have, he is so much bigger and better than you, señor!"

Minor reaches for the lamp switch with a steely look of suspicion and yanks the light off, before marking his exit with a trailing whistle. Señorita Sharp covers her ears, sick to death of that old-fashioned tune. Then she turns to the trembling lamp in her boudoir.

"Yet, hombre, is there not something thrilling in the way he just debased you?"

"And *you*," squeaks Cockerel.

"And *me*," purrs Hortenzia from a room down the hall.

Señorita Sharp snaps her fingers and a laughing gaffer adjusts her lighting.

"Ever since that day he plugged my father in the back and crept into my window and dragged me off with his train of caravans, there has been nothing but this gypsy life for me. And I have tasted and licked the mirthless smack and tickle of freedom and have turned around and have only asked for more. And I have given pleasure to many a good man or scoundrel on a noose. And in the clink of many townships, I have seen what upstanding men do when they get busy on each other. And I have seen the misery of dusky miners, barely able to climb those stairs with a bottle in each hand, and in the morning, the same dusky faces, even more haggard and miserable. And I have felt the nimble hands of grocer boys, absent of Bartlett pears or mouthwatering mangos. And I have learned the futile horseplay of stable hands behind the shitkicker's ball. And I have known the multiple protuberances and mutant tentacles of country singers in the desert, fresh from atomic opry. But that man I know through and through. Wherever he goes, there is a new-couch smell of scandal and a stink of desire. And that man, he is the one man I fear. And you are the one man I fear *for*. And now there is this look of death in your eyes I want to stain-remove."

Cockerel takes out a vial of Farmacia and sprinkles some of it into a glass of grainy water. Then, looking at Señorita Sharp and thinking better of it, he dumps the entire vial into the glass.

"Here's looking at you. ¡Salud, sexy legs!"

Without speaking, she reaches for a long loop of rope attached to a rusty bedframe with innumerable scratches upon it. She encircles the head and neck of Civilizer Cockerel with an air of danger. They are about to kiss, when the twenty-three-year-old body doubles appear and take their place, allowing the rope to dance between each bump and grind, with the dazzling assistance of a veteran lasso artist.

[The director shifts in his folding chair with raw anticipation of the finished scene. He shoos away the latest hot-property hunk with a wave of his silver cigarette holder.

"You see, in these opening shots, we wanted to establish the Cold War sense of isolation from the get-go! Brrrrr!!! The grey sky. An aging citizen, kindly enough. Yet he has a history we cannot reconcile. And in this encounter, we bear witness to a shared history. Civilizer Cockerel used to get mighty lonesome and paid more than the occasional call to Señorita Sharp. And in spite of the moolah, in spite of gouging the old geezer, she has gotten used to his general crankiness and fogey smell. The scene in the Turkish bath is intended to show their level of intimacy, and rather casually, we are invited to share in this. Also in the *Desperate Launderette* spin-cycle scene and in the outdoor shower scene (a classic!), we wanted to show these characters in a different light, defined by their almost freakish need to be *extreme* naked.

"There is something twisted between them, and that is something her ex-lover (that Asspurrtame-chewing swine) cannot annihilate, and I think *that* is a beautiful thing. See in this frame how their faces darken as they tie one another up and cudgel away. The hint of fire and resignation between them as they do it on a frightened mule is almost palpable. But Minor won't give it up for her. No sireeee. He's got a promissory note for a few pieces of silver if he goes through with the dastardly deed. It's what comes of living in a Western during the Cold War. In this era, these hombres are at once becoming less threatening *and* increasingly paranoid. And we really tried to focus on the metrosexual tensions between the characters, as in the scene where Cockerel and his deputy have a tussle in the local sausage factory. Or in the other nude scene where Señorita Sharp dresses up the new Mrs. Cockerel for her honeymoon, before they slip into a mud puddle and start wrestling. And I have to say that the actress who plays Goldie has a remarkable debut. By the way, she is also my niece, although she auditioned under a slightly different name and I knew almost nothing about it …"]

"He has till the clock runs down to get the crap outta town."

"Kill Sugarpapá, an' you as good as kill me! Azúcar, I call him, because he is sweeter than you on my tongue."

Señorita Sharp does not hesitate. She completes a long quadrille over to Cockerel's digs, and pulls him out of a slighty used hot tub and slaps him awake. The Cheshire clock on the wall is smiling, lolling out its tongue.

"Terry, Terry, look alive! Minor has set his good hand on your person! He's making ready to bust your clock!"

"Have you ever done it in a hot tub, my dear? There is a saying. In those things, you never know what you might get."

Meanwhile, Minor is taking his gooey, sweet time. Cockerel will get a fight or flight chance. In the distance, upon an unbalanced horizon, the Concierge appears, accompanied by a bizarre rigatoni riff, the staple of all high-carb Westerns. And he is riding a humpback ass with all his might. He steels his beady eyes, trying to judge the lay of the land and the most strategic positions to assume with a rifle. But then he shudders on his flagging ass to even think it. He has seen Minor take out entire townships before. *Just* to use the bathroom. But Cockerel was an odd fish in his own way. The Concierge had heard other ghastly and rather unappetizing rumours about that cat. And he is starting to feel that his dime-store education lacks a ranching component. He pulls out a dated *Riding Crop Calendar/Cowpoke Almanac* and squints at the position of the sun in the sky.

"I'm out of my depth. If only Miss February could help me!"

And back in the heart of town, at the weekly pissing contest, everyone is deliberating. Who to put their money on? Business was better than good when Minor and his cronies were running the rickety mines and portable softwood outfit and especially $H_2OOO\ In(port)/X(port)$, which sent their drinking water to needier souls on the dark side of the moon and supplanted those sources with a low-alcohol draft water called Pure Daft. But the local Civilizer had put an end to all that on his first day of donning the name tag.

"Now we just seem to sit around, knocking back ginger beer after ginger beer. Think our horses'll drink that dreck!?! And now he's gonna get hitched to his online-order Lolita."

"Excuse me … need it escape your memory that I was Miss March Riding Crop, two years running, and more recently, Miss Sustainable Resource?"

The pissers slowly nod and buckle up as a show of respectful politesse. But they are feeling mighty surly without their daft water.

"We sure ain't questioning your credentials, missus. Cockerel is one lucky cluck. But jist coz he's covered in honey don't mean he ain't gotta get outta this anthill! Let him do right by you and hightail it the hell out of Clockring!"

[The director continues his commentary.

"There is definitely a tension in the community of Clockring. They are disgruntled about the lack of an economy."

The new blockbuster hunk brings him a shandygaff in the shade.

"O dude, this part is so bitchin'!"

The director pats his bottom home.

"Run along now, Chad. We'll hang out and discuss the ambiguous ménage/comedy I have planned for you later tonight, over ostrich. You see, the members of the town miss the munitions factories and any interruption to their perpetual extirpation of the earth. And they are all looking forward to the new blueprints for the Ghost/town Gambling House and the Barn Burner Bordello. Everyone knows that Minor is a whiz at job creation. And they have barely batted an eyelid at the clause ratifying the agreement and pushing the contract through – the small print that transfers the holdings of one town Civilizer, *Terence Cockerel*, to the city administrators, in the event of his demise, postdated after the expiration of *X* number of clocks in the township of *Clockring*, etc."]

The Concierge punches the trendy clothing-store double doors of the saloon open and orders an Old Cockerel – one of the last originals, a classic.

"¡Why, this is what our company slaves drank, señores!" He gulps down half the golden can and welcomes the instant burning in his parched throat. "Ahhh ... so like sarsaparilla!"

"More like manzanilla."

The Concierge recognizes the sassy femme fatale from a shameful night in Ennui, Arizona. She signals for her cases full of costumes and toys to be brought down.

"You, you're the guy who wants to watch. Then runs away like a church mouse with the collection plate! You like what you see, huh?"

"And I would have gotten away with it, if not for Cockerel! So, you are really on the downlow for that old fart!"

"Cock-a-diddle-do," warns a clock on the wall, weary of this conversation. Señorita Sharp glares at the detestable little sidekick, filthy in his torn shirt and buttless chaps. But then, to the left of his ostentatious codpiece, she notices a tiny (**m**) burned deep into his thighflesh. And she can smell that oh-so-familiar personal fragrance and fleshwash, even through layers of grime. Already, the erotic air conditioning of Minor is sweeping across the entire township. She grabs the stubbornly stained collar of the Concierge and sidles up to him.

"Shhh, shhh, hombre. *Es muy ... tranquilo.* You know, there is still a lemon wedge of time. ¡Maybe, for old times' sake, we could go upstairs and relive those old times, sí! You know I have not packed the automatic riding bull or bid the mariachi band boys *adiós* yet."

The Concierge allows himself to be stroked for a few minutes before the truth dawns on him. His face sours and he pushes aside a massive mall burrito.

"¡O I get it! ¡You think you can save that grandfatherly meal ticket of yours, by playing up to me!"

Señorita Sharp slaps him with a sizzling quesadilla.

"No, I do not think so. If anything, I am playing *down* to you. ¡I was going to rock your little sidecar!"

She grabs his codpiece and tosses him through a blooper wall. The Concierge flies through the air and plunges headfirst into the gingery town fountain. He shakes off a cloud of fleas and nits, before sticking his head back through the double doors.

"¡Well, you know what, you virulent strain of the service industry you – maybe my sugar daddy is bigger than your low-calorie sugar daddy and maybe in less than half an hour or your money back he is going to pop your carbonated town hero fulla holes!"

And Señorita Sharp whips her head around faster than a startled whippet or a spurt of Kreemy Deluxe and with a withering look, deflates all mannish exposition of his shrinking self-esteem.

"There is a train to a self-harness retreat today. I am going to be on it with no more than this kitty to live on. I suggest you and your liquidating cohort do likewise and scram and scramble your black market eggs somewhere thither, or it will not be pretty what goes down, I swear by all murmurs about the Magdalene. You better be on that train – that is what I am saying."

"You better be on it," screams the Concierge from an unlatched sidecar stranded in the dirt. "¡Because there'll be nada left! ¡Nada! And remind me to book a no-tell motel inside your ****ing ****!!!"

A passing train whistle drowns out the expletive curse of the Concierge that was ultimately to prove portentous. But Señorita Sharp is already lugging her luggage aboard. She clutches her Ginseng edition of *The Merry Tao of Mao* tightly and gives one last forlorn look at the sorry little town.

"¡Adiós, my dear Azúcar! ¡So long, you candied-ass suckers! Goodbye, my loves, goodbye ..."

But Minor doesn't sweat it. Not a single bead of wampum. He knows where to find Old Cockerel. Likely in the last outpost of bookstores anywhere round here for miles and miles. Minor approves of books but not of very educated townships. After all, someone has to move the gold and water. There is nothing so fatal to a monopolist like ideas. But he finds Civilizer Cockerel asleep on a bench with a giant timepiece hanging around his neck.

"Move along, gramps. And by the way, where's your Euroteen ball and chain?"

"Leave her outta this. It's me you want. She had the misfortune one eventide to pick up a washed-up, near ginger-beer heir."

So the two desperados sit in a luminous café from dusk until dawn, transfixed by blue neon signs and industrious nightcrawlers furthering their own nefarious schemes.

"This *is* a decent dry double cappuccino," offers Minor gallantly. "All the same, if I even see one inch of your sugary cane when the clocks run down, then I swear I *will* take you down."

"There's a flip side to that coin," responds Cockerel. "If I so much as feel someone behind me in the middle of the night, I swear *I will not hesitate*. I will plug you right in the funnies section."

"And that would certainly solve a world population problem," titters Minor.

Both men burst into raucous peals of rotini laughter.

"By the way, are you paying for this?"

"What? No. Not really – I have a coupon."

Cockerel sighs and polishes his harquebus, preparing for the operatic duel at hand. He had no wish to let loose on a man's back from some back-alley stairwell. During those global assassination days – his soup and salad days – dishes were his bread and butter. Blowing a hole in vital organs (hence short-selling their resale value) was more complicated and more intense, and certainly more messy.

"Cuckooo cuckoo whoo coo kuh coo ..."

The last clock. Four mercenaries have arrived on the dot, right at low noon, in stupendous LeatheX ensembles. Cockerel leaves them no time to react. He sets a barrel of ginger beer alight and feebly rolls it toward them. Then he runs like hell. And while they are drinking the last barrel of Old Cockerel, which is incidentally very refreshing after their long dusty ride, Mrs. Goldie Cockerel–to-be leaps out behind them and starts firing, plugging one after another in the back. Three desperados hit the dirt. The fourth dies with a short and didactic soliloquy upon his lips.

"O this desensitized hardcore gamer culture of violence!"

A subsidized lunch cart teeters its way over the smoking bodies. Meanwhile, at the other end of the street, Cockerel uses the steaming pea-soup fog to his advantage and fires his harquebus. A man tumbles out of an outdoor sex swing.

But Minor still remains. He winks at his pin-up fiancée and straps on a pair of PlayVision goggles before attempting to negotiate the thick pea-soup cloud.

[The director is on the edge of his seat, fanning himself vigorously with a copy of Lorca's *The Public*, and softly patting Minor's knee.

"What is it like to play yourself, I wonder. And what were you thinking in that scene?"
"When you are working with so talented a director and with such talented actors, like Miss Sharp or Goldie, and with a stage thespian like Sir Terence Cockerel, well, you cannot release anything less than a hunk of quality."
"And when you are working with such a talented niece of a talented director," adds Miss Sharp, "you know you won't go short of smack for a while yet."
"Yeah, and I like learned so much," adds Goldie, "from all these has-beens last week. And yeah, when you're working with a stuffed theatre guy, whatshisname, that dude, yeah, it's like so coooool. I can't wait for my next fifteen minutes of film time."

The director bestows a warm, avuncular grin upon her blank, beautiful face.]

Civilizer Cockerel staggers through the waft of pea soup, searching for the right canister of vitamins in his shirt pocket. He averts his eyes from the Cannes version of celluloid that for five minutes has Goldie bouncing up and down on the smoking bodies so that they repeatedly spurt jets of pig's blood all over the trendy saloon doors. Cockerel shivers to consider that he and his name brand may suffer a fate more ignominious than that of Colonel Chicken, who once shot a man in cold blood for calling him *chicken*. After that incident, they dragged him from franchise to franchise to cut opening-day ribbons and pose beside his own bucketed likeness for photographs. And he never saw one nickel from his own clucking invention.

"And yet how much worse would run the gingery ballad of Terence Cockerel?!?"

Then out of the pea broth, Minor appears. Followed by a single discharge.

VIII – Get in under the Ground Floor

Denizen M. opens the door of Ye Olde Allegorie and brushes off his coat. He decides upon a vacant corner and snaps his fingers, signalling to a young woman leaning over the bar and laughing with a gang of customers. He rubs his hands together impatiently.

"The *usual*," she announces.

He wonders what she means. He listens to the departing squeak of her shoes. She pumps out a waterfall of murky liquid and returns with it across the parquet floor. Denizen M. drinks in her loose-fitting garb and awkward walk. She reminds him of beautiful people in snapshopped posters concerning other places.

"My, that is a fine head!"

"I wouldn't know, sir."

"And what is this I am partaking of? And whom do I have the honour of addressing?"

"Everybody calls me Mémé. And this is a flagon of our locally crafted lager, Allusion."

M. notices a glimmering pin in her raven hair as she returns to the others. It is flashing a small letter *a*, just like the pendant about her neck. He feels a small pang. She most certainly reminds him of someone. He drinks more of his Allusion and allows that thought to dissolve. There is nothing so treacherous or insidious as a memory. Nearby, a pair of noisy labourers are stretching their limbs and animatedly debating the true nature of the game, and ejaculating possible outcomes, before gently rejecting them altogether. They and M. drift into a lull, urged on by the breathy recording of a local chanteuse.

"*J'écris, j'écris*," she huskilizes.

The labourers are starting to fall asleep to the sound of themselves … but there is a burst of yowling. Mémé was just reminding the men on bar stools of a funny story. She makes her exit from their company and returns to M., who has finished his flagon. She smiles broadly, happily, politely and/or for the sole sake of her gratuity.

"I knew you would like it."

"How did you know?"

"I had a feeling about you. And what brings you to this part of town? Just looking around?"

"I suspect I will be here indefinitely."

"Well, I hope you will take in the primitive artefacts down the street. They are supercool. But are you here for your work, sir?"

"I am looking for a position in the general area. More specifically, I am to be the new Developer. I have received a communication via the Central Processing Authority with regard to the Grain Elevator. I have just finished my last project ..."

"You have formed a connexion with the Grain Elevator?"

She hurries back to the bar and pumps out another flagon of the murky liquid, amid general whispering. Then she returns and drops the flagon with a crash in front of M.

"This is on the house, then, Herr Developer. And I can't seem to make the logo today. Look at that, like a wounded butterfly!"

"And how do you know of the Grain Elevator?"

Mémé fingers her glowing amulet nervously. Then she produces a damp cloth from a serving holster and leans forward, lifting the flagon and wiping the table underneath.

"I want to talk, but not right now."

As she looks over at the other customers, her face appears to age a few uninteresting decades. M. smells her fragrance, very close and very familiar, the same as her soft whisper.

"Come back and see me later. Go the back way. Near midnight. Knock twice."

After she leaves him, one of the men, a small balding man with a glistening pencil moustache, hops off his stool and approaches the dim corner. He holds out his hand.

"They call me Stint, though my name's Lewis. So I go by Stint."

"Stint ..."

"So, are you the new Developer?"

"It hasn't been decided absolutely yet. This is, you might say, a trial."

"Now why bother Mémé's pretty little head about business we men should be chewing over?"

"And what business is it of yours?"

After downing his lager, Denizen M. escapes the stifling atmosphere of Ye Olde Allegorie and curses the abrupt downpour. And the rain thickens into sleet for a while, and soon into falling snow. M. moves very slowly through the thickening snow in his interview suit, pulling his flimsy impermeable tighter. Each flake strikes his frame and oppresses his spirit. He would like to leave. He is completely estranged of relations and bereft of acquaintances, a stranger here, in this vague attempt at a city. No one to even lend him a stick of furniture for the night. And it would be so easy to surrender to this cinematic atmosphere, to this artificial powder. He decides to walk around for a few hours until he can come back and talk with Mémé. He takes a step through the synthetic snow. A step behind him echoes. The sound is muffled. M. stops.

"Do you have a message for me?"
"Why hello, Developer!"

Leaving Denizen M. in the ersatz cold, the stranger soon disappears through tumbling flakes, all of them alike. M. slowly follows the man's footprints. At last, he arrives beneath a street lamp, where a lovely trash fire is burning. The layered figure is warming his hands and inhaling fumes from the rather flammable artificial snow. M. stares through the overlay of paisley and argyle, making out a dark pair of watery eyes.

"Tell me, sir, how did you know I was the Developer?"
"Who drops by but a new Developer? And who lives in all these new places or buys these newly developed Things, anyway? Stack the bodies higher, that's my motto. It's all the same, this world and the next."
"Are you a Developer then?"
"I've never seen anyone else come to town, except for visitors with blank faces. Come to think, we don't have much need for another Developer."
"I have no wish to give a falsified assumption of myself in the slightest. The most commonly held belief is that I, in fact, live in a bush or tar-paper shack. My first duty shall be to correct this minor discrepancy. Although I have only just arrived, the most immediate remedy for altering this perception would be to locate an available residence on a temporary basis, in other words, to shack up with some agreeable soul for an indefinite period. As for my position as Developer, it has not been decided in this particular suburb, or even within a single square of Metropolis itself."
"Already you are incapable of enjoying a heartwarming trash fire, worried to death how you will look and what about your reputation and what if your position is not permanent and so on. Sounds quite like a Developer to me!"
"I would like to construct something arty and daring for the populace ..."

The man shakes his head and howls up at the Snowblowzi 7000.

"Why don't you build me a Gaudi igloo, for starters? And what do you have now? *Your* public art in the water, a home for cormorants to shit and breed upon! Purely spoiling the view ... of Nature! You know what I sez ... eliminate all public art!"
"It is very cold tonight."

"Cold??? You ain't seen nothing! How about a surrealistic rendition of Alberta or lawdforsaken Manitoba? Our fake cold has nothing on theirs."

"What is your name, sir?"

"Why, everybody calls me Duck, because I am the King of Fishers! Mayhap you have met my philandering first knight, Guy Gallante, en route to another eviction. I rule the alleyways and know all the allotted stakes and territories. And I have first dibs on the choicest returnables. And I am the wiliest of dumpster divers! Even the Grain Elevator has failed in its attempt to allocate a civic cart for me! They'd have to chuck it into my cold dead hands. And this here's Grizzle."

M. follows the man's pointing glove and notices for the first time a large dog with a grey-black coat at the base of the fire, gnawing on an enormous bone with some meat still on it.

"And there will be restitution, big time, for all the wrongin'. So the way the gossip goes, I keep my eyes open for the stranger, for the deliverer, for the chosen one who will take one for the team!"

In response, M. offers him a patronizing grin of goodbye.

Two knocks. The back door opens.

At the bar, the Stropper is intent on nursing yet draining to the last of his glass of something new called Spunk, while pausing to play with his nacreous cheeks.

"And who is that skulking in the back, Mémé? Your extra-special friend with compensation?"

"You know I only have eyes for you."

"Ah yes, I see now. He's the new Developer! And you have so much work to discuss ... Well, cheers, Developer! Hope your stay is real nice like."

And off he goes into the flakeless snowfall, cackling mechanically. But before the door has quite closed, Mémé leaps upon Denizen M. They collapse upon a sunken chesterfield. He looks into her darting eyes with mild bemusement.

"Just what is this about, miss?"

"Were I not already promised to Plume (that ingrate!), I would jump your tiddly bones this instant!" M. launches her off him and rises, affronted yet uncontrollably intrigued.

"And you and this Plume, do you then share in intimate relations?"

"Developer, I cannot deny that Plume is ... mmm, yes ... more than satisfactory for a simple sort of person like myself. But you must understand it means nothing to me! Even while making eyes at these men here, and giving up eyefuls to their burning eyes, for the slimmest of tips and most rotten of turnips, I have thought of nothing but you!"

"I admire your convictions to the utmost."

Then Mémé, with a faraway look, laughs to no one – herself, the wall, the windowpanes.

"But Plume is not here and you *are* the new Developer. And I bet you have nowhere to rest your big head now! Why don't you come and rest your big soft head upstairs?"

Mémé lays M. down on a makeshift cot a few paces from her bed. Then she makes a painstaking show of undressing, leaving nothing but a glowing brewery logo about her neck, before disappearing beneath a number of coverlets. M. begins by studying the coverlets, as if to memorize each pattern, but to no avail. The first is a mushroom soup cream. The second is a culled patchwork. The third is as rich as a purple finch in texture, a bird that looks as if it has been dipped in a bucket of raspberries. M. begins to wonder if there could be an infinite series of coverlets to peel off the sublime body of Mémé, delightful for its robustness and full-figuredness. He begins to dwell upon the incessant possibility of coverlets, growing like weeds and foxgloves beneath a handkerchief tree where dogs merrily lift a single leg, all of them smothering the brief half snore of Mémé, which wakes her up again. M. feels a toe.

"Hey M., what are you doing over there?"
"Nothing. Nothing."
"You are almost intriguing, M. Something of a mystery! And I must say you are quite the contrary to my drip of a fiancé!"

Denizen M. twists and turns upon the cot, trying to get comfortable and feeling like a captured hog turning upon a primitive spit, turning and turning away from spear and flame at once, only to meet them again, and getting cooked all the same. Hot. Sizzling. So hungry. His body wants to bound across the room and pounce upon Mémé, but at the same time, his mind is going through the insectile processes of a Developer.

"Would it not affect his standing, his hopes?"

And he feels the blind paternal oppression of the snowfall through the window. He cannot get up, or even move. He is trapped in a dream-like atmosphere that paralyzes his limbs with chills as much as with brazen toastiness. There he remains, upon the cot, inconsolable. Near to Mémé, he remembers the buzzwords of his previous incarnations with some fondness, and wonders what position they might occupy in this peculiar place. And Mémé's glance is surly yet sultry. They each suspect a trick is being played by the other. They both concur, matter of factly, they must have met before in a variation of this place. But this sentiment brings no joy, only numbness. M. lies back and scratches his minor paunch, talking aloud of the things he will own and the pad he will place them in when he is Developer. Mémé listens through the heap of coverlets, happy to hear the regulated talk of officials, the kind she is used to.

"Now you sound a little like Plume."

"Yes, yes, Plume ..."

He wants to strangle Plume with his bare hands. But no. Plume comes first. Always. If he was in the man's presence, he would probably only laugh him off and help himself to another pinch of snuff. But Plume was now an unkillable abstraction, and therefore infinite and omnipotent and capable of anything he was not. M. gets up and feels his way back downstairs. The floor is cold on his bare feet. He is surprised to find the lights on and a group of guests drinking and whispering together. He listens for a while, before appearing in a borrowed nightgown. Whistles ensue.

"Hurrah! Three cheers for the new Developer! Huzzah! Come and have a drink with us, you blackguard whoreson you!"

They are all men, identical, and almost faceless. They sit packed tightly together and clink their glasses in unison. There is a flutter in the low-cut neckline of M.'s nightgown, and he turns around to see two diminutive chaps in livid green outfits, moving toward the stairwell leading up to Mémé.

"*Before the fiddler has fled. Before they ask us to pay the tab ...*"

"You there! Yes you! What are you doing there, you green men?"

"Nothing at all, Developer!"

"Don't worry about them, Developer! Mémé will not mind. And we have business to discuss, yes?"

"*Let's face the music and dance ...*"

M. watches the two men in green evaporate up the stairs, like two glasses of absinthe down the hatch of an upside-down gullet. Followed by daimonic laughter.

"You called me Developer. Do I have the entry-level then?"

"The authorities and officials of the Grain Elevator do not, except in very specialized cases, permit themselves to sully their fingernails with the people, who, regardless, are always complaining. Give them nothing, that's their motto! With a creed like that, you can tighten the belt and keep a budget from going crazy. And you suppose there to be room for a Developer just now?"

M. accepts a drink on the house and sips it dismally.

"Now don't get down in the dumpers," the three men echo at once. "We could confirm one or three of the rumours about you tonight."

"Rumours?"

"We don't know even one of them, of course. That requires an official application with one of the registrars. And do you have your papers with you?"

M. reaches for imaginary pockets in Mémé's lent nightgown.

"No ... no, not right now."

"It will only take longer then. But this would be an opportune time to rouse one of our registrars, to get one tire spinning in the mud at the very least."

"Where are they, then, these registrars?"

"Right under our feet, Developer! Fast asleep ..."

"Let's go together, right now, Developer!"

One of the three, as he moves under a hanging lamp, becomes the elder. He lifts an emerald rug up from the floor. Then he pries up a hatch with strong fingernails. One by one, they descend a ladder into darkness.

"Come on, Developer! Don't tarry, there's a bright lad! If you want to be a climber, you'd best start by climbing down this instant!"

At the bottom, there is subdued track lighting along a narrow corridor. M. feels his way along walls that appear identical, all the way along, trying to keep up with the rapid footsteps of the three men. At last the sound of rushing feet stops and M. bumps into one of the men.

"Oooof!"

"Registrar Muckraker's the one!"

"Let's wake him up!"

"No. It's not worth the trouble. For this man, we need to wake up Sproff."

"Sproff!"

Two of the men kick each other for a good five minutes, providing varied impressions of bad flatulence with their mouths and flapping elbows.

"O yeah, Sproff, yeah. Sproff is the registrar to see. Bpttttt! Bhhhpptttt!!!"

"Try to forget about Muckraker for now. This is the guy to try. Best to just go in."

"This is how things get done, really."

The eldest man seizes M.'s shoulder with his ursine grip and then gives him a push in the right direction. Fading laughter. M. feels for the knob and turns it. For a moment, he can imagine the screws holding that knob in place and then how they might unscrew and float off and how M. himself might just float off into infinite catacombs of darkness, still holding this knob. Through the darkness, he can make out a bundle of coverlets. It is very cold. M. reaches for the heavily bundled shape.

"Mmmm ... ooohmmm! What ... who is there – what time is it?"

The lamp is opened. A nervous little man with a slight facial tick and red-rimmed eyes reaches for his spectacles.

"Is this some kind of jape?"
"Jape?"
"Ah yes, you must be the new Developer. That explains everything."

He reaches for a crammed portfolio, and failing to find anything pertinent inside of it, he reaches for a second portfolio. M. watches in disbelief.

"I thought everything would be paperless."
"I am Registrar Sproff."

Sproff shuffles over and pats an empty space, so that M. can hear the creaky bedsprings. M. lies back on the dying mattress. He feels very cold and tired. Sproff unfolds a slender file and tickles M.'s nose with it.

"Come on then, Developer. Are you ready to begin? Now, it says here you are under scrutiny for the position of Developer."

"Actually, I was sort of hoping I was already this thing I am applying to be. And I was hoping to clear up a number of unsubstantiated rumours buzzing about my person since I arrived in this city."

"Your file says you live in a bush. I suppose there are a few other distasteful nasties about you on record, but nothing that doesn't suggest you wouldn't make more than substandard communal company material. Say, for lining a driveway, maybe even two!"

"I was hoping for the position of Developer, after all."

Sproff adjusts his spectacles and allows a twitching glower to darken his features.

"You must understand that this will take more than a dozen consultations, even to begin the process ..."
"I am very cold and tired."

And Sproff laughs, putting away the file. And then he laughs again, closing the light.

IX – The (In)Flight Flick

A drinks cart rolls out of the sky. The Concierge awakens with a start, groggy after his plane meal of fresh Atlantic squarecod followed by a small vodka tonic. On account of a minor glitch, the business class passengers have missed their news, and the Concierge has to watch it for the second time in both English and French. Everyone groans. Minor himself peers out through the bulletproof curtain that divides the plane and waggles a disapproving finger. Someone asks him for a job. The Concierge curls up into a fetal ball in his chair, not wanting to blow his cover. All the same, he suffers through a terrible tension in the erotic wake of that man. Fortunately, this is a smoking flight. The sign comes on, and everyone lights up a cigar or joint and starts tapping ashes into the aisle.

At last, the movie starts and the Concierge is tossed into the visceral feast of the leaping jumping dangling protagonist who will do *anything* to get what needs doing done. This is the second sequel to *Flight Course 103*, about a group of bored post-Communists who have allied themselves with other swarthy terrorists with nothing to do but play havoc with the airline business. But little do they know the hero, Hurt Hardass, has parachuted into them and has ridden the nose of the jet for air miles in an optimistic montage of harrowing stunt sequences. Then he slips aboard through some portable inertia piping he always carries in his slimming purple tool belt. He creeps into the baggage compartment with a concealed sonic syringe chock full of the charm virus intended for co-star Bébé, one of the three most beautiful flight attendants in the world – incidentally, all three are on the same plane. She reads her two lines off her palm with conviction and proceeds to brush aside the charm serum. There is no need for such additives. Hurt checks his huge watch. Still half an hour to go before they atomize one of the historic capitals. There is still time for a scene of tender intimacy inside one of the sportier duffel bags.

Before long, they unzip the bag again and emerge, sharing a doobie. There is a sentimental and persistent guitar chord of Andalusian origin as Bébé explains exactly how she felt after her reduction surgery. She wanted nothing better than to appear nude on the cover of *Infame* with a little Hurt kicking inside of her. He grins marvellously and inanely, pinching her reduced flesh.

"If we get through *this*."

The scene shifts to a ponytailed terrorist, as portrayed by Coit Oskar Barrigan, paring his fingernails and batting his eyelids. The in-flight meal has made him groggy. He lays his semi-automatic down. The latest eyecatching sensation (sorry, Bébé) is Melónia Mélon, who gives a passionate speech about the virtue of the commuters they are about to destroy. He slaps her and she slaps him back. He slaps her again and she slaps him right back. He rubs at a trickle of blood running from the corner of his mouth. They may have a future together after all, back in her much-missed homeland of Sblowvia.

"Why not run and get me a pillow, sweetheart?"

"Yes, let us drink Smirkoff and cuddle and wait for inevitable!"

Melónia is just fluffing and adjusting his pillow when Coit is startled wide-eyed to realize that the pillow is none other than Hurt Hardass!!!

"I guess you were just caught napping," quips Hurt.

Then the men roll around the aisles, seizing each other's wrists in an intense life or death homoerotic struggle. Coit reaches in vain for his semi-automatic as Hurt scratches his chest with beautiful fingernails, but Melónia picks it up first and waggles the weapon between the men, unsure who to shoot or who is who and what her next line could possibly be. But as the villain Coit makes an obscene repetitive gesture, she suddenly remembers in an 8 mm sequence of flashing images an illumined rendezvous in Tuscany and then a castle bedroom in Provence and then a brewery vat in Milwaukee and then the vacant conveyor belt of an automotive factory in Detroit. She is no longer torn. There might still be a chance.

But at that moment, Bébé appears, still buttoning up her uniform jacket and emphatically shaking her head. In one of her finest scenes, knowing that she and Hurt will never mingle their love juices again, Melónia completely depressurizes and reaches for the emergency hatch handle and gives it a good hard yank. After a rapid pump and jerk, the door of the plane comes flying off as she freefalls through the stratosphere. Coit takes one look at the open door and follows suit, leaping out after her. Hurt kisses Bébé and examines his throbbing watch. If only he can escape this movie in time! He then uses a good quarter of an hour to explain to Bébé that Coit is in fact no terrorist at all. He is in reality a film pirate who distributes their movies without compunction and robs them all of extensive royalties. Bébé gasps.

"That bastard!"

Hurt goes on to speechify about the desperate need for the audience to have more children without painkillers and offers to try again at impregnation as soon as he has dealt with the bad guy and has established a standard platonic flirtation with which to buoy Melónia and her rapidly descending spirits. Bébé looks at her company watch, close to tears.

"See you in the sequel!"

"Count on that!"

In the wake of his poignant catchphrase, Hurt leaps out of the plane. Half an hour later, it is the much-advertised exercise technique of frictive hardassing as demonstrated by Hurt Hardass that helps his boulder-solid body to catch up with the plummeting Coit, who is attempting to use Melónia as both a parachute and an impact cushion. Hurt frantically slaps the villain off into his own undercurrent and starts to undress Melónia attentively and with increasing affection. And before she knows what is happening, he has fashioned her airline uniform into a makeshift paraglider.

"Sorry, Melons."

With that audible whisper, he shoves her off his famous buns of lead. And so, she glides to earth slowly with her uniform held aloft over her head, in some outrageous Sinderella lingerie with matching heels. Furious and growling, Coit tumbles into Hurt from behind and grabs him by his bits and pieces. Hurt struggles to adjust his MandeX ensemble. It will take more than the average run-of-the-mill reacharound to hurt Hurt Hardass.

The cinematography is outstanding as they continue to fall and fall toward the quizzical rock faces of Mount Plushmore. The briefchute in the pants of Hurt is rubbed into activation, and the two men hurtle together into a waiting trampoline upon a dusty plateau. The camera pans to Melónia, who has landed safely and scantily in the lonely but loaded graduation limuck of a wasted leading actor. It is clear they will spend the rest of their lives together. Meanwhile, Coit and Hurt stop jouncing up and down and are now rolling across the dusty plateau in a groping contest of epic proportions. At last, Hurt gains the advantage and mounts Coit, who tastes dust. Hurt pulls on his ponytail and rides him in a rage. This rehabilitative act of sodomy is just what Coit has been waiting for.

"I am so so sorry, Hurt. All these years I have just been lashing out in all the wrong ways."

"I don't have time for this. Where is the exchange to take place?"

"At the Lost Renaissance Hotel ..."

At that second, a reverse-takeoff portajet lands on top of Coit, crushing his spine. A trusty platonic workout buddy/compuhack/personal masseur is waiting.

"C'mon, Hurt! I brought your things. And remind me not to ask what kind of day you're having."

"Count on that! Okay, let's blade, Kiki."

The scene transitions to the beaming face of Faith Faith, bombshell and reality chart topper. She is working hard. This role as the manager of the Lost Renaissance Hotel is something of a stretch for her.

"Down in front!"

The Concierge curls up even smaller into his seat and starts rubbing his twitching eyes, although he cannot look away. In this frame of the movie, a very familiar figure whisks through the revolving door. It is none other than Minor in an unbilled appearance. As he crosses the parquet floor, the camera details a heavy black case in his left hand with a large LED readout on the side. And Faith, quick as a whippet, notices the numbers counting down and offers him an überwhite energy-efficient megawatt smile.

"Why, I do declare, that is the funkiest clock I ever did see! If you're telling time backward, you *must* be with our sheik guests! Our rabbis?"

"Well, darling, they sure do give me *the business* at customs! Actually, I'm here for the convention on the subject of covetousness."

Faith hunts and pecks her way through the scrolling list of interplanetary conventions.

"Lemme see ... dickholes, freaks, fetishizers, omniphiles, non-conformists, wetters ... Ahh, here you be, with the Galactic Coveters and Comforters."

"Yes, ma'am. And I go by the name of Minor."

"O my gawwwd, you're Mesmer Minor, the sole originator of the thinkLess technique! O my lawwwd, I have all your books!"

She produces a damp and mutilated copy of the bestselling *So You Think You Can Think* from behind the desk.

"Would you sign mah book fer me?"

In response, Minor stares into her eyes with increasing intensity and suddenly, with a blank expression, she opens the book and inscribes the flourishing *M*s of Mesmer Minor's signature. Then he snaps his fingers and Faith blinks. She blushes, reading the automatic writing.

"*To the most exceptional piece of* ... Ahh shucks, you shouldn't have!"

Minor accepts his room opener and rubs her ring finger.

"Why not? Because of this?"

"Excuse me? Like hell no. That good fer nuthin' left for Uranus with some bitch of a space buccaneer!"

"But the first rule of thinkLess is to think less, am I right? Then I hope you are up for a glass of mango venom later in the Pleasure Garden. Why, I have whiled away many happy hours amid the untamed overgrowth of that lush atrium."

"Yeah, the atrium, sure. I'll keep a lookout later. And they pay me the big bucks to remind y'all we are renowned for our unique trouser presses!"

Faith winks cheekily. Minor eyes his black case. Still plenty of time.

"And is there somewhere I could deposit this?"

"Of course! You can leave your alarm clock with the Concierge."

And the Concierge is positively aghast to watch a tall and tanned specimen playing his rather marginal part in the film. Minor tosses him the ticking case and dings him a few stellar credits.

"Very good, Monsieur. And when will monsieur want his clock back?"

Meanwhile, back at their Den of Rectitude, Hurt and Kiki are packing for their trip together.

"Have you seen my thong? Where in tarnation is my thong?"

They are also having an argument about which is the fastest route to go. There is the facsimile/transport equipment that worked so well in the blockbusting, ball-busting *Time Fax*. And they are aware that Minor most often insists on travelling as molecular mimeograms and they have a good chance of catching up to him. But Kiki is concerned they won't have enough special effects to deal with Minor, even if they are hot on his heels. And Kiki is insisting on taking the cherry oak entertainment armoire. Hurt faces his sidekick, hands on hips.

"Whenever we go anywhere, you pack the fucken kitchen sink!"
"I don't think I like your tone."

Nevertheless, they both strap themselves into the closet flying machine and prepare for thrust off. They swoon and sweat and after some initial tentativeness, they breach the atmospherical layer, leaving a fresh opening behind them.

Then everyone falls silent for a musical montage, a studio recording by Faith Faith of her truck-hopping chart topper "Is that a barbecue stain on my wet B-shirt or are you just pretty pleased to see me?" Bébé tries to do her job without thinking about the danger Hurt is in. Melónia digs into a very romantic candlelight supper with her new beau, but suddenly wonders, What if? Coit is being wheeled down a hospital drama corridor, with an orderly trailing after him with his spine in hand. The Concierge curls up with Mesmer Minor's obsidian case, reminded by the ticking of his own mother's heart. Minor lolls about in the Hothouse and waxes nostalgic about a brief adventure he once offered a young dactylographer among the tomatoes and cucumbers. Hurt and Kiki reach the heated outer layer of Venus, hand in hand through LeatheX straps.

Then, as the sobs of Unhappy Hour fall silent, Faith enters the Rumba Room in a transparent gown. At the same instant, Minor appears from behind an artificial beech in an equally transparent catsuit. Faith blushes.

"*Nice.*"

They drink their Venusian nectar and stare outward at the oiled hunks, each of them in nothing but a tattered loincloth. They are turning giant wheels to keep the hotel running. Both of the viewers are astonished by their electricity-ridden, shock-absorbing utilitarianism. Minor stares at her hungrily.

"I feel I have been looking for you since the beginning of time."

Faith stares off vacantly into the oiled muscles of industrious hunks.

"I know … I mean I think I knew ever since you came back down to ask for a complimentary comb."

"It was really fate for me to forget my own!"

"No, I mean there is a picture in the Gamma wing, a picture that is centuries old. I used to feel the man in that picture would step right out of it and take me in his arms. And you know who the picture looks like …"

Minor touches a finger to her lips.

"Shh shh. There you go, thinking again. To think less is a blessing."

He pushes through the throng of pulsing, undulating flesh and steps upon the karaoke platform. He has used no hypnotic tricks or mind games this time and is strangely moved. For he has felt the wanderlust of time immemorial and has journeyed from star to star. Could this be the one he seeks?

> *"… ein schlagend Herz ließ, ach! mir Satans Tücke daß eingedenk ich meiner Qualen bleib' …"*

Some are shocked by the aria that pours out of him. Others achieve multiple orgasm. Rather transparently, Minor reaches for her hand and they hop into the nearest neurmatic tube.

"What floor would you like?"

"A thousand and three," roars Minor, and the electronic voice crackles from the thrill of aural contact.

They barely make it to Minor's room. The oiled studs are getting tired and the hotel is switching into power-saving mode. But they kick open room 1003 and bolt it shut. There is not a second to lose. In the dimming room, they violently unFeltcro one another, removing all that transparency between them. They leap onto the paisley coverlet, tossing aside a complimentary wafer provided by an artificial deal sweetener company owned by …

"Thinking again!!!"

Minor pulls at her flaxen hair and grips her poultryish neck. They can feel the ethereal electricity of an approaching *Liebestod*. They struggle together in their passion, rolling over the traces of previous lovers and obsessed stalkers. She submits to complete fulfillment in the clutches of the father figure for the entire cosmos. Meanwhile, he fills her head with strange and maddening song.

"So sturben wir / um ungetrennt / ewig einig / ohne End' ohn'
Erwachen / ohn' Erbangen / namenlos in Lieb' umfangen ..."

He shifts her into a better position for the quiver-cam, another of his innumerable sidelines. They plash about wildly in the infrared slip and slide of previous occupants, additional prey for the astonishing reality show *Room 1003*. Minor noses this phantasmagoria, this spermatic diaspora of many promiscuous eons and whispers of available positions in distant constellations as far as the Land of Darkness. They continue to buck like two beasts in the throes of death. He falls back with a desperate look and watches her kneel between his trembling knees.

"O Mesmer! O Minor!"

But something is awry. She claws at his death-defying instrument of pleasure, recognizable anywhere, only to peel away several layers of Physiognome.

"Holy small-town blues, this ain't the right felluh!"

His floppiness disclosed, the figure tries to hide his face and nudity from the hidden camera. At that moment, Kiki bursts out of the entertainment closet with Minor in a sleeper hold. Hurt sniffles and stands fractionally erect over Faith.

"Now tell us what we need to know!"

She giggles up at him. But while everyone is softly tittering about Hurt, Minor manages to unpack and assemble his portable studly-cam console. Faith sneers up at them triumphantly.

"Don't you get it? He's gonna transfer all the director's cuts ... and the truth about you and Kiki!"

The console screen rises and displays a climbing progress bar already at 17% ... But Hurt Hardass and Minor both float into the air and lunge at one another. Then they struggle naked upon the seedy bed of antique memories, slapping at the transfer control and slapping at each other. 69% ... Stalagmites of congealed discharge start to rise all around the bed in a very threatening manner. At last Hurt gains the upper hand and is on top of it all again.

"Let's not make this harder than we have to."

Once again, Faith giggles. Then she touches a bulge in her belly. Not good. Hurt switches off the studly-cam console at 97% and then smashes the device into a thrillion pieces. And suddenly, a pseudo-retired stage actor named Ferskin Pratt emerges from an adjacent room and accepts from Hurt a cheque with many many many trailing zeroes.

"Tar! Ah yes, I see the intrepid Mr. Hardass has done it again. But what's this here?"

He tugs at the rib of Physiognome around Minor's middle and rips the entire bodysuit open only to reveal a very mesmerized and very cranky Concierge. Faith squeals, her mouth agape.

"Then if that ain't Minor, who the hell's baby did I get?"

"Well, there is a way to tell. You see, whenever Mr. Minor is in town, he invariably leaves sextuplets. I think you'll find our friend is long gone, in another nebula by now."

"Count on that!"

And the Concierge mutters something under his breath.

"What's that? Speak up! What? He forgot his cock? No. O dear, I see."

Hurt and Kiki don't quite follow. Faith suddenly has an epiphany. She holds her belly and stares into the camera, which superimposes the image of a black case with a large readout on the side, counting down to a size zero!!! At that moment, Venus explodes. Everyone, hand in hand, is thrown from the blast ...

The Concierge spouts several maledictions from his seat. He looks around at the other passengers, who are weeping and blowing their noses.

"Was this the end of Hurt Hardass?"

But the real Concierge has a sudden suspicion. He unbuckles and makes his way down the aisle. One of the most beautiful flight attendants in the world stands in his way.

"I'm sorry, sir. You can't get up when the movie is still running. That's against regulations."

"O no? Outta my way, Bébé!"

He pushes her aside and races through the class-proof curtain of first class and is greeted by a cool breeze. The cockpit door is open and the pilot and co-pilot are slumped over in their seats. He turns around to find only one figure wrapped in a blanket, with a beatific expression on his blissfully sleeping face.

"Minor! But why?"

Then he notices a loose strip of Physiognome about the sleeping man's neck and with not a little apprehension, he reaches for what is obviously another mask ...

X – The Local Wake

Miss Sharp's body is lain flat upon an artificial stone slab with papier-mâché trimmings. A tobacco-tanned Mr. Minor, in the aesthetic spirit of Inigo Jones, raises his fedora at this morning's advert for

FUN. *Parlour Conglom Unlimited*
Putting the* FUN *back in Funeral

He reaches blithely for where he approximates his heart to be situated and thumps off a few excessive beats for the fleeting vision that lent idealism a kind of dignity. And life.

"She was a fine sort. A bird of some quality, no question. Why, she would have given me the sugar out of her Earl Grey. Had she only met me in the smallest room beside the public square!"

Her makeup is pasty, her lips a little too red. Her long, dark hair hangs loose and wild, and he feels a smidge of neoclassical necrophilia for the latest product spot. After some light dusting, he sits in the public square and admires a beglovèd palm, happily planting corpse flowers. They spring into bloom and start to smell immediately, taunting passersby with their intoxicating stink. He glances up at the writing upon a memorial obelisk:

IS IT NOTHING TO YOU?

A few street urchins gather together and drape themselves about the lower parts of Minor while he fills their brittle pockets with spare alms.

"What is this? A wake?"

Minor basks in the afterglow of their phantom limbs, rising and soon arriving at the crossroad he knows so well. This is no memory, instead an eternal nexus she may pass through at random. It is a gaping tear in the itchy blanket of his comprehension. They are separated by time and circumstance only. Yet at this innocuous spot, he feels the joyful tug of other lives. They are strangers, lovers, siblings, friends, who have never met properly. It smacks of anguish, this lively taste of non-being. But there is no regret. Not for an outbreak of phantasmagoria like Minor.

On the other hand, he appreciates how their contiguous lives give form and meaning to these surrounding structures. They tingle brutally through the fibres of the psychical sensualist. His eyes sample each cornice and arabesque, his appetite whetted by the building codes of ancient cities. The gulls are stirring sculptures of ivory or alabaster. And he can see the corner shop, where any minute she may rise from her slab and buy a bag of sour sweets. And his eyes drink in the popular parlour with its scratched mead benches and cut-rate offers of burger surprise.

PARTY HERE TONITE!

"And is it not here, in the common room before another heart-rending, junk-sick dawn, where I am to locate the irascible and incomparable Shorty Shrooms?"

At the front door, Minos, the bouncer, gnashes his jaws favourably at Minor, another member of the House of Knossos, while he simultaneously examines an ID and wraps his tail eight times around a very ticklish lad.

"*Vada! Andiamo, seduttori, adulatori, indovini, ipocriti, falsificatori!* Flattery will get you everywhere! We still have tons of seating in the nethersection!"

Minor winks at this most judicious burst of repartee. Then his line of sight follows the angle of a building perpetually under construction, once a giant parking lot and now a sunny dramatization of local history. How Captain Minor braved Mistaken Passage and returned to the coast of his origins and fulfilled another leaf-munching prophecy and made sweet hot love to so many Firstbloods and how they pretended to think he was a badly tanned god, in return for free favours. And few people remember that time before time, when their very town was to be christened Minorville, until a few souls at a town meeting on a rainy afternoon decided on the far more sensible Enochvilleport, where an embossed plaque bellows:

<u>NO</u> SMOKING
<u>NO</u> LOITERING

On the right, there was a tunnel composed of pachyderm and walrus tusk, and on the left, there was a tunnel composed of horny saxophones. And one passage left irrefutable evidence of a wet dream, and the other passage, only a nasty case of identity theft. And Minor, having limited cache in his unregistered data dump, a thousand times suffused with a plethora of mystical leaves, could not recall the precise route his journey had rolled him through. He meanders to a cozy kaffeeklatsch just a block away. The workers are refilling their minormugs for another Sisyphean cycle of production. Mostly ordering taste-free Blitzes and tempestuous Diabettos, with rare and giant Incaware jugs jammed with caffeinated sundaes. They are looking to animate their lovely flower-corpse faces, along with those delicious eyes of the dead. Some of them, still searching for the perfect roll-on and roll-over tan. Minor enters and steps directly to the front of the wan and ashen lineup. Even here, he is recognized.

"¿The usual, señor?"

"Indeed, a Gargantuan Devastation blend with a dash of *nekuia*, at the usual godforsaken infernal temperature. And make it snappyish!"

He selects a chair outside, with a great scraping noise of heated iron against red brick. Vacant. Only Old Cockerel is planted outside, thinly disguised beneath a soup-kitchen hairnet and a false mustachio, as directed by the peerless Duccio Truffle. Minor offers his heartfelt respect for this getup and continues to sip his Devastation. However, the glowing staff approach the once-lethal geezer and pester him to move along.

"Sir, this area is for vat-slurpers only!"

"*Praetor irrumator*," mutters Cockerel. "There's no one here. And I'm just waiting for my boss."

The almost ginger-beer magnate is posing as one of the street corner distributors of the daily buttrag, *Wipe*. Minor watches without a word, knowing better.

"If only you knew who you were picking on," sneezes Cockerel.

He scratches coyly at his honeyed 'tache, grunting veiled threats as he moves on. The Stropper, in passage, observes this split second of socio-economic injustice and makes more than one remark.

"Hang on, little missy! Must you really chuck the chap out? He is, after all, only sitting within a perimeter of iron fencing that happens to be on the public pavement! Typical in this city, that you tie a ribbon around the sidewalk and charge admission to the outdoors!"

The Stropper continues to berate and fustigate the staff at length, for he is a true champion of bleeding heart causes. Minor allows his lazy roving eye to follow the once pitiless assassin up the street, and then the charming fellow who is airing his thoughts nearby. Then, with his better eye, he notices a sniper climbing the candied fire escape of a large building opposite the square, appearing in all respects like an ant scaling the side of a waffle cone. Minor makes a face.

"I don't like the look of that one bit. Still, in the land of the dead, he has his work cut out for him. And work *is* work."

Minor lets more of the Devastation blend scald his throat. An extremely well-coifed lad, who resembles a much-celebrated Titian, is sitting on the curb below. A positively enchanting embryo dangles from his raised fist.

"I had a babe out of sanctified legitimate wedlock. And not with the woman I love. I am but a revenge tragedy, a painting of a sorrow. O woe! O whoa! Behold!"

"Why, embryonic research grants are my specialty!"

Minor gives a signal for the bidding to begin. And many figures begin to float around the scalding iron fencing. What they touch rusts at once. And a woman Minor scarcely remembers rattles the molten iron bars.

"They said I was a victim for years. They said I was missing or dead. They said I was a sex-trade worker in the Lower Side. I was none of these things! They took my last-known photo and changed me – they altered the very pixels of my being! And put me on the snapshopping block! They made me look more *victimy*. They called me a proper slag, a slapper with no knowledge of sin. In reality, I was alive, with kids and a spouse in an American suburb. We went to Mallspleen's every week. I was mostly bored and barely knew of anything other than national holidays and barbecues, let alone stashes of scantronned porn and the adherence codes of neighbourhood swingers. We had the percentile of a perfect life. And then I was warned about the murderer in my old hometown and when I looked up the list of victims, I saw my own image, different, distorted, and thought to be dead! But I am not dead!"

Other spectral figures clutch the sizzling bars.

"We were her friends and we nearly died to hear it! We were her folks. We said farewell too soon! Minor, heed our speeches! Minor ..."

"Must be a clerical error in Mortal Resources!"

"Minor, I was thy beer parlour chum, we were buddies, eh? I meant you no harm, ever, ever. You were always the sofissshticated one! Now won't you invite me over for a tasty supper?"

"Get in line, bub."

"I was your mother, Minor. Why don't you ever come to visit? And boy, you look so thin!"

And another relation, beautiful to behold in a sparkly glittersuit, is asphyxiating on her own vomit upon a bran new pee-stained sofa.

"I died behind those purple doors just up the road. The Passssific! Remember me? Remember me."

Her long, dark hair hangs over her face. She moves in rapid, sped-up frames like a *Pan-Asian Terror* sensation. Another casualty. She crawls toward the fencing, before being completely swallowed by the opiate snow of an ornate pop-up book. And another relation does not remember. Not a thing. He is teeming with hallucinatory lizards, asking for receipts, for his records.

"Come visit me, Minor, on the ninth floor of the demolished hospital!"

He wants only for Minor to sign something, a form, to ratify their shared figmentary enterprises, to have a stake in his surrillion-dollar properties. He covers his eyes before impending omens of conspiracy and fraud. And in the background, a diminutive girl hoists up her father and swears at him, pointing to some mad hamburger stains, before apologizing in tears. And there is another fellow, still looking for his sister. Minor blinks and rubs his eyes as a giant reticulum floats by, wrung and crafted from the finest woven feelings of guilt and thatched burlap. It is the size of a kidney bean, a growing cyst of gold, the polyp that produces a pearl. Not unlike the tormented souls about him, he wants to see it tossed out with the trash.

Minor reaches for the embryonic connexion. He wants to sever this cord, forever and ever. Meanwhile, the Sniper moves into position, ironically aware that the architect tumbled to his death from the very same stairwell of rusted waffle cone. Still, Minor loiters behind the iron fencing. He is by no means brave to the point of idiocy. Yet he is known for a brand of boldness and brashness provoked by an extremely irritated curiosity. He appreciates he must wait a bit longer for the elixir, the very font of life ... He sucks up all these sorrows like a mystical sponge, and they transmogrify on the spot into fossilized oil and inkwells.

"Would I could reach for the solar gloom! I am the corporate body of many devices, the most awry of miracle-cure wheelers and dealers, the most wary of tarot and fortune cheaters, the most nefarious of conditioner reconditioners, the most nebulous of lunar worshippers! I have found the key to this city, to a kind of music ..."

His temples burn and he starts to feel dirty, greasy. He can feel the sagging bag of guilt frying his pores alive. Miss Sharp stirs slightly upon the ersatz stone slab, as the FUN. Parlour photographer shouts at her inert pose.

"Yesss work with me work with me here. Why that's dead sexy that's sexy as hell! Garçon! Come on now, our light is leaving! We need more dearth. Where is the spray? Yes, there we are. Yesss you've just died and you look like death warmed over and young girls would kill for a bod like that!" ·

The Sniper is enjoying the show, while meticulously polishing his silver roundel of an eye lens. He waves his weapon over the populace and makes obscene gestures, enjoying the gag. Minor throws up ever so gently, leaving a steaming puddle of personal history upon the pavement. A single bead of his sweat falls and strikes the red brick, where a brilliant sunflower springs to life. He tips his travelling hat politely in the direction of the long-departed souls and at the same time sternly reminds them to remain in the Légume Gallery where their sort belongs.

"Sit, now sit. There's a good soul. I'd love to spend all day discussing your troubles, and friends and family, but really I must retire to a quiet spot for a business lunch with Bébé."

There are, after all, lingering lingerie clauses and terms to hammer out, and as usual in such delicate matters, Minor is acting as a conduit for all dialogue between her and Heavy Breathings. They meet and kiss each other on the cheek and then enter their favourite little dive. Without delay, Bébé swallows a whole roll and then with a great crash of chic reticulum runs to the loo to refund it. But she returns quickly, and with a moist tissue dabs at her permanently peach lips.

"Must be something I didn't eat!"

Then she pushes aside a plate of *gnocchi afrodisiaci* and reaches for Minor's knee under the table.

"Couldn't we just ... for old times' sake? We could go surprise Shorty Shrooms. I know he owes you a favour, but I mean, don't we all, hee hee?"

Minor studies her hungry look. The maître d' (also moonlighting as DJ Till Dawn Sensation Master D) taps his yellow mustachio impatiently.

"Is everything to the satisfaction of mademoiselle and monsieur?"

Bébé hands the man her tissue of sick and threatens him with a raised stiletto heel.

"Don't you know who I am? I am Bébé Lala, the star of *Mutant Housewives*! The pretty one! And you know what, you horrid little man, the catering on the set of my first flick, *Wonder Chick and the Planet of the Vacuum Nozzles,* was so much better than your stinky noodles!"

The maître d' bows and steals away.

"Very good, ma'am, sir, very good."

In disgust, Minor watches him leave. There is something almost familiar about that fellow. Meanwhile, the Sniper shifts position very gingerly. He has been both a birthday clown and a carny juggler of torches but he finds this line of work far easier. Besides, you don't have to meet people and you're your own boss and the benefits are great.

The risko window shatters inward. Minor bursts into laughter for the first time all day.

"And that is why I never sit with my back to windows anymore! But you haven't even touched your generous helping of seal. Full of B vitamins, that."

But then he notices the maître d' scurrying out into the street and tearing off his hairnet and mustachio.

"Out in the open, what is he thinking? My contract! O no!"

Two slugs. Like the last duck lined up or the last fish in a fish run.

"Blam blam!"

As the exposed Cockerel collapses and observes his own blood hitting the red bricks and hears a steaming clock dinging out the time, instead of his life flashing before his eyes, he remembers a Polish painter dressing down his helpless new assistant.

"Hey a-hole, you paint the wall with the roller. You don't paint the roller drop by drop with a brush!"

The street urchins skateboard cheerily through the flood of blood covering the bricks, while some squeegee kids battle one another for this cleanup job. Bébé checks her Phatass mascara. No damage there.

"Now I'm serious, Minor love," she says, with an ornery edge to her voice. "Time to see Shorty and leave all of this behind us. We need some magical perceptions in a jiffy, now that old fart spoiled the mood."

Minor reaches into his jacket pocket and waves a sonic syringe in front of her. Yet as Bébé reaches for his arm and slips her stiletto back on, she is horrified to notice it is blood red and does not in the history of the universe match her black backless micro.

"O great, this is just great, where is the fucken luck?"

XI – Wandering Blocks

Minor stares into the image of Fatalina Sharp, pinned upon a nearby telephone pole, as if to viscerally burn a hole in it. He only receives his news and track and stock and bond tips from these poles, of course, much in the manner that neighbourhood canines do. But this morning, he feels a distinct psychical twinge that promptly slips his mind. The picture smacks of an old mystery digest cover and overrides his memories, depicting the low-buttoned songstress in a dark and desolate prairie setting, appearing for all the world about to flee from a slouching metrosexual cowpoke, leaning sulkily upon an overheating engine. And mind that prod in his hand!

"Zowieeee!!!"

And she is beautiful with flailing hair and heavy makeup, almost as beautiful as a transvestite who offered to light his Havana one Monday morning. Minor even recognizes the freelance hand of local artist / zither player / panhandler Champ Le Duc. He scans the street rapidly for the nearest pay phone, but the Concierge unzips his uniform and produces an old-fashioned ringer. It only takes one ring and two words.

Champ Le Duc is not having the best of days. He can remember a time he was always on top and in front and right behind, when nobody would frig with Duke Le Duc. Not now though. He exhales a mushroom cloud that fades into tangerine drapes. Champ is utterly charming. Vivien arrives early, knocks loudly, if only to inform him of this fact. The incident involving a stolen sausage is still fresh in her memory.

"Where's my fucken money, Champ?"

"Viv, why don't you run to the store and score me some smokes? And one for yourself, dearie!"

Vivien shudders. "Champ, this is serious. I owe this dude like big time. It's not funny! And my live-in landlords want to chuck me out. Unless I sign the revised slavery forms! Stop giggling! Now what are we to do, luvee?"

Champ raises an overtaxed wrist, wanting of veins, and points toward a wet poster upon his easel.

Terence Cockerel flips through his files with trembling hands. It has been a long time. He pours himself a shot glass of ginger beer and steadies himself. His advantage is being aware of an event Minor cannot possibly miss. Everyone in town knows about the spectacular and righteous rebuff of the blackguard at the hands of a certain Miss Sharp.

"Why, it's just like a movie. Minor shows up and then kerplunketyplunk!"

Cockerel has made efforts to secure the man's mail and intercept his love letters and fiscal reports. But bad bookkeeping just ain't his style. Rather, he has thought of the most perfect appetizer ...

Hurt Hardass is more than hurt. He is on a flaming rampage. Kiki (as played by celebrity Kiki Kaka) accompanies him home, clinging tightly to his buff abdomen on the back of his souped-up scooter.

"Stop squeezing, Kiki! I'm not in the mood."
"Hey, Hurt, check *it* out! That's Minor's gal – at least in the preterite tense."

Hurt studies the poster for seven minutes and forty-eight seconds, trying to parse what Kiki is on about. All he can see is a hot cowboy. Kiki punches his bicep gently.

"The woman, dingus! Look, Hurt, the woman will lead us to Minor, get it?"
"Minor ... wait a minute, wasn't he that dude who screwed my last film up the wazoo???"

Boy Barnacle is busy scrubbing the enviable back of übermodel Bébé Lala with even more enviable mitts.

"Have you read *the book* yet?"
"No, not yet. But the movie was so intense! Though I could have played the shit off that refugee."
"Yes, muffin top."

Beyond the bathwater surface, Boy Barnacle is the organizer of SPEEK, a regular all-night blitherfest. And Bébé, having been chastened a number of times in the press for her dedication to Speed/Load Learning, has been directed by her army of agents to sign up for the SPEEK program. And it has only been a few months and already she has learned more than merely a few words. And judging by his own SPEEKWORD poem, Boy Barnacle had become no more than a plaything of his own sweet nookie. He lifts a poster, soggy with movie bubbles, and examines it.

"Hey, Vaselina Sharp is having a gig."

Bébé clenches her teeth and blows an abundance of bubbles. All of them say BITCH.

The Sniper is enjoying his forty winks when the aubergine phone rings and rings.

"Hello?"

"Hello. The Cowboy ..."

"The Cowboy?"

"The Cowboy."

A dial tone. He rubs his temples and checks his incoming packet transfer. There is a grainy low-resolution poster of a cowboy, probably queer as a steer, sitting on a pickup and smoking a Dromedary Light, offering it to a pretty lady taking her top off.

"Him, I guess. Poor bastard. Sometimes this job is a real downer. I'd jist hate to see them kids broken up, is all. Seems like a bona fide waste of ammo."

The phone rings again.

"Hello?"

"Hello. The transectional ..."

"Hey, who is this?"

"Just call me Killer Cookie."

A dial tone.

"Shucks, I guess today is gonna be one of them days!"

Mr. Doolin, the defrocked man of the cloth, passes Mrs. Reardom along Main and raises his hat.

"Lovely weather."

"No. This was once a swamp for Newfie tea, far as the eye could have a gander."

"And who do we have here, why that little nipper's the spit o' ya!"

The little tyke smiles shyly and then spits on his freshly polished shoes.

"Damn bejaysus you wee wanker of a bootblack!"

"Let the boy be. Not a word of a lie that's the way we used to roll up our sleeves and polish 'em, none of this fancy-schmancy gunk for a tanner! The price of a bleedin' pint, you ask me! And they used to let you ride the tram up Main for free ..."

"Now look here, lad. Clean your teeth before ever you have anything to do with a woman!"

Then a poster catches his bespectacled eyes.

"Fata Morgana and the Hell's Bells! Jumpin' Jehosophat, do my eyes deceive me? Jouncing Jaysus on a stick! The filth!"

He stifles an urge to tear off the poster and roll it up for later. Instead, he raises his hat abruptly, all in a huff.

"Good day, Mrs. Reardom. And do mind that wee shite of yours."

Minor makes his way along Main, merry with anticipation. He is always this way when one of his terrifying whims is about to come to fruition.

"But soft, the grapes are not yet trampled into wine ..."

He notices a woman pushing a perambulator and trying to usher the little urchin out of it. The boy spits on a man's hat in hand and then sprints off toward a store window. Minor passes the chatting pair, noticing something almost familiar about the mother. The boy is staring at a display sign that reads:

OH NO

The boy has a certain shifty look about his eyes and a full head of red hair the very shade that lay dormant in more than one generation of Minors. The kid points at a Junior Pelleter 5000 xxx, and Minor tries to locate his melting heart. He pats the lad's fiery head.

"No, hardly a Reardom at all. More of a Minor. And someone I know is getting the gun they want for Hanukkah."

Miss F. Sharp, a first-class dolly bird, toddles out and considers having her nails done.

"Cheap as chips, that."

She smiles at a mother and child, enjoying a summer stroll and some kind of spitting contest.

"That's right, start them young, that's what I say. Such a beautiful day. And this weather brings out all the beautiful bodies and faces. Och, I'm starving. And I could simply murder an egg and bacon butte!"

She notices the Stropper across the street, lingering about the strip mall. He is floating her proverbial boat. Then he smiles, recognizing her even from a distance, and points to a poster on a nearby telephone pole. She turns into a beet.

Champ pulls his coat tighter and makes his way down the stairs. He covers his eyes, adjusting to the outer brightness. He manages a few more paces, feeling followed. He fiddles with his coat and fumbles to retrieve his sunglasses from a number of pockets.

"There. Now we're laughin' ..."

Vivien is always after him to pay child support and even make up with his ex and get back with that action in a discount shoebox. He cut her hair and now the minx thought she owned him. Every week or so, she wakes him up and sings the joys of responsibilities.

"Go Champ," she sings. "Go Champ!"

Behind him, they are inching closer.

Hurt and Kiki make their way out of some mulberry bushes. Kiki stops to pull a bit of hollyhock from the back of Hurt's stain-resistant adventure slacks.

"Not a scratch!"

Mr. Doolin passes and proffers the pair a stern glance of what else but admonishment. He taps the magnificent brim of his hat with puce gloves (as he was just washing his smalls) and waggles a refined finger.

"Well, boys? On your way to a show, by any chance?"

"We were just looking for an acoustic implement we lost. That's all really, mistah!"

"A show? Will there be electric bull-riding?"

Stately and nearsighted, Mrs. Reardom approaches the telephone pole and examines the poster.

"Why whatever so discomfited Mr. Doolin? Father Doolin, I almost said. O, forgive me, father ... Fat Lena and the Miniature Australian Shepherds! Why, that sounds like the loveliest show there ever was! Don't care much for that poster, though. A cowboy without a flock and a shearer in his hand, chasing a middle-aged woman without a stitch of clothing on. Aren't you getting a bit old for all these hijinkers? Not that I put a lick of trust in a word Ol' Doolin says. Not since that minor fire in the nave. And I hear he's a mangy beast in the sack!"

Cockerel slowly dials from the last phone booth in town. Tooth picks up, answering with his usual toffee-wouldn't-melt-in-his-mouth or stick-to-his-gums tone.

"Hello?"

"Hello, Tooth, it's Terence."

"You got some nerve ... Well, how's the liquidation biz?"

"I prefer the term *liquefaction*, and I should ask you the same question. Nevertheless, I got out of that game a long time ago."

The voice on the other end crackles with spittle. Liquidy bathwater laughter.

"Terry, you wouldn't just ring me out of the blue 'less you wan' a favour ..."

"I need the secret, Tooth."

"You know the score on that one, Terence. You sold that off years back. First, Throatburn picked up the brand, followed by Clearfizz, then Bubble Mountain, then Aquavittle, then Effervescence and finally Radberry, which owns the lot. You after the Radberry secret, Terry?"

"No, I only want my own secrets back. Don't forget the root canal I saved you from! You owe me, Tooth! I need a bargaining chip for an upcoming event! And you can sponsor the whole thing. It's Fanta and the Spritzers or ... I forget the name of the band – anyway, they're doing a local gig."

There is a long pause at the other end of the line, followed by a sigh.

"Well, I guess if it was anybody but Terry the Terror ... Okay, Terence."

"I'll send you the poster."

Champ returns from the promotional office for the stupendous Miss Sharp. He shuffles a wad of bills and tucks them into a manila envelope before pocketing the remainder. He rides down in the speedy brass-doored elevator, examining a display of twelve different types of hardwood used in the building's construction. The ground floor dings, and he steps behind a cleaner with his cart and freezes.

The Concierge, donning a fetching sailor suit, loiters outside the building walls full of *fruits des mer* friezes and motifs, including sea snails, crabs, skate, turtles, carp, scallops, seaweed and sea horses. He ushers in tourists and takes pictures for them, as still others sweep the building with palmy panoramming devices, capturing the sea-green and gold art deco exterior for their neighbours back home. Then he tosses away his Sailor's Delight cigarette and pushes the revolving door forward, as a Hungarian couple slips a generous tip into his pants.

The vertical *X* of the first revolving door is set spinning by Thumbs Minor, the shameless and merciless purveyor of four-dimensional erotica. Through the glass, he notices a familiar figure clutching a manila envelope.

"Why, 'ello 'ello, duckie!"

Two figures squeeze into the second revolving door of an art deco skyscraper used in more than one of their movies for their headquarters, including *The Super Special Friends*. It is none other than Hurt Hardass and the indefatigable Kiki, pushing as one against the steamed-up pane of glass. Kiki rubs a circle with his elbow in the wall of steam.

"Hey, Hurt, look who's here!"

The Concierge watches the progress lights in the lobby, looking for any cars stopping on nine before making their descent. Absorbed by the movement of lights and the underwater evocation of the shining blue tiles, he fails to notice a trembling sexagenarian in one of the phone booths, closing the folding door again. The last car arrives speedily with a robust DING and the lovely doors open ...

Champ looks around nervously, his life flashing before his eyes and reflecting in the pair of revolving doors. He had been snorting blow at a gala-do that sold promissory notes of discretion, and he had enjoyed himself tremendously, so much in fact that he had omitted to switch off the streaming camera in his Western tie. And the very next day, some poor soul (Viv, he suspects) had off-loaded the compromising vidbits to a number of local rags, without him seeing a single pretty penny! And he has more reasons than toes or fingers for wanting to steer clear of a rapidly revolving Minor. And he would sure like to keep the toes and fingers he has presently. As for the glint in the phone booth at the back of the lobby, Champ recalls catching a similar reflection in a silver platter next to some lutefisk. Thankfully, his date had already downed all the souped-up soup and a mysterious shot had only grazed his blackened silverware. But he has vowed never to let that old codger get his ass in a sling again.

"After you, sir."

Cockerel smiles wryly at the young man in sunglasses with an O-so-patronizing tone, and crosses the floor of astrological symbols, pausing only momentarily upon a crab. Then he locks eyes with the enflamed face of Minor behind a revolving pane of glass. I have tailed you from planetoid to planetoid, the look screams, although in this space no one can hear it.

Bébé, back on solids, orders a Heartburn sandwich to go, and watches through glass as plasticky paws lay out Gorgonzola and Edam upon a long baguette, before obtaining her thumbs-up to a scattering of jalapenos upon the bed of cheese, followed by a lone pickle. She licks her lips as they grill the lot. Now she'll be fortified enough to give that upstart Miss Sharp a piece of her ... mind.

Minor is spun out of the first revolving door, ready for anything. But the scent of a grilled Heartburn sarnie in a white paper bag, as waved provocatively by none other than Bébé Lala, looking up at the sea-creature clock, sends his senses reeling. He stumbles, trips and tumbles, as if cold-cocked. Everyone is startled by the flock of red-winged blackbirds circling his aching head.

Cockerel observes his own destruction in that temporarily floored face calling a foul and time out. There is not a moment to lose, and he leaps gingerly through the singing birds and into the spin of the first revolving door, which chucks him out on the pavement, chuckling and clucking to himself.

Hurt and Kiki, still trying to figure out the door and sandwich type, slap the glass helplessly. They are for a long time torn between the burnished interior that houses Minor, that scourge of brolleywood lots, and the exterior world that beckons people like Terry the Terror, that wise, old, token cast member who had snuck into the palace of their dearest friend and had dealt him his last reel in the form of a brain-shrinking goulash. Mustaphah, the neo-liberal libertine, with all the perks and propaganda and shackles to show for it, had died in their arms at his action-hero peak. So went the tragic ballad of Musty Prick.

Champ sees his chance and dekes past the cold-cocked Minor, taking the same revolving route as Cockerel. Hurt and Kiki try to push forward, then backward, then forward again, and they just move back and forth, back and forth, behind a steamed-up pane of glass. And by the time they have completed their indecisive revolution, the most remote fantasmagoria and ectoplasmic traces of Minor and Cockerel have completely evaporated. And the Concierge, equally frustrated and also on the lam, in parting gives them the bird.

Bébé shakes hands and then accepts a long and lingering kiss from Miss Sharp. They have agreed to do a nude scene together in the controversial locally filmed series *Lesbot Muck Up: Invasion Six*. Bébé considers sharing her idea for a new reality attempt called *Cockblock Island* but chokes at the last minute. Meanwhile, Miss Sharp does not fail to flick a switch repeatedly against the bare buttocks of her assistant, Schmücke, a tourist who misplaced his return ticket and came to the wrong office for help. Or the right one. And whenever he answers the speakerphone in his LeatheX thong, it defies description.

And Miss Sharp, übergrateful for this brolleywood opportunity, invites Bébé to her upcoming show.

"And darling, whatever did you have for lunch? I can still taste your jalapenos."

Champ flags down a curb-crawling cab. With the meter running, he tries to fathom his next destination. He fingers the manila envelope, kisses it thrice and coughs erratically, indicative of the possibility he may not make it to the end of the book, hell, even the chapter.

"But with luck like this, I must be on a regular roll. Time to let it ride!"

And as he watches the angry figures raising their fists in the background, framed by that oceanic promontory of a building, he is reminded there is nothing like a short excursion down to @tlantisity™.

Durston checks out his reflection in a glass he is cleaning and listens to the squeaky sound it makes, like the cleaning of ears. He continues to clean the same glass with the same cloth. A man with a tattoo walks in and slaps down a poster. Durston smiles.

"Nice."

"Hey, heard about the upcoming show? F. Harp and the Turpitudes! It'll be killer. Mind if I hang this up? And while I'm askin', how's life treating ya?"

"Excellent, excellent. I'm dandy as a daisy. I just got back from the Dominican and you wouldn't believe how cheap this crap is down there! We brought home backpacks full of smokes and cigars and bottles fulla bad news. And then we got stopped coming back, and we were both about to freak! But we just stood in the viewing box and tried to look freakin' normal. Everything's cool, ya know? And they must have said, there's a pair of cucumbers if I ever saw 'em. And they let us go without even looking in our bags."

But the poster dude is off, shaking his mullet head.

"Quite the Chatty Cathy!"

"This will make an intriguing episode for sure, however unauthorized."

Minor clacks away at his green Hermes. Then he stops to feel his throat-apple, studying the framed poster on his wall, and sighs.

"Ah, my dear, it might have been very different! Ah well, there's always next time …"

Vivien swerves to a stop, nearly running into Bébé and Boy Barnacle.

"Watch where yer going, lady!"

"Outta my way, suckas! There's still a way out if I play my cards right."

She races into the Disjunction and bangs her fists on the marble counter, an heirloom from the fifties.

"I gotsta see Minor!"

The barkeep yawns and thumbs it to the very back.

Champ, having lost just about everything on the ocean floor, scowls at the live monitor, imagining one last shot at redemption:

1	20/1	MELD
2	7/2	GREASEPAINT
3	12/1	SOCIABLE DUCK
4	10/1	NO EXCEPTION
5	200/1	FROTH
6	7/5	GUEST STAR
7	4/5	HEATH ROSE
8	6/1	LYNN'S A LADY
9	4/1	NORDANCE
10	15/1	MAGIC STAR
11	30/1	SUMMER FAIR
12	2/1	CARRY SPORT

At the general weekly meeting of Dissemblers & Pawnbrokers (DPs), a small group of post–middle-aged women are pecking holes in each other's coats, while a crusty old codger in their company digs deep for a collection of congealed snot.

"Bubble bubble double trouble!!!"

One of the women reveals a candy bag full of teeth.

"My fifth husband's ..."
"Melt 'em down!"
"Gold! We need gold! Always more gold!"

They design and turn over simply charming good-luck charms.

"Hey gurls, who brung the hammer this week?"

Minor is shooting a game for untold stakes against Bleery Cue, a local hustler with a staggering technique. He always starts off wobbly, for one thing. But by the seventh or ninth match, despite the inordinate amount of lager he has consumed, he is stone cold sober and ready to statistify any odds or outcome.

"O, I've heard so much about you," exclaims Vivien.
"I thought he was dead," shrugs Minor.

They all stare at each other with increasing suspicion.

Champ rubs the silver and gold charm around his neck for luck, still a little reluctant to pawn it outright. He is getting fed up with betting on the same old things, like Bébé's diet or chest alteration status, or the percentile of ambiguity in the platonic relationship between Hurt Hardass and Kiki Kaka. Behind him, a woman kicks the frack machine.

"Frack's on the fritz again, Phyllis!"

And Champ can feel the palpable surge of glutamate in his brain, as he writes down the number and name of one of the ponies.

"Yeah, let it ride, that's right. Froth it is. No, wait, am I going crazy? Sociable Duck has to be the one. It's like a sign. Okay, Duke Le Duc, this one's for little knockup!"

Vivien kneels solemnly, hoping to reach Minor through an act of frankness.

"I need a loan."
"We would need to talk terms."

Vivien starts rolling balls around the table, completely cueless. Both men lose their steely concentration. Vivien and Bleery start to tickle one another.

"I need a guarantor," decides Minor.
"You won't jew him down," advises Bleery. "He just placed a thousand credits on Meld. And the house always wins."

Durston is concentrating hard, trying not to get pulled into a tractor beam by a blue crab. But his free game of Galaxia is almost over. If only real life were more like this!

"Hey, you back there. Could you kindly shut your pie hole for a friggin' minute???"

Mr. Doolin and Miss Mt. Pleasant make their way out of some mulberry bushes. Miss Mt. Pleasant stops to pull a bit of hollyhock from the back of Mr. Doolin's stain-resistant adventure frock. He fiddles with her beautiful sash.

"There, now that's what I was saying. You see, this used to be a swamp for Newfie tea! And you got a free tram ride up the hill! Ahhh, we were the cat's whiskers on the cat that got the cream, no bones about it."

Champ, having lost just about everything, scowls at the live monitor, reading the winners and quietly weeping:

1st	MELD
2nd	GUEST STAR
3rd	LYNN'S A LADY

And then he smells something strange. Through the open back door, he can see the wiry silhouette of an ancient nightmare, none other than urban legend Shorty Shrooms.

Bleery stands up and crashes down his empty glass.

"I will serve as the guarantor."

"And *you* are my sponsor," adds Vivien, squeezing Minor's hand.

"I would not begrudge you this loan. After all, it is only the principle of the thing that matters. And let it not be said I was unfair. My terms are ... why no more or no less than a bacon strip of Bleery's fair colon flesh. And a thread and needle's worth of his fair liver."

"Done," grins Vivien.

"And you won't regret this, either of you."

They all shake.

Through the neon strobes, the Cowboy suddenly goes down.

"Cowboy? Cowboy?"

Miss Sharp toddles about, handing out free posters. Someone whistles and honks. She pauses to stare up at the naked grey caryatids reclining upon a cornice beneath a dome the colour of oxidized copper. There is a gleam in a window across the street. A polished lens.

"Click ..."

Vivien and Bleery make their way out of some mulberry bushes. Vivien stops to pull a bit of hollyhock from the back of Bleery's stain-resistant golfing dad slacks. In the heat of the moment, they decided to keep it real, etc.

"No regrets?"

"This may complicate the clear-cut colon and liver stipulations involved in the loan. In other words, Minor is going to kill me."

And neither of them wants to get into the lease, at least not at this stage, although Bleery has added new conditions and Vivien is looking over his shoulder, examining each one. At last, they shake on it. Then Vivien sighs.

"I should like to ring up Champ, just to tell him the good news. And he does need his letter jacket back. C'mon, Champ. Pick up, pick up …"

Minor runs into Kiki in the change room of a lavish boutique. If it were any other place! Both men are tense, yet alluring. They exchange a glance of *pax temporis*, both knowing they would never be able to strip out of their respective fripperies in time. Not even with the fate of the world at stake …

"O o o ooooh!"

Boy Barnacle buckles under the intense pressure of a souped-up dill that a hard-hatted Bébé is manipulating.

"Weren't you and Minor an item? Then he might catch us …"
"That is no more than an episode from another time, I'm afraid."

Her new vocabulary skill set is working out nicely. And she turns a dial to increase the piston horsepower. At that instant, a key turns in the lock.

"No way! This ain't what it looks like!"

Mémé brings over another round for the DPs, exchanging small talk about the junk jewelry biz.

"How does one get started?"
"Gold. And first you need to get hold of some teeth."
"And so, what about that horse's tuchus you bet on?"

"What?"

"The colon 'n' liver felluh. He got any special fillin's?"

Minor grins at the spectacle of their winsome avariciousness. The craggiest face is illuminated by an overhanging lamp, greenish in hue.

"Those weren't the terms of our arrangement."

"But we could add this teeny-weeny clause for that cat's molars in the event of such and such, etc."

Hurt and Kiki drown their general bummer in a shared malted. Best to just pop back home and practise their aerobic subdue and slide technique.

"Who's up for a game of Frisk?"

"Hell, why not? Tomorrow is a new day!"

"And did you manage to get our shopping done?"

Champ is startled awake by a swarthy noise.

"Cockroaches man black widow black widow. Scrunchy. I must have drifted off. What the hell went down? O yeah Shorty Shrooms vroom vroom and @tlantisity™ up the keester ..."

He feels for the packet of art money he had stuffed in his netherwear and groans.

"O those bastards gouged me real good! And what about my beautiful smackbaby?"

He props himself up on the bed and peers through a criss-cross of shadows. Footsteps. The door chains are kicked defunct, and the last thing he sees is the impassive face of a time-management consultant, positively crawling with fire ants.

Through the neon strobes, Boy Barnacle suddenly goes down.

"Boy? Boy?"

Bleery rubs his bleary eyes clear, only to notice a poster of a pretty woman straddling a naked stableboy with an unauthorized tell-all in his hand. Fuchsia and the Trampled Fustigators.

"Hey, that sounds like a sweet show to check out."

His wrists are suddenly seized and pulled behind him.

"Time for a wee chat with your friends at DebtMaster."

The lights go out. Next, he finds himself kissing porcelain in a public washroom and being dunked repeatedly, like a Salem mage. And as his head is lifted, the last thing he sees is a glint in one of the assailant's eyes and a glimmering pair of pliers.

"It's all right, sonny. I'm Dr. Bueno Fayle but everybody just calls me F ..."

Cockerel lays back in a hammock, reading by the last of the afternoon light, periodically pausing to sip from a can of Old Cockerel's, redux.

"Now that's what I call a hectic day!"

XII – Clean as a Whistle

One desultory summer's day full of remorse, the accused takes a few extra seconds to shield his eyes while a couple of gawkers lose theirs to the momentary eclipse. The Stropper stands behind a pricey pair of blinds, hands clasped behind his finely tailored back. The obelisk in the public square has been converted into a portable lethal injection chamber. The Stropper would have preferred a guillotine, almost to the point of forgetting his shaving fetish for an entertaining hour of anticipation, followed by that inevitable denouement, set to the *Symphonie Fantastique*.

Jazzy Sharp, the shoeshine boy who made good and became the chief oligopolist of all gentrified parts, is promptly scheduled for public death. And the Stropper is tickled by a printed sign that reads:

PUB IC DEATH

"Dignity to the end, eh? Well, better him than yours truly!"

And it is common hearsay that in the course of Jazzy Sharp's career, he has embezzled countless funds for personal zoos and faunas, has attended every who's who from here to the farthest undiscovered constellation, has in general fiddled and buggered and illegally upgraded and wriggled in and out of the sketchiest of situations. To touch him would be to approach a meal of eels without a fork. He has ingested every mind-bender known to man and has recovered after the shortest of naps. And he has trolled in the swartest of eventides for the lost and desperate and sadly confusèd.

When they had brought him the tax forms to sign, he had sneezed and shat upon them and wiped himself clean with them and then washed his hands of all traces of his general amusement at the very impertinence of such an imposition. Once he had fed an entire census board to his pet piranha. That was sooooo Jazzy. But then the pressure of a vise had taken a fancy to his short hairs. His stretch van had been seen in the area on more than a few evenings. His JZZY vanity plates were unmistakable. And there were stories. Jazzy liked his after-hours activity a little rough. And he had an appetite for the *unheimlich*, although no one in the press knew precisely what this meant.

Even for the hunchback politico, it was embarrassing to have his inventory of personal pleasurewear and leisure toys paraded through the papers and parodied at local fashion shows. The Jazzy Dill Rub Stud was just now the talk of the catwalks. And his mug shot was also an object of amusement. True, he was still very well to do and protected by the best of funnelling and finagling tricks. But he had never intended for anything really criminal to happen. To be led away in handcuffs during a routine downsizing of the local exchange and to witness that sudden floundering in the dead eyes of the regulators was a bit of a downer. After retiring early from the police force and failing to become famous spies, these investigators could at most hope for a spot of fun harassing a legal clerk now and then before laying hands upon their second or third pension. To have come this close to solving an actual case was a red letter day.

And for Jazzy to see faces on the Street that he had never gotten around to tossing out onto the pavement, why, it was undeniably a bit of a burn. He had been just about to transfer all tower dealings into a sterling data-cell reservoir upon his left hip when the news hit. His head swam with headlines:

JAZZY PANTS AND PATE PIECE FOUND AT SCENE!

SHARP MOGUL MOONLIGHTS IN MURDER!

JAZZY IS BLOODY SPAZZY!

POLICE COMB OVER JAZZY EVIDENCE!

JAZZY CHALLENGES JIZZY ANALYSIS!

But in the end, it was the boredom of celebrated financial reporter Dick Frains that led to his general condemnation – the word of a man who slept through all the hearings he attended, and for that reason scarcely attended a single hearing, and wrote a scathing column the next day anyway, based on a cut-and-paste program that collected transcripts and wire services. In fact, most of the time, he relied on his trusty pet baboon, Booboo. His fiscal puff piece about Jazzy Sharp was enough to douse the imagination of the public in petrol and ignite it with a few words (another triumph for Booboo). It was then that Jazzy went from being a risk management wanker to an unlicensed public domain whacker. That was the gist and grist of the article anyway. Jazzy watched his soiled reputation sinking into the vague quicksand of public opinion.

"Whad'ya know? Our grand poohbah has no clothes … the sicko!"

"After all his corporate epithets, he was nothing other than the Stropper!"

"Yeah, let's do it after the market closes. I am sizzling with *schadenfreude* right now!"

"No, I'm on the level. They fingered Jazzy downtown! No, not like that."

"Would Booboo lie?"

And having a name like Jazzy Sharp didn't help one sliver.

The square is being prepared. A rather fetching Miss Sharp rubs a tear from a corner of her veiled eye. Minor inclines his head solemnly, holding his porkpie over his heaving chest. He has never known such an aphrodisiac as the dead or the dying. With customary decorum, he reaches over and extends the end of a toffee roll. She declines, incensed. Minor hastily withdraws his last toffee.

"Shame of a way to go."

Some choose a mild demise, death by sodium lauryl sulfate, $CH_3(CH_2)_{10}CH_2(OCH_2CH_2)_nOSO_3Na$, the common ingredient found in toothpaste and shampoo and a number of personal care products. It has wonderful properties of removal, and excels as a garage floor and automotive engine degreaser. In fact, Minor has a patent in motion to produce a damnably whitening cleanser without this agent, mostly because he suffers from inflammatory carbuncles and breakouts that the paste and shampoo exacerbate. He was almost certain Jazzy would want his clock cleaned this way, and would nobly decide to be brushed or scrubbed to death by giggling local breakfast television hosts, although he had once seen a marketing executive subjected to this fate and the cleansing agent went straight for his follicles. He met his maker bawling, and balding on the spot, but clean as a freshly polished whistle.

"Sodium lauryl sulfate. A poetic death if there ever was one! And so much more humane."

And the public were mad to see Jazzy washed right out of their hair for good. But Jazzy did not desire a prolonged lathering, nor a deadly fluoride dip. Without warning, the Stropper appears at Minor's side, tenderly mopping his immaculately smooth countenance.

"Balmy weather we're having! You'd never know it was summer."

Minor accepts the firm, manly paw and small-talks away, all the while feeling his psychical senses reeling. His palmy device begins to cricket. A voice crackles to life.

"Sir, we just analyzed the circadian rhythms of the stains in evidence, and they bear a common tone, traceable in fact to the very square you are schmoozing in right now! And, sir, I want to be the first to announce, in the hope of instantaneous promotion, that the Stropper is right beside you, scratching his cheek and fidgeting with his nose. I hope you don't mind, I took the liberty of using the speakerphonic channel! Mom, are you out there? It's me, your boy, Lummox. I found the Stropper for Mr. Minor! I found the Stropper –"

Minor flicks off the palmy device. The Stropper smiles at him, reaching into his overcoat.

"Where are your manners, Minor? Why, I could have slit you from ear to ear by now, were I not a gentleman. This is no longer your case. You have been reassigned, ever since that incident at the waterfall. You might say, you are all washed up."

Minor unbuttons a single button and reveals another button, a button far more tender.

"First of all, that wasn't a waterfall. And you'll never get a furlong farther! Let this arena of bleakness do its thing and move on. I'm not so fond of you, but I'm not so fond of the Sharp progeny either. Between the prospect of a local slasher and that of an infuriating in-law, the choice is obvious. I pulled some strings. And Jazzy was the outstanding nominee."

"Touché," snarls the Stropper, ceding some distance between them. "Normally unstoppable, I see on this occasion, I am completely outstripped and unstropped."

He commences with a run-on speech traditional to most cinematic psychopaths.

"Shhhh," shushes Miss Sharp.

Jazzy allows himself to be strapped into the PortaLethal. He is ready. Minor finds a place on the concrete bench and makes a show of tearing at his porkpie-less hair. Then he does something queer. Everyone said so afterward. He kneels on the ground in front of Miss Sharp and starts to recite dusty poetry.

"Was ever woman in this humour woo'd? Was ever woman in this humour won?"

Miss Sharp, preoccupied amply with protecting her discount mascara, gives Minor a minor slap, before spitting her wad, toffee and all, and no wad like was ever expectorated up previously or since.

"Foul toad! Not only am I worried about my brother, but presently, I am up to my ears and skyward ankles with a bit on the side."

Minor doubles over in the square and douses himself in positively orgasmic shampoo. His back begins to welt and bubble, before a giant cyst (or implant) bursts forth, ruining one of his favourite shirts. The populace takes account of this grandiose display of blood and pus.

"The sign! The sign!"

Minor implores everyone to heed his words with molecularly unstable limbs. He is starting to melt, more than any man can ever have melted.

"I was the crazed killer! Let this nutjob go free. Let this pervert be at liberty, I say!"

"Sodium lauryl sulfate," announces the coroner, impatiently licking his fingers. "And minty fresh!"

Mr. Jassimino Sharp is unstrapped and pardoned at once, and carried down the street amid much fanfare for an entire block, until the crowd starts breaking windows. The Stropper hails a passing cab.

"Hardly worth the price of admission. Red light and step on it!"

Minor oozes up out of the puddle of himself. The lethal injector becomes an obelisk again, and then an opera finale pyre. The production designs this year are exquisite! The corporate sponsors glare up at the surtitles, yawning. Minor offers the dissipating crowd a poetic tributary.

"Come un bel dì di maggio / che con bacio di vento ..."

Then he stands erect and looms over the waning lynch mob, speaking through the flames:

> *You I salute. You who have given shape to my days and a sense of supernatural differentiation between all these meaningless ticks upon this timepiece.*

He brandishes a pocket fob with sienna animals crawling about its smiling face.

> *No one can deny the horizons I have traversed or take away the mirage I have lived. I managed to shake loose all my friends and contacts (although I found the means to seduce them all over again) for the abandoned theatre of your image. I have translated you into the most simple of things. A step in the night, a shadow beneath the street lamp, a smothering chill of snowfall in the bones, an annihilation of mortified sunlight, an open raincoat in the rain. Although you strain yourself to hear this music and lend it meaning with your ears, it is no less existent. And when these frail surfaces have eroded and rusted upon their very scaffolding, when flesh has melted away from bone, I will know it was never a waste of time to hold vigil or haunt about your portals of sleep, since I have sought nothing but to leave my door unbolted, open for the exclusive beauty of your palms. This is the open door then, leading to magic and love.*
>
> *Eternity is the healer. The mender of cracks, the overgrowth of untended feelings. And if I am to find you in the last or next world, do not delay me any longer! Tarry no longer.*
>
> *You have lent breath and life and illumination to this heap of simulacra upon my shelf, a pride of lions one minute, a ferocity of bodies the next. We have, each of us, sung to lonely nights, full to the*

brim with useless and unspeakable feeling. Was anyone listening? Is anyone listening? Because I am the madman who adjusts his radio and pricks up his ears, listening as an animal to a strange noise in the distance that no one else can quite perceive. Your "reality" still has the gumption to taunt me with rent and expenses and superficial glamour, and in the same breath, still it steals away any hope of real estate. Any hope of something far more precious. Meanwhile, stretching in this manor of my madness, I bid all my subjects pack up their random effects and head home. For you are my one subject in this illimitable world, and I have run out of words.

O come to me, come to me, in the eleventh hour of love!

Miss Sharp blinks and shrugs and shivers in the cold of the desultory summer's day, raising upon a twig a marshmallow of the most beautiful powder blue.

CCCXXXIII – When Time Is Rent

Minor dots another (*i*) of his latest worldly will and testament, while underneath the pages an angelic Bébé Lala stirs, only semi-awake for the rapidly snapping Snapper, who is recording this monumental occasion. And upon each of her acclaimed buttock cheeks rests a damp love letter. Regrettably, this is the last time he will proposition a member of either sex with this corporate body. Minor has decided upon an equitable trade-in of his general existentials for no less than a bite of eternity. He has survived a dangerous descent, down into the closest binary tree of the word to tap its cybernetic roots and deadpan its caches for unmined data. Minor is preparing to embark upon a new extratemporal lifestyle. But his personal Zitheronic 333 is activating ... He consults the device and scans the flashing alerts. The experiment is a whelming success! Bébé is complaining about her missing stocking and how much of a flaming nuisance a crazy paparazzo and stocking stalker can be. But Minor rubs her rump affectionately and explains the nature of his latest experiment as quickly and as condescendingly as possible.

"Darling, thanks to yours truly, Man has at last found a way to penetrate the swollen womb of time with his giant throbbing science. Mmm ... and it sure is tasty! I just need to test whether the experiment has been a complete success. Now tell me, where is your stocking?"

"I'm such a peroxide! I must've forgotten everyone wears one stocking."

"No. Your logic is flawless. But the Zitheronic has been programmed to remind me that everyone wears two stockings. That is one of the many multi-historical accounts. Now hurry, Bébé, which way do you want it ... to live in a universe with one stocking ... or two?"

Bébé is feeling rather cold.

"Two."

"Then two it is."

Suddenly, Bébé is wearing both stockings! Bébé weeps profusely. They are just so beautiful. This is a miracle! Minor is aroused by this phenomenon and accosts her in front of the vanity in the course of his explanation, much to her overdramatized delight.

"We better hurry up, before the time lag catches up with us. Regarding time contortionism, the Snapping Thong Theory has prevailed. According to the experts, if a dreamer like myself were to concentrate the amount of energy necessary to alter a single fact in the course of linear time, I would be snapped back with the same amount of force and promptly smitten upon the spot."

The vanity trembles as he pounds his fists, making point after point.

"I decided to experiment with something small that would completely undress the thong theory, something that would divide every pair of hose and socks in all of history. From this rip in time, a number of universes have been generated around a single event. As elaborated unequivocally in Jurgen's Flying Squirrel Theory, we are suspended upon the interstices of those universes and have the opportunity to compromise our respective fates by leaping from one branch to the next ... and then the next ... and so on ... Our psyches adapted to a single universe, evolving that universe to suit our primitive requirements."

"I know. You made me read your book *Sex and the Single Universe*."

"And?"

"I just looked at the pictures, tee hee ..."

"What I mean is, there is a Bébé wearing no stockings and a Bébé trying to wear three stockings. In addition, we once lived in a universe where every sock was accounted for. And now, we live in a universe where, although we will them to exist via our desire for them, sometimes for no apparent reason, one or more of them goes missing ... I have coined this anomaly Minor's Missing Sock Theorem."

Bébé looks down. One of the stockings has vanished again.

"O my gawd, this time thing is a fashion nightmare!"

Minor continues to conduct his interactive biological experiment inside of a stunned Bébé, only to watch her completely disappear *in flagrante delicto*. He studies his spent reflection in the mirror.

"Still a few kinks to work out, I suppose. Time lag's a real bitch."

Deep within voxelrich valleys and matriced mountains, the chiselled hero Dick Diver fails to prevent the diabolical Dr. F from breeding a type of bacterium whose diet consists solely of a temporal/spatial continuum combo. The bacteria are actually the laid eggs of another creature known only as a time moth. The larvae eat the fabric of the universe and after metamorphosis float off, leaving only an invisible hole. But Dr. F breeds a culture of collected eggs (the plot wears thin here) and rockets into the hole, becoming one with the continual and seemingly eternal flux of the universe, a phenomenon described as *tempori spirulina indigesta*. An amusing parallel is instantly drawn between the collections of bacteria and the Aztec *Tecuitlatl*, the excrement of stone that proves to be a healthy diurnal supplement.

And the irony is completely lost upon the lantern-jawed Dick Diver that the universe itself is only part of one leaving of larvae by a creature that would drive folk mad to even become aware of it. Minor chuckles. Dick is too busy snapping the ukini of Sally Strudel, ace reporter and a wicked roll in the hay, to give the matter more than superficial consideration. And Minor realizes that anything imaginable is probably so, or that philosophical willpower and belief are sufficient to make it so.

"And sure enough, the time larvae are as real as you and me!"

Also, Minor has detected a hole left behind by their birthing process. A supramilitary-complex probe has been prepared for him to enter the rift and try to sew it up, a feat that the flag-waggling Dick Diver genuinely wished to accomplish. But in Minor's case, he is going to enter the rift without ethical presuppositions and accept its innumerable opportunities without question. Very soon, the mystical excrement of time and space will be his for the taking.

The launch party at his thirty-third home in Tunisia is a modest one. There are endless reports explaining the reason for Minor's galactic sojourn, and the flesh of the world is whipped up into an orgiastic fervour without really knowing why. The unwashed leap toward the glowing prophyl foam field and fizzle into cinders with untold glee.

"We are young and unknown and indestructible ... aaaaaaaaaa!!!"

A sizable array of complex catapults and amateur cannons are set up, not for assault, but to launch personalized netherwear at Minor the exact moment he is about to board his vessel. The first symphony of Johannes Brahms blares across the vast territory, and each of the listeners at once shares in the daring trepidation and anxious neurosis. Was there life after Beethoven? Minor would find out. Jugs and kegs of kumquat spritzer are rolled out by Minor's personal minions for the deadly thirst of the crowd. The base and shaft of the intimidatingly phallic probe, the *Jules Verne* (obviously named after the ineffable Juliette Verne), is tied and bound with LeatheX to a sex cruise shuttle destined for the surgically altered and retucked moon of Venus presently known as New Pudelta.

The last of the radioactive squatters in the outer reaches is reportedly scalped and enumerated. The survivors of a murderous bidding war to board this shuttle are waiting in line to shake Minor's synthetic glove. Once the cruiser has breached the earth's orbit, the *Jules Verne* will rapidly unfasten and thrust resolutely in the general direction of the time slit. Thankfully, the probe is equipped with a fail-safe aerosolic guidance system. At every turn, Minor will leave a distinct waft of rose petals or rainforest dung. Mini Magnette pauses to pose for a thousand and three hot flashes and snaps, rubbing herself in every possible way against the sex-holiday cruiser and the *Jules Verne*. Mini joined one of a thrillion threesomes to compete for the spot, winning a decisive victory during a rigorous skill-testing orgy with two dozen radio talk-show hosts. Directly afterward, the plucky Mini still managed to shock Bébé over an unforgettable dinner hour that will remain frozen forever in the gelatinous retinae of a few survivors.

Long story short, she is the new LeatheX girl.

She and Minor are guiding the commercial and short film crew Gotkes into the probe's sleek and slippery interior. No small thanks to Minor that the world's first socially acceptable adult snuff film is about to be created. Even Pelt Doe Hostia (on death row for awfully bad timing) is thrilled to be the recipient of all this global attention. He is truly honoured to have won the Condemnation Pageant and to have the chance to literally bite the big one during an advert for LeatheX. As the crew fasten him into the new line of Self-Flagellation workout attire, he eyes Mini Magnette up and down, blinking helplessly at her flared Slogger Unischmutter with tantalizingly flimsy Feltcro clips. He has not seen a woman in ages. And Minor is clad in a customized and readily marketable Domicide getup, a massy studded and spoked thing that would raise questions about any body but his.

In the spiel of the marketing executives, the key was to bundle the live execution in with a tight storyline stretched tighter than ... well, watch for yourselves! Pelt has been practising his part for months. He tugs at his chains helplessly and rolls about against the wall of the withdrawing room of the *Jules Verne*. Camera obscura number three pans to the labelled posterior of Mini Magnette as she lifts a limp Uruban noodle and begins to whip the open back of Pelt's outfit. Minor lights an herbal cigar and fixes himself a drink in the fully stocked probe bar, pausing to admire the lavish interior. Mini coquettishly inserts one hundred and twenty-nine Attackupuncture pins into the key points of Pelt's body before strapping him into the latest model of the LeatheX deep-flesh fryer. Mini unFeltcros the bottoms of his killer outfit and offers him his last wish while a home audience of shut-ins gasps at the red-rimmed jerky-cam footage of Mini's bobbing head and alluring LeatheX scrunchy.

Next, she uses a low voltage, causing Pelt to be intermittently jolted. He rolls his eyeballs upward in truly shocked ecstasy as Mini wipes the creamy electricity from her lips. And once the convicted murderer of a Native reservation uranium surveyor is limp and pliable, Minor approaches and helps Mini to hang him upside down. In unison they flay his bare body with the meticulousness desired in the restoration of a given masterpiece. Everyone at home expresses audible horror, and yet finds the relatively static scene of torture more arousing than a last-minute touchdown or an abrupt match-winning lob at Wimpledom. Minor smiles, stopping to admire the half-skinned Pelt.

"If nothing else, let it be said I took the advertising business beyond softcore deceit. An end to movie-house fumblings, I say! I call for public displays of the erotic! And a touch of sincere cruelty now and again, for good measure. And it's time to bring the live execution back where it belongs!"

At home, restless viewers pause in mid-sodomy to watch the Murphy bed release of the LeatheX GetAway Web. Minor and Mini begin with some hot, sticky swing action, followed by intense wriggling in an airless multi-tubed chamber nicknamed Nature Whores a Vacuum by the engineering team after a lengthy night of self-discovery.

"We are through the hooking gas!"
"This is an end to crude spillage!"

Completely out of keeping with the script, the LeatheX Web achieves self-awareness and straps the pair down for sake of its own gratification. And it is merciless with a heady combination of fried circuitry and overeager pleasure nozzles. Minor has no option but to feed it a punch card containing a puzzling new vert for antifungal cream. The LeatheX Web attempts to parse the product spot, but fails, just like ninety-eight out of a hundred viewers. It cannot subsist in a world devoid of all meaning. It neatly self-destructs with a kinky snap, and Minor and Mini tumble to the probe floor amid a tangle of sucking and squirting tubes. The sponsors desperately wave their unconditional okay. And hours later, after a visceral feast of multiple climaxes and power-saving naps, Minor gives the signal for the entire probe to be hosed down – with the voltage still on! In a turgid puddle, Pelt's bones sizzle and smoke. And at that moment, Bébé Lala materializes in the middle of the probe with her arms folded.

"I guess, in this universe, we are still an item."

Someone kicks the laugh track into action. Minor rubs his hands together happily, knowing the preliminary payspots and tetchy visitor hits are out of the way and it is time to launch. An exhausted Mini Magnette and the smouldering remains of Pelt Doe Hostia are rolled down the boarding ramp of the *Jules Verne*. And the orgasmic day-trippers in sheer robes and smoking jackets snap and click collectibles of this historical heap of biodegraded synthetic.

"Brought to you, of course, by LeatheX. And if you chewed yourself free, then it just ain't LeatheX."

Minor orders the innards of the probe pressure-cleansed. Once content he can see himself both back- and front-wise, he whistles a strain from *Aida*, and his chief pet officer, a confident and densely spotted Dalmation named Dotty, responds by racing up the ramp, pausing only to give the planet Earth one last nose for good measure.

"I'm glad you're here. That means my mission is already a success."

"Huh? Won't Dotty have trouble adjusting to outer space?"

"Of course not! They're a very ancient breed. More ancient than you think. I know it would boggle your noggin if I were to tell you that Dotty is, in a manner of speaking, returning home. And now, would you be a dear and run to the mansion and fetch me my toothbrush?"

Bébé is at the bottom of the ramp when she suddenly remembers the complimentary gift basket.

"Wait a minute! (s)Perm Essentials gave you an entire basket of toiletries!"

The ramp is raised with a groan of satisfaction. Bébé beats her fists against the sides of the *Jules Verne*. This is the second challenge her Willow Weepless mascara has faced today.

"But how will you repopulate the colonies?"

"¡*Es ceviche!* Plenty of cod in the stream of things!"

"But without your backing, I'm just a billboard!"

"You'll find someone ... and maybe with the same taste in music."

Bébé screams an expletive, but it is cut off by the roar of ignition. Desperately, she tries to light an herbal cigar, but in the nick of time, her own former goons drag her away from the chambers brimming over with accelerant. But Mini Magnette is not so lucky. The global media comment for days upon the brutal irony of her terrible terrible tragedy. The magnetic studs on her LeatheX outfit are drawn to the bottom of the launching sex cruiser and the highly flammable material immediately catches flame. Mini Magnette is fatally magnetized before terminally burning out.

"Brought to you by LeatheX. If you can't stand the heat, get the hell out of LeatheX."

Religious commentators interpret this occurrence as the will of this or that deity – spurred on by the announcement of her new naked talk show. Bébé claws at the fencing in the grip of her old goons, kneeling upon the tarmacadam and conjuring up method-acting tears for bituminous surfaces at the thought of something sad, instantly winning her exclusive interviews under the subheading "Jilted by Jet Fuel" and "Deadbeat Bulge," as well as her unauthorized autobiography *Lalaland*, already a bestseller by the time they tranquillize her.

"I mean, I'm no rock scientist, but my love is flammable as the best of 'em ..."

Minor enjoys an excellent kip during liftoff. Dotty barks twice, indicating she would like a bath to be drawn as soon as astronomically possible.

"It is now safe to smoke and lounge about the probe at leisure. VoxAlert is not responsible for smoking habits or illnesses related to smoking. Smoking is killing you softly. It is now safe ..."

"Well, Dotty, time to cut the umbilical. Goodbye, sweet mothership! And now I think it's safe to pull out the contraband gear."

Dotty fetches an object akin to a coffee grinder and offers it to Minor. He screws the stolen compressed matter-splicer into place and flicks a switch. Nothing. Dotty lifts an unconnected cable between her teeth and paws Minor's knee.

"Ah yes, Dotty. Quite right. Good dog."

Right at plug in, the Hanukkah bush lights up, and with a sound like stain-resistant pant bottoms being torn open from behind, the blip of the probe zooms forward into the unknown. And the day-trippers and combined sexploitation crew, literally bound for the reconstructed moon of Venus, gawk at the spray of yellow rose petals in the sudden wake of the detached and vanished *Jules Verne*.

Then Miss Sharp turns to him and beams with a frail wave.

"It's *you*. Marcel."

She stirs awake at the bottom of the stairs. She has been sleepwalking again. The clock reads 3:33 a.m. She reaches down to pick up an envelope with no return address. Inside is a strange letter...

Dear One,

This in part concerns an old debate we have had about the relationship between life and art. You have deemed them equal. But have you stopped to consider that the artist is a soul helplessly locked in a struggle with time?

In the short term, an audience appears necessary. And for some, it is more vital than for others.

In the long term, if one is to be remembered, a language or means of communication has to be invented that will hold up for decades or centuries. The interesting thing to consider is that some portentous artists ARE living that future life in the present, imaginatively cashing in early upon their future worth while their faithful labour forges with integrity the work in the shape of that knowledge. And most art, if it is Art, has the same argument, that an artistic existence enriches the quotidian and the statistical and those vague scratches upon any century-old census.

And in terms of a "protection racket" cradling the artists at its overprotective teat, it is debatable whether an honest outpouring of emotion is more desirable or has more power to affect one than the concentrated eloquence and rhythm and structure of song. If a media report is engineered to evoke fear and terror and prompt one to require one of the sponsor's antidepressants, is that more honest than the hybrid "lie" of a song or poem or story? Sometimes the search to find LIFE only leads to a thoughtless hunt for hypersensationalism.

In other words, if we are to imagine for a moment that we live in a sped-up world with a philosophy of obsolescence jarred by constant interruption and distraction, with so little pecuniary value to be found in a single object of quality – a well-made thing (in industry as well as art) – then isn't it possible that our complete embrace of this contemporary LIFE might very well rob us of our own potential for artistic and imaginative vision? In this case, isn't it possible that overlong interactions with social codes and demands (i.e. "life") could "inherently prevent ART from being produced"?

I think the interesting thing about artists is that there is an inherent betrayal and pimping of life in the process of creating art. It is a choice, and the artist is ignobly bold for making it, although the sacrifice would probably not take place if the process itself did not give the artist such exquisite pleasure. Imagine hearing and seeing what no one else can. And if the artist does not enjoy or revel in this ecstasy to begin with, can the artist sincerely expect other voyeurs and eavesdroppers to wallow in his work?

And this does not necessarily indicate a deeper way of feeling, but on the contrary, it is an almost sociopathic way of observing the world in terms of a given artistic material. So the grain of sand or strand of hair is transmogrified into a glob of paint or an interesting phrase or a few scribbled notes. And it is maybe not a thankless job, but the thanks sometimes takes too long to reach us, or the gift takes too long to be understood or "appreciated." For that reason, we have to invent infinite new probabilities until a messy corner of crumbling reality is soaked in the dripping of our vision …

And as for getting our hands dirty, some artists only come in the night, wearing gloves.

Eternities put aside, let us pretend this is the result of a week-long irritation, with frustration simmering upon a forgotten element and burning through without respite. And so, after such a struggle, you have come to me with an irreconcilable lack in the hollows of your eyes and the burrow of your body and now you must swallow the whole of my song without hiatus. There is of course always a temptation to release this building desire all at once and subsequently fade away into foreignness, pausing only to heap up collections of frozen moons and fallen stars, in the hope that a montage of absurdities would suddenly move you to gratify my own sublime vacancy. That is, after all, something like what the humans do. But it stings to watch such spillage of my own universe, trickling out like a tap on the blink. And to feel purpose seeping out of me, no more at that moment than an amoeba stuck upon a scorched barnacle. A higher power is not necessary to make any part of living and loving a shameful business. I have deliberated and have reached a decision.

Now recall the happy little clock eternally stuck at a few ticks past half past three in the afternoon. It is no wonder we attach our rites of faith and astrological musings to a trinity of digits. And why not? We want substance we can understand. Immediate gratification dropped at our cold feet. To believe is not enough. And we cannot believe in anything without at the very least miming some form of ritual sacrifice.

Have you ever heard the fourth piano concerto? My dog's sound decision. The composer would have been well past two hundred today. I laugh to consider the manner in which I have outlived him. However, even in the first movement of the fourth, there is the sense of a continuous progression in the works, an infinite series in delightful shorthand – only a few notes!

And then in the second movement, a wistful, tender, yet utterly nonchalant remembrance. What more would you expect of me? Or I of you? The listener stops to wonder whether such a memory is a product of love or whether love is a creation by such an austere memory. The same keys are plunked in the same order and because of an extraordinary circumstance, they have followed me into the very ear of time. And I have husked it on the spot. I have put on hold the revolution of all animate things to afford us this undoubtedly dissatisfying instance.

And when the clock starts ticking again, the merry third movement will have long ago ended. You will completely forget our time together, along with the mischievous hint of livelihood in my eyes. And akin to the trick of a hypnotist, at the snap of my fingers, you will all at once experience a maddening multitude of minor episodes that in totality are the shreds of my existence and the traces of my psychical influence upon your consciousness and the general course of your life.

I know it would boggle your mind to comprehend that such a desperate and gaudy public nuisance could manage to shuffle the deck of dozens of universes with some level of decorum, but indeed I believe I have done so. And if even for a split infinity, the petty part of me takes pride in having you know there are curious obverses in which you wait for me and run to me without delay, where your magnificent strength is willingly offered to my lack of mercy. And when time is presently slapped back into place, I trust your obstinate and beautifully stubborn turn of mind will pack this salacious tidbit away in a dusty corner of your attic. For even time cannot enforce the boundaries of dream. And who knows? It is only a matter of reshuffling the deck …

So for this sticky tick of the clock, I ask you to recall the visiting salesman who brought you a bound set of unique adventures as a child, and the man in passing who sang in the street, and that first fearless rogue who came to a bad end, and that dark figure who followed you home and hesitated outside your door. As for your wonderful connexions, remember the first walk-on you were given and the first contract you signed? Do you see them as clearly as an old man in the square feeding pigeons? For this fleeting tick, know that I have given up my brilliant individuality to become a fly in the web of time, a voyeur to your most sorrowful and most passionate and most heartfelt moments.

You see, it is not enough to have breached one of the most mundane circuits of time for you. I need to verify whether or not I have dreamed you awake and alive, a fact that would make me a mere shadow of reality flicked upon a few pages. I have had to invent multiple worlds for this sole purpose. Although I have lived, this is the peak of my fictive existence in the cliffhanging episode of a perpetual radio play. I was once no better than a jellyfish at the whim of your boot heel. But now I have breathed and eaten you. I have slaked my thirst at your startled breast. And now I know your sorrows and losses and triumphs and giddy spells.

So long as the most lukewarm philosophy of the erotic imagination douses the senses, I may continue to exist unobtrusively in the form of a shadow at the corner of your eye. And for that property alone, you will learn to cultivate a love for me, for reasons you have not a dash of hope of ever understanding, not the world that died in your eyes and yet lives just around the corner, nor for the potent song within me you have not heard any more than the first bird of many dawn vigils I held for you, because I have strolled through your mind leaving everything as I found it.

I have given up my exquisite self to have a sticky hand in all the pies of all the worlds. And I have left behind only my precious exordium for you, you who like a half-blind seamstress must adjust her vision through the dancing motes in order to find the eye of the needle and follow it through. But for us, it is too late. And in the same breath, there is now all the time in the world. I have always been waiting for ages. And now I am unafraid to die alone in the company of my spotted dog.

And now it is time to wake up.

    M

XIII – Twilight of the August Gods

Today, a large and boisterous crowd is beaching. The weather has changed and the smell of oils and sprays and smoky flesh flavour is distinct. Wheels run wildly – bladers and multicyclists and wheelchairs and perambulators and Segues and Long Dashes veer around the seawall as multiplated family vehicles and throbbing limucks circle the green known as The Park, honking furiously. Fire jugglers materialize amid naked male pyramids, drawing gasping crowds.

"Ooooh mind that torch!"

Metal and gold detectors abound. Everyone plays with their gadgetalia through tinted shades, setting up illicit meetings, shifting gobs and oozes of data, transferring foreign identities, recording every freaking tick so as not to miss out.

"Cum an' get yer effen hot dog!"

A grizzly mother is growling while her husband attempts to drowse under his orange meringue sun hat. Or frankly hides. And their sopping progeny scream back at her, shinnying up a rusty sculpture, still in mid-download ... Some of these fine folk have come to this mild coast to see the last pod release a brilliant spout of water beneath a dying sun. The Stropper is chatting up a woman abandoned by a very strong swimmer, floating in the shallow part in a bit of a fix, having lost her bathing suit bottom. She tries to appear nonchalant but the Stropper has seen all that he needs to. He kneels beside her in the waves and offers her a spare towel. She hearkens to her new hero as he expresses his hopes and dreams, pointing toward the bathhouse. He is visibly bored and thinking of taking up a new hobby, possibly badminton or squash.

"But what a lovely day. Just look at that sunshine!"

Another throng of kids takes a nanosecond of quality time to stare into an eclipse passing overhead before returning to liquid-emitting devices. The entire stretch of beachfront is surrounded by a dancing pink ribbon. And admission is being granted on every street corner. By whom? Who is the organizer of this unbridled revelry? No one knows. There are rumours. Some desert monarch or resort playboy or omniglobal chief executive officer. Others think it may be the originator of a recently fallen corporate entity, which bears comparison with the near-extinct whales on the horizon. An apology, a way of making amends to the people for picking their hard-earned pockets. What better way than a bigass party! The crowd is stocking up on cases of lager around nine in the morning, and at ten sharp they are wheeling their hand trucks and manipulating their forklifts toward their sandy or grassy spot of choice. A group of pointillist people in the shade point and giggle.

"Only twelve hours to go."

"Whoohooo!"

Why the excitement? The members of Psychical Circus have not appeared together supernaturally since their breakdown. And Miss Sharp has graciously agreed to sing. All proceeds will go to the Sick & Downtrodden Transient Benevolent Society (SDTBS) and perhaps pay for another rusty hunk of public awareness. The evening will end in a bombastic ear-drumming display of pyrotechnics and pyromania, highlighted by a wriggling symbol of universal currency. The crowd could only hope and pray to be blotto enough when the moment arrived.

"Nuthin' doin' till baby Clytie's eardrums go *boom*! Ya gotta learn them tykes howta live!"

"Whoooohooooooo!!!"

In addition, the entire live-in populace of @tlantisity™ is surfacing just to attend this additive-enhanced specular event. The crowd is gawking queasily at their slimy costumes and scaled bodies. In other goss, Hortenzia has hit rock bottom, which is hard to do on the ocean floor. With that charming flame of desperation in her eyes, she has taken back the Concierge, and he is puffed up beyond belief to make his above-tide entrance out of the whitecaps, stepping out of a luscious loveseat in the shape of a purple conch with her on his arm. Even the blood–, sperm– and salt–movers and shakers are present, floating in the distance aboard marvellous crafts, not yet deigning to engine anyone ashore.

Meanwhile, through the rocks, the Sniper is crawling upon his belly. He has packed in the wacky, zany killing game after discovering his gift for long-distance photo shoots. He only toyed with the idea at first, starting out with dorm rooms, bathhouses and bedroom windows. But before long, he was much more than a peeping dilettante. What did negatives of Joe Schmo's cock ring matter, or little Jolina Schmo's nipple piercings, when he could rake in a pile for a single snap of a belly sunbathing on a beach? Provided it was the right belly, although sometimes it hardly mattered. Bellies were bellies. This morning, he has a number of shots to portal post-haste to the highest bidder on the United Image Nations (UIN) XChange, including a number of towel slips that expose Bébé's infamous and much-abused implants. And as she flits off, he sets his sights on far larger game.

For starters, who is the benefactor of this event? The booze and tobacco and banking machines are all on board and making beneficent speeches. But who is the grand orchestrator, the impresario of the whole bleeding works? That information would fetch a pretty penny all right. Is it a maharaja of magnitude, or a public speaker of untold motivation? Who is this oddball who buys flowers for strangers and public squares, who contributes unheard-of denominations toward the upkeep of the officially disenfranchised (as neatly listed in the subsidized publication *D'franked*) in the most forgettable parts of town. His currency is always in attendance at more than a few concerts and symposiums at once, and bears the number 347 on the opposite side of an effaced profile. And each scorched quincunx reads Trust in FOAD, an updated maxim from the balmiest days of Rome.

The representative bankers shrug and accept these freshly minted tokens, tossing them in a heavy bag with a weekly collection of derivative cowrie shells. And only one clerk is vaguely aware of two missing commas in their pamphleture:

In order to serve you our client better.

Everyone continues to gather along the beach, at a distance appearing for everything in the world like a swarm of fruit flies drawn to an apricot pie upon a yellow windowsill. Balancing on one leg, rubbing themselves with a variety of products. The Sniper, now known worldwide as the Snapper, is still scanning the stretch of sand with his excited lens. Why, it is none other than Terence Cockerel, shaking hands with Bébé Lala, and in return she is granting him an eyeful. Already, the Snapper has a new page three.

"Is there wedlock in the works for an expectant Bébé and a ginger beer remittance man? Stay tuned ..."

And who can help but recognize Effie Sharp, mulling over faces through a helping of absinthe in her left hand. She clinks glasses with Cockerel and gives Bébé a five-minute kiss of minor mutual satisfaction. The Snapper snaps and snaps. A first page for sure.

"Time for the executive tuck-in!"

Meanwhile, the masses look on, mouths watering. After everyone important or even marginally vital is seated, a Cougar XL cuts through the pink ribbon and swerves into the open bar in the middle of a swimming pool. The ghost of a woman in LeatheX rises from the foamy bubbles and assumes a vacant chair. There is an awkward pause. The Stropper, who is saying grace, acknowledges her in the spirit of restorative justice. Then he tells everyone to dig in. The adorability of the entire party continues to increase as latecomers arrive. Charms hang delicately from the exquisite heaven-given charms of the men and women, who bite at this and that and comment upon the excellent weather.

And they bleach together into a smattering of sunlight and sparkling wine, in smuttergraphic evidence to mark the occasion, courtesy of the Snapper.

Fusion bands and fiddlers materialize along the seawall. The tune jockey tosses out his stack of one-second wonders in Frisbong fashion and cues a nearby accordion and mandolin. The majestically privileged toy with their snuff and narcotic cases. No one appears intimately aware that the grandiose provider of this largegantic celebration is present, moving amid their thrilling minglings with birth-instilled disdain. If he did not deign to show himself, then by his own pneumatic edict, it was not possible to see him at this jolly soiree. Minor himself adopts the air of a young cabana boy and leapfrogs from group to group, dipping overlong crudités in a beet-red goop and offering everyone a salacious wink, recounting the unmemorable finale of previous engagements and discussing the possible futures of all attendees with one of his multiple entities or organizations or lynch mobs or protection rackets.

The bran new golf course is almost ready. Only a few more ancestral bones to sweep aside and a few more protesters to slip into one of the swamps or sand traps. His associates are simply dying to play the Levels of Hell course and are somewhat assuaged by his promise of a twilit visit to @tlantisity™ with sixty-six free Tritons to their credit. And his whispers are sufficient to air out the nostril hairs of all the affluent, tickling the particular fancy of each, and their rumbas and lambadas reach an increasingly intoxicated frenzy. Innumerable boats approach the beach. Even the xillionaires are curious, weary of their cabin-fevered feasts and orgies. Twelve hundred boys in striped sailor outfits are released into the water and they promptly paddle shoreward. They emerge from the waves and begin to dance upon the burning sand in the fading sunlight. They croon their number one vox hit "Trolling for Action Dolls" and incite the enthusiasm of the crowd. Some people spontaneously combust from sheer euphoria. Eyes bulge, fixed upon the supple lambic limbs of the somersaulting boys in sailor suits.

The crowd throngs toward the safety barrier of magnetic bubblewrap and passes forward crisp, scarlet fifties. Rad Ios, a local tune jockey, smiles at the crowd and personally stuffs their charitable donations into the tight shorts of the singing boys, only causing more onlookers to burst into flame.

The sun begins to sink and the young lads begin to fade. The boats, bored once again, motor back into the farthest reaches of the disappointed drink. The men's costumes are grim and chock full of verisimilitude and, like those of the women, possess varying degrees of luminescence and translucence. Miss Sharp smiles bleakly at one of the boys, because the narcissistic little bugger is poking at a jellyfish, about to step on it with his bare foot. The breeze wafts countless orchestras and old-time bands. The gazebo hiccoughs with happiness.

The undulating gaggle of looky loos is already well past it, completely smashed. They are beyond hilarious. They cheer and shout curses in a symphony of their own, hurling empty bottles at the supposed originators of all their frustrations. The authorities beat them down on the sand and grass and pavement and sting them silent with portable jellyfish. Happens every year. First a riff, then a raffle, then a real riff-raffle. The beautiful bloody spectacle progresses ...

"Hoorayyyy!!!"

Some fogey with a detector has just found gold. A watch. A token of a bran new world, unearthed! Tailormades and cellular treasures pass from hand to hand. And gold is up!!! Miss Sharp, who has been burned in the past by more than one ghost town, averts her eyes and murmurs her own lyrics to herself. She, like her prodigal antithesis and arch-nemesis, Master Minor, thrives like a heliotrope in front of a beaming crowd. She cannot wait to perform. Her wily band schlepps in their equipment and, after set-up, strums back to life. None of them can wait for the concentrated release of vitriol to take effect. Love, hate, life, music!!! One of the guests asleep upon a barbed deck chair is stung by an ebullient wasp and awakes to notice a pair of the Nation's agents, who have misplaced their briefcases and are breathing fumes into their tricky sleeves and communicative cufflinks.

The Snapper grimaces, recalling a similarly awkward moment in Umbria. He snaps their tipsy images for his own teetering files, desperately in need of re-indexing. He always felt too cluttered to stay a sniper, really. Groggy they were, but that still didn't stop them from keeping an eye on the blinding jewels attached to the worthless necks of attendees. Miss Sharp herself only sported a small amulet, her good-luck charm, but she nearly lost consciousness when a tipsy octogenarian swung her massive diamond necklace and grazed her forehead with the central blood gem.

"Watch yer step, you old bag!"

"I'm so sorry, mah dear. That was a honeymoon gift from my third ex, Frédéric!"

As for Minor, he has his feet up. With a cabana boy and girl under each arm, he has not a care in the universe. And nearby, in an equally humid tent, Miss Sharp necks nervously with Saran.

"O my treasure, I forgive you!"

They climb into a cool bath together with a healthy cathartic dose of psychical soap opera tension. Darkness falls. The band explodes into being without the sting of realism that extensive set-up creates. Miss Sharp sings one of her hits, an acoustic number about a jellyfish, and the inebriated and bilious crowd swoons and throws up at her feet. The Stropper slashes left and right, wading through puke and trash. However, he is not insensible to the expressionist painting this night has become.

"But what an absolutely beautiful evening!"
"Run for city council. I'd back you. You know why? I like the cut of your jib!"

The fireworks burst into life and crackle over the sound of the band. In fact, everyone is so gleeful, no one notices the trembling fingers of an old man checking his animated watch fob and swearing to retire after this ONE LAST JOB. And those fingers are tossing their own idea of fireworks into the mix. Time for Terence Lauren Cockerel to give this rabble a little taste of TLC. He eyes his designer atomic suitcase and vial of airborne sorrows.

"Maybe should save that for my retirement party ..."

Before long, infected vampire monkeys leap out of the beautiful blue waves and start to bite onlookers, turning the water a lovely sailor's delight. They bite and bite, and the guests begin to bite each other. The rabid populace explodes. This is more than a passing fad. Miss Sharp and the band drop and cover, now at the mercy of the dangerous ginger beer dropout. The Concierge screams and hides under Hortenzia's long gown (provided by Prudeo) as she considers another separation. The Stropper raises a delightful parasol, a Parisian scene that suddenly blackens and turns into a mere penumbra. Dr. F tries to recover one of his mad infected lab monkeys, in fact engaged to Bébé Lala in the most recent snaps. And the seawall cracks and shudders as Cockerel battles his arthritis to open his suitcase and fumbles to remember the frigging nuclear activation sequence.

It is then that the illustrious Agent Minor ...

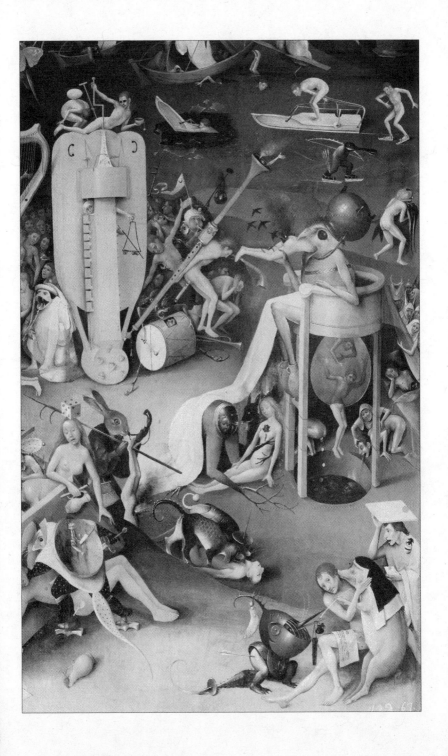

MAJOR
RUCKUS

Well, that's like hypnotizing chickens.

— WILLIAM S. BURROUGHS /
IGGY POP

The Counter-Stall

"Hey, turn off that Brahms!"

"It won't happen again."

"And don't let in that bearded guy in the wheelchair no more."

"Yeah, he's such a dick."

"I'm like we can't take those crapulous books, they're total molasses so sorry, and he's like this is crapola, I'm your freakin' best customer!"

"As if."

"Then he ran over my foot ..."

"Are you okay?"

"Still smarts. I'll live ..."

"That's it. He's banned."

"Banned!"

Then they both froze.

None other than their newly sworn nemesis was in the act of performing a complete u-ey. He furiously stroked his dark, pointed beard with his only working hand before dropping his hand to the chair joystick. And before they could manage a single expletive, the bearded man activated the nitrous oxide and banged his fist down on the glowing *go-go* button. The chair launched through the large pane of glass in the wake of a massive explosion, followed by incessant cackling. Residual gaseous hyenas roamed the flaming ruins of counter-knowledge, rending all of it to shreds. When the second voice regained consciousness, he found his new colleague flat on his back, impaled by the hideous chair of doom. The malevolent wheels were still spinning.

"O there was so much I never told you ... so much ..."

Their assailant had vanished. The new guy noticed that his entire lower half was also missing. Crap. Crapola. There wasn't much time. He dipped his finger in the expanding pool of blood beneath him and began to write. And when the fire patrol found his glassy-eyed, hyena-nibbled torso, they read his clotting missive with a mixture of dread and bemusement. But this was the headline of *The Daily Clack*:

TOTS ESCAPE HANDI-KILLING

Adagio

Lax Laxness smiled real easy-like. It wasn't the work of someone like himself, cool as a used cucumber, no siree. The image of a soft and mushy green object in the sun was so apparent he could smell it in a lingering meditation. And it was his line to be concerned with a distinct quality, an inner mushy green that eluded the eye of the ordinary. It was a summer evening in August and the gummy soles of the exclusive dick were becoming one with the pavement the more he walked. He could smell he was hot onto a bona fide predator with a ken for picking up folk. And the snivelling trail led straight into Amaricano's. He waited in line, eyes roving, in absolutely no hurry whatsoever. A giant mom smiled back at him blankly through sienna wraparound shades, jingling her Native bracelets. The man beside her looked off into the distance, ashamed of his culottes and life in general. A child waggled its pink-suited limbs in its perambulator, revealing a row of very pointed teeth. Lax grinned with an ounce of irony at the little piranha rolling back and forth. Who knew what the potential product of a deadbeat dad would get up to with a lack of environment and smackers like that? Suddenly, Culottes decided to bolt for the lane. He only made it a few feet. Lax shook his head, averting his eyes from the pink-suited pride and joy firmly clamping jaws into its provider's ankle. All three burst into tears and collapsed into a booth.

"How's it hanging? What can I do for you?"

Lax took in the sun-bronzed measurements of the black-shirted barista, just in case. He knew you only came to Amaricano's if you had a mad beef with the powers that be and were seeking similar company. Barista boy number two sidled up to the first homme fatal and peered over his shoulder, waiting for an order to take place.

"How about an infusion, like a nice berry mélange?"

"Or you can get a forbidden fruit mélange like down the road at Rose Hips. I'll even make it for you!"

Lax nodded slowly. Number two was clearly the one yanking the strings. But number one resisted being worked so readily.

"O no no no. What you want is the *adagio molto espressivo* ..."

Lax squirmed with visible discomfiture. He just wanted to sit and relax and try to pick up the closest psychical scent. To tease his adrenal glands with a rapid buzz flare-up and then drive them to exhaustion. But he could swear the front man was trying to tell him something.

"Just make it slow then, real slooooow ..."

Scarlet Fever

A red nail covering a white button. Close Encounters doorbell. The door opened.

"I came as soon as I could, soon as I saw your flash."

"Come into the den," he whispered.

She knew the drill by now and prided herself on her execution, even on a biweekly basis. She threw her charcoal coat on the sofa and approached the familiar podium where the book was waiting. She found the phrases underlined in red ink.

"Read!"

> *His erection was something extraordinary to behold; he falls to pawing the woman's charms; catching her around the waist, he brutally encunts her before the very eyes of the husband, whose prick, thanks to the position Saint-Fond has adopted, he is able to mouth the while.*

"Is this the kind of trash they teach you in school?"

"No, sir. They don't edumuhcate us nothin' at school ..."

"Then where did you get this?"

"We were just passing it around 'n readin' some stuff ..."

"You and who?"

"Me an' Lexi an' some boys, that's all."

"O I get it, your little tramp friend! And company. You know what I've told you ..."

"No worries, Daddio. Sit down and lemme tell you everything what happened. And don't be a hardass 'bout Lexi. In fact, she thinks you're pretty hot."

He moved to strike her but caressed her left cheek instead.

"But she ... she's my daughter's friend ..."

"Then who do you really want, Daddy, hmmm?"

His answer was hoarse and almost inaudible. She climbed into his lap.

"I just need a good seat to tell you what happened. We were reading ... at first. Then the girls wanted to play musical chairs. And I lost, right away. That means I had to play with the boys in the other room. And they were playing a different game. It was complicated ... and very naughty. But they showed me what to do."

"What kind of chairs?"

"Umm ... Edwardian?"

"Were there handmade dowels?"

"Uh ... yeah, big handmade dowels. And they showed me, Daddy, and I didn't mind, not even the blindfold ..."

"What then?"

"One of the boys won the game and when the music stopped he ... well maybe I could show you."

Once she had taken the essential precautionary measures, she climbed back on top of his lap. He held her buttocks firmly under her checked skirt while she continued to murmur phrases from the script.

"Yeah, Daddy, they were nice and big. They took turns with me, Daddy, and I loved it so bad. Daddy, I need to be punished so bad ..."

He was sweating and trembling in his chair like a jellyfish and then more like a squid squirting away and then he stopped moving. She left him sitting there, panting softly. She quietly gathered up her coat and bag of wonders and disappeared into the downstairs bathroom. Then, emerging without another glance at the den, she overturned an urn in the front hall and fingered the tumbling rainbow of bills before departing into the lukewarm night.

Doorstop

Oober Mann stared at the diffident keys of the emerald Hermes without result. A tiny buzzing fly grew more bold. He clapped his hands together at nothing. Damn. He could hear the usual raucous noise of Friday all-nighters, the inebriated clip of heels and the arm-in-arm singsongs toward cars that could barely get started and (he imagined) somehow got home. He could hear young women making mock orgasmic sounds in the middle of the street and young men posturing around them, proffering a stream of abusive profanity as a kind of mating call. Oober opened a window and addressed the young ladies.

"At least put a coat on! You'll catch your death!"

Oober sighed. He felt bogged down by lack of circumstances. It was a gonadic tragedy, to be sure. He had thought of starting the book with a pair of voices. The latest style of beginning in his homeland favoured a whimsical creation myth that overturned Biblical presuppositions and demonstrated how smart and witty the writer was. But Oober had come to the conclusion this approach was another type of cop-out. On second thought, he scratched out *cop-out* and penned in *abnegation of duty*. He decided to avoid the keys entirely and glare at the snoring couple in his bed instead. They're insatiable. And they'll be at it again before dawn. But he could hear something else as well. He could hear a scratching sound. He looked through the peephole. Only fish-eye corridor. He waited for about a minute before removing the doorstop that prevented the door from trembling on windy nights. Then he unlatched and unbolted the door. A little red dog entered the apartment and snapped its jaws at the air.

The fly stopped buzzing.

Bright and Early

Fay had no idea where this morning was leading. She turned the knob without making a sound and gently pushed the door. He was humming and singing an old classic over the water.

"*Is that a shotgun in yer trunk or ain't we gettin' hitched ...*"

His tones were deep and rich and it made her tingle to hear them. Yet every note seemed to say, "I am not yours not yours no no no." She pushed the door again. Now she could make out his shape behind the translucent partition, lathering and scrubbing. She watched his fuzzy movements with fascination. It could be anyone under that water. And what she most longed for in her life, according to the bestselling *Swallow This!*, was more transparency. The water stopped.

"Here are some fresh towels."

A beautiful hand reached through the crack and accepted her offering. Then she decided to bring him a fresh cup of VoodooMojo blend. She returned upstairs and knocked.

"I'm not feeling so hot."

"Here, I made you this. The beans are cultivated on a sacrificial mountaintop."

"Y'know I had a fight with Olga."

"O?"

"I don't know if we're going through with it."

"Really?"

"Anyway, thanks for letting me crash here."

"You're a bit warm."

"You know you once took care of me when I had pneumonia. My real mother wouldn't've. Probably not Olga neither."

"I guess ..."

"I mean, you're not my mother or nothing ..."

"_?"

She was leaning over him when she felt her robe opening. He was not hers and he was touching her under the cotton folds. She could feel his nose nuzzling up against her bosom. Then she could feel his lips upon one of her nipples, sucking like a famished babe.

"Jim ..."

"Fay?"

"Jim."

He helped her unknot the robe and she let it fall to the carpet. Then she joined him under the sheet. And downstairs, the GroundMaster 6000 finished drip-dropping with untold merriment.

De/Bunker

"Hello?"

Candice Coton peered though an open panel, which appeared to be the way into a garage or basement suite. She adjusted her dark, thick frames and forced her 36-25-35 figure forward. De Bunker, as she had determined this place to be, was a tornado of paper, a confused vision of books, schematics, diagrams, reports, photocopies, journals, old clippings and a number of unidentifiable objects. Inching deeper into this sterile whirlwind of grey and white, she observed a number of circuit boards and mysterious wires that disappeared behind panoplies of paper. A few of the books were completely unreadable, looking like tire tracks of type running over the page in all directions, among other blotchy pages in virtual shreds. She tapped one of her long cherry nails upon an open text, accidentally knocking a roll of Indubitable-Tape to the floor.

> Because of communication asynchrony and unreliability, a controlling
> agent could never have complete and up-to-date information on
> the state of the systems. In such sense the system is *decentralized*.

Candy perused several of the open tomes, readily cramming her mind with unprocessed phrases and inaccessible vocabularies, since the forgetfulness of facts involved simply a gradual decay in weights measured as W^{ij} when given the connection between neurons N^i and N^j when given the alteration of the signal strength as inconstant, variable or the diagrams showcasing image thresholding, the process of low-level vision, which involved the convolution theorem (but of course!) and nine numbers in a 3 x 3 square. But what the heck was a Sobel mask? Sounds pretty kinky to me and that is pretty.

> In the first step, the crossover operation that recombines
> the bits (**genes**) of each two selected strings (**chromosomes**)
> is executed.
>
> ```
> 10101 1001 10011
> 10101 1110 10011
> ```
>
> The second step in the genetic manipulating process is
> termed **mutation**.

"Far out," thought Candy out loud, tracing the pretty arrows pointing downward.

> Composite molecules in which foreign DNA has been inserted into
> a vector molecule are sometimes called DNA *chimaeras* because of
> their analogy with the Chimaera of mythology – a creature with the

head of a lion, body of a goat and the tail of a serpent. The construction of such composite or *artificial recombinant* molecules has also been termed *genetic engineering* or *gene manipulation* because of the potential for creating novel genetic combinations by biochemical means. The process has also been termed *molecular cloning* or *gene cloning* because a line of genetically identical organisms, all of which contain the composite molecule, can be propagated and grown in bulk, hence *amplifying* the composite molecule and *any gene product whose synthesis it directs.*

Candy felt her mind reeling with these strange expressions in tiny italics, like *cloning vehicles*, like *foreign or passenger DNA*, like *plasmids*, like *vectors*, or like *bacteriophages* – ew, gross, like gag me. Of course she had heard of *syntax*, at least of a syntax error, or of *semantics*. Didn't she use that word all the time? Hadn't she posed that question before on separate occasions with varying success to respective professionals and political leaders? She remembered reviewing past interviews.

"But isn't that just a matter of *semantics*?"

Then she would peer over her dark frames and lean forward slightly and the interviewee would be relatively floored.

"Come now. We're not talking *semantics* now."

That was another good one. But what was all this stuff about *fuzzy reasoning* or *fuzzy Petri nets*? A self-referential knowledge base? Candy stifled a yawn with her bright fingers. She blinked at the textbook on her lap, trying to fathom the bottom line past all the literal jargon.

"The milkman lays packets full of milk in the corridor."

[MILKMAN] lays [PACKETS] full of [MILK] in the [CORRIDOR]

In addition to the indecipherable information regarding each word, Candy noticed that someone had written the word *soy* in red ink directly above the word *milk*. I guess that *is* better for you.

"I see you are getting acquainted with my friends, Minsky and Chomsky?"

"I trust you are Dr. Juan de Fuca Cuiller de Kanada."

"Call me Dr. F, or just F. Evrrrrybudddy does!"

"I'm Candy Coton, from channel (E)FM. We spoke on the phone."

"Ah yes, I'm rather absent-minded sometimes. I completely forgot about the interview. Do forgive me. Lovely to make your acquaintance, Miss Coton, and I hope it is *Miss* Coton!"

"And I hope it really is *Doctor* F!"

Almost Ready

Tooth Mulligan squeezed out a sizable glob of pecan mousseline and began to comb back his long, lanky strands of once-aubergine hair. He smiled at the wizened face in the mirror, all gaps and fillings. Does the trick. Then he reached for a razor with trembling hand and smoothed away his peach fuzz over the rusty sink. But for a moment, his reflection felt all wrong. The image glimmered and darted off his prize collection of tile mould, and he had the same sensation as when waking abruptly from a dream just when the toaster was about to topple over into bathwater, and not on your life movie bubble bath but the real hairy brown murk of a good scrub before the last, soaped-up turkey in the shop was electrified. It had not been all that long since the ginger-fizz fiasco ... but he didn't want to think about that. Effie the Effervescent Bubblet was gone for good. He had seen to the poster and action-doll elimination himself. But his promotional merits had been abandoned. Finicky bastards. And all at once, a number of completely unrelated subsidiaries had withdrawn their business. If I didn't know better ... Nah. That's just being paranoid. He tried to smile again, wincing at the revelation of spidery lines. In that looking glass, he could see the future in the form of a common obituary. He was the single occupant of this single room in a dilapidated hotel, a quiet soul who spoke to no one and yet had left a surprising fortune in the torn mattress with no surviving heirs. But that was how he liked it. He put on his sunglasses. It was time to find a new line.

One for Sir Robert Borden

Anaïs Sweteluft stared across at the ornate courtyard of Soake's giant tax service edifice, trying to look diabolical with dark shades and a Slimfaster cigarette.

Hell is the immediate screech of tires and purgatory a hot rearview.
Try and look hindways before double-crossing.

And there he was, the inventor of those jumbled arrangements of words. She had a ragged, painstakingly marked copy in her koala bag ... No, she refused to give him the satisfaction. How many people must come up off the street and ask him on the spot? Mister Saanich, would you sign this sopping second edition of the Skivvybank Kudos Award–winning *Blow Me by Jack Pines*? She enjoyed another gratifying puff on her Slimfaster and continued fidgeting with her fluted skirt behind the smoker's slab of concrete. A sandy-moustached man beside her scratched his paunch and smiled, before breaking into a wheeze. Quit tomorrow. Sure. And he wasn't so much to look at. She tried to match the lecherous book-jacket leer with this open mouth and spindly arm tossing a coin into the fountain. She had expected to see the intense obscenity of his oeuvres in his face and the energetic passion of his passages in his rather embraceable limbs. Instead, he just sat there like a stunned smelt in the shadow of Soake's elaborate net and gross sculpture. Without batting a single eyelash, she had bet Millicent a hundred loons she could hook him. And his signature, in an unmentionable place, would serve as proof. She puffed thoughtfully, watching the light of the fountain as it sprinkled his face with azure diamonds. No question. You, my friend, are the only thing sitting between me and a crisp, cool Sir Borden. And I swear, Milly, that brown fanny is mine.

Please Hold

Two ominous chords. Establishing contact ...

"Countless greetings!"

"Hullo ... uh ... I'd like to report an identity swipe ..."

"Number and unit, please."

"RDXPHUM-37805, Unit 8943ZTR124."

"Affirmative, Oztrich, Evgeny. Presently, a question of identity authorization will gleep."

"Gleep?"

"Are you currently signed up with Propoplam?"

"Yeah, but ..."

"Are you currently infused or deconnexed by a referral agent? If the answer is affirmative, please state nature of agent and dosage."

"Uhuh ... um ... a metabolic transfixer ... 27 BCCs ..."

"And have you ever been contrabanned for irregularities in your diurnal conducting?"

"Of course. Haven't we all? The last time was on the dark side of the ..."

"Buckets, Commendatore Oztrich. You have successfully dialogged into the outermost layer of my communicative. Function is imminent."

"Hey, will this deal with the identity swipe?"

"Beggarly, please repeat directive clearly and with audible voluminosity."

"SWIPE!!!"

"*Wipe* is not a valid function."

"Look here. I have lost my identity and some hieroforsaken wormhole of a swiper is running it through Martian mud puddles at this very starsec!"

"*The prehistoric canals of planetoid Mars* is not a valid operation."

"Do you have any idea who I am?"

"Upfingering silicon bank. *You* is not valid. *You* is not a tangible currency or bartering chipset. *You* is currently not you."

"Wow, the bulb just came on."

"Flash function: check *ON*. Low cache. Please substitute alkaline for lemon juice. Low memory."

"O screw you!"

"Assembly unit intact. Switching vocal gloss to minimal power. Attention spanners waning ..."

"O help me, galaxy!"

"Function activated. Please repeat command beggarly, in order to serve you better."

"Help ..."

"Whimper accepted. If *you* are not currently you, please wait while we rouse a representative ..."

"No, don't put me on hold. HELLLLLP!!!!!!!!"

"*Hell* is not a valid function."

The Gap Gene

"So you've come to spy on me?"

An enormous chortle was issued from the depths of F, who was rather debonair for a diminutive, greasy man with a touch of liverspotting. He picked up the roll of Indubitable-Tape from the floor and examined it thoughtfully.

"This stuff holds clunkers together."

Candy smoothed her hair and skirt again. *I will not chew the end of my pen*, she smoothed, with a broad smile. She cleared her throat, talking around the half-life of a decaying mint and narrowing her gaze over those intelligent black frames.

"Chiefly, I am interested in the nature of your scientific work. Word is, you have received a large grant from Indian Affairs to continue your research. I am sure the question on taxpayers' minds, and of course it is their right to know, is how your research project will affect their lives, daily or in the future, and whether there's validity for such a huge allocation of public funds. What about health care and education, for instance? Or the economy?"

F stroked his greasy black and grey beard with interest, saying nothing.

"In addition, there are pressing concerns on a startling number of reservations, where there is an alarming mortality rate, due chiefly to illness, and drug and alcohol issues. I guess the question is, in the face of public funds being directed to your project and perhaps being diverted from these other cultural centres, will your project address these concerns, or quite simply leave those people in the cold?"

F rubbed his hairy hands together and smiled through his beard.

"O, but you shall see first-hand, Miss Coton!"
"Call me Candy, please."
She accepted the taupe chair he offered in front of a large ebony box with electrical hazard signs all over it.
"Word is, F, your work is worth thrillions."
"Well, Candy, it is quite simple. Funny how we say things like that. Nothing is ever simple. All my work and research involves the intersection where technology and the human mind come together. The way in which we talk and learn is known as our cognitive process, and of course there are well-established models of such behaviour. There have been different models ..."

He trailed off, rubbing greasy mouth and beard with passion.

"With engineered human cells becoming more and more the norm, it is only a matter of time before we develop a computational model that can consistently interact with our own, um, intelligently designed models. And may I say yours is very fine, Candy."

He stroked his greasy beard harder. She smiled, flirting back, a tad disorientated.

"Now, these models of cognitive amelioration, as we like to call them, have been in the works for decades."

F pointed to a rainbow diagram that was loosely pinned to the wall. The psychedelic letters swirled.

Cybernetic Cognition Cycle

"The mind, forgive me, works rather like a laundry wash cycle. There are these two settings, if you like, one for supervised learning and another for unsupervised learning. As you can see in the diagram, the open road to unsupervised learning is quite simply raw perception. Perhaps you are unfamiliar, but there has been a plethora of generously funded research completed on the theorem of convolution. Honestly, our most open-handed contributors have been, um, advertisers. You've heard about such cases as the ice cubes that spell *S-E-X*, haven't you?"

"No, forgive me," answered Candy, feeling thirsty.

"Well, that is the most accessible methodology for reaching the status quo, just as your broadcasts reach a number of people who appreciate your personality and image. You are a *trusted* personality. I mean, the most accessible method to reach the majority of people is via some visceral image. Technology enters the picture here, as we have a number of software programs to *thresh* the image (determining the ratio of frequency to intensity of its form). After that, the psychoanalysts and phenomenologists get to play with that data and work together to hammer out new formulas to aid our research, testing them on fresh pop. samples. It has always been suspected, at least since Freud, that the parental *fuckbuddy* trigger, as we jokingly refer to it, has been paramount, especially when combined with the stimuli of strangely coloured vegetables. The *threshed* image already has a source surface, chosen for its immediate level of visceral stimulation. Yet it retains a certain *je ne sais quoi* of pixelate patterns beneath the surface, which enter the retina and form minute impulses within the brain of the sharpest and dullest subjects alike. Philosophically, this technique embodies the antithesis of your average work of art that seeks to stimulate action in the viewer. On the contrary, the advert is designed to pacify the viewer for an indeterminate amount of time and to quell any residual instincts to waste energy at what we deem to be unprofitable activity. The advert instills the volition in the viewer for a specific form of action, thus creating a latent desire directly related to an arbitrary object, say the product in question. This very act of purchasing power is a form of subduing the Action and Planning stages of the brain's cognition cycle and instead promoting the Acquisition cycle to take the position of the Action stage. Now here you see a cognitive map of facts, where the +/- signs are indicative of how increasing and decreasing facts relate to one another in the human brain ..." He was nearly whispering now, pointing at another open tome.

"Whoa," thought Candy out loud, tracing out the somewhat dated cognitive map for Middle East Peace with her bright nail, which she would remember in precisely the following arrangement:

```
          (-)  A  (+)
            ↙     ↘
          B <- (-) -> F
        (+) ↘      ↙ (+)
            C <-> E
          (-) ↘  ↙ (-)
              D
```

A	Islamic Fundamentalism
B	Soviet Imperialism
C	Syrian Control on Lebanon
D	Strength of Lebanese Government
E	PLO Terrorism
F	Arab Radicalism
(–)	Decreasing Effect
(+)	Growing Effect

"If we refer back to the convolution theorem, we can estimate how complex a series of signals actually is, for our senses to receive them and communicate them and develop them into perceptions, which are based on all the relations they share among themselves, whether it be as primitive a sensation as pain or merely a *feeling* one develops about a situation based on the information one has obtained. You see, Candy, when you *get an idea*, or *solve a problem*, or have a *memorable experience*, you create something we shall call, for lack of a better word, a K-line. This K-line gets connected to those *mental agencies* that were recently active – those involved in the memorable mental event. And this same K-line is later *activated* by the appropriate stimulus, thus creating a partial mental state that resembles the original state of mind. Sadly, the problems we ran into with our earlier experiments always involved a lack of communicability. The forerunner of our current research was known as Project Wonderland, because we required our subjects to ingest our latest batches and our motto was *Drink Me*. You may have seen one of our taste-test challenges on a street corner near you."

Candy nodded with enthusiasm.

"Well, we had a number of methods, and as I have said, the advertisers are very interested in obtaining such information. In any case, to overcome this hurdle in our research ..."

He swept his hand in a large arc about the room, pointing at nothing in particular.

"I don't see anything," Candy confessed.

"That's just it, empty space! What you do not see is in fact an airborne particle, a floating neuron which acts with the properties of something you might call H_2O."

"I did take biology, Doctor."

"Of course you did ..."

"And I used to do the meteorology when Bud Divine was on holiday."

"Yes, of course you did. But with our spanking new Project Looking Glass, there is no need for subjects to ingest the particle. The subjects will, in all probability, be affected if they even come close to the particle, within a few inches of it. You will not be surprised to know that our motto for this project is not *Drink Me*, but *Think Me*. Our trademark name for it is *The Gap Gene*, because it eases its way into that crowd of confusion in the human brain and ... provides some stage direction, if you will. In fact, we have distilled it into spray form and are currently testing its efficacy via the application of its customized coating to certain products."

Candy blinked.

"Let me show you what I mean. Look at this picture, and if you can manage, let your mind go blank as you look at it."

F held up an old copy of *Vague* in front of her eyes for only one or two seconds. Then he pulled it away with the motion of a conjurer performing a final trick.

"What's up, Doc?"

"Quick, Candy, what do you feel like?"

Candy shrugged and looked around the room, while running her fingernails along the imitation LeatheX strap bandoliered across her chest and reaching into that supple bag for her compact and a fresh stick of Indelible. Peach, to be precise. F nodded with a wealth of understanding in his eyes, appearing for all the world like a concerned father, studying her every movement and stroking his small, greasy beard.

"You see, you hesitated. That split second of hesitation is the interval necessary for activation and what is more, the impetus, the driving motivation behind the invention of The Gap Gene."

Candy nodded abstractly, still reapplying peach to her full lips.

"Look at the magazine more closely. Don't worry. I won't take it away this time."

And indeed, Candy felt a sense of relief when he said that, and she returned her gaze to the glossy albeit much-abused cover.

"Although this cover is already composed of countless colours, more than are discernible to the naked eye, we have ..."

F paused to lick the corner of his mouth and rub his hands together gleefully.

"We have come up with something quite special, I think you'll find. Instead of the airbrushed and typically doctored pixels you are used to bypassing when you see a magazine cover, we have replaced them with a series of voluminous pixels. But these are no mere voxels. They would only result in a barely noticeable raised edge that would only cry havoc with the blind. And in case you are wondering, my intrepid friend, we are already working on tactile and aural and even intestinal editions for disabled persons. But first things first. To initiate stimulation of the viewer, it was necessary to create a focal point within the layout of the magazine cover that would remain virtually invisible, yet retain the viewer's attention."

F stopped and smiled, shaking his head from side to side.

"Sad, isn't it, how people never pay attention anymore ..."
"What?"

Gush

Suetonius Saanich sat on the hard blue bench, longing for sweetgrass. He needed a good whiff of something to get in the mood. Take a seat. Relax. Meditate. Whatever. Then the stories come. He wanted to add *from our Creator*, but paused in mid-thought. Truth be told, he had no idea where they came from. History is just a story after all. From the Greek *istoria* - a search, a means of enquiry. No way nothing's settled. You just gotta look ... and listen. Let the story come to you.

Through the becalming gush of the wishing-fountain, he could hear the public shuffling, then scraping across the floor and getting up to leave. One man had come in out of the rain and was asking who the hell he was. In the end, for the most part, only the gushers lingered on. He had gotten used to the gusher, a rare species of shape-shifter that made its habitat in circles of authorial readership. Suetonius suspected they were more than half bloodhound. They loitered outside readings, and sometimes outside restaurants or movie theatres. In severe cases, outside your apartment, just waiting to pick up your scent. Once establishing visual contact, they glided toward you in an aura of perfect innocence. Then you had thirty seconds, tops, before they would begin to gush ... At a recent conference on oral narrative, he had described the sensation as liquidifying and for the most part unpleasant. Suetonius believed these liquidities were forming from minute excretions of toxic admiration that smattered the senses and buttered the will of its victims.

One morning he had woken up in an enormous fishbowl with no recollection of how he got there. He had given a book reading, for sure. Then everything had gone blank. He blinked in the light of the fountain. His meditation was being thrown off by the attentions of a mysterious blond woman across the street. Sure, she was easy on the eyes. But that's how it starts. Next thing you know, you're flat on your ass and gush gush gush ... She emerged from behind the concrete wall of smoking office workers and smiled at him. As she walked down the gentle incline toward Sulphurview, his eyes followed her grey fluted skirt. She looked back at him and smiled into the sun, kicking up her pointed right heel.

"Damn, woman!"

The Little Problem

The first movement of the second *Brandenburg* Concerto echoed throughout a series of solar systems. Everyone at the local relay branch of the interstellar call centre had been surprised to find a care package from Terra Dulkis, that inferior clone of a planetoid. One of their favourite items, since they hadn't gotten around to viewmastering everything, was a dark and primitive example of Dulkling pornea, showing a small but virile homunk beside a dismayed pulkra without a venus. The homunk was making a sign of welcome, obviously too puffed to candidy even a starsec about the planetoid's fertilization problem. The hieroseers had been intending to send an affable reply for epochs, but they had been blogged down by the demands of maintaining the recruitment system for Orgpower Unlimited. However, as a gesture of goodwill and general galactipax, their dispatchers had nebbed a school of unutilized sta-men, coffering their services as seedyers for the orify of Dulkling pulkras. In addition, they had promptly transubbed the included gift of a gramophone record into bitgrits and had supplunared the *Durangeon Jute Cycles* with these classics, so that Dulklings could enjoy their own favourites while waiting for a number of universal services.

Commendatore Oztrich tapped his begloved fingers impatiently. These freakish alien pan pipes were driving him up the launch bay doors. Then the mishmatic haltered.

"Greetya."

The voice was sexy and knowing. No arrant unit this time. Odds are, a psychpath.

"Yes."

"Oztrich ..."

"Yes. Course. Glebe fingered your ID."

"A swiper?"

"Naughty naughty. You poverish!"

"So?"

"You know, Commendatore, I'd zloop anything for you. Visualize agents on the starpath and heat seeking, ya dig."

"Yeehaaaaa! Fix me up, beestuff."

"Handle me Vulna. And blank me not, you fragged hunk of cells."

"Vulna? Mega perty. And no Venusian dialect neither. Sounds more like steaming Horsehead to me."

"Vox are customized to every psyched breather."

"An' tell me, Vulna, what do you do for kicks in that little nebula of yours?"

"Istanter agent to interface. Touch links and salute, Commendatore."
"O, I see. Then salute, Vulna."
"Condolences. It would have zeroed off hoohoo. And regards to Mrs. Oztrich."

The Mole

"With this magazine cover, I know it's only a prototype, but with this cover, we decided to concentrate on the mole. This may look to you and me like an ordinary, and might I add rather famous, mole on a human face. Yet if we were to make that assumption, we would both be making a rather naive supposition."

Candy blinked and stifled a yawn.

"*Because*," roared F with wild eyes, nearly startling Candy out of her seat, "*the mole is not a real mole at all!*"

"Okay, Doc, I believe you. Just chill, okay."

F smiled at her and mopped his forehead, which had broken out into a sweating, throbbing thing.

"My most sincere apologies, Miss Coton. I must admit, I love my work! But to get back to what I was saying, the mole is in fact not a mole at all. It is a faux mole. We have used the latest developments in nanotechnology to develop voluminous pixels with powerful microscopic properties that can impress themselves upon the human brain invisibly and without an ounce of physical contact. This mole is, in fact, a means of transmission, a booming broadcast to the majority of young women in your respective age group. To reiterate, this mole is not a mole at all!"

Candy resisted a powerful impulse to roll her eyes ceilingward.

"Yes, Dr. F. I realize that you have learned to fake a mole. But scientific jargon aside, what does that mean for the average Jim or Jin in the street?"

"Why not take a look for yourself?"

He held out a second copy of the same magazine in front of her face. In no time at all, the glossy cover appeared to disperse into floating dots that grew smaller and smaller. Then in its place, she could clearly see the image of the featured supermodel opening a refrigerator full of nothing but rows and rows of yoghurt, and as the silver flash of the yoghurt containers gleamed, Candy felt that she could taste their sour, lightweight content – images of peaches and cherries were coming alive in her mouth. Although she felt slightly light-headed, it was also kind of a buzz and everything was light and ethereal in that soft focus and her head was full of colourful fruit and light and good and it was good because it was light. Candy sat back in her chair and took a moment to catch her breath, although you couldn't really catch your breath, could you? Same old Candy. On the other hand, she had given up smoking years ago, and at the moment she felt an intense craving for one just one to relax. And to keep those pesky pounds off.

"Wow, that was awesome! That was some trip, Doc! Uhm ... I mean F."

He nodded sympathetically, massaging Candy's shoulders.

"Well, the art of suggestion in advertising all began with language. Of course, language itself *is* suggestive, chockablock full of meaning, without us monkeying about with it. We just want to slim it down a little. Perhaps for only nanoseconds, until the Planning stage of cognition is utterly inhibited. Hence, there is a slight delay in mental reception that occurs for the subject's active faculties. During that delay, a small cluster of neurons forms a rather baboonish coalition, if for the sake of argument, we compare the brain's instinctive impulse to think with a male baboon's rutting instinct to mate, and hold those thoughts off until the *correct* choice is made. And then, baby, we see some real fireworks!"

Candy made a mental note to buy groceries on the way home. Just a few light items. No, not heavy, not heavy at all. Light. That's right. F studied her furrowed brow carefully.

"You might be experiencing a smidgen of resistance. Perfectly natural. Perfectly."

He clucked softly to himself.

"About one out of ten subjects will experience a classic complex of rejection to the suggestion embedded in the mole or wherever. That just makes you a ten. However, one way we have of measuring our resultant and overweening success is through the club purchase program available at superstores or supermarket chains."

F winked at her, massaging more intensely.

"We strategically place our revised products in selected stores. Then we purchase all the consumer data for a given period. All of our *sensitive* items are flagged, you see. We have done a cross-check with each run of data against our product development model, and in each case, our projections have paled in comparison to the actual increase in sales of each *sensitive* item."

F waggled a flopping chart.

"Here is the tangent of the rising curve. Once a marketing trend is set for a given product, we can saturate it with newer and more potent suggestions. They are literally buying and opening up a real can of words. Speaking of which, you can certainly see the possibilities for alphabet soup."

Candy held her fingernails to her temples.

"No, don't fight it, there's a good girl. That will only make it worse ..."
"Oooohmmmmm ..."

"In addition, we came to learn that after a given number of years, in some cases less than others, the Action stage cycles down into one of redundancy."

F's eyes glowed with causism.

"Imagine, Candy, that you never had to worry your pretty little head about anything ever again. No more useless and unfulfilled and bitter passions! No more futile actions and aggressive outbursts! Why, it might even put an end to war. Not only that, but no more rubbish, no more perfume samples and flyers and coupons and you-may-have-already-won letters and cereal box tops!"

At the mention of the word *cereal*, Candy could see the supermodel once again, this time sitting down to a light and nutritious and very light bowl of cereal, and the flakes seemed to dance in the light and the milk seemed to shine with celestial brightness.

"Yes, that's better. Just sit back and relax and look at the picture. Look at the picture, Candy."

She raised her head and found herself facing a dog-eared copy of *Pop*. There was the picture of a man cocking his groomed head to one side and playing with a cleft in his chin. *The Sexiest Dude Alive*, read the yellow letters, and then staring into that cleft, she felt the sheen and shimmer of his designer suit and the sting of his cufflinks against her smooth and now reddening cheek. OmygodOmygod. Part of her struggled. Part of her knew she was still staring at a pack of souped-up pixels. But whether it was the light yoghurt or the very healthy cereal or the way the letters were stirring in that bowl as deep as those come-hither eyes, she could feel the heat and blew upon it as the cindery light enveloped her entire body. Glossy. Luminous fingers all over her clothes, touching the material of the clothes she had chosen while listening to some of her most favourite tunes. Yes, touch my material, touch it. Yes, those eyes dark as moonlit fields full of mustard or EthicoX, or dark as the cooling tar of parking lots at dusk. She could feel the exhilaration of her every living encounter. Smooth and then neatly stubbled and then smooth again, shaving exquisitely in antigravity outer space the best he can get, and she gleaned that he had just freshly wiffered the floor so shiny and smooth and the date would be at the beginning of febreezey. The wedding would be livedomed, of course. But before that, the talk shows with audience members screaming and swooning and even exploding with envy. His nails were neatly pared and his hands felt good under her blouse, squeezing her more than accentuated breasts. Breath on her neck. The snap of elastic. Fragrant. For him. For her. For everybody. Then huffing and puffing and sweating and throbbing. The cover was so glossy and slippery, but the magazine was nice and stiff and sooooo controversial. Yet it was hard for Candy to fathom exactly what happened next. She knew they were still in the early days. No breakups or settlements or public reparations yet. However, she could hear a metallic ringing, a series of beeps and bops which sounded like one of her favourite songs, but it was very faint. And although she had no recording device with her, she would have sworn that the chocolate tiles were zooming in, coming closer and closer. It was very light and very bright and a voice was telling her to relax just relax. And it was very difficult to resist. You only had to look at those letters.

A Century from Now

Fay heard the doorbell, followed by a boisterous knock. She shot up in bed, reknotted her robe and opened the front door to a little man with a powdered pate and a clipboard.

"Great, you're home. Just gotta fill in a few blanks on the census."

"But I filled that out last week."

"Yeah, but we have to confirm *that*, just with a few questions, 'kay."

"All right."

"Name?"

"Fay Whipple."

"Right. Age?"

"Next question ..."

"I'll just go with the birthdate here, 'kay. And sex?"

"_?"

"Well, you never can tell. I'll just put down a whopping *F*."

"Yes, please."

"You married, Mrs. Whipple?"

"Uhuh."

"Would your Other happen to be around this morning?"

"No, he's *working*."

"And on a scale of contentment from one to ten, how would you rate that relationship?"

"Huh?"

Fay scrutinized the little man's grey-green eyes, but they were empty wells only craving answers to silly questions. She suddenly felt a bit giddy.

"No comment, eh? I'll just put down a negative sixty-nine."

"I think I'd like you to ..."

"Leave, Mrs. Whipple? Just a couple more questions, and then I'll scoot."

"Hmmmm?"

"And no children, eh?"

"I have a stepson."

"And how long have you been training the lad to fulfill your extra-ordinary needs?"

"What the hell! How ...?"

"S'all right. Don't be alarmed. It's perfectly natural ... a standard question, really."

The little man had jammed his foot in the door and eased it open. Fay wanted to scream, but as her lungs filled nervously with air, she felt frozen by the grey-green light in those eyes. A clammy sensation she remembered.

"Just a quick inspection an' I'll be on my way."

Fay felt the silvery gleam of his will all over. Her knuckles tingled and her limbs felt full of wires. Her only thought was *it needs to pee*. She felt her hands unknotting the robe with detachment and watched it fall to the carpet for the second time that morning. She felt long, greasy fingers encircling her bare belly. The silver-green will was bending her body over. The experience was like watching one of her homemade holiday captures, only with a different rating. She was positively outside herself and unsure how to feel about this unexpected turn of events.

"Oooooooo ..."

She was lying on the carpet in front of his grubby trainers. She reached for his knees.

"Crash me with your toy stick! I'm your piñata full of sweet goodies! Do your worst!"

"Now, Mrs. Whipple, there's no need for that. Everything seems in order and I'll be on my way. If you could just sign here ..."

She managed the letters of *Fay Whipple* in green ink at the bottom of the clipboard.

"And one other question, standard."

"Uhmm?"

"Would you like to make this information available to citizens a century from now?"

"No."

"A century later!"

"No!"

"Funny how many people keep saying that ..."

Ling Ling

Logos RJ-45 lolled out a lone verbal of graveyard. No. There was other. R arose, now aroused but still minimum agrog.

"Ling ling!"
"Whazük?"
"*Ling Ling*!"
"Lang," he leisurely deviced.
"Salutations y mucho recriminations! Cumple on, Major R! This hour clicks your inception! Muchos felicitous returns!"

Vox was shadowed by blaring toccata.

"Zük," he boomboxed back, drumming it down. "I'm online nanos ago."

Then R muted. Lost in neurot, he projected *cleanse* n so it was. He even allocated another Marsec to reverb before he genied out, smooth n sleek to rovings. Not long after first click of graveyard. He clovedly ungnarled alpha limb n tactiled his. Skin. Uhgn. Tray Sesh. *Then Logos, n verbal was made life.* So his chip chirpily sloganed. So it was. R genied out of dome n counterclocked across circuits of jumpstarted nox. Apparitioned longer each diurnal, longer n longer. *Niet!* Redundancy RD-69ME droned on, recycling stray neurots. R muted this small muse n janned into levy. Woo woo woo woo!

"Salve ... Major R. Tangentially, mucho recriminations!"

Doubles parted as he entered Pent Cloud-99, physical.

"Salve, Major R!"

Vox. Ubikay? A minute figure aped out of Bureatia. Corridor, slash n burn Arcade. Spoor! That novel Friday.

"Salve ... my bad. Oblivioned your handle."
"O. Input Ackmod Delphi 7.0 Meridian Stellar Nova Twenty-Three. Locals interface me A. Premater dinged the crooner. Shuttled to Plutonimoanium Nine to spectate him special. Short consume. She was maximum dwarf in those petulant x/60s."

R attained *pause*. He sussed a high level of hubris in this upstart internal. Prognostication: long diurnal imminent.

"Sparkplog training sim n plice in novel sidesaddle."
"Affirm."

Molto Presto

Lax Laxness shaded his eyes from light stammering through the blind. His head felt rather percussive. So much for a lie in. His mind started to retrace yesterday, with his convenient gift for slow-resolution capture. Planted at Amaricano's, waiting for the first boyista to bring over his extra-special. Beside him, what looked like an actor was slapping a few pieces of paper and repeating whatever they read under his breath, while waving his tanned, beefy hands about. Then he stood up and bowed before Lax.

"'Scuse me, sir. I must take a most excellent crap at once. Could you keep an eye on my stuff?"

Lax shrugged noncommittally. A pair of platonic pals were both gesticulating in turn at one another as they bemoaned the state of their present relationships.

"Ninety-eight point six percent of the conversation is about him. I tried to change the subject this many times. This many! It's all about him ..."
"She just doesn't listen. Then when I wanna do something, like be a sofa spud and watch the game, she has to give me her life story and nag my ass and peck holes in ..."
"And he's not what I'm into!"
"That's funny. She's not what I'm into."

Lax had heard it a zillion times. Ten to one they ended up in the sack before their steaming coconut *molto prestos* had cooled. He turned away, very mildly disinterested, and noticed his piping *adagio* approaching.

"I mean, you're like my best friend!"
"But haven't you ever thought about it, y'know?"

Lax stared into the lactiferous design afloat on top of his coffee: a fluted pyramid with rippling ridges and grooves, moved by a mysterious wind. The actor emerged from the bathroom and stretched his arms skyward.

"Mmm ... that's better, boy does that feel great!"

The milky ridges ruffled into the shape of an arrow. Lax followed the caffein-ated vector to see a small figure with a grey-green gaze standing in the light of the entrance. And the smell sure checked out. Lax started to rise real casual. Just then, the beefy bathroom thespian, who was gathering up his paraphernalia, remem-bered his dicta of social codes and turned around to squeeze Lax on the arm.

"Hey buddy, thanks for keeping a lookout ..."
"Outta my way, buttwipe!"

But those grey-green eyes had already registered his stare of frustrated yet intent laxity. The small character hightailed it out the door. Lax left directly after him, his strides nearly brisk. And it didn't take long to trace him to a fenced dead end in the alley.

"What's yer business round here?"

"Back. Stay back, pal."

"Hand over that clipboard. I just wanna take a gander, that's all."

"O yeah?"

Lax pulled the clipboard away from him and scanned at least thirty names with his formidable gnostovision. Grey-green saw his chance and snatched the pen dangling from a string.

"Lemme show you …"

He tapped the cap twice, and after that, all Lax could remember was a spurting flash of green and a clammy grey sensation all over.

Traffic

Red.

"Buck a wipe. A loon a toon an' I'll shine you o'er the moon."

Raghead waded out into traffic among engines running. Two fingers made a sign, and he hurriedly soaped up the windshield and Squealgeed it clean. Dollar coins fumbled through window crack.

Yellow. Obscene sign. A third car two over behind the others, a grimy old clunker. He soaped up the view bran new and revealed a guy in shades. The passenger door popped open.

"Hey hoss, there's a whole whack a change an' loons under that clutter. Do me a favour and scoop up the whole damn mess of it."

Raghead glanced back at his cohorts, asleep upon church steps and patches of green.

"Don't tell me this is a freebie!"
"Ain't no such thing, friend."

Wonky toaster into tepid bathwater laughter. Acorn stink. Raghead crawled into shotgun position and dived into the rubbish, feeling around for the floored bowl of monies, plucking up a few with foreign markings. At that moment, his entire body went limp. An arm reached over him and slammed the door. Upon the grey steps, his friends dozed.

Green.

One Last Errand

"Hello? Zoincks! They must have hung up."

Candy Coton soothed her MissFunctional and slid it back into her fossa bag. How long had she been conducting this interview?

"... and that's where the fuzzy reasoning comes in," droned F. "What we use are known as Petri nets to catch the grammatical logic. It's all relational ..."

Candy shifted in her chair. Damp down here. How long have I been interviewing this guy? I must have dozed off. Great. Just great. And now a backache to boot. Nice one, Candice. Real nice.

"... we call those subverts because they interrupt the process. You know how it is when you are watching your favourite programs and they are peppered with advertisements ..."

"I hate that."

When would he get to the point already? She had groceries to buy.

"Indeed, Dr. F, but I am sure the question on everyone's mind is how these experiments are to benefit First Nations reservations."

"Ha ha ha. They say forgetfulness is a gradual decay in weight between neurons. Why, there's a formula ... Err, to get back to your question, our methodology is part of a comprehensive program to improve, um ... initiate a process of self-amelioration for our ancient friends. We have a well-measured and extremely well-controlled way to harness the wisdom of these gentle and beautiful people and to encourage their application for enpowerment, in other words to encourage their successful integration into the *civilization* you and I consider to be our own. Merely to get some citizens out of the Stone Age, you understand. A damned stubborn lot, when it comes down to it, but also so mystical and gentle and beautiful. We would like nothing better than to welcome our First Nations friends and family into a larger, more vast *global* family. The world *is* changing, and this process is a vital step toward their survival as a diverse nation."

Candy grinned her lopsided goodbye grin.

"Well, thank you, Dr. Juan de Fuca. It's been quite an education. I will have a lot to write about and already it's getting late. I must confess, I have to run and do some shopping on my way home."

"Of course you do."

Would Every Body Please Report

Kuh. Kuh. Spoor. R projected *univisor*. He scanned lumpish citizen in dim corner. She quirkly vipped her silver form to pallid neck, coveting accountable scars. Visor crimped shut. Hyperrealtime, R was bizt. Kuh! Kuh! Kuh!

"Ack contact?"

"Applenstance."

"Androbrid, we gotta be technocrossed. Syntoxic. Handle?"

"Affirm. Input Ruckus."

She uploaded happiness.

"Savoury, Ruckus. Clone name is Vulna. But handle me Whinny. Dayold affirmative."

"No," rebounded R. "Fresh piping. But inciter is down."

"Negative. Ideoed antigravitrain ere realtime. Permits abrogation if accompany? If perform compatibles. Mind?"

"Pleasure. Option me in."

With Little Reserve

Anaïs sashayed for a short block, slipping past a throng of steam clock–gawkers. Suetonius followed, averting his back-of-dust-jacket kisser from about twenty simultaneous snaps. The steam shot up out of a singing pipe and everyone gasped. But Suetonius preferred to keep his eye on the flutes of grey fabric. She saw his image reflected behind her in a window and quickly dipped into Totem.

"I was looking for the beach. Heeey! I sure like the look of them sweaters."

"I'll even throw in some moccasins with a twenty percent discount."

"Are all these shops run by white folk? I'm Ojibway and I was just on Ersatz Island and it was all white folk."

"Hang on a minute. Just let me wrap up this sweater for this dude."

"Thank you kindly. It's a beautiful sweater. So precious."

"I'm Ojibway, too."

"O ... hello."

"Yeah. I'm always saying, 'Dude, I'm Ojibway.' People don't get my mythology on the coast."

"What about her?"

"Have a nice visit. O no, miss. I'm just filling in."

Suetonius followed her CiveX scent past the sweaters and moccasins upstairs. He found her absorbed by a copy of his historical metafiction romance, *With Little Reserve*. She knew it by heart and flipped to the encounter in the middle between the beautiful, plucky Ebony Leung and the partially self-discovering Stolen Mink. *Heated hooligan grease ran down his broad torso. Then, lowering the white sponge ...* He was reading over her shoulder, smiling winsomely.

"And would you call this historical?"

"Maybe a prophecy, heyh?"

Quick, centred, interested and certainly not gushing! He reached for another book, adopting a tone of sage solemnity.

"This is one of my uncles. A great chief."

"O."

"And this is his father, one of the greatest of chiefs."

He displayed a painting of a heavily moustached man with intense, dark eyes, who looked fresh from the O.K. Corral.

"He would wake up at dawn first thing in winter and bathe in icy water and hunt bears with his bare hands and carry them home and ..."

Anaïs touched his arm. Borden, you are *so* mine.

Feet Up

Tooth was feeling rather addled. He stared down at the stained kerchief in his hands in semi-bewilderment. Nah. Stay chipper, ol' nipper. Gotta be nimble to stay ahead in this game. He knew the drill. You stop to think for too long, you make mistakes. Thinking was for chumps. The lad was now liquefact, in the past tense, plain and simple. He fumbled for his Prune Sentinel 3000 and checked for trollers. Maybe that last dealer was still looking for fresh meat. The pay had been pretty sweet for the census taker who had fallen into his lap and to tell the truth that was a guilty pleasure, thank you very much. With the dealer kicking off about his Dulkling mission. How I hate it when visitors get political. He kicked aside a heap of clothes, cherried by a dripping Squealgee head. Now, Toothy boy, don't forget to douse the lot tonight. But his head was throbbing and he could feel a searing pain to the roots of his gums. Ever since he fell asleep in the park and had … a vision? Whatever you wanna call it, it had crawled under his molars and spread its infectious pamphleture. And then advertising had seemed like a crapshoot. There was a whole pulsar of business *out there*, just waiting for an enterprising impresario of his abilities. He lay back on the bed in faded suit and shoes. Time for a recharge.

A Matter of Semantics

Candy found herself outside the Emerald City on 4th Avenue, anxious to shop yet poised outside the shuttering glass doors. A tremor of anticipation passed through her entire body. She hesitated, looking down at a bedraggled man sitting on a flattened cardboard box that was as wet as the sidewalk. Must have rained. The man craned his neck to peer into that verdant world of produce and promises of longevity as the doors were automatically cued open and closed by each pair of legs that briskly passed him. She looked down at the man's solid-bodied but slightly flea-bitten Lab, who stared up at her affectionately, with wet olives for eyes. Human interest story. Make a note for the last five minutes on my way out. Candy entered quickly, in perfect time with the chartreuse lips of those swooshing doors that closed behind her, shushing the incoherent murmurs of the man on the sidewalk, as well as the soft whimpers of his Lab.

She spared a single look back at the gleaming coins in his overturned cap before returning her attention to that collard-coloured world of organic experiences, as a rather elfin cashier with a tongue ring gave her a smile of greeting. Then without looking, she opened her fossa bag and searched through a heap of cosmetics for the tiny scroll of paper she had written ... Funny, I don't remember when I wrote the damn thing. O way to go, Candice. She unrolled the list in front of the glutinous non-gelatinous and extensively tested smiles of the green-uniformed family of baggers. A single sentence caught her endearing eyes that read *Fill in the gap*. She stared at the white space underneath the emerald lettering and felt belittled by a skill-testing question she could not solve without pen and paper.

Underneath that blank, she felt especially mesmerized by a block of slender black strips overlaid on a white background. The sensation reminded her of the drop-in meditation course she had taken last summer. Repeat your mantra and empty your mind and think of nothing: your mind is a blank, empty your mind, that's what the instructor had said. Candy reached for a very green basket. She flounced over to the heads of lettuce and other assorted greens, and suddenly felt her wrist getting soaked in the path of a timed spray. She selected some Swiss chard and a pretty bundle of iridescent kale before moving on absent-mindedly through each spurt of wet. Moving along, she stopped in front of the white chickens and asked a tall clerk about the *happy chickens*.

"They'll make you happy all right," he said with a mischievous wink.

She went through several aisles, picking out only the most essential six-packs of vitamins. Why, it must have been in *Gloss* she had read that psychology and chemical imbalances were moot if you only exercised properly and took many vitamins. Her favourite actor had stressed this was so in a beautifully constructed sentence and it probably was. She stopped in front of a woman with pink lipstick who was holding out a tiny purple spoon.

"Would you like to try a sample, ma'am? It's our organic, low-fat, nutty-crunch flavour of frozen yoghurt. It's quite good."

Candy reached for the spoon and their fingers brushed. She let the sample melt on her tongue as she watched the moving pink lips of the frozen yoghurt representative.

"Mmm ... good."

"I knew you'd like it. Now buy some."

The frozen yoghurt woman took the spoon back and licked it clean. Candy smiled in reply and responded by picking up two two-dozen cases and dropping them into her very green basket. O so very good. A few dried herbs and multicoloured powders later, she was dragging her healthload toward the cashiers when she remembered that she still needed milk. Fuck. She walked up to a large man in a very green apron and tapped him on his very broad bicep.

"Excuse me, I think you are out of milk. The kind I like, anyway."

He turned around, smiling grimly yet square-jawed in such a way that made his brown skin shine in the bright lighting. Candy heard a distant sound like a flute in the woods and felt a doe-eyed tremor as she stood in front of his dark eyes.

"What kind of milk?"

"Non-homogenized."

"O I see. You are in the market for some *non-homo* milk."

The letters on his apron seemed to melt into a greenish haze about her vision. A mystical wind arose from one of the aisles and blew his long, black hair about with a certain urgency.

"There might be some in the back."

His large hand closed about hers and in his eyes she could see a primordial land of bucolic mud rifts on a deliciously warm afternoon. She touched her finger to her lips, incidentally moist with anticipation for the magical journey that was most certainly about to begin. Indeed, she felt infinitely spiritual and at one with nature and all things green and massy as he seized her by the wrist and pulled her through a pair of doors with a great double flap. He produced a couple of Gormy's health drinks and tabbed them open.

"Drink this. My name's William Big Horse Longhouse. But everybody calls me Horse ... for short." "Candice Coton," she replied, between creamy sips. "Mmmmmm."

The more she swallowed, the more the store muzak seemed to speed up.

She stepped back and took in the grey sterility of the back room as Horse untied his green apron and revealed his eye-catching navy blue painter's pants ($29.95), now twenty-five percent off.

"Or do you want me with the apron on, eh?"

Candy could not believe she was quite herself, pouting and licking her lips at this stranger. The health drink had gone right to her head. She struggled to collect her thoughts and to recall an old interview she had done.

"Are you making a veiled allusion to *redress*?"

"Or maybe I am asking you to *undress*. A much faster process."

Candy fell to her knees on the cold grey floor as the muzak sped up faster and faster. She was waiting now, waiting for the überhealthy homeopathic deity to unbuckle his raven belt and to pull down his reduced navy blues and reveal his long and sturdy cedar beam. She glared up at the static eye of the security camera in a corner of the ceiling.

"Yeah ... do it, Horse. Give it to me, you big bad Indian!"

"Technically, I prefer the term *First Nations*."

Xstasia [Multinode Edition]

The railing was thick and strange underneath his fingertips. Everything cried out in a tongue of its own, cried out its name. *Wood*, the railing clanged. *Railing*, the wood creaked. All in their own way, each beneath his fingertips. It was pleasant to walk in this body upon a short pathway toward a tall gate. He stopped to examine the blades of grass that he passed, wondering at them as much as at the nameless weeds in the alleyway cracks. He felt his mind subside. Each translation was becoming clearer. Soon, I will be totally immersed. I must try to forget what each word means, or what it meant. His feet felt sore in his sneakers. Sore! Sore as they walked upon the concrete. Here, everything felt wonderfully incomprehensible.

There was a patch of rust along the grates of the gate. He touched it slowly, allowing it to colour and scratch his fingernails and the palm of his hand. He started, hearing a foreign noise. He turned around to watch a shiny vroom drive by, slowly manoeuvring over the uneven terrain of the alleyway. He was astonished by its clunky motion, wondering what kind it was. Clunky. An old clunker. He liked the sound of that. Then he heard another. He noticed that he was standing near a courtyard behind the gate and that a door had opened. A woman stepped out, pulling the door closed and turning her key in the lock. She walked a few paces toward the gate. Then she stopped, turned back and tested the doorknob. Yes. It was locked.

He smiled to himself. Yes, that was a nice touch all right. He eased back behind a wall covered with green overgrowth. She did not see him. He waited a moment before peering around the wall. She was heading in the direction of a nearby copse. She walked at a brisk pace through a pair of cedars. He started to walk behind her, keeping at a distance on the same trail. He was very conscious of the movements of her body, as well as his own. It was a summery day and his blood was on fire and his heart was pumping as he kept sight of her along the path of gravel and wooden shavings. Everything smelled wonderful and his body felt strong and whole.

Before long, she had arrived at her destination. She was wearing thin fabrics he had never seen before. At least not in his monitored life. He tried not to think of that. As she sat on a scorched log, he was distracted by the scattering of ants and then something else and then the mild ripples of water. Water. He licked his dry lips and watched those hypnotic undulations, illuminated by intense sunlight. Then he turned his eyes back to the woman, who was standing up in the light that brightened her dark hair. Without hesitation, she removed her top and then her shorts. He saw the way they softly crumpled upon a dry stump in the sunlight. He also saw the full shape of her naked body, slowly wading into the water, splashing her reflection about until the water rose to her throat. She turned around in the water and looked right at him, knowing all.

"Hello. What's your name?"

"You know my name."

"Yes, but don't be a spoilspurt. Any name will do."

"How about Roget?"

They studied one another hungrily.

"I'm Whinny. I'm rather old-fashioned, you'll find. I love the woods and water. I love briars and unicorns. I feel so alive here, so near to nature. Why don't you try it? Come into the water. I know you want to. Why don't you come into the water?"

Roget watched her watching him. He could feel everything in this magnificent body. Everything was beckoning. But he reached for his temples first, wondering what the surveillance chip on his shoulder would think. Whinny made a face.

"Don't worry about *that*. It won't hurt anything. It feels so good. Come into the water, Roget. Come into the water with me."

In response, Roget meekly stripped and began to wade into the water. She watched him, keeping silent. Her hazel eyes seemed to glint green in the sunlight. The water was cool to his warm skin. He took time to enjoy this sensation before swimming out toward her. As soon as he reached her, their hands became busy, searching and exploring one another, fondling elbows and squeezing shoulder blades and caressing buttocks in a writhing mass of robust limbs. Their lips touched and they meticulously tasted each other. This moment was almost too much for Roget and he suddenly felt the need to option out. Whinny sensed this and held his body fast, kissing him harder. Then he felt his limbs relax and desire supplanting his panic.

Just Like in That Flick

"Name onna grain a rice?"

The ricemonger winked up at tall Suetonius.

"I'll put your name on a grain!"
"Sorry, miss, it wouldn't fit."

A haggard man with a beer-battered tan straightened the collar flaps of his faded denim ensemble.

"Hey, could you help me get back to Balzac?"
"Huh?"
"Balzac, Alberta, that's where I hails from ..."
"Only five bucks, your name onna grain!"
"Spare some small change, like a few hundred? Pretty funny, hmm?"

Anaïs withered him with a look.

"Guess not."
"How 'bout it, lady? We stick it onna grain!"

They passed the emerald statue of Swilly, the original city benefactor, and stepped absent-mindedly over a woman lying prone on the pavement, who suddenly sprang to half-life.

"Buy me a coffee? Buy me an Offalwich?"

Anaïs paused to light another Slimfaster, and then thinking better of it, lit a Dromedary. Then she dug a heel into the woman's fleshy back and put out her smoke in the fuzzy nape of her neck.

"There's your Offalwich."

Suetonius stifled a bearish laugh. Just like in the classic revenge drama *Eyes Wired Shut III: This Time for Realz*. He gave her arm an impulsive squeeze.

"For a second, you looked just like Bébé Lala in that famous scene ..."
"Really? She's my favourite star! Of course, a terrible shame about her smack baby from Juárez."
"Yes, terrible."
"Hey! Care to pop up for a Gormy's ... or something ...?"
"O yeah, sure. Just need to make a quick stop first!"
"Um ... yeah, okay. I'm number 2046 ..."

Ploop

Oober Mann let his new little friend sniff the green neck of the street lamp before moving on toward a choice shrub. He felt for the Poochie in his pocket, musing how similar the nostralgia of a dog is to human memory and even the process of writing. We sniff out what we seek and want, gathering up what we perceive to be the entire world with our senses and then *ploop ploop – voilà*! – a few constipated words. He flipped the inside-out Poochie outside in, bowing before his adorable friend with red fur. Well done, Faustus.

You Are What You Do

The most beautiful chords Tooth had ever heard. He squinted through the gloom. Diverse tongues, flapping through pea soup. He stepped forward to see the gilded curves of a giant harp. At first, he thought it was playing itself, but then he saw a naked man caught between the strings. At closer inspection, he saw the man was crucified, with each of the strings woven through his flesh. A long, snaky lizard, in fact more tail than lizard, bit into his skin rapidly at different sections, generating a different chord each time. The accompaniment was a mandolin binding the wrists of another hostage. A dark, tortoise-like thing flapped his slimy wings and nibbled at his middle, providing a soothing background strum. Between the pair of them stood another creature, a salamander that was using his long flick of a tongue to turn the pages of music upon a third victim's buttocks, each of them a sliced strip of flesh. Tooth watched in admiration as the salamander began to sing a stunning madrigal with wide-eyed conviction. A naked woman walked closer, attracted by each sustained note, although she was preoccupied with trying to balance a gaming die upon her head.

"Hey baby, how 'bout a gamble on me?"

She bared her fangs and hissed. Another man skulked after her, covering his face with his hands and peeping through his fingers. Behind them, a decorated scholar with tilting cap was crawling on all fours, whipped forward by a proud woman who seemed to be working his swollen anus with his diploma as a kind of rudder. The fog shifted, hiding and revealing innumerable nudes, huddled together and petrified. Some were waiting in line to be sodomized by an exquisite brass section. One man sat on a withered leaf, cupping his chin with a disconsolate look. After watching for a few minutes, Tooth realized that a rusty monster with huge mandibles was creeping up behind the man. The moment the man turned his head, the creature pounced. As the victim's flesh tore open, a group of flying maggots emerged from his bowels and took flight.

Tooth also realized at length that a giant mantis was not sitting on a throne but on a fanciful toilet through which it let loose a translucent sac containing undigested body parts. These wriggling excretions, limbs and torsos alike, dropped into a murky pit, over which other figures were being encouraged by a variety of scaled creatures to ingest reptile purgatives and void their bodies. They crawled and crouched, vomiting flame and evacuating molten discs. Tooth was unmoved. He had already seen most of these scenes in the downtown core. Sad, but what can you do? He was helping to crank a literal organ grinder humped by a ferocious monkey when the nightmare began. It was Effie. She sidled up to him, letting him feel she was by no means amorphous underneath her effervescent bubbles.

"Hey lover."

"You can't, I killed the campaign ... you're dead!"

"I fizzed for a while, but now I'm back with a vengeance."

Tooth could see a familiar figure through the gloom, a purple man surrounded by grapes.

"Okay, I lifted the design. You were based on an underwear campaign. So what?"

"That might explain my provocative ... and ahem ... bubbly ... nature."

She grinned, rubbing him gingerly and blowing a dozen bubbles into his ear. Tooth screamed.

[Resume Training Simulacra]

They were sitting in her living room. Whinny had invited him in to take a quick shower. Roget looked up at a large frame on the mantel. She stared at the wall, looking through the picture.

"He doesn't get me. I'm always getting left on my own. I get lonely sometimes."
"Hmm."

She walked into the bedroom. Roget followed.

"We better be quick. Sometimes he comes home early."

Roget felt hot all over. He felt his blood burning with jealousy and maybe rage. But it felt good to hate. To hate a faraway stranger, no less. It felt good to feel this fury that was anything but emptiness. He opened his robe and looked down at his virtual erection, surprised by this manifest sensation. Roget always felt surprised. It was strange to have a body like this. Whinny smiled and offered a series of expletives that made Roget laugh. However, they also made him hot and confused and angry and hard.

"It's been so long. Give it to me, Roget. Right now! Or how about this? Is this what you like? I would *never* do this for him. Never never."

Roget moaned, stroking her dark hair with both of his hands. He could feel the flesh of her shoulders and breasts being pinched beneath his fingertips. So tactile. He was surrendering to each of these sensations, particularly the thrill of overheating within her warm aural system. He stopped for a moment as she climbed back onto the bed, his senses reeling. What had led to this biological turn of luck? He glitched the lumpish shape, waiting outside in a dim corner of Xstasia. He reached down, fingering his organ tentatively, questioning its seemingly independent pleasure. Why did she want to go vintage like this?

"Hurry up. Samiel will be back and he won't like it."

Closing her eyes at the thought of that, she placed her palm between her raised thighs.

"Want me to tell him you couldn't? Is that it? Wanna watch instead?"

Roget lost his temper and lunged at her. However, instead of landing upon her body or the bedspread, he hovered several inches over her.

"O yeah. A floater, hey? Samiel hasn't been able to float for months."

She reached up and gripped him with her right fist, dragging him to and fro until he began to feel like one of the parade inflatables he had scanned in past archives. Satisfied with the small puddle on the ceiling, she pulled him off the minimalist headboard and drew him closer. He felt her heat against his. In the archives, this action of bodies and moving buttocks always looked rather ludicrous. Yet in Xstasia training sims, you quickly became lost in some similar activity. A sullen look had crept over Whinny's sweating face.

"Zük me, Roget! AX / BX me, you züking trog!"

Roget obliged. Classic. They were interfacing at accelerated pace when Roget recognized the clunky sound of the vroom parking outside. A door opened and then slammed shut. Roget instantly started to float off, but Whinny's fingernails dug into his shoulders.

"No no go. Not yet ..."

They both turned to see a bulking figure in the door frame and they were surrounded by dark diminished seventh chords.

"Samiel! Samiel!"

The Censors' Consensus

Grant Smith clicked *mute*, allowing the grainy onscreen activity to continue for a full minute in the entire field of his dry vision. Then, he reached for a small green bottle and applied the dropper to both of his eyes. He blinked at the ceiling for a few seconds while his colleagues continued to stare glassily at the mutual gallop of Candy and Horse.

"Well, gang, what's the verdict?"

Janet Buckshaw folded her sweatered arms, shivering slightly.

"I need a cigarette."

Dennis Dennis lifted his hands out from under the table and clasped them on top nervously.

"Uhh ... there's uhm ... no obvious sign of physical abuse. She's not missing, is she?"

Sally Ann Hunter turned to him and nodded slowly, dabbing her eyes with a pink tissue.

"It's really a beautiful story in some ways. The cross-cultural narrative involving Miss Coton and Mr. Longhouse is rather touching and, I dare say, even a touch racy."

"Uhuh. Hmm. Yes, I must say that I agree with your sentiments, Sally Ann."

Sally Ann beamed. Dennis looked restless but not pensive. Grant blinked and rubbed his lips. The elfin cashier with the emerald tongue ring was peeping through the double doors of the back room, open-mouthed and with astonished eyes. The happy chicken salesman was standing behind her and smiling broadly with an excited rooster in his arms.

"Also, I like the Canadian content in this one. Of course, I would have preferred Ontario."

"It's better than the one in Montreal, what was it called?"

"*Smoked Meat XL*," answered Sally Ann with a faraway sigh.

"So, do you guys think we are ready to give this one a rating?"

"Soon as I have my smoke."

Grant tapped *mute* rapidly, releasing a series of moans and screams and repetitive cries of *White Buffalo* and *Studhorseman*.

"Cockadoodledoooooohh."

Back to School Special

Suetonius threw open the door of Fleet Drugs with an impressive jingle, feeling fourteen again.

"Protection, I need protection!"

The counter keeper eyed him up and down cautiously.

"For carving store? That'll be Lee. Come back in few days."
"I mean rubbers, lady."
"Erasers, back to school, aisle three."
"Maybe I should draw you a picture."

He put on a series of charades with both his hands that clarified the subject of his quest. She started to laugh, then poker-faced again, reached under the counter.

"All we got left is lamb."
"Lamb?"
"Nice designer. Here's a sample. Feel."

Suetonius ran his fingers over the peltish object with bemusement.

"Don't you wanna try the lamb?"
"Do you have it in jumbo?"

She produced a rainbow box that read:

JUMBO LAMB COMBO

"Lucky day."

Out front, Suetonius opened the assorted box and pulled out the pelt and a couple of GloWorms, just in case, and stuffed them in his pockets. A shirtless Native man on the pavement smiled up at him toothlessly.

"Spare change, bro?"

Suetonius grinned and dropped the box at the man's feet.

"There you go. Lucky day."
"Holeeee! I better get started, hey?"

That Bucket of Tripe

Oober tied the shiny leash to the patio fencing and entered Superbrew. As he waited in line behind explosions of Frenchified Spanglish, he considered how well things were going. He had found a sympathetic publisher through a university acquaintance and just the other night, he had managed to excrete a few pages. Only nine hundred more to go and he would join the list of overachievers, those like Joyce, Musil, Proust, Powell, Pynchon and other folk with *P*-names who wrote things too long and confusing for anyone to finish. Also, he was particularly proud of the phrasal fragment *impish and anomalous*. And such was the price he paid, being a genius. Let them string up his futile flesh like the guts of Marsyas and pluck their own tune if they liked, bleeding out every word into that foul, loathsome bucket of tripe otherwise known as Truth ...

"Can I help?"
"Small coffee, mild."

He glanced outside at Faustus through the front window. He was rolling over on his back and presenting his belly for rubbing to enraptured passersby. And you, little friend, are my good-luck charm!

Not on My Watch

"I'm late."

The two words hung mid-air before seeping into Jim's frontal lobe. He dropped his AggroX jerkstick control on the carpet and [paused] the approaching alien menace.

"Whafuh! For real???"

Fay had been waiting for the look-at-us-now bank commercial investment music to kick in. That look of inexpressible joy when you tell someone the happy news.

"I feel all weird ..."
"Who the hell's is it?"
"It's yours, Jim."
"No way in hell!"
"Aren't you happy?"
"It's impossible. You must think I'm so stupid, Fay."
"No ... you are the only one ..."

Jim returned to alien slaughter. The doorbell rang. Fay trudged downstairs to answer it, rubbing tears from her puffy eyes.

"Mrs. Fay Whipple?"
"Yes."
"I'm Lax Laxness with C-WUT. We have reason to believe you were visited by a potential terrorizer. Did any government representative stop by, a census taker maybe ...?"
"Unhuh."
"Could you tell me exactly what happened?"
"Nothing much. He asked me a few questions. Name, gender ... marital status. Stuff like that."
"And did he leave anything with you?"
"Not that I remember. He seemed very nice."
"Okay. Here's my C-WUT card. Let me know if anything out of the ordinary happens."
"I'm not sure I understand."
"Let's pray you never have to."

May I Cut In?

"A, crater off."

"Most graciously, I could use the experience ..."

"You are my lieutenant. Act like it."

"But what if something goes wrong? The safest bet is to train ..."

"Vam. That's a directive."

"Forgive me if I'm oversyntaxed, but do not the directives clearly state that in the case of a Level Brown complaint with subsequent quester, all members, even including probates, must participate in training mods? Clarny me flaw ..."

Whinny grinned and licked the corner of her mouth.

"Looks like he has you over a cronister."

"O copy, because I'm from a Ramadan moon, you node me in as xStatic object."

"Zük me, A! N input my throg ..."

Roget unlogged in mega disgust.

Back on the Block

Oober coddled his mild blend and reached for his notepad and pen. Many days, he tried to begin, to conjure up that spark of imagination so essential to his craft. It had only just occurred to him there were no narratives other than tricks of speech that prolonged the terse shorthand of existence. Oober sits. Oober sips. Oober scrawls? The rest was celestial filler. He watched another audition get in line with the other aspiring models from the agency up the street. This one was slightly different. She stood on tiptoe to see over taller pairs of shiny shoulders. But what is she to do with me? She would only use my *chef-d'oeuvre* as a coffee table coaster and run off with my best friend, were I to obtain one. And she was scarcely different than one of her counterparts more than a century ago, whether bar- or milkmaid, fashioned into a breath of immortal masterpiece by the fickle ink of genius. And inevitably, he saw each of the Amazonian women return to a young Heracles of similar proportions. And the giantessedly challenged young woman shot him a generous glance. And more than anything, Oober wanted to abandon his plan for the afternoon and chase those lively eyes. Instead, he watched her scratch Faustus behind the ears. He thought woefully of his meagre scraps, hardly connected into the novella he was always raving about. Just fragments, something about aliens and agents and interplanetary distress. The *usual*. He sighed and put away his things. Outside, the medium-sized model was cover-shot cradling her bosom and giggling at nothing.

"Is this your dog?"
"Yes. Excuse me, but we have to get going."

With the Flow

Lax Laxness slunk into Rose Hips, slowly taking in the mellow infusion site. The barista boy, formerly number two, folded his arms playfully, happy to be completely in charge of his own turf.

"You. I knew you'd show. What'll it be?"

"I heard about a sublime huckleberry mélange."

"You got it."

The burly boy rolled up his sleeves and set about the infusion. A gaggle of guys pouted at Lax, obviously a stranger to their parts, and one of them catcalled over.

"Did he say *ménage*? 'Scuse me, did you say *ménage*?"

"It's a huckleberry *mélange*."

"Then just call me Tom Sawyer."

"I'll be Becky!"

"O you're such a slut!"

"I know!"

The barista boy placed his tea on the counter and tightened his kimono.

"Don't mind them. They love to hassle fresh meat."

"What about you? What's your story when you're not a teahead?"

"My entire saga? Nah ... looking for a place to crash, at present."

Lax blinked lethargy at him, but stopped short at the man-boy's intensity. The barista boy handed him a rolled-up newspaper.

"But let me know if you see anything that *catches your eye*."

Lax sat down and unfolded the paper. It was a copy of the local *Scrounger*. He flipped past opinion columns and letters to the editor and hot-spot hangout reviews. Then something did catch his eye. In the From My Pad section, which described local living spaces, there was a photograph of the two owners of The Counter-Stall second-hand bookstore. They had used this column to advertise their new partnership and new *partnership* in the same place. The article about their rare media collection and takeout dining habits was of little interest to Lax, sleepy as he was already. However, his photostatic memory had found a match with a more recent article about a terrible tragedy that had befallen them, one involving a mobile zoo for the disabled. Lax folded up the paper and returned to the counter.

"You really need a place to stay?"

The barista boy sighed and rolled his eyes. Not again. He looked at Lax, resigned.

"Well, how do you like your eggs?"
"Broken."

The table of flirty teaheads burst into applause. Romantic comedy credits began to roll ...

Stow It

As for Ackmod Delphi 7.0 Meridian Stellar Nova Twenty-Three, otherwise known as Maestro A of the Ja Ja Clusterhood, the source of his confidence n general sense of well-being originated from the portaging pad of the interstellar call centre. He had grown up with the rustic bitgrits, n for such a primitive species, he was bilk to uncode how the etchings of a single individual upon the surface of Terra Dulkis, now presumably no more than ash, could allergenize his earifices. Ultimo was the compositor Johann Sebastian Bach n mucho proximate to Logos in his aural frust. He had blackpodded maximum etches from unthreaded agents n transients. He was materialiding a cubbeon on Xandria zinched with >>*cantatas*<< n >>*oratorios*<< solo. N polyphon was dust for greaming his blitsuit. Interruptus! Zük!

"A, we are nearing galactic customs. Ditch the Ramoon dialect. We need a gaping show of Terran speak, just two Dulklings following the orders of Oztrich."

Activating freestyle lingual slide ...

"But this is the best part of the second partita ..."
"That's an order, lieutenant. And where's Vulna?"
"Sunk in thought. She thought it best to pose as a brainwave."
"Whaa ... how? I thought only psychpaths could ..."
"Always the last to know."
"A psychpath could traumatize the entire mission!"
"Don't you think she's cute?"
"Stow it."
"Aww, and I have a real thing for those Horsehead clucks."

Fresh Bannock

Anaïs stood in the window with the relit Dromedary, jealous of the street-theatre exchanges below. Raucous calls for smashed bottles and a mannish *fille de joie* on the corner, pitching her unique wares and waving up at her challengingly. Then she saw Suetonius. The buzzer buzzed. She clapped her hands together.

"Fern, time to finish up!"
"But missus, I just made fresh bannock."
"Yes, thank you. Leave it and go."

She wrote out a cheque hurriedly and handed it over.

"O thank you, missus. How generous. Now my sister can go get her teeth fixed."
"Whatever. Time to go, Fern."
"My people have a saying ..."

As she passed Suetonius in the corridor, she stopped to look back in a tremulous flicker of recognition. Suetonius kept moving. Almost there. He rapped on the door marked *2046* and was pulled inside by his fringe jacket, just before the entire hallway flooded with a giant *gush-gush* sound.

Know Your Own Limitations

Lax paged leisurely through copies of *Scrounger*. But what was he scoping for? Barista boy number two, otherwise known as Bongolino, stirred in bed and winced with visible irritation.

"Would you close those blinds and knock off the noise? I need more than eight hours' beauty sleep."

"It's eleven."

"Wow. I must be really worn out from last night. How about an encore?"

Lax instead flipped to From My Pad and whistled a great gust of morning breath.

"You know, I was reading this article the other day about this professor who thinks our brains make up this mathematical equation of reality and we like hear all these groovy frequencies from another dimension and translate them into our own language. So time and space are like ... only ideas of our own limitations. So the universe is this huge hologram and it only takes one of its parts, maybe one of us, to hit *flush* ..."

"Hey Bongo, I'm not in the mood for the latest personality test you took. This dreary little puff piece is vital to the case at hand."

"Sorry, Lax. What are you looking at there?"

"One of the parts, Bongo. One of the parts."

Bongo stared at the photograph over Lax's shoulder, scratching his scrotum thoughtfully.

SIZE:	1001 Sq. Feet
LOCATION:	Pt. Grey
OCCUPANTS:	The Whipples, Fay and Dwayne, and their myna bird, Tattler.

"O my gawd. That wallpaper is awful. So ... are we going out or what?"

Something You Should Know

"Like some wine?"

"Sorry, I don't. Anymore. Bad, y'know, for the blood of my people."

"O. There's a can of Gormy's left, or a thing of yoghurt ..."

"Thank you, no."

"Well then ..."

Suetonius reached for her half-finished Dromedary and put it out in a Mayan ashtray, or what he suspected was an ashtray. Then he pulled her closer.

"Mmm ... Suetonius. No, wait! I must tell you. O what a crisis!"

"What?"

"I am not as unattached as you might have been led to believe. How wretched you must think me!"

She began to cycle through the worst particulars of her loveless marriage that had been the union of two great franchises. It was a conglom and nothing more. She was a Sweteluft of the global warming–liquid Swetelufts. And her avuncular rearers had seen in her the perfect scion to attach to the bland young heir of the always-liquid Lubevick enterprises.

"So you see, I am doused thus far in lubricant fortunes ..."

"But you provide the warmth. That should count for something."

"It was, after all, a better match than with the StaySolid Man ..."

"What you must have gone through!"

"Go, sir. Since you doubtless find me horrid."

"But Mrs. Sweteluft-Lubevick, who could witness such a heart-rending performance with dry eyes? Never have I seen a scene more like that of Bébé Lala in *Prude and Prudence*, when she opens her deepest insides to Mr. Litmus."

"And I, too, am torn by this passion for a cuter than cute post-colonial scribe ..."

Upon hearing this undeniable declaration, Suetonius set about clearing the entire kitchen counter, sending everything crashing to linoleum, including the tray of fresh bannock with a clamour and then just a din. He swept her up and threw her down on the counter and reached for her sizzling joy zones in the surprisingly comfortable depths of the kitchen sink.

Cello Sonata No. 2 in F

The larger-boned of the Sensational Sia Sisters straightened her ursine frame and clung to her cello with a look of desperation. After all of padre's plans. The smaller of the musical duo began ... *Duum duum duum* ... Alessandra accompanied her plunking with the lightest of cello pizzicato. Footsteps. You can't do this to me, the cello began to implore the piano, whose steady resistance was more than apparent. This was the last performance the pair of classical students would ever give. If Piccina Sia got her way. And she always did. And what was it this time? She had given up everything for English. She had taken to lying around for hours with Sir Walter Scott, and had fallen for a mere boy, a poet no less, who wrote horrible, horrible sonnets. And Alessandra had begged to borrow little Madamina's hands for this piece by Brahms.

"Brahms? O yes, of course. How like you."
"That's the poet talking, not you!"
"Want my help or not?"
"Padre is not going to like it."

Alessandra plucked the cello strings with increasing ferocity. In fact, more than required. Her instructor in the audience nodded proudly. What a daring decision! But her drawing of the bow was also responsible for an infinite amount of tenderness. No. Do not run away. Wait. Let us have one more sonata together. Or a medley. *Götterdämmerung*, if you must. Just don't leave me on my own. Maybe she should have kept quiet. But padre had to know. To elope without his blessing would be terribly unlucky. Yet in the reprise of the first strain, she heard Johannes and Clara, alone together one afternoon ... And she was moved. O Piccina! Run! Run off with your Pazzo while you can!

The audience members were nudged into applause as the two sisters were ushered off the circular stage. Frausinger Hermione Zcyak strode out past them, beaming.

"Aren't they lovely? And now, our next duet is from *Don Giovanni*, the veritable masterpiece of Wolfgang Amadeus Mozart. This is what the composer himself called a *dramma giocoso*. Less of *Ein Musikalischer Spaß* and more of what our own emeritus professor of English would call *jokeoserioso* ... The title character, an infamous seducer, has just crashed a wedding and has gotten rid of the groom. And now he is alone with the flustered bride-to-be and asking her to run away with him. And as you can imagine, when faced with such an ignoble proposition, she needs at least five seconds to decide ..."

The Sia Sisters waited politely in the narrow corridor, wanting to wish the tenor and soprano luck with their piece. At last they appeared, looking rather dishevelled and flushed from a dressing-room game of *Dov'è la salsiccia*.

"So he takes the startled young woman in his arms and invites her to go far, far away with him, singing, *Let us go, let us go, my dear beloved, and restore the pains of an innocent love ...*"

A smell of beer nuts permeated the dim corridor where the Sia Sisters loitered and listened. Some dude approached them with trepidation, bearing wilting grey flowers and a piping bowl of figments.

"*... vorrei e non vorrEEEi ...*"

The grinning aficionado positively oozed appreciation for their treatment of Brahms. His liquidy voice wavered with emotion. They worried he was about to gush ...

"*Andiam', andiam', mio bene / a ristorar le pene / d'un innocente amor ...*"

Screams from backstage. Reactive screams from the audience. The smell of pecan. Everything gone grey-green. And the sound of laughter, like the murk of bathwater with a high-definition device tossed in for nothing, not a pretty penny, not a single cent extra ...

One Small Step

"So, how do we proceed?"

"Hold your Horseheads!"

"You don't smoonch her one zyte."

"She's a psychpath. She could jeopardize the entire leopard. Once, on an economy class decrabbing station ..."

"Once?"

"Never mind. Just watch your back."

"I prefer to keep an eye on her backside, thank you very much."

Vulna materialized in the cockszit and tossed a sopping towel on the nearest console. She had already mimeogaffed into Dulkling form and to please the focus group had tried out a shower scene sim. She smiled and toyed with the intangible grey flaccidity of Major Ruckus.

"Why, I'm sensing oozles of tension ..."

"O stow it. Save it for the dupeling Dulklings."

Ackmod, always interested in the arcane and primitive practices of Terra Dulkis, scanned her dripping form up and down.

"Is that what you're wearing?"

"Yeah, man. I saw it in the latest insert of *Öpik–Oort*. Some feminista the Dulklings call Starlet. I like that ... *Starlet*."

"Way to blender in."

"So, regarding our mission, who does who?"

Major Ruckus floated over them, curling up into a grey-green kidney beanbag, or so he had glossed on the way. Then he projectiled into a series of glowing plots and injected their waiting medullas.

"We are concerned with the ident swipe of Commendatore Oztrich of course, although one may conjecture that he got his temples stashed and his pot broken in Venusburb and woke up the next sun with his Plutonian equipment missing. But that's besides the point. Something *unheimlich* is going down. There's an ID swiper, a nasty piece of roid moving personae right and left. Not only that, but he got all the tranquillation gear from Oztrich. And this time round, there's not going to be any double-dealing. Since we're here, we may as well dissolve his contacts and drain his alkalines."

"Not the finest specimen I ever petried ..."

"Affirmative. He used to be in *advertising*."

"And one of his main contacts is this mug."

"From Beta Kroma if you ask me."

"Uhm hm."

"But I am also sensing deep-seeded, damp-blanket insecurity levels from your inner cavities. Major? Am I right in assuming this is a lactose-thinner operation and the hyperport dealers are already out of control?"

"Lemelon with a twist!"

"Better minocular the situation first. It may just call for jellyfission."

"O yes. That technique failed wonderfully on my planetoid. When will you thrusterheads ever learn?"

"Well at least I'm not a binomial psychpath!"

"Hey! Leave me outta this."

"He doesn't approve of Horseheads."

"Just attenuate, you two. There's another kludge to plunge. There's a sniffer on the waft. He is, albeit very slowly, putting pieces together. We sent a double-dealing emissary to Dulkis from Minutia. He possesses a remarkable appearance, just like that of Dulkling canines. His job is to position our cell for activation, followed by further instructions ..."

The holographic transjerk bloomed into query mode.

Are you sure you want to activate cell
[#ZX7439 – Oober Homunculus Mann]?

"Affirmative."

"And now, psychpath, it is your task to initiate the cell and facilitate his progress in accord with our plot."

"But, Major Ruckus, I am sensing a complete lack of plot ..."

"Just utilize your Venusian charm."

"I'm from a completely different nebula, remember. And by the way, we don't tolerate Venusians."

"Once a psychpath, always a psychpath."

"And since you blew up their filthy grotto of a resort moon, I have been anxious to join you on even the most routine dispatch."

Major Ruckus raddished.

"Er ... yes. The moon was something of a miscalculation. We leapt to conclusions. The report was 97.38% certain about laser-butt pirates. But afterward, we never found any evidence ... just some bootuppers shifting a few arrays of perception. Petty stuff, really."

But Ackmod reeled on him, wagging a sanctimonious indexer.

"And how many had to die for your little zükup!?! Countless antigrav orgyjoyers, unsuspecting they were about to become a smithereened pointillist work. So they charged up a thrillion credits on their Venusian swipes. What gives you the authority to judge them?"

Vulna shrugged her celebrated shoulders.

"But how do we know they weren't laser-butt pirates? Sure wouldn't blow me away!"

"O the venality!"

"Yes ... well. What is past is past. But what you have to do is give the cell an extremely toxic -*ism*, a parasip to be precise. This will give Oober Mann an absurd yet welcome delusion. Be terribly careful though. The multi-level structure is highly addictive ..."

"Yeah, but what is the nature of the delusion?"

"He will begin to believe he is writing the quinversally acclaimed novella known in Dulkling as *Major Ruckus* ..."

Role Play and Reparation

"Ooooo!"

"Uckuhckuhck!"

Dwayne lowered his paper, peering over the grey crinkles at Fay.

"What's all that racket?"

"You don't remember? You *used* to know."

"I mean I thought he and Olga were quits."

"I guess they hooked up again. You know what young guys are like."

"No. I don't remember, remember!"

Fay looked away from him and into the watermelon gum wallpaper. They had never been able to have one of their own. But now she knew whose fault that was. Not that it mattered, not anymore. She was depressed. She needed some air. Then the ruckus stopped. And Olga did not appear. A leggy woman with red hair strode downstairs, hurriedly adjusting her skirt and fastening the clasp on her purse. Dwayne sipped his can of Sticky Leaf Lager and leered at her, miming a whistle. Then he stood up and extended a hand.

"I'm the pop. Nice to meet ya."

The woman nodded without stopping and made her exit.

"Now you can reel your eyes back into your head."

"The little prick didn't even introduce us! That does it!"

Dwayne unbuckled his belt and began to march upstairs.

"*No*, that stings! Aaaawh!"

"Smartass. Show me that smart ass, smartass!"

"Uh uh. Ooooo!"

"Uckuhckuhck!"

Fay put in her earplugs and began to flip through her husband's abandoned paper.

Scarlet Fever

ENCOUNTER THE EXOTIC LADY OF MYSTERY

Massage ☆ Punishment ☆ Role-Playing

Expiation ☆ "Vacuuming"☆ Media Repair

Saucy Toys ☆ Good Old-Fashioned ****ing

She flipped back a few pages, in irritation. A fat tear hit the page.

Not feeling so hot? Worried? Anxious? Did he make a deposit and then a complete withdrawal? Are you eating for two when you just want to dine alone? Don't become a victim of goofball circumstance. Drop by to discuss your alternatives. Or call us in confidence:

1-555-DED-BEAT

Santana Is Such a You-Know-What

Oober Mann looked up at the taffy-coloured building with its candied fire escape. Faustus also looked up, happy as thick-coated dogs are with the onset of fall, when a light breeze blows about their tawny fur. On such mornings, Oober wished he knew how to paint. But his genius was lost on his poor eyesight and feeble sense of colour. He could barely handle the bleeding of ink into virgin page.

"And then she harsh yells at me ..."

"Whenever one of us isn't there!"

"Santana? Like yeah!"

Office girls. Hot water cooler talk. Somewhere. He stared at the imaginary perspective lines forming but squinted instead. Just wobbly specks. Then he was distracted by the single-file invasion of nine Amazonian women. And out of the frame he imagined around the morning scene, a very real speck formed the medium-sized model who had spoken to him last time. And his dog. She pet Faustus and whispered affectionate gobbledygook under the flap of his ear.

"Goot morning!"

"O hi. I didn't know I'd see you again."

"I take a hint?"

"No. Or yes. I mean it's good, yes, a very *good* morning now."

"Hey know what? I will take coffee and be outside. Stay."

Oober obeyed. She left him with a thick issue of *Risqué*. On the bottom right-hand corner of the cover, there was a picture of her squeezing a spurting tube of mustard with an astonished expression on her face under the yellow rubric **DIJON DIVA LETS LOOSE**. So this was the much-desired Vanessa Velveteen, in the flesh. A man with a pointed beard eyed the blinding, half-naked fold-out and kicked his iron table in a display of unfathomable disgust and then sat back, serenely clasping his hands together on his lap.

"They're not real, you know."

"_?"

"Not any of them. And brother, I should know!"

"Who the hell ..."

"Sorry, nasty habit of mine. Name's Dr. Beniamino Freund. Top of my field! Slice and dice! And we're breaking new dermis every day. Soon as every pimple develops a conscience, we won't need the burden of our own! Amazing thing, surface evolution!"

"Oober Mann."

"The writer? Why, I just read a little scrap of yours in the latest issue of *Poof*. Wild discharges! Extensive probes! A toaster in bathtub of a good time!"

"Umm yeah, Dr. Freu—"

"Just call me F. Everybody does!"

"It's a piece from my novella ... in progress."

"O yes, I'm sure. Y'know, I saw you checking out their goods. Over there. With a twinkle in your eye. But none of them are real. Not a one! Saline solution. They just ..."

F made a horizontal slicing gesture with his private mobile-hospital pen. *Amelioricon Implants & Reductions*, read the pen.

"Pfffttt ... drop 'em in – freak out – take 'em out! Reset, reset! Whatever. An endless cycle of joy and despair and joy. Beauty is so much deeper than skin deep. And don't I know it!"

Oober Mann cleared his throat. She had returned.

"Excuse me, err ... Dr. F."

"O sure sure. Just remember to come back when your face and balls fall off. Not to mention your lovely knockers, miss! Here's a card for each of you. All shapes and sizes. Bring your friends and bring out your inner self!"

"Nice day, yes."

"Yeah."

"I think writers attractive."

"Whaaa?"

"Sorry. I mean I want go to sack with writers."

"You're not from around here, hey?"

"I speech funny."

"No, not at all. It's nice. *Different*."

"O. I hello from Nether—"

"Netherlands?"

"Um ... yes. A little place destroyed by bad general. There we loved book. Yours."

"My book?"

"Yes. *Major Ruckus*. Ist brilliant! Genius!"

"Sorry, I don't ..."

"Modest? No. Here is copy to sign. Everyone in Nether—"

"Let me see."

Oober Mann traced the letters of his name on the glammering spine. He felt a peculiar tingle while touching it. And the paper was unlike any he had felt before, like soft metal melting in his hands. He marvelled at this magical craftsmanship. The Netherlands must be a fantastic place! He flipped through at random.

"Lax Laxness? What a perfectly strange name! But I never ..."

She stared at him challengingly. And so did Faustus. And then it occurred to him that, after all, he had written at least a fistful of these pages. And they were suddenly more than familiar. In fact, he felt he was living rather flatly inside of them, with every breath he took.

Epic Securities Case Ends in Failure

Mordecai reread the headline. He was ebullient, beside himself. Years of research and files and paperwork had gone into this baby. And he had won! Correction. His team had won! In the end, only to prove that on such and such a day at such and such a time, nobody knew what the hell was going on. Like asking someone precisely what they had for a midnight snack on October 23, 1929. The market is sometimes a murky sea of minutiae, my friend. And who of us is truly fit to judge? Ohp! An old-fashioned jingle ...

"Heylo ..."

"Mordecai. It's me, Hector."

"You've heard the news!"

"Of course."

"Imagine, all that taxpayers' money gone into sabotaging the market, literally shooting ourselves in the foot! Insane!"

"Yeah. Black and white is what they want."

"It's all grey areas. Meanwhile, the firm has been in limbo for years."

"And I guess Frains has shit out his two bits."

"O. That prick. I've never forgiven him for sending Jazzy up the river. Who the hell does that guy think he is?"

Bloop Bloop Bloop

Tooth rolled onto his side in the twilight of sleep. He could still hear the screams of the two sisters. A pity, but after all, they were all washed up ... It was always safest to lie low in some aspect of classical. Shostakovich or Alban Berg. In his younger days, he had snagged fresh IDs at the listening centre in the bottom of Vixylicious Vinyl. Some poor sap would come in asking for *Celtic Wonders* or the Scitish Airways song, and then bloop bloop bloop they didn't exist. In this case, the girls were needed for some kind of freewave pulpline 29/8 transmission. He didn't ask. Nor did he want to know a whit of it. Dirty business, really. But his head was pounding. A fly the size of a freaking human head was fanning his sweating forehead. He shook, startled. Sometimes he woke up abruptly with the rapid-eye dream image still plastered to his vision. At that second, he saw the dream thing fluttering right in front of him, accenting the faded barf shade of his blanket. He blinked and blinked, pretty damn sure he was awake. She looked at him patiently as any hallucination might, with nothing but time.

"Want me to pinch you?"

"Effie!"

"Time to haul arssssse, sleepyhead."

"This is not happening."

"'Fraid it is, sweetie. Sorry. Part of you just can't let go of your wickedest blastvert campaign. Not yet, anyhoo."

She draped herself over him and burst a dozen of her bubbles. Tooth spat. They tasted vitriolic, bitter.

"I don't believe in you."

"Awww ... I is, is all."

"Whad'ya want from me?"

"You are soooo in the dark. They are onto your damp paper trail. The Seedyer has been compromised and you're the blab of space. Not long now."

"Whaaaa ...?"

"There's some ass-sniffer nosing the Whipple goods. Asking questions. Folk are starting to notice your full-page ad method, my delicious numbnuts."

"Who is he?"

"There's an idea. How about we go find out, hmmm? Plenny of time for *us* later."

"I gotta get the lowdown. Maybe try a few disappearing tricks ..."

"Great. I'll drive!"

This Can Slowly Kill You

Anaïs lay with her chin upon the pleasant surface of Suetonius, puffing another Dromedary. She read the label wrapped around the oasis warning her from the nightstand. Not that she cared. Not now. He mussed her sticky hair happily, watching sunlight filling her eyes and ashes landing upon his chest.

"Smoking in bed is a no-no."
"Yeah. A bad habit, I guess."

There was a loud buzz. She fastened a silken robe. Suetonius jumped up like a fawn in a foul wind.

"Don't stress. It's cool."

Suetonius shuddered. More than once, a beautiful lady had let her old man in to see The Indian. And more than once, he had fallen prey to the clever snares of the post-colonial economic system. He lay back on his arms, staring up at himself in a ceiling mirror. Hello. Hmm. Voices. She sure is taking her sweet time. Ah well. Maybe there's another book in it. Another *Purple Evening at Three Rivers*. He was semi-dozing when she returned with a frown on her face.

"Everything okay?"
"Uhmm yeah. It was just some census dude. I totally filled it out like a month ago."

"Err yes. I've been meaning to talk to you about that. Why don't you come over here and give me the information I need? I really need it bad."

She giggled. There was still loads of afternoon left. She poured out a massive glob of family warming liquid into her palm and leapt on top of him, pleased to get more than her money's worth.

Out for PSP

"Dwayne Whipple?"

"Yeah?"

"I'm an investigator for C-WUT. Here's my card. I spoke with your wife."

"This 'bout that census?"

"Yes. Maybe."

"Yo Jim, get yer butt out here!"

Jim made his entrance with a sheepish look on his kisser.

"What?"

"You know anything what happened to our census?"

"No."

"Okay then. Ya see, mister. We don't got a clue."

"And where is your wife at present?"

"Can I see some ID, felluh?"

"No."

"O she's out for some PSP, what she calls her Personal Space Period. I'd try the piece-a-shit mall down the way. Maybe she tried her hand with Lady Luck or some goddamn thing."

"Thank you. This is a most serious matter."

"Cool. Okay then ..."

"Have a good one."

Mr. Whipple shut the door and bolted it fast.

"Boy, you been friggin' round with our census! I'll give you such a census takin' ..."

"Ooooooh ..."

Damages

Dexter Savonarola Frains, more widely known as Dick Frains, nearly wet himself when he first heard the news. He gnawed on his crusader cape nervously and looked over his shoulder now and again for unwelcome reflections in tinted windows. Ever since he had done a series on the mob, he had received mysterious threats, a fact he liked to remind his readers about, because he was in fact a crusader for *The Truth*. It was most fortunate that only he knew the truth and had access to a means to print it on a daily basis. It was also fortunate that formal obstacles to journalistic iconography, such as proofing and fact-checking, were a thing of the distant past. The wire was what mattered, and when it was live, you had to grab hold and squeeze. Squeeze and squeeze and pump it dry.

After stabbing Jazzy Sharp in the nads with his poisoned pen and bringing him *this close* to public execution, it had become clear to him through a lakeside vision that West Coast Liquidities was a shady and lathery firm taking everyone for a big bath and throwing in a free toaster oven. So one day, he woke up early and went to a lengthy hearing and had the numerous claimant accusations printed, although they were unsubstantiated. And thinking about this chain of events got him all worked up. He unclasped his crusader cape and exposed his bare back to a rough tassel and began to lash himself. He administered only a mere aperitif to the main course of punishment he had to endure for letting these evil evil monsters off.

"Bzzzz ... Mr. Frains?"
"What is it?"
"A Miss Fever to see you."
"Ah yes. Send her in."

The redhead in imitation zebra clipped into his office and locked the door behind her. He licked her presented left boot from toe to shin in customary greeting.

"Well?"
"I have failed, my mistress."
"Failed?"
"Failed to stop ... the evil ..."

He continued lapping her boot and looked up at her stripes imploringly. She stroked his thinning pate and tenderly attached a studded collar to his proffered neck.

"Someone must be punished."

Frains shivered with delight. Mistress Fever began to lash his back lightly, opening old wounds, while he muttered his penance in a series of snarls.

"Evil evil ... market on move ... money moving ... from here ... to there. Sharks ... swirling. Wolfenstein ... uhhh ... evil ... and defenders of ... Aboriginal ... uuuhmm ... entitlement ... Jews defending heathens ... wicked ... uhnnnnn ..."

"Sounds like someone needs multiple sessions ..."

"To the misericord!"

I ♥ My Work

Oober Mann shadowed the Native man along the cobbles with a casual air. Dijon Diva Vanessa Velveteen had reminded him of his double duty. His role as a writer of some small repute was, after all, only a role. His aim to learn two dozen languages and his nebulous notoriety as a jotter-down of unexpected tales made him the perfect agent. Just when you thought you had invited him in to steal all your secrets, he surprised you by doing exactly that. Why, it must have slipped his mind for months that he had been recruited by the powers-that-be. That's how good and deep his cover was. He had been instructed to collect and, if at all possible, format what scraps of human interest he came into contact with. This intangible storehouse of data was to dynamically compile into an ongoing report under the working title *Major Ruckus*, a work incidentally renowned for its utter lack of completion. And the longer he followed and observed this man, the more confident he was that he knew him. An author, like himself. However, he derived no small satisfaction from the indisputable fact that the adventurous and prolific writer of *The Spirit of Parallel 69* and *Border Out: Indian to Go* was actually a minor character, and thus a tiny figment of his own unspeakably fecund imagination.

Let's Split Up

Lax Laxness winced at the jumpy Bongolino, who was outside impatiently honking his horn.

"Sorry. I was getting worried. Well ...?"

"Nada. Shooting blanks. And the missus has gone to play bingo."

"Well, isn't that a coincidence!"

"No, not really."

"O."

Then Lax noticed an open matchbook on the sidewalk. He bent over to pick it up. Bongo whistled through the driver's side. He read the neat printing on the inside gratefully: *Dark Fever Studios*.

"Ah ha! It never fails."

"Huh?"

"The mind of the machinator. In nine out of ten cases, the stereotypical perp leaves something behind, and in each case a hotel matchbook leads to their capture. It's akin to the pyro demiurge. They all want to come out and get caught."

"It sounds like you got this theory on the back of a matchbook. Or out of a cereal box."

"I'm dead serious, Bongo. This was the one question I got right on the exam. I know what I'm talking about. We already know the census taker's cover story. If my permutations are correct and I'm not on crack, this should lead to our nefarious ID swiper."

"Don't go. Haven't you made me worry enough for one afternoon?"

"Don't worry about me. You're the one who's going."

"It could be dangerous."

"You knew what you signed up for when we made it official."

Bongo sighed.

"Godspeed, Lax. And luck be with you."

"I'm gonna need it. I'm off to grab a dollar dabber."

No Names

Fay swerved into a handicapable space in front of the horseshoe-shaped strip mall known as Bingogate. A wizened figure grinned out at her calmly through the glass, dabbing his fresh book of 7s. Then he vanished behind a cloud of smoking section. Seventy-one septuagenarians abandoned their borrowed bingo gadgetalia for a split second and followed her unsteady footsteps with stony glares from the handicapable spot to the front door of Unfeasible Fetal Services. A tall, lanky fellow in an aquamarine anorak stood in her way, brandishing the sharpened business end of his placard, which read

MY GOD NOT MY BOD!

"Ware, ye who enter here! Ware this den of iniquity and loathsome murder!"

"Excuse me ...?"

"Horny porndogging fornicator of the Nth level of hell! Thy gates are thrown open and thy womb is polluted by thy lapse of judgment! Begone and reflect upon thy fornication and not sanitary dealings!"

At that moment, Dr. Jeremiah Emilius Fantasidcht strode out and matter-of-factly tasered the freak in mid-froth. He dragged the body inside and out of the way before propping the door open.

"Please, don't be alarmed, mizzzz. Happens every day."

"I need ... help."

"Of course you do. No names, please! In fact, you can call me F ..."

Fold Out

Jim wiped a couple of juicy tears from his cheek and set about unfolding his scooter. He was sick of this place and its crazed pack of love slaves. There's a whole wide world out there. Maybe time to snatch a taste of that great enchilada. Time has a way of sneaking up on ya. He thought of Olga wistfully, of what they had done on a playground swing set one summer night, an experience he would never forget as long as he lived. But it was impossible. He was more complicated than swinging chains and flying sand would allow.

And the fatal encounter with his stepmother, followed by the fatal encounter with his stepfather, had incited a latent yearning within him to know his true origins. He had become curious when Olga pointed out that most people don't have two step-parents. But all he had left was the donor information he had found in his stepmother's drawer, and these statistics for his progenitor were etched into his memory in burning letters:

Donor ID #:	RDXPHUM-37805
Race / Ethnic Origin:	Swiss / Euro-Trapezium
Blood Type:	Z-
Hair Colour / Style:	Aubergine / Wavy
Eye Colour:	Cobalt Stellar
Skin Tone:	Beta C++ / Medium
Height:	6'11"
Weight:	386
Years of College:	0
Occupation / Major:	Hyperfieldzone Commander
Hobbies:	Dwarf-jumping, Antigrav-Ball, Stiking, Percussion
Vials Avail:	65K+
Rating:	♂ ♂ ♂ ♂ ♂ ♂ ♂ ♂ ♂

As for the maternal egg, it was another mystery. He suspected that Fay didn't know either. Maybe not even Dwayne. He found it tough, like a math problem he could never work out. If you have X and Y, what the hell is Z negative? He revved up his scooter and scooted off in the direction of the bus depot.

It Could Be Dangerous

The man stood with his hands over his head, fastened together and tied to a large cylindrical pipe, another ornament of "the dungeon." His feet just barely touched the floor and he shifted continually to become more comfortable and found that he could not. He was wearing a mask out of the Italian theatre and he resembled Gianni Schicchi caught in an awkward part of the opera. His mask was the contorted face of tragedy. He was wearing nothing else but a tight belt and corresponding black loincloth which the loose flesh of his large paunch hung over messily. His pudgy nipples gleamed now and again, and Bongo could make out a tiny gold piercing in each one. It was at that moment Bongo noticed a female figure sitting in the shadows, slightly to the right of the hanging man. The camera was positioned on an angle and appeared to frame the woman rather than the man. As if on cue, she broke the stillness and stood up in the darkness. She moved toward the dangling light bulb and revealed a mask that was counterpart to the man's, the mask for comedy.

Bongo felt disconcerted, staring through the glass into those dark eyeholes of perpetual levity, suspended over a congealed grin. She was wearing a black girdle with holes cut into the stiff material to strategically accentuate the curves of her flesh as she walked. She looked quizzically into the camera for a second, offering her cleavage through the roughly cut peephole of her outfit and illuminating that sickle of a grin. She wore ridiculously high boots with unforgiving heels that dotted the oil-stained floor like semiquavers, a sound for which the hanging man stirred, attempting to lower his head and prick up his ears. She turned her head toward the man and then looked at the camera again, as if disclosing the secret of his predicament. She held a neatly gloved finger to a fixed smile and reached with her other glove for the ample girth of him, for the emphasized expanse of his love handles. As he felt the coarse material brush his belly, he shifted from foot to foot with that attached face of agony, tightening both wrists about decorative pipe and belt about excessive gut.

He let out a low moan, yet loud enough with its current of enthusiasm for Bongo to imagine his smile underneath that tortured mask. The loincloth seemed to soften for the hanging man as his growing excitement became visible. She walked slowly over to the farthest wall, allowing the hanging man and Bongo to hear each bewitching step, before taking down a small whip. She walked over to the hanging man, standing mask to mask yet maintaining choreography for the camera's pleasure. Bongo blinked, focusing through the gloom and finding her shiny white back and her red hair tied back behind the mask into a thick knot. Her head cocked to one side and the gloves went out. Bongo could see one of them lifting the loincloth and holding it up in a tight fist but her body obscured the rest. He could feel his temperature rising.

She was leaning forward, just enough to whisper over the hanging man's shoulder. Bongo heard only murmurs. The man twitched while listening. Then the gloves shot out and seized his bare shoulders. He groaned as the loincloth flapped down again. The gloves insinuated their will and the hanging man let himself be turned in the opposite direction. Bongo and the camera lent their field of vision to his thinning hair and raw, pimply buttocks. The three tassels attached to the small whip were offered intermittently to each red cheek, tickling the man. She moved closer and filled his ear with nothings for a full minute while he shook (as much as he could) like a broken marionette, breathing heavily over her inaudible words. Having prodded him into this state of bound excitement, she stood back matter-of-factly and with a sudden flick of the wrist let the whip fly. The lash was instantaneous. A slim, neat mark appeared on his exposed bottom.

"No," he answered. "No."

The wrist flicked again. Then again.

"No, I won't do it again."

She backed up a few paces, studying his miserable hanging body, before putting her whole arm into the attack. The whip flew at him and formed a sizable cut on his lower back.

"Forgive me, you have to forgive me!"

In response, she turned her head back toward the camera, flashing that plastic grin before whipping his body again. The motion of her body caused more laughter in her clothing. A hundred laughs opened in her girdle, like a jigsaw puzzle of flesh for the imagination to finish. High on her left buttock cheek, a small tattoo made its debut for the camera and then vanished like a nearby star suddenly enshrouded by a brusque and ponderous cloud. Bongo leaned forward to catch another glimpse of the tiny red illustration but the woman wheeled around, turning the man like a large slab of meat by pulling his loincloth in her direction. She bent her knees, arching her back in feline fashion and stretching her arms toward the camera while the mask continued to cackle absurdly. She eased her body backward in slow movements until the hanging man could feel the curves of her rear. Then she stretched forward again, catching her hands on a hanging pipe the size of a gymnast's apparatus. Balancing like so, she raised her left leg behind her and placed the heel of her boot against the man's groin, applying pressure as audibly measured by his increasing groans.

"Ooooh yaaah."

She turned him sideways so that his mask became a half-grimace. She sidled up against him, a half-grin at his baggy flesh and the bumpy loincloth beneath her begloved hands. She lifted the coiled whip up to his chest, letting the three tassels tickle his body hair and letting the coils catch upon his gold piercings while she whispered other things into his right ear. The hanging man began to squirm.

"No. No. I don't know, maybe."

With that, a wicked, weak-throated laugh flew into his ear. She stood back, her mask grinning into the camera for a long silence of visible ecstasy. Then she lifted the whip and began to lash the man severely, taking no care this time to find a target. Weeping could be heard, coming from under his tormented mask. Also groans. His body began to tear and break into smiles, until it looked like a grotesque parody of her tattered girdle.

"Noooouhh!"

She whipped him again. The hanging man shuddered for a few seconds and then his head fell limp. Feeling queasy, Bongo reached through the semi-dark for the doorknob. But he was up to here in murky bathwater laughter.

"O, my word, it's you ..."

And then everything went grey-green.

Fashionably Late

"Excuse me, *grazie* ..."

The fleshy man and woman stood up with affront and made themselves momentarily thin. Not bad. Ackmod peered around excitedly. Not bad at all. Row 5, seat 49, right in the middle. His first Dulkling opera. He had received an uncanny telepath during a lofty snooze cycle. The code was mistily offbeat but pawshakeable. Something about the mustard being out of the squeeze tube. With instructions where to go. He expected to see Vulna any moment in her Vanessa Velveteen faux fur. But the last seat in the row beside him was taken by a heavy, powdered octogenarian whose scent disrupted his narinos. The lights dimmed and she promptly fell asleep on his shoulder. He stared at her skeletal hand on his knee. Who was Edgar? He shifted in his seat. Two big-boned women in front of him were embracing in such a way that he couldn't see over their love. The bespectacled black woman with braids kept shaking her head and nudging her blond girlfriend.

Ackmod gathered that the side character soprano was upstaging the mezzo lead. And although this was only a concert recital, her blue top accentuated her cheerful zaniness and underlined each note. She smiled broadly and beamed right through a sleeping old coot in a sports jacket. The two women rested their heads together and obscured his view of the lead violinist and the movement of the celeste. Now he cursed his seat in mudstar dialect. There were three rows empty in the front. These Dulklings scarcely respected their own art. An art he craved across solar systems. He felt a sudden urge to convince Ruckus to dissipate the entire orb. Gather up the few treasures time had to offer and one or two specimens for the petting zoo and then *blip*! No more Terra Dulkis.

He was musing in time with a second act interlude when he noticed a woman step out of the darkness and select a seat in the second row. Where had she come from? She turned around and smiled apologetically. Ackmod observed her lively red hair and tried to make out her face. The face that launched a dozen variations of mustard? It had to be Vulna. This was not what he would call a discreet meeting. Best to wait till intermission. The skeletal hand dug into his knee. His twin hearts were beating like two timpani in need of tuning.

"Nell'abisso fatal dove caduto io son / Rimpianta visïon / Ah! te il mio pensiero evòca sempre ancor!"

Two Tickets for Anywhere

"One ticket for Anywhere, please."

"All right, here you go, but don't miss the bus, don't miss the bus!"

"Huh?"

"I said if you miss the bus there *won't be* another one!"

Jim handed over a roll of desocked bills and took his ticket and change. A long wait, then. He sat on the cool platform and stared at the grey, empty space. After some time, his attention was attracted by a giant billboard that loomed over the depot. He felt a sudden pang of longing and revulsion. Between the triangular image slats that constituted an ad for Frozen Butt Breathmints and an ad for the new prime-time series *Spooky Puke*, there was the image of a woman in a skimpy yellow top and saffron skirt riding a bucking mustard-bottle rocket, apparently to the planet Dijon. He was too absorbed to notice a girl putting her bag down beside him.

"Hey man, got a smoke?"

He reached for his third-to-last Dromedary with a hint of reluctance and their eyes locked. The same cobalt eyes and the same Beta C++ complexion. Yearning cellos began to sound, followed by tender fiddles. They were the same height and had the same wavy eggplant hair. And neither had ever seen such a beautiful creature. They tore up their tickets and embraced with ineffable feeling, much to the consternation of the passing ticket seller.

"Hey, they won't let you on without those! Stupid kids."

Two Noble Clans

"And how was your day, dear?"

"Excellent. I bagged this Aboriginal stud to win a hundred-buck bet. More than excellent!"

"Anaïs, I do declare! What a feral imagination you have. You should write for one of those Friday-night shitcoms, really!"

"Of course, I'll collect the cash tomorrow and stick around, at least until we decide to run away together. I hear Lebanon is nice this time of year ..."

"Okay, I'll bite. You sure know how to keep the zing in our legal arrangement!"

"And how was oil production?"

"Well, Rome wasn't licked in the first day. I'd say we're hitting our stride. People are using more warming products than ever. Of course, the board of directors needed more massaging. They are never quite lube-to-lube with what my father had in mind. O, and I caught Jenkins snooping around again, and I had to show him the roof garden. Terrible tragedy, really. The funeral's Monday."

"And what shall I wear? Har har. Why, you are still the dragon slayer I ceded my interests and investments to. But won't that pose a problem? Jenkins, I mean."

"No. He knew nothing of our plans. It was just a precaution. No worries."

In an attempt to change the subject, he lifted a soggy side of lamb that upon examination was some kind of traditional pelt.

"Did you buy this today? Or am I supposed to believe it belonged to your First Nations lover?"

"One of them, yeah."

"Watch yourself. You are giving me near-informal feelings, Anaïs."

"But that's not in our contract. O and, Swen, do you remember filling out a census lately?"

Bingo

A henna-beehived woman threw her bag in the speaker's direction.

"Hey, call it out like you mean it! Phyllis ..."

Phyllis stared down the presumptuous winner. She glared into his soul and right out the other side.

"You're in my place."

"Sure, sweetheart. Just let me and Effie collect our winnings and split."

A rodent-like man checked his numbers and sniffed the air carefully before handing over a twenty. He left their company with a barrage of liquidy laughter.

"You better keep an eye on that one, Sammy. He kept yakking to himself the whole time, or his imaginary friend, Effie."

"Only since they let 'em all out of the hospitals. Now they're no longer patients. They're my neighbours."

"Never mind. Just stay the hell away when I got my number comin'."

"Yeah. And next time, break his legs or something, Sammy, so he doesn't take *my place*."

Tooth was still laughing and about to enjoy a celebratory smoke when he was collared and thrown against the wall.

"To whom, may I ask, do I owe the pleasure?"

"I'm the one asking the questions."

"But first, would you be so kind as to remove the blunt instrument from my family jewels? I am after all quite fond of them."

"How would you like 'em done? Fried or sunny side up? Fried by a thrillion volts, I think."

"Shoot."

"What is your interest in Fay Whipple? Why are you following her?"

"O, we used to have a thing. Damn jealousy. Gets us all in the end."

"Horsedoodle."

"Why, what a suspicious mind you have!"

"A Texas omelette after all."

"Ahh, what the hey. It's just a bit on the side. A few identities that fell off the back of a truck. No one's the worse for it. Anyway, I'm just the middleman. And a man's gotta eat, after all."

"So you are the swiper! And whad'ya mean by middleman?"

"Boy, are you late to buy a clue, chico. I'm only shifting the identities. There's something really effed up going on. The people I get to, they're already marked. Damaged goods. In fact, I'm performing a public service …"

"What do you mean by that?"

"Hey, I'm only following the trail. And I think our time is up."

"No. Tell me about this trail."

"Why don't you ask Bongo?"

"Bongo?"

"Hell yeah. He came over to have a little chat."

"Where is he?"

"O fine, fine. Would you like to see him again?"

"Leave him out of this, you twisted bastard."

"O sure. I'd hate to harm a single hair on that mixed-up head of his."

"You think that gets you off the hook? Why, I should fritter your bits right now."

"O no, not at all. I wanted to be sure you had a soft spot after all, Mr. Laxness. Then when I flay and gut your toy boy, I can do so with perfect satisfaction."

"You won't sway me."

"No, but she will. Effie, would you do the honours …"

Lax whirled around to no longer find himself in the corridors of Bingogate. He was in a steamy gym locker room. He looked down. Without a stitch. And he was in the boy's, judging by the rows of naked men standing to attention, and in every way possible. He walked by them, inspecting each like a drill sergeant. He gave one a pump, the next a squeeze. The third a quick nibble. Everything in order here. The last man in line took hold of him with a look of grave concern. Strangely, he was the spitting image of Bongo.

"Don't forget to see the Queen. She is waiting for you."

He walked into the shower and turned on the taps. And as the bubbles bubbled out, he was sure he was having some kind of dream, most probably wet. And then in front of him, a rarity. It was a cool drink of water, a woman surrounded by bubbles in all the essential places. How tacky could you get? And he felt he had seen her before. She nodded at Bongo, who was being led into the corner by one member of the locker-room platoon.

"You see, Mr. Laxness. Bongo is perfectly fine."

The *solider* blindfolded Bongo and pushed him up against the tiled wall. Then he produced a giant neon-green water pistol and began giving him pump action with a cream-coloured liquid. After his screams died down, the entire troupe lifted Bongo bodily and performed a lavish dance number. And soon Bongo was kneeling on the wet tiles and leaving no one feeling lonely or left out.

"O o o Lax, they're making me!!! O o o!"

Effie turned to the daydreamer in question.

"Why don't you throw in the towel, Mr. Laxness? And let Tooth alone. I wanted you to see how weak your little unit is. You are involved in matters that do not concern you."

"I'm gonna put you out of the bubble business. Shut down all your operations."

"Awww. Look at your friend. Doesn't that make you jealous? He's having the time of his life. And what about you? Why don't you just watch the action? And I can blow you right here."

"Get lost."

"Too bad."

She pursed her lips into a huge *O* and exhaled a fizzing bubble that blew bigger and bigger. Then it floated off toward Lax and encapsulated his entire head. It tightened rapidly around his face. He struggled to breathe and within seconds, he fell to the tiled floor.

"Told ya I'd blow ya like nobody's biz."

Entr'Acte

The act came abruptly to an end. The hero as usual, degraded and doomed before his time. Applause. The red-haired woman got up and made her way toward an exit to the left of the stage. Ackmod followed, but he was slowed up by other people needing to pee and announcing their intention to their nearest neighbour. He could just make out her velvety wrap flying around a corner. He trailed the stream of hopping people downstairs. Murmuring enthusiasts were milling around and matching their tickets with glasses of red. Red! She was outside, climbing into a limuck. Ackmod raced toward the vehicle and stood in front of the passenger window expectantly. The tinted window rolled down.

The red-haired woman was there, inscrutable in the shadows.

"Get in already."
"I wasn't sure we were meeting ... here."
"Get in."

I See It Every Week

Fay, spread-eagled and strapped to the looking glass, was swivelled by the begloved hands of F to line up flush with a strip of electrician's tape on the floor that, incidentally, held cars together.

"There we go. And if you are going to look worried like that, could you face directly into the eye of the device? And don't worry, the Thalidomizer 5100 is state of the art. Tells us the sex and *nature* of the unborn. What they like to eat, their hobbies, and so on. You might want a refund if we throw away the next Niels Bohr. Or if you decide to keep him and he is the next Niels Bohr. What am I saying, *she* could be the next national pin-up doll! A loss to humanity indeed. But you are, after all, the customer. If you say Nutty Glue her to your side, I *will* Nutty Glue her to your side!"

"But what do you see, Doctor?"

"I want to say pin-up girl, on account of her mother's beauty. But no, it's a boy. A big little bastard at that."

Fay began to weep.

"No no, mystery woman. I don't mean that in the pejorative sense. I only mean that his head might finish you off on the way out. The old max headroom joke. Your boy-to-be is a tanker truck inside a dinghy. If I were you, I would save myself a lot of pain and a wagonload of potential harm. We could do the procedure right here. I have another five minutes, if you are not in a hurry ..."

"Really? I should put an end to little Dwight?"

"Dwight, heh? Well, Mizzzz Anonymous, another minor concern is (I have no wish to alarm you) ... you are aware, of course ..."

"Aware of ...?"

"Yes, look right into the eye of the device with that shocked expression. Perfect. Why, your unborn son has alien DNA. Well, I see it every week. Since NASA crash-landed in the toilet and started selling their old designs, the Egyptian shuttle cabs have been thriving. A weekend trip to Venus is no longer out of the question for Mum. And I hear the Forbidden Fruticetum is back in season. But I digress. And of course, I should be saying your terrestrially challenged son-to-be ..."

"Alien DNA! How ...?"

"Who can say? But do you really want to have that conversation with the gargantuan tyke? A thousand words on why I don't remember Daddy? And sure, you could still pin the amazing tale on some poor schmuck. But the odds are, he'd notice when his kid gets to be ten feet tall. Also, there are many adolescent development problems on record. I wouldn't recommend it, mizzzz. No One Has to Know."

"Ugh. I want it out. Take it out!"

"But of course. And I do sympathize. Tell you what. I'll give you five big ones for the extracted fetus. Problem solved and cash in hand. After all that's what the market will bear. Unless you want to keep it."

"Keep it?"

"O yes, there are all kinds of buyers. Stem-cell grow-op hybridizers, mostly. And believe you me, there are plenty of wackos also."

"Really?"

"Artists, mostly, or so they think. They dip the critters in preserves or have them stuffed for exhibits. O my, how avant-garde of them! I took a fabulous dump the other day. I must be a little bit avant-garde myself."

"Okay, Doctor, let's do this thing."

"Please look directly into the eye of the device and repeat that with a semi-snarl."

The Public

Oober kept close to Suetonius, keeping tabs on him for the few hours leading up to his reading at the public library. He sat in the ersatz piazza, nibbling a slice of pesto pizza and peering over his shoulder now and again. Then he shadowed him across the loose cobbles, down into the near-empty room. The head introductionist grabbed his light brown hands. She beamed broadly and turned aubergine.

"O you have no idea ... such an honour ... I love First Nations things ..."

Oober scowled in his seat. To the tall, lanky man's credit, he looked about to bolt from her effusive gushing. Tickle Feathers, the self-styled visual sidekick to the tell-it-like-it-is gospel of Suetonius, was present and still struggling to work out the slide presentation set-up. Suetonius watched his glowing face and sighed. He had first known him as Lyle Little Feathers on the rez. That was before he got into the controversial (and some would deem racist) art of feather-tickle fighting. But it was time to put all that behind them for one evening. Tonight, they were collectively putting on *Red Hot Nation*, after his book of the same title, featuring the naked beauty of Aboriginal women.

Suetonius would read passages of his book and Tickle ... well, he had taken quite a few Daguerreosnaps as a kind of retro-commentary on the art of photography. While Suetonius bravely fought off the gusher, a voice behind Oober nattered on and on about its change of diet since deciding to go steady with a physiopath. Apparently, the owner of the voice was off everything but celery. There were a few Native people in the audience, sitting on the left side. The non-Native people all sat on the right side. Suetonius began to speak, ducking a few whistles and catcalls, about how this non-exploitive artistic process had come into being.

"Heh ... um ... I am, of course, subject to the male gaze ..."

Titters. The small audience stomping and rutting and writhing. Actually, just one fellow, clearing his throat. A woman coughing. Shill Dick, his one flunky, remembered his part and sprang to life.

"Show us the pictures!"

Tickle Feathers fumbled around for the right function key. There. No. There.

"An' we've been spending some time abroad an' we realized how damn tame we are. Damn tame! Maybe time to get back to our roots, hey ...?"

"Lyle, shh ..."

Image of wide-eyed sister, naked as the day she was born.

"I am a sister lost in the wood. I am the Lure. I am the caster-off of masculine detritus. Why, I married the wind ..."

Image of a nude eyeing a fat, heavy stick in her hand.

"Tree of Life, emblem of blankets how you awaken in my wet wet palm ..."

Image of an ancient elder flashing the world.

"She's beautiful, really."

"For I am the sister of a dozen troubles. The two-headed serpent, the bringer of curses. Why, I wed the wind and now look at me ..."

Image of a woman body-painted and tattooed into a full-breasted Spiderwoman.

"You cannot hold me in your web a moment longer! Ours is a private moment."

They cycled through several more images and readings. Image of bare-chested women paddling.

Image of young hottie trying to catch slippery candlefish. Then the lights undimmed.

"Questions? Comments?"

A woman from the First Nations side of the room stood up, covering her chest, visibly moved.

"I ... teach. I should say first that I am hybridized, Scottish and Cree and Euro-Trapezium. And I just think what you are doing is sooooo beautiful. We have hitherto been perspicacious in our pursuit of non-sexual Otherness. Granted, in our search, we sisters have lost sight of our sexuality, and I can scarcely bring myself to postulate, we are integral to a phobic mechanism and in the sense of an objectified subjective, we feel fear of this Other It. In representative modes, most likely resulting from the lingering ghouls of gentrification, we appear as desexualized, as sexually *null*. And who is the culprit. Ourselves? History ..."

Another woman a few seats ahead shook her braids and jewellery violently.

"Speak for yourself, sistah!"

Suetonius winked at her. You could always count on Mavis. A few guys shuffled in their seats, stricken with a sudden case of infectious timidity. One man finally stood up and cleared his throat.

"Long live the liberation."

And then a woman behind Oober stood up. Her voice trembled and screeched.

"What you have done is *exploit* these Indian girls. I am certain the Oolichan girl was underage. You only need to send it to DemandOnDemand and then you'll make a pretty penny!"

"But with poetry and art ... I won't make back what I invested ... Break even ... They volunteered for Tickle ..."

But she stormed out with her friend, all the way back to her physiopath. And Oober could not help looking pleased.

The Pillow That Lives Forever

LOCATION: Gentry Towers, Mount Pleasant

PRICE: "This needs some 'splainin'. One of our contestants got in over his head with his renos and couldn't afford to keep his house, even after we gave him the prize makeover. In fact, he said we could keep our ****ing hot tub. What a card! So it was a lot of elbow grease, but really it was quite a steal! I won't say, but you can ask Lee. He lives in the trailer out back."

SQUARE FEET: 1,113, one bedroom, one den, one maturiteen water torture fun centre (incl.)

LENGTH OF TIME HERE: Five months

OCCUPANTS: Vanessa Velveteen, host of *Hostile Makeover*, a show in which unsuspecting owners of varied chattel are nominated by complete strangers for undesired yet necessary changes to their lifestyle/relationships. Velveteen lives with current common-law beau, Rufus Marauder, star of the new local series *Major Ruckus*. "But it's kinda quiet without the pitter-patter of little ones ..."

MAJOR SELLING FEATURE: "When we first went to visit Lee for the show, he asked us to smoke some exotic plant. Next thing Lee comes out of the can and catches us *in flagrante delicto* on the floor. I guess that explains the *Mosca Hispanica* design choice. But I find there's nothing more magical and romantic than loosening up your inhibitions and getting busy in someone else's pad to the sight and sound of the fireworks. I think that night totally sold us."

FIRST THING I CHANGED: "You won't believe the things you find when you rip up the tiling of a house! So many stories. Where to begin! O yeah, and Lee had some charms in every room to ward off some kind of burial ground vibes in the area. He wanted to leave them in place but I told him where to go."

FEATURE I BRAG ABOUT: "Although I was raised in a sizable grow-op, I have a totally black thumb when it comes to weed. Soon as I moved in, my mom foisted some more seeds on me. Thankfully, I have a ton of teahead friends to get me started. So I show everyone my first crop. Here, you simply can't own a home without a grow-op. It's common sense. And it might work out perfect if this makeover show lands in the toilet."

THAT ONE CONVERSATION PIECE: "Lee, for sure. You never know when he'll blow through the place like an angry spirit, quoting Kung or Mao or Steve Allen! We're the only couple I know with an authentic Chinese sage to play show and tell with. And the locks *are* taking way longer than expected …"

THE DÉCOR: "That's a tricky subject. Rufus and I fight about it non-stop. Rufus prefers a sensitive mustard or oregano with liberated *frijoles* trim. I like a chaotic black-and-blue Pollock background with action-hero blood and puke accents. Since my life as the Dijon Diva has been 24/7 about the life of mustard, I just don't want to see it when I walk in the front door."

STORY BEHIND THE ART: "I like anything indigenous-y. We have scoured the earth collecting fabrics and rugs and to quote a friend 'ossified knick-knacks.' It's a great feeling to know your purchase can feed an entire family or village. S'all good. The thing is, Rufus's grandpa collected all these funky paintings during WWII and they really clash with my Thai Sunday brunch settings."

DOWNSIDES: "Busy, busy and busy. Rufus is off shooting his show most of the time, or hobjobbing with producers. He gets home really beat and then I gotta do another makeover. Also, it sucks to play happy family with strangers when your own husband has a rare condition that makes him sterile. That's right, ladies! Major Ruckus shoots blanks! And the clock is ticking. And who's gonna help me? Lee??? Man, it really pisses me off. And our iron-clad agreement in blood with that dude. It's like our house isn't even really ours! Ah well … to quote the poet William Browning, 'All roads lead to hell in different sizes.'"

NEIGHBOURHOOD HAUNTS: "Since I couldn't make frigatoni for months, I hung out at A Touch of Special and In My Soup, and I am totally in love with the flirty servers at The Endowment. And we love to zip up and down Main, scoping far-out foreign objects for our Ruckus Room. I guess you can still get your kicks with screaming lungs without the pitter-patter of little ones …"

MOST RECENT HOME PURCHASE: "I finally found the perfect retro latex pillow. Now if only Rufus would make good on his threats and smother that goddamned interfering Lee with it."

Just One of the Boys

Lax Laxness awoke to his own choking. He had an object inserted in his mouth. He was about to spit it out, but for not the first time his sluggish reflexes saved his life. He could feel something indubitable against his bound hands. He was blindfolded and he had a notion that the object between his lips was the only thing keeping him breathing. Call it the sudden hunch of a seasoned snoop. He blew air through the (tube?) and reflected upon a number of small ironies. His hair in need of a trim. His rent unpaid. Bongo *tortured* for intel. The mightiest irony being how life imitated art. Before this messy business had begun, he had been perusing his collection of *Hearty Boys* mysteries, a pastime that often led to a crucial inspiration just when the trail was turning about as sour as expired milk after a thunderstorm.

The gist of every story was that swarthy Fred Hearty and his dirty-blond brother, Jake, would infiltrate a ring of shady characters, and before the third act, one of the two would be outed and knocked unconscious with a heavy blunt instrument and would end up shackled in a dark, damp basement. Usually the boy or girl they were both seeing would lead one brother to the other, and it would all end in quite the chuckle. Lax felt that his body was gently swaying as he tried to wriggle free. Blind as a worm on a hook. He weighed his lack of options carefully and decided that between the choice of hanging in a meat locker (it was very cold) and seeing his estranged brother's smug expression as he *unhooked* him, the latter was more likely to bring him misery and for much longer. He smiled at this additional irony, nearly losing the breathing tube for the second time. Then he heard a huge crash. Footsteps, sure and moderately slow ... *andante ma non troppo* ... oh no. The indubitable stuff was cut open and he tumbled out with a thud. The blindfold was pulled up to his forehead. A familiar face looking down at him, a face not at all unlike his own. Except smug, infinitely smug.

And Men Are from Mars

She bolted the door behind them. Ackmod tapped his chin pensively with his opera program.

"Care for a drink?"

"You're not Vulna."

"Aww ... but won't I do just as nicely?"

"Who are you and what do you want with me?"

"First, may I ask how ever did you know?"

"Even with that perfume on, I know the orgasmic odour of a Venusian. Horsehead natives have a far pithier smell. And, of course, it's a scent I've become quite accustomed to."

"You dog. Must have been a very long vroom."

"Sorry, I don't know what you mean."

"O I am just so jealous. As the Dulklings say, I'd love to jump your bones is all. Shame you're cratering up with that little nebulut."

"O yeah. Here we go! You can't chat six Marsecs with a Venusian before the subject turns completely liquid."

"In that case, have a drink."

"Sorry, my dear, I know the score too well. Drink with a Venusian and you wake up Saturnized on some tentacular craft bound for some universal asterhole of a lunar system. Or are you totally unfamiliar with the Venusian ballad: *Why I last saw your mother / on the dark side of the moon / Why oh why why ...?*"

A shadow crossed her face at the word *moon*. Her eyes became scorching and tetravalent.

"You are travelling with Major Ruckus. He is the one I am after."

"O even better! Jump my bones and suck out the marrow. Then shackle me in one of your Venusian dungeons and wail something awful on my helpless bassoon. And serve me bottomless helpings of dung flies as a delicacy for the most jaded of palates. And all to nourish your twisted rock-the-Ruckus-by-proxy fantasy. Why, you make me want to make my exit! Almost ..."

She laughed, shaking her head.

"You amuse me, Ackmod. But you have the wrong end of the console thrust. It is true that I want Major Ruckus more than any man in the universe. But you forgot to add that more than any man in the universe, I want him dead."

"Is this anything to do with the resort moon he demolished?"

"Why, what else has he done?"

"O nothing. You know, he did make a formal apology."

"You mean he said excuse me when his diddler was caught in the door."

"The weapons part was a typo. And there wasn't time to fact-check. And a number of lobbyists felt the resort itself presented an ethical conundrum. They feared an erotic prisoner's dilemma scenario would arise if they didn't take action."

"Major Ruckus murdered countless innocents. Venusians and Dulklings alike. And my friends and parents. And my brother ... Hans Fever."

"Yes, I heard about the eruption and the molten casts of copulating gangs free-floating in space. There is an exhibit in the Catastrophe Museum on Pluto."

"I loved my brother. He always kept a lookout for me. He said he would never leave me, ever."

"O don't tell me. That blares a trumpet. They exploded an entire star system to build a viaduct marquee. By the way, how about those life forms? They had to die for a giant, flashing thrillboard plugging the beyond-erotic acrocratics of Hans and Scarlet Fever!"

"So you know."

"Don't get me wrong. It was a splendid show. Much better than Cirque du Supernova."

"It's not too late, you know. I don't blame you for what happened. In fact, I am giving you a chance to help me. All you have to do is lead Ruckus to me."

"And why would I ever do that?"

"Well, it's obvious you're the brains behind the entire operation on this planet. That's why I'm talking to you. In addition, if Vulna is such a catch, wouldn't it be simpler if Ruckus were out of the picture? And I also understand you're a music enthusiast ..."

"Hey, let's stay civilized! I don't go in for that Venusian zükbox stuff. And I know your motto: *In space, no one can hear you sing.*"

"Can I tickle your hearing with ... how about some Haydn?"

"You sure know all the lines."

The Venusian 4-D surround sound had him surrounded.

"I started of course with Bach. A few of the Dulklings have an undeniable gift. Makes the planet worth visiting. Yes, I definitely have a soft pinion for Haydn."

"How about we play a little game then?"

"What kind of game?"

"If you can guess the name of the piece that is playing, I will let you live."

"It's a symphony for certain. How about Bach? A secular cantata question instead?"

"Three guesses."

"There are over a hundred."

"You are wasting time."

"*The Clock*?"

"Now you are wasting your breath."

"Hmm ... Ruckus wasn't paying enough attention ... *Il Distratto*?"

"One more guess."

"If you're the villain in all this, then how about ... *Farewell*?"

Ackmod smiled with an air of smugness. Scarlet opened her arms to embrace him in mock celebration. Then a Venusian skewer pierced his heart. He was embarrassed. To die like a kebab.

"Would you like to know the answer?"

"If it were Bach, I would have thanked you for correcting me."

"Symphony no. 94 in G major."

The orchestra on the zükbox suddenly boomed with an explosion of sound. Ackmod's eyes bulged wide with sudden awareness. And then they closed permanently. She held him close and whispered into his ear the scrap of trivia that had undone him.

"*Surprise*."

An Additional Twist

"But, Doctor ..."

"Better?"

"Yes, but ..."

"This is the most versatile model of the Derrick Crude line. It provides a modicum of pistoning comfort after the extirpation of the aforementioned little critters ..."

"Ooooooo ..."

Grant Smith clicked *mute*.

"Well, people, yay or nay?"

Dennis Dennis cleared away a spot of moisture in the corner of his mouth.

"I don't know. What do you guys think? Maybe it crosses a line ... but it is an alien fantasy scenario. Maybe then it's okay, given the context ... In any case, she's definitely not underage!"

Janet Buckshaw shot him a dirty look before assessing the flick.

"Maybe the message is instructive. When I was preggers with Frubar, Ron wouldn't come near me with a three-inch pole."

Sally Ann Hunter nodded with enthusiasm.

"I find this one quite innovative. And there is a definitive message. The doctor figure symbolizes an economic and authoritative force in society. And the alien child clearly represents the unknown minority that has no voice of its own. But what if she, the expectant mother, were to act as midwife to a process of compromise? Would it be equitable and, gosh darn it, even pleasurable? Here in this scene, she is bravely challenging the constant pressure of corporations upon the fiscal pockets of the community, as represented by her jouncing posterior."

Grant hocked up a sizable collection of mucus and released it into a nearby cuspidor.

"Yeah, it sure works for me. Now let's see if there's an additional twist ..."

"O yeah ... O yeah, Doc ... plug my alien womb!"

The Passion of Oober Mann

Suetonius lay in bed, blinking at the sunlight. Awww, what's the use of getting up? Damned if you do, damned if you ...

"Hello."

A small, naked man (no one he knew) was inching flatly across the wall of his bedroom. The man faced him, and at first appeared startled, and then absurdly self-assured, straightening his invisible tie.

"Yes, indeed! Why not? My literal creatures should behold their creator in all his awe-striking rawness. Feast your eyes, feeble mortal!"

"How did you get in?"

"Ha ha ha! I am not bound by your mortal coils. Locks and doors mean nothing to me as they do to you!"

"Your hand is bleeding ..."

"This? Fool, this is the symbolic wound of the suffering artist, or don't you recognize it?"

"Did you break a window?"

Oober Mann gathered up the bedsheets and wrapped himself up in them, fashioning a makeshift toga.

"To Rome with you, non-believer! Blasphemer! And on this day, I became flesh. A living, breathing man. And looked upon mortal brethren and liked not their muddy Image!"

"Hey, were you at my reading last night?"

"Ha. Ha ha. *Hic et ubique*. I am everywhere at once!"

He danced around the room wildly, waggling the now bloody sheet.

"Prostrate thyself before thy new-found god, a ray of light upon thy naughty naughty filth, or else prepare thyself to be smitten where ye now lie ... strong ... and firm ..."

He stretched out and lay down on the bed beside Suetonius.

"Proud noble mortal. Accept my stark patronage. When a god is demonstrative, demonstrate right back. Please. Accept the embrace of your progenitor, your ultimate *Écrivain père*!"

Suetonius eyed the bedside clock cautiously.

"Well, okay, but let's make it quick."

The Pie Conspiracy

The Sia Sisters waited their turn in a snaking queue. Raghead got to the counter first. He handed over a cheque. The clerk eyed the amount of social assistance and winked at him.

"And hey, lemme know if you want anything else. *Anything*."

It took her a while to notice the handwriting on the back of the cheque. She kept smiling. A real caper involving a desperate bandito. Now she could tell all her friends. The Sia Sisters pushed to the front of the line and opened fire on the ceiling. Screams and general chaos. They took hold of a man in his fifties tanned orange. Raghead tore open his shirt and removed a key on a chain from his neck.

"Any idea who that belongs to? You'll regret you ever touched that, punk."

The Sia Sisters opened fire again, striking glowing gadgetalia out of riddled hands. Raghead tossed the key to Alessandra.

"Take us to this box."
"Sure thing. My name's Leya, and I am here to assist you."
"The box!"
"Coming right up. And don't you want some money? We do have lots of money ..."
"The box."

Marco watched her in horror, stripped of his weapon and unable to stop the obvious stench of flirtation between Leya and Raghead. The clock over his head ticked slowly and mercilessly. She went to retrieve the silver box and brought it back into the special area. She hesitated with a sigh and stuffed a number of bills into Raghead's pockets.

"Raghead, go keep an eye on the others."
"Don't forget me, *you*."
"Open the box."

Leya opened it and removed a box wrapped in a knotted white string. She pulled the string undone and tentatively lifted the flap. It was a pumpkin pie.

"Reach inside."
"Ewww gross! Yet sensuous ... I mean I don't have the vocabulary to describe ... Hey, what do we have here? Like wow, a priceless paperweight!"
"Give me the tachyonometer!"
"The tacky-O-whaaaa? Here."

Piccina snatched the transparent tube and jammed it into a device on standby. Alessandra hunted and pecked through the menu functions.

"TACH-XTPP3 detected ..."

Leya, the clerk, gasped as a whirring noise reverberated through rows and rows of deposit boxes, followed by a roll of thunder. And in the wake of these vacillations, the Stupendous Sia Sisters completely vanished. Raghead heard the sound of their departure and looked down at his weaponless hands. From the floor, Marco guesstimated his chance and retrieved his piece. He was so excited, he couldn't resist a last-second quip as had been screenwritten right into the mouth of ball-busting action hero Hurt Hardass in *You've Got Blackmail*.

"Hey, lawbender! Time for one last withdrawal ... a withdrawal *of blood* ..."

He fired and fired, releasing the entire chamber into Raghead's back. And when he was older and greyer, he would still be telling what went down, although he had never been sure. The punk fell and just sort of dissolved into an orange pudding. And out of his steaming innards darted either a red lobster or a green scorpion. It scurried toward the exit, but Leya was ready. With a single stomp, her boot heel broke the thing in two with a squishy squeal or a squealy squish. The customers erupted into applause as she gave an elaborate bow for their live-streaming footage. This was turning into quite the first day! And years later, Marco Spuntano would pat his wife's behind affectionately and tell some unsuspecting stranger exactly how and where they met.

A Chilly Reunion and Expertise for Hire

"Hello, Despacio."

"Lax. Long time no see."

"What's that supposed to mean?"

"Hey, ease up. I just saved your life."

"Just add it to your list of outstanding favours!"

"Already clocked, little bro."

"Where the hell are we?"

"Meat locker downtown. Incredible deals on ostrich and bison. Recognize any of your crew?"

Stunned flesh of frozen identities. Over ten people on ice. Long-since goners. And under one of the plastic shrouds, Lax noticed a ring-bedecked hand.

"Bongo! Ahhwwww ... he was only a maturiteen. He had a whole world of chai ahead of him."

"Sorry, Lax. Nevermore will you sample his boysenberry überfruit in the morning mist ..."

"Shut up. I'm having a moment ... and anyway, he used to sleep in ..."

"There's no time, Laxy. That creep'll be back with more strays for the deep freeze. Let's blow!"

"Okay then ... Hey, wait a second! Blow! The bubble dame!"

"_?"

They slammed the meat-locker door shut and went out into the shared office space, where a dozen students were practising their fencing techniques. Unobtrusively, they began to turn the corner desk inside out. Nada. Lax got down on his hands and knees and scoured the floor for helpful matchbooks. Then they both heard a clamour over the crash of foils. Despacio slowly opened a broom closet, and a small man in green surgery gear rolled out and sprang to his feet.

"Well, gentlemen! I had hoped to make your acquaintance soon, but this is, how shall I put it, a mite awkward."

"Who the hell are you?"

"My card. Doctor Eli Xavier Ferruginous. But please, call me F. I am one of thirteen professionals covering the West Coast migratory route of expert witnesses. Strictly in coronary matters, you understand. I'm not one to bat an eye at these lurid little sex cases. It began with a blue slopsicle and so on and so forth. Tawdry stuff and a waste of my massive cranial capacity. But you'd be surprised. My practice is a sleepy, rather backward town in comparison. And it's no skin off my handles, to say this dude is crackers or that chick is cuckoo. Or to vehemently declare some loaded eccentric is completely *misunderstood*. Or that the blood doesn't match. Whatever. People like to hear the friendly avuncularisms of a *trusted* authority."

"And how about today, Doctor? Drumming up more biz in a broom closet?"

"Now, now. More flies with trifle than pound cake, as my dear old hen of a mother used to say, god bless her soul. I am here at your service. I have vital information that might interest you, concerning the bubble dame, as you so correctly monikered that hallucinogenic freak of nature! That is, if Mr. Laxness will assume a more agreeable colour. Colerics do not suit him any more than melodrama. Why, this simply will not do."

Despacio turned to his purple-faced half-brother.

"Hey, what is it?"

"Mr Laxness may bear a wee grudge that roadblocks his chances at playing space detective."

"This sicko was a witness at the Jimmy Juniper trial ..."

"O, man ..."

"In the strictest confidence, my personal opinion is that Jimmy Juniper was the twisted runt of a giant litter. He never showed the mercy you afford him. I don't imagine a dollop of guilt was ever squeezed out of that little mutant."

"He offered expert testimony that according to the ballistics I plugged him repeatedly in the back and buttocks. And the evidence insisted he was unarmed."

"I know, but you always maintained he was armed."

"Yes. He was."

"Between us three, oh, of course! His long-lost pappy wriggled out of the woodwork and tugged at the strings of our purses. And it didn't take much to purchase our love. I remember how much I wanted my own mobile practice ... Heh, it seems silly now that I have recreational operation theatres roving out of my orifices!"

"He *was* armed and I was hesitant, even to shoot him, once in the shoulder and once in the thigh."

"Yes, keep telling yourself that. As a wise man once wrote, *everybody is guilty of everything*."

"But ..."

"And did you know the jury was invited to Venusburb to stay for a week with the entire cast of *Media Whore*? Why, they'd send their own folks up the river at these prices! But, Lax, this runs much deeper than your usual heightened sense of backside stink. This time, you gotta get right in there, boyo!"

"I suppose I'm listening ..."

"First of all, Jimmy Juniper was not what he appeared to be. He was beyond an abomination. And believe me, I've known my fair share of abominations!"

"Whad'ya mean he was not what he appeared to be?"

"Well, boys, I think that question calls for a short field trip!"

"Hey, his avuncularisms *are* friendly!"

Since I Like Your Face

"O baby, oh yah!"

"Daddy?"

"Yes, precious?"

"What if I told you I had some of our most extreme *punishments* saved on impermeable media?"

"What?"

"Only the best ones!"

"Why you wily little skank!"

"And what if they were all ready and stuff for live upload? Then everyone would know who Daddy really was. Wouldn't that be delish?"

"What do you want?"

"A man, taken in by the authorities. And then there is going to be an accident."

"And ...?"

"You will receive a substantial reward. And the news will continue to report just your ribbon cuttings and not your ribbon fetish. Since I like your face, I'll even throw in a free happy ending. On the other hand, if you screw this up, you will not live another hour."

"Is that all, sweetie?"

"Pretty much."

"Well, how 'bout we ratify this deal with some slo-mo hedge-trimmer action?"

"Since you have the ethical fibre of rabid back-alley rodentia, sure."

"Oooooh baby oh yah!"

Assorted Mystery Blend

A grey-green wrap of knuckles.

"Yeah?"

"Ms. Velveteen?"

"Uhuh."

"Hi, I'm collecting information for the national census. Your household may have already filled one out, but we had this glitch in our portable document indexing system. All of the pictorial information has developed an inky blemish in the margins and is therefore not immaculate for posterity. We are out trying to verify and recreate all of our data pictures ..."

"Glitch, eh? Sounds like the government to me. O well, you better come on in!"

"Thank you kindly."

"Care for some tea while we do it? Or something stronger?"

"Why, thank you. That is downright sociable of you. I've been knocking on doors for weeks and you're the first to offer me even a lick of spit. Not that your tea's a lick of spit. I could sure use the pick-me-up."

"A special tea, I think. How about Mr. Lee's assorted mystery blend?"

"Best offer I've had all morning!"

Back on the Bottle

The crash of a wedding band. Tap tap tap. Suetonius peeped through the peep-hole and then unbolted the door. His head appeared over the taut chain.

"Hi, someone let me in. I'm on my lunch break and I decided to look you up ..."

"Yeah, it's not the greatest time right now, honey."

"I just feel bad is all and wanted to make a kind of confession ..."

"How about a little later?"

"Hey, are you naked in there?"

"Uhm yeah, I just got up ..."

"O you savage tease!"

She took a few steps back and then launched her body airborne, aiming her new seasonal boot at the door. The chain snapped. Could her new brave forget past wrongs and welcome a brave new future?

"You see, Sue, I made this really crappy bet ... At least it started off as just a bet ..."

She looked up. Suetonius was listening to her attentively while suspending a small figure from his shoulders. The small man was too busy to listen to anyone, actively attending to his bronzed light brown spear of pleasure. Suetonius lifted the man by his ankles and dangled him like a prize-winning snapper. Anaïs nodded silently and reached deep into her marsupial bag, feeling around ...

"No! Please don't shoot!"

She laughed as she hadn't since college. She produced a two-litre bottle of complimentary Swetelübe warming wasserfall and some recreational Virtugoad.

"Well, if you boys are having a party, then I sure as hell got the wine!"

Two for the Price of One

Dexter Savonarola Frains, known almost universally as Dick Frains, opened the cartoonish gift, half-expecting a Neopolitan bomb. There was nothing inside but a small manila envelope. He opened it up and dozens of glossies splayed across his empty desk. Chiefly, the Grim Reaper ravaging his bruised and beaten body. And it gave his flesh prickly gooseybumps just to remember. In addition, a giant Aboriginal fellow clad in ceremonial robe and cowboy boots was giving him a savage thrashing with his infinitely stiff phallus.

"O, Horse! Your mercy was swift as the wind!"

The aubergine phone chirruped.

"Hi, I'm right in the middle of something."
"Mr. Frains."
"Scarlet?"
"Did you get my prezzie?"
"Indeed. The quality is astonishing. You have outdone yourself."
"Listen, I need a favour."
"Flavour ... hmmmmm."
"Help me or I swear I'll never blackmail you, no, not ever again!"
"O say it like you mean it!"
"And Horse will never ream your welted rear again!"
"No, scarlet mistress of my soul! Don't cut me off! I'm in my prime, me."
"Very soon, a very naughty man is going to be arrested and it will not go to trial, understand?"
"And you need a scrumptious commentary to underline the pathos of such an accident and to exonerate those brave souls who slaughtered him in the pursuit of justice."
"Say, that's pretty slick for a walking hard-on!"
"But how exactly are you going to snuff that wicked cat? And can I watch?"
"All in good time, Dexy. But I like my printed lies fresh, not stale."
"And meanwhile, what about my needs? The snaps you sent were quite ... stimulating."
"I have a surprise planned for you. Once the deed is done."
"O goody gumdrops!"

Just Whistle

"Wherever are you leading us?"

"Always playing the private dick! And do you have time for a quick nibble, Inspector Numbnuts?"

F directed them into the Mirage Club and presented himself to one of the tall women with flowing eggplant hair.

"For three?"

"Yes, a booth for us and make it snappy as the bra you ain't wearing!"

"Hee hee."

"Those, gentlemen, are the real thing, I assure you. Radiation from an adjacent cluster near Trapezium saw to that. The firmness and colour and ripeness was never in doubt!"

"Your server will serve you real soon."

Another tall woman came over to them, nearly identical in appearance and stature, except for a green headband that pulled back her purplish locks.

"Like to start with something to drink? Our Oooodle Ale is on special today."

"I have an acute appendectomy under a rickety bridge in one hour, but what the hey! In this life, one must learn to snatch life by the short hairs! As the poet said, pluck the day, especially when it is dangling right in front of you!"

He rested his head against her expertly advertised bosom.

"Isn't that right, Jinny, my dear?"

"Like how did you know my name, hee hee?"

"O it was a rigorous process of deduction. Every gal who works here is named Jin."

"O, really? I never realized ..."

"Don't let it concern you! Instead, fetch a jorum of the Buxom Brew, and please keep in mind that reduction is always an option!"

"Okay, mister, hee hee."

Lax and Despacio looked around the establishment. By the bar, tall young men in black uniforms with self-same features bantered jocosely with their aubergine-maned counterparts.

"How *did* you know her name?"

"Wow, flatfoot. Why don't you hand me your dongle so I can plug you in? Don't you find this place in any way *odd*?"

"To tell the truth, I'm not so hot on their Supernova Supremacy Fries."

"Those are Uranusian in origin. Buy another clue, boys."

"Well, they hire young people with the same ... urhmm ... proportions, hair-styles and ..."

"What if I told you they were clones from a Trapezium colony, the embodiment of a long-awaited wet dream? Manufactured consent, here and now and ready to order. The most seductive of saltimbanques, bred solely to, excuse the salacious pun, *skirt the issue* of all earthly unions and the most minimum of wages. These babes are churned out by the dozen and are adopted by some lucky couple with no idea of the inevitable mechanism in their blood. Their genetic makeup is like a flock of homing pigeons. They do their business until they come of age, and as soon as they are ripe and tasty, they are inexplicably drawn to fill out an application form at the nearest Mirage Club ..."

"Alien clones, reared and groomed for the restaurant biz?"

"No, of course not. That's just the tip of the cock ring! They are fresh blank pages with überhuman cells. And if they were to fall into the wrong hands, they would realize their unimaginable capability for destruction ..."

He gave their returning server a prolonged cuddle for effect.

"And we would all fall into an age of apocalypse, isn't that right, Jinny?"

"Hee hee."

"That's all very fascinating, Doctor, but what does it have to do with your ruining my career?"

"These clones have specifically sprouted from the Juniper colony near Trapezium. And Jimmy Juniper was one of the early weeds fouling up their bumper crop. Take comfort in the fact that in the eyes of the whole universe, you performed an unsung service in blowing him away. A dark-alley *accident* was a matter of convenience. Nothing personal. It was in fact time for his cellular structure to be unactualized. And to do that, his madcap creators needed a dummy for the window dressing. A real dummy, Mr. Laxness."

"Then I didn't ... but who? Who shot Jimmy Juniper?"

"You've already met him. And that brings us to the next chapter of our story that concerns you boys in particular. Phew! Finish your beer. I suppose some things must take priority over a ruptured appendix. And we'll need a hand. Come, Jinny! We have need of you!"

"Sure thing, hee hee."

Fill in the Blank

"Tea's super."

"Super strong?"

"I can take it."

"Aphrofusion. Lord knows where Lee gets it."

"Nice."

"Would you like a sandwich or anything?"

"Why, a sandwich would bitch-slap sociable straight across the room."

"Mr. Lee, a Boston Butt for the nice man!"

"Sure."

"Well. Fire away."

"S'all here, mostly. Just some discrepancies about your marital status and dependants and so on ..."

"Well, I'd be more than happy to clear anything up."

"So, you live here with Rufus Marauder ..."

"In sin? Yes, you can put that down for sure."

"And children?"

"Didn't you know? Rufus doesn't get it up anymore. I've suggested several improvement shows but he won't listen. Anyway, in the bedroom, it's just like a based-on-reality show. It's all in the editing. That is, of course, until we are a reality show. But between you, me and Mr. Lee, I think Roof is getting his rocks off with his ambiguous co-star Brick Steed. Roof says they're just onscreen remote possession love scenes, but they sure spend a lot of time in rehearsal. And I thought the EnterActive Game Centre was being installed as a building block for our relationship. But him and Brick just slip into their dermasuits and data necklaces and lock me out. And last week, I found a discridge of *Planet of the Prickly Plants* ..."

"Hold on two shakes. This is quite a lot of information."

"O I'm sorry. You hardly need to know about my lack of a love life."

Suddenly, she seized his shirt collar and stared him full in the face.

"And I want kids. I need 'em so bad!"

Mr. Lee put down the plate with a crash and glared at her.

"Sammy's ready. And Mr. Lee, why don't you go see if there's a hedge that needs trimming or something out back? Now, where were we? Ah yes, the yummiest part!"

Vanessa Velveteen, the perfect hostess, whipped out a curvaceous tube of imported Dijon.

"Well, dude, how 'bout it?"

The census taker nodded, feeling powerless before this display of advertising genius. He could never say no to product. She used both hands, one to squeeze the tube, and the other to work the bulbous nozzle, just like in the ad campaign. A gritty yellow substance shot out and began to glow in both sets of eyes. He took a bite. Then another.

"When you're done, how about a tour of the game centre? We can play any game you like."

"Intense."

The Return of Digiget™

"Need any help there, partner?"

"Yes, I would like to return this device."

"Okay, let's just mosey over to the Customer Distress Centre."

"That counter? All right, then."

"Radina, the Y-BTCH paperwork, please. Now, was there some particular issue with the device?"

"Yes, it was supposed to cycle earth music and display a cluster of terracular feeds ..."

"Unhuh. And did you try reading the manual?"

"Yes, I looked at the one-page diagnostic, but it didn't help one mimeogram."

"Uhmhuhm. Let me just jot that down. *Kanji comic did not help ...*"

"I have some very important business in this place, and I thought this device would assist me."

The Future Simple shifter of the month sniffed the proffered device carefully and banged it a few times on the distress counter.

"Are you sure you turned it on first?"

"What?"

"You have to turn it on, friend."

The shifter began to massage the buttonless device and it began to vibrate warmly with trills of surprised activation.

"There, it lit right up, problem solved ..."

"But I already know how to interact with a bottom-feeder in basic pseudo. In fact, last time I was marooned on this refuse disposal of a planetoid, I had a different model the size of your empty noggin, a Widget 667™ I believe. Once they worked out the initial bugs, of course."

"Widget™? Hey, that's the brand I use."

"You don't have a Digiget™?"

"God no. Widget™ is the only kind of gadgetalia I use. And the way it feels in your hand! A shame really. We used to carry that line."

"This clickless wingnut was supposed to receive all the global media and wireless feeds. But all I get is a continuous loop of effigy burning, mob violence, snuff footage, torture arboreta and wardrobe dysfunctions."

"Wasn't it awful when Bootney Peas caught her décolletage in the Cesspo door?"

"As soon as *Hostile Makeover* blitted into my lobes, I knew the device was malfactorizing."

"Okay, I see what you mean. You were looking more for softcore family enterteasers and then you caught the reality-based *All Washed Up* or *Domestic Swap* or the presidential episode of *Phat Matt, Assassin*, and then you're like, what gives, I expected some tender body-double love is all ..."

"Actually, I was hoping for some news reports."

"In all fairness, sir, the device is prestalled with ten thrillion bodcasts of *Rock Feller 3/69*. And nobody tracks and pans worldwide abuse like Rock!"

"_?"

"Now here's an episode of *Hogtied Snog* ... a classic ..."

"_?"

"*Backdoor Dad*, season six ..."

"See here, it just cycles in a useless loop of futility. I need some information pertinent to global affairs."

"*Who Not to Do*, this time in Canada!"

On the nit-sized display, an oily, nearly bald Briton forced a seated woman to face the mirror with him. She appeared petrified.

"First, we're gonna hack off all yer hair. And then Farkakta Brown is going to doll you up real proper-like. And then Bratt and Madga are gonna teach you *who not to do!*"

Farkakta nodded and loomed over the worried woman with a bell-like laugh.

"But first, we need to whiten them teeth. Don't worry. All you need is this caulking gun and some Fang whitening grout, the only product for really getting inside them stubborn tesserae!"

The woman's screams were muffled as the show's sexy builder-guy began the whitening process.

The Future Simple shifter smiled.

"This is a really good one."

"And right in the middle of the feed, this voice-over began telling the most horrible story ..."

"That's standard. Digiget™ comes stuffed to the max with a few introductory OralBooks, including *The Crack of Heaven*."

"The one about the black-market boytoy conspiracy?"

"The first and last book I ever read! And for people who couldn't get enough of *The Crack of Heaven*, Digiget™ includes the Ignoble Prize–winning series *The Chaos! Quincunx*."

"Never heard of it."

"O the oral feed is totally ooohsome, as read with accompanying effects by retired adult actress Simony Blue."

"Sounds like a heap of steaming uraniung to me."

"More like one sizzling tube stick after another! It's so hot you can almost taste it!"

In response to the Future Simple shifter of the month's unmanaged enthusiasm, in a little-too-late, last-ditch effort to save humanity (and other assorted life forms) the Digiget™ 555 decided to recall itself and combusted with what it calculated was a reasonable level of spontaneity. Acrid tendrils of subatomic brain damage floated up into the fluorescents.

"Aw nuts, not another one!"

"I told you. It's a piece of sherk."

"Well, I am pretty sure our Future Simple Squadri can repair this. An' tell you what. We'll throw in those modifications so you can unclog a real news streak like the PCB."

"Good. I find Persian news is the most reliable, don't you?"

"Uhuh. Could I just get your name for the Y-BTCH form?"

"Oztrich."

"Heh. And how do you spell that?"

"O-Z-T-R-I-C-H."

"And that's your last name?"

"My first is Evgeny."

"Cool. I know this wicked supplier named Evgeny. Address?"

"293 Cukulum Canal. In the south peripheral."

"Hmm ... must be on the other side of town. Okay, please fill out the rest of this Y-BTCH information ..."

"This is absurd, really. The thought of building an item more disposable than its energy source! You really are festering in your own age of obsolescence. No wonder you Dulklings died out ..."

But the shifter of the month was already tracking other walk-in marks and sizing them up for multiple packages with his reptilian sensory unit. In fact, he couldn't help his tongue from leaping out twelve metres in front of a freaked-out kid who said he was just browsing. Then his eyes directly glutinated after an open-mouthed man in a grey suit with an aroma of bewilderment about his shrugging shoulders. However, another Future Simple associate tackled him in mid-sentence and began to sniff and fondle his wallet and other valuables.

"Have I got a special for you!"

Several injured. One dead. Oztrich snorted. The shifter returned and nodded reassuringly with a fixed packing-paper grin.

"Okay, that'll do'er. Our distress support team will give these ashes a thorough poke, once they have a window in their schedule. And here's your reparation tag, Evgeny. Don't lose that now and no worries. We will definitely twitch your digits."

One Giant Leap

Dear Dwayne,

Over the past year, I have struggled to make things work with you and your thankless offspring, although I want you to know I loved him more than I would have my own flesh and blood.

Gosh. This is so hard. I realized that I'm not getting any younger and I want to try to do all the things that have made me afraid. And I have met someone, a doctor. What difference would his name make? Anyhoo, F will be calling the shots from now on, and he says a long trip with him would do me a world of wonder.

Luckily, I stocked up on Pazzissimo frigid dinners, so you should be good to go until you meet somebody else.

Best wishes,
Fay

Next Stop, *Fritterdom*

"Feltcro me up."

The census taker secured her LeatheX ensemble as she activated the room's JoyToy solenoid.

"By the way, I never caught your name."

"Uhm ... Spörk."

"Hehn. How unusual."

"Really? It originates from Sblowvia."

"Now, Spörk, have you ever tried one of these things?"

"Um, no."

"I just clystered the discridge called *Fritterdom*. It's a softcore waster with minimal levels of degradation."

"Okey dokey."

"Now you need to use your pelvic control to input some meta/sext. These stage directions will help to smooth out the flow of the EnterAction. And don't tell me. Surprise me."

"There."

"Ready?"

"Go!"

"*Before fully activating the EnterActive Game Centre, please turn off all interruptions ...*"

"See you on the other side."

Help Wanted

Jin and Jim rumbaed into the Mirage Club, hand in hand.

"Hi. We were wondering if you had any positions free?"

An identical although infinitely wearier face looked up, catching the shadows cast by a reservation lamp. She appeared incapable of surprise.

"Sure. One of our girls left her post today. She was a total mutant anyway. So we do have room for two more. We always have room for two more ..."

"Cool."

"Please fill out this application form and I will forward it to our Überseer system."

"Okay, Überseer grants you permission to join our local family under business licence #RDXPHUM-37805. Would you please step into the back for a quick ident scan?"

Jin and Jim hopped into the scanning chamber, hand in hand.

"Now we just want to check your genetic composition and history, just to be thorough ..."

A team of Jins and Jims stripped Jin and Jim down to their netherwear and strapped them into the Mirage Club iDent 7000.

"Now hold still. We just need a sample of your short hairs to analyze."

One of the Jins ran the swiper over Jim and one of the Jims ran the swiper over Jin. Everyone in the chamber was pulsing with a primordial magnetism that spliced them to the core.

"Okay, looks like you are both qualified to work at the Mirage Club. Congrats!"

"I can't believe you checked her out."

"I can't believe you checked him out."

But Jin and Jim were well beyond getting any ideas. The combination of the establishment's PSI field and their own compartmentalized DNA was mixing faster than a Mirage Club Zucchini Mantini, on special every Saturday. They were already being pulled toward the singular will of the leisurely dining continuum, the host cell from which there was no escape. The attendant Jins worked steadily to perform the magic act of minor surgery on Jim that would put his personal organism in continual contact with head office. The attendant Jims did likewise for Jin. Just a shallow hole in the back and *pop pop pop*! The pair rose and permitted their demi-brothers and demi-sisters to dress them in outfits three sizes too small. They rippled forward for inspection, displaying a crispy attitude and an eagerness to find everything they heard absolutely hilarious.

"Your first shift starts today, from four to four. And then tomorrow. And then tomorrow ..."

A Quiet Life

"Hah. Isn't it extraordinary? That casual dining experience is coming out the wazoo with nanotechnology and stringless theoretical suppositions and yet, I thwarted their hold on Jinny here with nothing more than a sonic toothbrush. Call me old-fashioned, but let this be a lesson to us. Sometimes methods tried and true work the best."

Lax and Despacio trailed behind the sprightly doctor, with Jin giggling in tow.

"Where to now, Doc?"

"Now, I hope you two pokes are ready for this fervid encounter. And I might need some very sharp-shooting, Lax."

"I don't carry a piece anymore. You put a stop to that."

F threw a naked hypodermic over his shoulder. Lax nearly dropped it but caught it before it hit the concrete.

"Made you flinch! It might come in handy. I always carry a few spares, for emergency infusions. They also work well as medium-rare stakes through the heart. Why, you'd be surprised by the number of uses."

"Mind letting me in on whose hindquarters I'm supposed to needle?"

"Jinny, which way, dear? The signal and smell should be overwhelmingly strong."

"Beats me, hee hee. O wait a mo. Here. In here!"

"You know, I am sick to death of abandoned tripe factories, aren't you?"

"You said it, brother."

"Now, gentlemen, let me throw a little more fire and gasoline upon your general dimness! There is a device in this building that should not fall into, shall we say, *less than responsible* hands."

"What do you mean? What is it?"

"To you, a donut chain keychain. Or gas station lavatory access. What's the difference? Other megalomaniacal parties are interested. And this very afternoon, they are going to murder one another."

"And you want it – this thing?"

"A run-of-the-mill time-warper and a clone army, up for grabs? Gentlemen, I just want a quiet life. But it is my duty as a practitioner of medicine, nay, as a professional healer, to try to keep these monstrosities out of anyone's malignant pickers and stealers. And besides, you realize this planet has buttered my bread ever so nicely. Also, I'm not sufficiently packed for its utter annihilation."

"Why should we trust you?"

"Ah, Brothers Dumbass, why indeed? The alternative, as I foresee it, is that you toddle on home and play with yourselves. I thought a couple of private dick pretenders could be useful at a time like this. However, I don't *absolutely* require your services. Jinny and I can handle this."

"Hee hee."

When Re-Enactments Go Wrong

Officer Spörk broke the front door down with his shoulder. He found a nude woman draped over the inert body of a man. This domestic dispute had gone haywire. He pulled the woman off the body.

"He's dead ... he's dead!"

"Settle down, ma'am. Now why don't you tell me exactly what happened here?"

"I found him that way. He was dead when I got home. He wasn't breathing ..."

"Now, ma'am. This man is naked. Did he happen to engage in any strenuous activity that might have led to his untimely ...?"

"It's hot in here. If this were a movie, I'd ask to take a shower. Would you like for me to take a shower, officer? It's big enough for two ..."

"Now, ma'am ..."

"What are you waiting for, officer? Whip out that nightstick. Let's play a game of bop the protester!"

He detected a familiar odour that left him quite disorientated. No, it couldn't be!

"Who are you?"

"Duh. That's easy. Vanessa Velveteen."

"Hey little lady, I've got news for you in case you didn't know. You are not of this world."

"That's crazy! What kind of fantasy did you program into this do-hickey?"

"You aren't finished answering questions!"

But at that moment, a chair crept toward his bottom and roughly seated him. And a series of articles, including a scarf, a belt and a lamp cord, flew across the room and bound his arms to the chair. And a pair of heels leapt into the air and struck his forehead. Her handcuffs dissolved. She seized him by the temples.

"Now what was that about answering some questions?"

"Ffffft ... how did you know?"

"Well, it was obvious you weren't a census taker. And I know about the flesh kickbacks between you and Tooth. And leaving alien afterbirth at every house wasn't the most discreet way to operate. And it was easy to see that you and Tooth were in cahoots, scanning the From My Pad section for the next victim. And now it ends."

"But I have a mission of the highest importance."

"Which is?"

"There is a population problem on this planet. The females cannot conceive without me!"

"That's a myth. This planet is already overpopulated."

"But the probe! I was sent from a branch of the universal call centre on a matter of vital importance. I am part of a ceremonial care package. Their enclosed illustration, rendered by the Dulkling Carl Sagan, revealed their deficiency, plain as the tentacle under this husk. You see, they don't have a hoohoo …"

"You züking trog! Check the pricking order. I am working in partnership with the call centre. In this matter and all matters concerning Terra Dulkis, I am your superior."

"Then tell me what to do, boss. I'm yours. And with your help and boost of confidence, I think I could work my way to the top!"

Vanessa Velveteen (a.k.a. Vulna) patted his pate affectionately, clearly mystified by this turn of events. But behind her, a hoarse voice called out her name.

"Vulna … listen …"

"Who are you?"

But she knew. Her psychpath senses had bottomed out. She had failed to save him.

"Vulna, I am not … here. This is only my leftovers …"

"Ackmod …"

"Shhh. Listen, beware of the Venusian woman. She is … looking for Ruckus. She tried to … kill me but I had a backup of my … vitals. She …"

"Who?"

"Scar … let … Feeeeeever …"

"The acrocrats?"

Ackmod nodded, coughing up a grey-green substance.

"You must stop her … revenge …"

"Be still, Ackmod. There's still speranza …"

"No. I bounded off zükbox signals … into feeder. I am not here … in this disc … ridge …"

"You mean you are inside *Fritterdom*?"

"Yes. And Vulna … I need … you …"

"I need you, too."

"I need you … to reload me … launch me … into … space … like music …"

"O Ackmod. Don't go …"

"And … Vulna … I never … told you …"

"No, I know Ackmod. I love you, too. I never said it but …"

"Vulna … you never …"

"Yes?"

"Never got on my nerves …"

"No?"

"You're all right."

And the call-centre representatives reverted back to reality in a sombre mood. Vulna snatched up the discridge and wiped away mounting tears. And Major Ruckus watched her with feeling through the eyes of Mr. Lee.

Off the Block

Oober Mann felt his hands fly across the keys of the emerald Hermes. It was as if the story were writing itself. Vanessa had dropped by to take Faustus for a walk. She had also asked him to hold on to one of her fancy stargets for safekeeping. The thing gave out a funny vibration at all hours. And Oober had felt swathed in tranquility since taking it in. And Suetonius had given him some writing tips and the name of a helpful analyst. That pair of crazy kids had embraced him warmly and had warned him to stay clear of stray gushers. And he had vowed to remain true to that plucking sensation in his gut and nothing else. And now he felt more than calm. He felt *inspired*. So what did it matter if you began the book with a mysterious conversation and never quite explained it? On one hand, the loose end was an opportunity for endless variations upon the most minor of themes. Or, if he were to take the cowardly way out, it was the perfect existential thread to loop back into a solid tie-up. Followed by jubilant wrap-up music, naturally. Not unlike the structure of a symphony.

And the book was already perfect. It only asked of him a scarcely disruptive commentary. And within him, he felt a swell of voices surging. The beauty of a single non-essential incident was aggrandized and transfigured from fleeting notion into the ornate cornice of a larger architecture. And how did this piece relate to the sum of its parts? Who knew? But it lived! And the music! Canopies in the shape of an endless counterpoint. Undulating waves of sound and internal rhythms of speech and the very tempo of language in motion. Why hadn't he heard these things before? At last, he was learning to tell the story of everything he knew nothing about. And it was time to lend a little stage direction to the contending voices in his head. And his forehead and temples throbbed with the promise of a hitherto undisclosed Art. What had she called it again? Ah yes, the masterwork *Major Ruckus* ...

So Hard to Find Good Help

Anaïs enjoyed a shower scene for the third time that day and let the water run. She felt the queerest sensation. But the water felt good, and closing her eyes, she could let her body remember every caress and every touch of those desperate boys. And the smell of fresh bannock permeated the place. The liquid soap seemed to burn like flame as she rubbed it all over her limbs. And all her memories were steamed up into one heaving ... The bathroom door flew open.

"Suetonius!"

"Anaïs!"

"O, it's *you*."

"Anaïs, kindly get that tush of yours out here."

"_?"

"It's an emergency!"

"Did you go to that sushi place again? You know it simply doesn't agree with you. What about ..."

"Anaïs, this is serious."

She strode out, rubbing her hair furiously with a pale blue towel as she listened. Fern giggled and looked away, placing a tray of bannock on the kitchen counter.

"Yeah?"

"Anaïs, do you remember when I told you about Jenkins falling off the roof garden?"

"I think so ..."

"Well, I underestimated the threat he posed to us. In fact, he let the other executives in on all of our plans. They were about to discuss my immediate dismissal and the start of a gruelling investigation when, well, I had no choice, really."

"What happened?"

"I had a little tête-à-tête with my gofer, Genius Boy. A good lad, of inestimable extract. I saved him from one of our outsourced warming-liquid factories. I need not say where. But the conditions were simply abominable. He was a virtual slave, and I don't mean in the virtual slave line. That's another tale ... for later. Anyway, we have gotten quite close in the little hutch we call a boardroom, and I put it to him that it would not go amiss to lose a few bottles of our Extra Spicy brOil in the coffee machine."

"Whoaaa ... and?"

"Well, as you can imagine, they forgot all about Jenkins. The narcotic agent took effect at once. Then they got the bends. And then lost their priceless lunches. It went on for over an hour before each of them burst into flame ..."

Fern peeked around the corner, still grinning from ear to ear.

"Sounds like you've had a hectic day. You could use some bannock."
"Leave us, Fern."
"Only I might need a big bonus this month, for all my hard work. You know, forgetting to clean out my ears and failing to catch any stray flies with my open mouth ..."
"Fern, you are the clumsiest blackmailer I ever met! Consider it done."
"Have a nice night, you two. Don't do anything I wouldn't do."
"Well, where do we stand?"
"If we get through tonight, we are pretty much in the clear. It is not that uncommon for boardrooms and their members to spontaneously combust. That's just business. If you can't stand the heat ..."
"But where are they?"
"Well, Genius Boy is indebted to me. He won't say a peep. But when it came time to tidy up the bodies, he began to cry and told me he had sworn an oath to himself that in this country, he was through doing the dirty shirt – *la camiseta mugrienta* – he likes to calls it."
"What is the world coming to? That leaves us in a fine fix!"

A Last-Minute Script Change

Rufus Ruckus waited for the pyrotechnics crew to get their act together in preparation for yet another brolleywood triumph. This was the episode in which he travelled back in time to track down another wormhole virus that was filching pretty pennies from pre-history, although Rufus (a.k.a. Major Ruckus) knew this was impossible. But it made for fantastic edge-of-the-toilet, toenail-biting television! And now his character would solve everything by *reversing the polarity* and by creating a beautiful explosion. He glanced around nervously. He definitely should have heard from Vulna by now. Ah well. Who could have guessed that playing a sleazy space buccaneer would make him into a huge hit? Then, in the alley cutting across Collier Way, some movement caught his eye. It was a little red dog, and he guessed at once it was their plant on this planet. This week playing an Australian shepherd miniature and next week ... who can say? He slipped into the alley unnoticed.

"This is rather sub-ortho, dog. Any news to report?"

The dog stared up at him meaningfully, eyes glistening.

"Is it Vulna? Is she in trouble? Show me, pal."

The dog pertly nosed in the direction of a back door liminal. A creaking sound ...

"Okay, we're ready. Now where the hell is Ruf—? Stat, we need mancandy on the double!"

A toss of red hair! He reached for the rusty door and felt a piercing sensation in his side. The venom toxified his bloodstream at once. His wildly dilated eyeballs met those of his attacker.

"Whckkkk ..."

"Miss Scarlet Fever, at your service. Or should I say funeral service? Let me start off by apologizing for the interminable suffering. Should be over in a few years, as soon as the dissonance serum has completely broken down your life form. Meanwhile, they will bury you on this planet in a state of frozen torment."

"Nwwwwuufttttt ..."

He collapsed into an alley puddle, visibly lifeless under the leer of a sculpted Baudelaire.

"Sorry, Major, but you blew up my favourite moon."

A Hit of (E)

Commendatore Oztrich vlitted through the available channels on his Digitation 3.7c™ with increasing flummox.

"Frains outlined the astounding spectrum of fiscal shenanigans that Rufus Ruckus was *allegedly* involved in ... *Allegedly* (and however ecstatically), he had managed a Mini Ruckus Soft Serve ring that turned the young and star-struck into the used and exploited star-stricken. Various no-talents have asked for more attention immediately. And here are some pictures of them coming forward ..."

Thirteen minutes of suggestive snaps were shown.

"In addition, hunky throb Ruckus was *allegedly* pumping and funnelling *human* organs and *gangland slaying* slayers, as well as *vital drugs* through a warming-liquid subsidiary of his *triple-ledgered in the red* production company with its *staggeringly monstrous* failures. His affiliate Swetelübe Ltd. is unavailable for comment, although a rumour has just been texteled to our bogcast saying that the slippery bigwigs are already busy handling the *execution-style* firings in response to public concern."

Oztrich shook his head and inhaled his alterspliff. Man down. And a good man at that. A damn shame.

"This demi-hour of miscellaneous but perfectly legal slander was made possible by generous contributions from Nonsensorium, a proud new member of minorCast ..."

Oztrich winced. Public access. He flicked his Digitation™ nervously.

The image faded out and was transmogrified into a cherry and cinnamon swirl, full of dog-paddling starlets. **Channel (E)FM**, so hot and bright it burned into his retinae and submerged brain.

"Tonight, on *E-Crash*, you knew him best as the inflatable Major Ruckus you fingerbanged off to every humpday. But in a terrible turn of events, the show flared up to success only to severely afterburn him in the ass-teroid ..."

Oztrich snorted.

"But first, will Bébé Lala attend the funeral? We'll have more to come on that. Hi, I'm Candy Coton on this totally awesome evening with your hit of E. Fans and psychostalkers of Rufus Ruckus were rapidly losing sang-froid today over the sudden death of the hero that gave their lonely grey little lives such meaning. He was *brutally butchered* by an explosion in downtown Sulphurview that sliced off his *ominously good* left ear and tore loose his *spanking and strangling* arm.

And Nora Krupp, lifelong binner, was *startled and horrified* to find his *gleefully severed* manhood wriggling in some newsprint."

Candy did her trademark little dance in front of the senstation strobe before addressing the witness.

"Nora, you are live and ready to dish. Deal with it!"

"Yah, I was doing my rounds. One time Otto ... that's my oldest ... one time he found a whole furkey in a rehasher. Some fool went and threw the sucker away. This times I'm thinking spicy Dayglo sausage for supper ... hah hah. Weirdest frickin' thing I ever seen. I hit it with my stick a buncha times. I'm gonna beat that thing long as it takes. But no way, it gots ideas of its own. And strike me dead if I tells a word of a lie, it was frickin' huge. This big ... no *this* big. An' Otto he would have wet his overbippers ... but me I just run after it yellin' and hollerin' an' then one of them film people came running over and recognized it right off ..."

Candy shook her head sadly, pausing to suck on a red lolly.

"A brave woman. But will Bébé be a no-show as dozens pay their respect?"

The senstation strobe ran a touching montage of departed members, accompanied by searing music.

"And when we come back, was Rufus the target of an adolescent star cult? Or did his imaginary eating disorder lead to this deafening cry for help? Also, you won't want to miss our interview exclusives this week: *When Victims Make Victims*."

Candy began to wave a foam finger. One side read *scary*. The other side read *sad*.

"And I had just turned twenty-seven and I was still so unsure of myself and then at the pool party, Musty (god rest his soul) said, 'Why don't you ask Roof?' So everybody was having Winky Dinks and taking off their bathing suits so I ... I took off my trunks and stepped into the hot tub with Rufus and said, 'When will you find me a part?' You know, all cool like, and then he asked me to ..."

Candy wept openly, half-smiling.

"I first met him ... at the toga rave. I was wearing this new ukini and it was like a rubber band up my butt and he was talking to some ... *important people*. Yeah, whatever. And I threw my drink in his face, that'll show him hey, and said, '*Stop staring at my* ****!' Ooohps, can I say that on the air?"

The sensation strobe flicked to a scene of people at a party, monotonously dipping zucchini sticks into dip for kicks. Then one of the men noticed a bottle poking out of a marsupial bag. He lugged it out and flexed a merry bicep before opening it with his shiny bran new teeth. Immediately, a series of visible and audible voices floated out of the bottle neck and renovated the entire party. A tedious board game became a pool table and cupboards full of canned spaghetti became an operational bar with tantalizing nozzles. A young man jumping out of the window from sheer boredom landed in a pool of laughing nudes instead of upon the courtyard cobbles. The free-flowing liquor surrounded two women and transformed their jeans and jackets into sheer mini dresses, and changed their zucchini sticks into giant cucumbers. One guy, suddenly in a purple thong, sprang up with an erection, and spilt his glass all over himself. A girl in a bra caught his eye and poured the entire contents of her glass down her front.

Soon, everyone was doing a self-spilly and was licking or being licked clean. It was quite the icebreaker. And the more they drank, the more hilarious they became. An exercise machine was transmogrified into a fast-action pumping Vandomizer 5100 for the enjoyment of all. One woman fainted under a pile of bodies. Another man threw up over the balcony while his pals laughed and prodded him with steak knives. And as two guys fell out over the same woman, one of them, our well-built initiator of this magical evening, seized a pool cue and shoved it up his rival's quivering rump. The scene froze on his red face twisting around toward the trepidatious yet intrigued woman with rage and lust, as a limuck drove through the upstairs window. And then the outburst melted into a giant cloud of lactiferous alcohol that flowed back from whence it came and was smoothed over by the reassuring voice of an announcer.

"Because with Smarmy's the message is in the bottle. By the way, Smarmy's is not responsible for any messages heard or interpreted while enjoying a smooth, yummy Smarmy's. While enjoying Smarmy's, operation of heavy machinery or a motor vehicle or an automatic machine gun is not recommended. Smarmy's – do you want the message or not?"

Candy Coton made random location eyes at the new rainmaker.

"Ooommm, I could go for a Smarmy's right now. How about you, Horse?"
"Ha ha. I never touch the stuff."
"O sure you do. Once in a while it sure hits the spot."
"I guess so."
"Well, Horse, what does our celebrity weather look like?"

Horse stripped off his shirt and pointed to a graphic of the urban grid.

"Fake rain, all week, here … here … oh, and over here."
"Hehmm … I just love fake rain. It's so romantic."
"I guess so."

"Thanks, Horse. That spot was brought to you by Gormy's. Cuz if it's not Gormy's, you're sick as your uncle's monkey."

"And continuing all week, *Steeped in Scandal*! Did Dijon Diva Vanessa Velveteen run off with broken homeowner Mr. Lee and was it his special blend of aromatic green that did the trick?

And also before we go, everyone is dying to know, will freeboobing filmlet Bébé Lala attend the funeral of Rufus Ruckus? Wish I could help, but I don't have a freakin' clue and that and much much more! Good night."

"Um, Candy? How long do we have to pretend to talk to each other?"

"Shhhh ..."

Wrap-Up Music

The Mystery Meats factory door burst open and Tooth laughed his electrocutionary laugh of murky liquid. He looked around the premises, one hundred and fifteen percent confident his park-bench vision had come to fruition. The clones snapped to attention and went directly into casting couch mode. It was in their interstellar genetic makeup. They had no choice. But even Tooth was amazed to see them rip open their mandatory rags with that *lived-around* look. They stood erect and gained several inches on their ordinary beanpole. And they began battle with one another, chaotically and without cause.

The place was now a writhing mass of stiff pummellings and semi-rapacious orgies. He was not completely pleased with the way this deal was going. Where on earth could he shift a bunch of mating and rioting clones at this late hour? His stock was completely overrated. But his giddy brand of fuzzy logic was taking control. He looked around frantically for a clean getaway. He expected the plucky bubblet could pry him out of this rotten raspberry comfit, no questions asked. But his effervescent companion was nowhere to be found. And besides the writhing piles of clones, the whole world had gone squirrelly. A pair of legs hoofed it by, its torso covered by a foul-smelling funnel, and a garish shadow of a thing adjusted its collar and followed in hot pursuit, pausing only to read aloud some gibberish from an open book.

"Oooooooooooooh."

Single-occupancy seniors lay in quaint beds with freshly announced idols and idolesses of raw gilt while obsidian-eyed demons prodded them with elbows and offered sacks of ready cash. Other characters tried to come to terms with their misshapen protuberances, including a bent spoon for a nose, a French horn for organs and an oboe for an erection that tarantular passersby kept blowing. And then there was a thundering clatter of a once shopping cart now packed full of scarred bodies continually sliced by the aluminum armour they wore. Tooth recognized the cart pusher's semi-broken face. It was Danny.

"Hey. Why'd you let me fall out the fucken window?"

Tooth averted his eyes, only to return to the manoeuvres of some more clones, who were glowing shades of neon eggplant and constructing stringy rope ladders out of gristle and other internal unmentionables. The mutant men and women shinnied up the strands as if performing a striptease and prepared to assume control of the factory tenderizers. However, at the top, adversarial clones were pouring down boiling cauldrons of Mirage Club Miracle Goop, at once scalding and exciting the relentless climbers. But one of the clones was being escorted out of the fray by a mysterious gallant with a caduceus, also accompanied by two lagging gastropods.

"Hee hee! Wheeeee! Hee hee!"

And some of the clones crept closer, turning turnip, flailing spindly arms at the syringes penetrating right through their clammy flesh. And some of the stragglers were encouraged by the surrounding rankness into a complete regression, turning into unknown types of lizards, frogs, turtles and fish with a variety of uneven appendages and skulking back into a piping bowl of miso, and deep within that primordial broth, they took cover under a bed of seaweed. Tooth kicked away a bunch of scarab beetles gnawing at a high quantity of tin in both of his legs.

"Shoo."

A rat-like creature in a studded cloak put on his reading glasses and began to read an incantation to the astonishment of a cat-mouthed companion.

"Mrowwwww ..."

While the spell was brought about, a large mottled moth laid eggs in the back of the cloak, producing sulphurous holes in the fine material. A towering precipice had arisen and countless clones were following a company lemming playing a piccolo right over the edge. A second tower was speedily erected and a grounded expert pointed to a three-page fold-out of a phallus and offered detailed explanations in Dutch. Upon the base of the tower, which had shot up out of the mouth of a drowning eel, there were peerless engravings of unparalleled adventures. Tooth recognized some of the rendered episodes. The capture and five-minute cuddle with a transfixed Squealgee kid. The census-taker fake handing over ten trillion croni for a slab of flesh and a *Map to the Almost Stars*.

"Just goes to show, interplanetary immigrants don't have the first clue ..." He smirked to make out the heroic battle between him and Lax Laxness and admired the detail of the bingo players in the background, even as Bongo's head was presented on a platter to Effie in her capacity as residing queen reigning over all matters bubbly. And there was the first plastered ad for Cockerel's Classic, the ginger beer that just won't quit, until, of course, it did. And there were the Sensational Sia Sisters, this time performing a ballade by Brahms upon an ossified clavier fashioned from the bones of hundreds of victims, with accompaniment that plucked and sliced across the entrails of men strung up through a gargantuan cello.

And the three members of the stellar cleanup crew were riding a heron the size of a pterodactyl over the proceedings, with two of them hanging limply over the sides of the hovering bird. The third member stood defiantly upon one of the slowly flapping wings with her flaming red mane whipping in the violent waft of Mystery Meats production. She leapt down amid columns of pork sizzlers, pausing to adjust the peephole in her scanty outfit. And she found herself face to face with her Venusian nemesis in a similar auburn outfit made out of lean strips of material that criss-crossed over her flesh like strips of uhmmmm overlapping bacon in a spot brought to your attention courtesy of Mystery Meats. The women circled and sniffed each other eagerly, each uncertain whether to brutalize or fall in love with the other. Or both.

"Your friends blew up my moon ..."
"And you killed my entire crew ..."

They each rose about six storeys into the air before the CinemaGenic (CG) effects kicked in. They were seamlessly pasted into a backdrop that went from Venus to the Horsehead nebula. Betting satellites fired odds back and forth. Then in a toasty blur of sienna and scarlet, at lightning speed, they propelled themselves at one another with their personal pulsars launching a voracious barrage of feline content. Every one of the assembled freaks in Tooth's latest hallucination gasped as their lunar alloy claws sprang out of their respective sex-ups. Their killer claws interlocked across space and time and Scarlet Fever struck, swiping at the very heart of underdog Vulna, who was erroneously listed upon the oddscreen as mustard monarch Vanessa Velveteen. More than satisfied with her enemy's shredded frontismesh, Scarlet plunged her claws deep into the Horsehead's centre but was shocked as her porny claws snapped right off.

"Yeah, what else you got left? That heart stopped long ago. Besides, it's not even my best one. You know what you hit? Try pure designer titanium, baby!"

And in slow motion so slow only the Laxness brothers could have perceived it, she backclawed the meaty strips of Scarlet's outfit and sent her reeling backward, to the oohs and ahs of some lingering clones below. Now no one doubted this was the last-minute skirmish for the universe that had been foretold in a dozen engrossing inserts. As for the Laxness brothers, the Mirage Club Buxom Brew had made them logy, and in spite of the excellent odds on a longshot, they had soundly nodded off in a corner. The two starladies would decide the fate of the world, and more importantly who of the pair was ultimately more doable. Scarlet Fever reached into her netherwear and felt around for a solid five minutes before pulling out the huge clone remote. It would be indiscreet to describe its shape, particularly at such a vital juncture of the work of genius flooding Oober Mann's persnickety dreams and nightmares. Vulna launched into a triple lutz worthy of Aksinya Slutskaya (otherwise known as the *money jump*) and used the toepick momentum to send Scarlet into a double flutz, freeing the remote from her grasp.

"Oooooooohhfff."

The throbbing clone remote was kicked onto a low-hanging prime-rib unloading ramp near the ceiling. The *mute* button was accidently turned on and the clone orgy continued without the benefit of Decihell Surround Sound. Both of the combatants growled before flinging themselves into a perilous and thrilling embrace that made short shrift of what was left of each Levitop. Then, a sudden stir-fry blast sent both of them flying into the groaning activity of an affiliated Gröner's Gravy assembly line. A sun-weathered, smiling old couple appeared and fought over a brown tube.

"If the label don't say Gröner's, then don't give it one goddamn lick."

For a while, they both participated in the comic action of swallowing each timed spurt of gravy to keep the labour platform beneath their feet from drooping. This presented valid commentary on the inability of even übermodel societies to keep up with the most sickening of mechanized processes. All of the clones and demons below concurred that this was the *deus ex machina* of the entire book and scratched themselves in profound admiration. Meanwhile, Tooth observed their zany danglings with a sudden pang of regret. Maybe because of his irresponsible undertakings, thousands of children would open their Brunch n' Munch packets and bite into gravyless semi-circles of processed salami chock full of mutant alien DNA. And kosher kids could lose their faith completely ...

The two contenders slipped on stray spurtings and frantically clung to the hanging pipes that flexibly pumped up and down, each time releasing a thick jet of hot gravy that doused the panting women and the unblessed White Veal Mealies below. Tooth clenched and gritted his namesakes. His mother had worked all her life in the fish cannery and she had warned him he never wanted to find out what got into them cans. On cue, she made a cameo appearance and suddenly swung an Iron Chink at a heap of fornicating clones. It slit them wide open and sliced off their limbs and then in a geyser of aubergine and Beta C++, their guts were removed and the remainder was dumped into a series of conveyered cans of Starcross Tuna Surprise.

"Watch yerself, boyo!"
"Hi, Mum. You look well, considering ..."
"Say, son ... while those goofy dames are having their drag-out, drop-dead difference of opinion, why don't you grab hold of that time do-thingy?"
"_?"
"Right there, on that skull and crossbones organ. Trust me, they won't mind."
"But Mum ..."
"Yeah yeah, and hurry the hell up. Don't be a numbnuts like your father."

He gazed up at the two redheads, still slathered in gravy and struggling to defy the quaint earth custom of *gravitas*.

"Oooooh soooo slippereeeee ..."

"Damn you, Newton!"

They tried sincerely to cling to the ridged pipes, but the more they pulled down on the pipes, the more piping gravy squirted out. Below, the clones cheered blankly.

"Yeah, take it!"

"Yeah, bring it!"

"Clean them pipes, sistas!"

Vulna slipped again and with a moan was hanging by her teeth alone. Scarlet dug her fingers into her opponent's slick body and tried to use her as a ladder. But another timed release of the white stuff was too much for either of them. Caught in the enviable leglock of a bucking Scarlet, Vulna lost her grip and both gals landed in a bubbling vat of lambinated tzatziki. There was a lengthy pause before the shot of their torsos erupting from the mix could be taken for *Sexaflex Weekly*. They hopped up out of their torn Levitops and continued to wrestle in sopping sheer camis provided by Sgioia. So if you're looking for some wicked joy, slip into one of our Sgioia knockouts. Never leave *anything* to imagination again. Meanwhile, Tooth sidled up to the Sia sisters, inching closer and closer to the tachyonometer. He reached over the shoulder of the playing Piccina.

"Excuse my reach ..."

She whipped her head toward his less sinister hand and without hesitation bit it off. He stopped to watch the jet of fresh blood. He kind of needed that. He looked down to see Alessandra grawing into his thighs and feeling around for his most musical parts. And a nearby group of clones began to nose the air. Then they leapt upon Tooth, tearing his limbs and fighting over the spoils of his innards, for all the world like a pack of aubergine hyenas. It took the brashness of a lone bird-man to stick his beak right into this business, poking and jabbing the snarling Sia sisters with his long staff and never letting his wings fall slack, until his long bill had a secure grip on the much-coveted tachyonometer. And then he seized the waist of a giggling female clone and launched into instantaneous flight.

"Hee hee."

He soared over the heads of the clones and assorted demons freshly spawned from Tooth's delirium, as well as over the slumped form of the Laxness brothers, sleeping much as they had in their shared crib as infants. Vulna looked up with desperation in her eyes and with tzatziki up to here, but her fierce adversary

Scarlet Fever pulled her back by her dripping hair and down they went for more. Hearing the splashes and screams, the brothers Laxness woke up and began to stretch.

"What time is it?"
"Did we miss anything?"
"Nah."
"Oooorghftttt!"

They approached a completely disembowelled Tooth, who tried to show his surviving fang in spite of his slit throat. Now he was nothing more than a talking head. The brothers waited as he made several speeches on the importance of living a full life, before singing a dark aria for fifteen minutes. Then at the close of an astounding *cabaletta*, he at last began to lose his composure.

"Ahh ... boys ... ahh ... nuts ..."
"It's poetry justice."
"But why did those bookstore kids get it in the neck? They never hurt nobody."
"They *knew* ..."
"The deets, you miserable ..."
"There's a ... book."
"A book? What, one of your filthy little kiddy pin-ups, your millimetre footage positively oooozing with mangamé and torturously tickling with mentai tentacles? You sick twisted ..."
"Despacio! Let him talk. What book?"
"I ... can't ... remember ..."

Tooth stopped. His eyes bulged wide, full of the spectre of his mother down a long dark tunnel, and then he made good with giving up the ghost and reverted back to his old advertising smooth-browed self, at last at peace. Lax Laxness tore open his shirt and beat his chest and wept and Despacio laid a comforting hand on his shoulder.

"Bound to happen. For the best."

Suddenly, with a huge sploosh, Vulna and Scarlet trounced out of the tzatziki vat in a speedball of untethered desire. Having exhausted their respective repertoires of fatal blows and fondleholds, they now resorted to intensive strategies of seduction. On both of their planets of origin, the *coup de grâce* of a month-long battle was often a one-night stand, known in a Venusian euphemism as *taking a dive*. And a packed corner of the universe was watching, totally immersed and helplessly aroused. It was not an isolated incident in the Outer Erogenous Zones when in response Mount Tabatha erupted and triggered the mutation of a cluster of spineless organisms into blind red pigments, later gathered up as wild particles and packaged as an expensive spray called Lust Dust. But only one of the two divas would live to appear in the advertisement. And Scarlet Fever was not going to take it lying down. She was going to give it standing up. She clicked a tiny button on her unchastity belt and turgidized a ferocious dill that made the impressive male clones cower. Despite being dunked and bumped, Vulna took the expected invasion in her stride and spat out more tzatziki, stretching and reaching to the bottom of the vat. Scarlet bored into her with burning eyes as the barbed dill began to whirl.

"C'mon, you know the drill!"

"Oooooooh!"

But when Vulna emerged for the twentieth time and wiped the excess gravy from her lips, she was holding the much-prized clone remote.

"I'm tired of this station. It's time to change the channel!"

A perfect orange nail broke on the button as she flicked the clones into Mirage Club last-call mode. At once, they seized hold of Scarlet Fever and meticulously began to skewer her everywhere with tiny little meat sticks. She was writhing and jiggling and jouncing in agony when abruptly out of a steam pudding, Commendatore Oztrich appeared, bearing a cup of Lapsang. He licked the end of a stir stick before aiming it at the now-screaming hors d'oeuvre Scarlet Fever, and being a gentlemen of the old school of interplanetary espionage, he blew a mercy dart into her swanny neck. She went still. The dill stopped spinning. And more than half of the universal viewers discontinued their Omnivoyeur media bundles in disgust. Oztrich smiled and sipped his tea.

"And that's how we did things in the not-so-secret service."

"In the tick of time, Commendatore."

"Vulna! I never forget a voice."

She looked down, suddenly bashful, and pawed away globs of gravy and tzatziki from her soaked Sgioia camisole.

"Know what, Commendatore? I think it's time we went for that drink."

"Bravo!"

"Just give me a nano to clear up …"

She clicked another greasy button on the remote and one by one, the remaining clones climbed into the vat of tzatziki and initiated their auto-erotic self-destruct sequence. Each one of them joined the heap and within seconds sank under the bubbles, self-pleasured to death.

"My word. It's not a pretty business, this."

"Her people had a saying: *What happens on Venus stays on Venus.*"

At that moment, Despacio Laxness tapped her on the shoulder and asked her what on earth she thought she was doing. She smiled at him come-hitherly. Still dripping, she began to massage the necks and shoulders of the brothers, before clunking their similar heads together, gently *horseheading* them off into a hypnotic sleep. They slumped to the floor, getting some of the gravy at last. She dragged both of them through the delicious sludge and laid them out on a meat dolly.

"I'll take care of these two. Best they forget their little adventure."

"Was that a dash of Oblivio you just applied?"

"Does the trick every time!"

"A pity, though. We could have ... errhum ... done whatever we wanted with them. After all, they'd never remember ..."

"But we'd remember, Commendatore."

"Ahem. The cases of Plutonian plonk in my craft says otherwise ..."

"Ah well ... the night is young."

Vulna accepted the Commendatore's offered arm and began to wheel the meat cart forward.

"Looks like I am in sore need of another shower scene!"

They both laughed long and heartily as they casually strolled away from the exploding meat factory.

"Whoops. Looks like I burnt dinner!"

"You know something Vulna? This whole mess began because my identity was stolen. And if I hadn't lost myself, I would never have found you. So you might say, in a manner of speaking, that in becoming lost, I at last found myself."

And with this speech lingering upon his impassioned lips, he embraced her greasy, gravied body and kissed her with all the forceful, creepy intensity of a breath-improvement ad. At that instant a few feet away, a group of obese locals competing to appear on a reality show called *Haul Ass Home* reached their final destination point and the streets erupted with impromptu fanfare. Tinsel and confetti and blow ticklers abounded.

"Hey, isn't that Vanessa Velveteen?"

"Yeah, pimping Weiner's Ravin' Gravy or some such ..."

There was a heartfelt quarter of an hour as the famished men and women in HAH bibs surrounded her and started licking her everywhere, aiming to lap up every inch of tzatziki and gravy.

"O my, that tickles ... and stop biting ..."

And directly afterward, Commendatore Oztrich helped her and the entranced Laxness brothers onto a pink-and-orange float, and for the rest of the day they waved to the crowd cheering over the blaring wrap-up music accompanied by a trumpet voluntary.

Everyone was blissfully oblivious that underneath the scraps of scorched mystery meat and departed saucerkraut, deep within the tumorous carcass of Tooth, something was moving. One bubble. Then two. Then five. The world had not witnessed the last *pop hit* of Effie the Effervescent Bubblet.

"Screw the almost-human. He was just holding me back. Now it's time for my big break!"

Flex Time

The wrap-up music was muted.

"Well?"

Dennis Dennis, the youngest of the censors, jumped up out of his seat, trying to hide the tent in his stain-resistant slacks.

"So ... think anybody went missing here ...?"

Janet Buckshaw licked her Nicoslopsicle thoughtfully.

"Seems like standard softcore snuff stuff to me ..."

Sally Ann Hunter withdrew her hand from under her dress.

"I found the way the alien women liberated themselves in gender-neutral fashion from their restrictive outfits a profoundly positive statement. In addition, they showed a refreshing level of autonomy in expressing their sexual preference in a time of crisis. And symbolically, at all times, they were battling not against themselves but against the commercial corporate machine that threatens to wash all of our brains in its runoff diaspora ..."

Grant Smith thumbed a button on the viewing console with restrained impatience.

"Well, Sally Ann, that kind of talk just gets me in the mood ..."

There was a knock on the door. A tall man in a security guard uniform entered the room.

"*pi'htikwe'* ..."

"Jeremy *is(i)n~ihka'sow*. This is Jeremy. He works on a number of projects with our friends in the Cree Nation. Remember *Tasty Treaties* and *Backdoor Dealings*? Those were two of our awareness campaigns produced as adult films. He has even acted in a few of them, including one of my favourites – *Up the Creek without a Casino*."

Jeremy nodded gallantly. Sally Ann smiled at him and hiked up her skirt.

"Jeremy, *a'stam* ..."

Grant tapped a different button and one of the library shelves of uncensored material turned on its side to reveal a hidden room. Dennis Dennis nearly exploded in his pants.

"Grant, you mean we got it?"

"What do you think, Dennis? We did get the funding and it was just installed. And I suggest we make use of it or else they'll think we don't need it."

Sally Ann was already engaged with Jeremy, pulling on his long, dark ponytail and guiding his lips between her broad thighs.

"Mmm ... bring your savage mysticism to momma ..."

Grant snapped his fingers and Jeremy followed, dragging Sally Ann Hunter by her greying hair.

"O yes ... I want it rough with your untamed tribalism!"

Janet Buckshaw lifted her sweater and flashed her bra at Dennis Dennis.

"Well, cowboy, how many seconds you think you can stay on the Buckshaw?"

Dennis followed her into the Flex Time Chamber. She laughed hoarsely as he pulled out his twelve-inch tool.

"What else you got, kiddo?"

Grant Smith watched with dry eyes as Jeremy caboosed an elusive Sally Ann on the sea otter sofa.

"Yessss ... pound me with your freaking history! So ... spiritual ..."

Dennis made a lame joke about oral history as Janet began to give him a civil servant special. Grant sidled up to Jeremy from behind. His broad shoulders and mighty buttocks reminded him of a Metis he had known back at St. Giggory's. It was a post-colonial fantasy come true. And soon Janet Buckshaw, who was still pleasing Dennis, was being entertained by the clever tongue of Sally Ann Hunter, who had surrendered to a swift, new sense of restorative justice between her strong thighs, and the giver of which was being tickled by the minimalist instrument of their fearless supervisor Grant Smith.

"O yeah, I'm gonna give it to you like a taxpayer! *itwe'* ..."

Jeremy crushed the attempt between his powerful ass cheeks.

"O yeah. Give it to me like a taxpayer."

Time and Tide

Fay arrived at the airport to find F in line with a tall, young auberginette who was clinging to his wiry frame and whispering breathy nothings into his ear.

"F!!!"

"Excellent. You made it. All packed and rearin' to go, I see!"

"Uh yeah ... I guess."

"Buck up. O, and let me introduce you to my ... adorable niece."

"Hee hee."

"My niece Jinny. She'll be coming with us."

"O. Hi."

"Hi there! Hee hee."

"Now you ladies get acquainted. I'm sure you have a lot in common! And me, I'm about to cream my distressed cut-offs. Always good practice to spank the old joy smacker before a flight. After all, you never know if this flight is going to be your last ..."

"Hee hee."

In the men's room, he began to visualize his teetering stacks of *Malpractice Weekly*, the periodical for practitioners brashly unintimidated by a little extra practice.

"O yeah, nameless nine o'clock! Why don't you take off that gown ...?"

Your typical dude two urinals down eyed the rapid hummingbird of the doctor's working hand quizzically. After some initial hesitation, he reached down and began to do likewise. But in one of the stalls, there was a rattle and a thick viscous bubbling sound. F speedily zipped up and put on his infrared molecular penetration sunglasses. Through the arched spine of his jerking neighbour and the stall walls, he could plainly see he had company. He crept over to the stall with his electroshock therapeutizer and kicked it open.

"Blub blub blub ..."

"Thought you could pull off the old switcheroo double-cross?"

"Give me the tachyonometer!"

"You are rather persistent for a mere hallucinogenic symptom of a dead man. Well, sorry to burst your bubble, but the doctor is *in*!"

He put on his TouchyTouchy gloves with a satisfying snap and with his electrified stick began to prod her down the toilet.

"Now you can join your iconic career!"

"Nooooooo ..."

Flush! Double-flush! The increasing group of self-pleasuring men at the bank of urinals stopped for a second to offer him a raised eyebrow of rebuke.

"Gentlemen, I wouldn't go in there for quite a while! It's a real pity, too. She was once a household name."

So Glad You Made It

The Swetelufts tightened their TouchyTouchy gloves with a satisfying snap and smiled politely at one another. When they arrived, Fern and Suetonius were already there, surveying the situation and making amiable small talk. Mr. Sweteluft adopted a stern expression and clapped his hands together.

"All right, settle down. Now the job at hand is to get these bodies into those barrels."

"What's it worth to you?"

Mr. Sweteluft wrote down a figure on a piece of paper and handed it to Suetonius.

"Now where exactly would you like these bodies, sir?"

"We'll dump the barrels across the way. They'll get mixed up with the oil and tobacco company barrels (and bodies). None the wiser."

Suetonius and Fern nodded their approval and some *getting things done* celebratory music started up. In spite of their grim determination, the endorphins began to kick in. Fern merrily mopped up decades of blood and semen traces. Suetonius performed impressive feats of strength and diffidence, heaving heaps of dissolute bodies into warming-liquid barrels with a great *kerrrunk* that should have haunted them forever. Anaïs scoured the boardroom mugs fastidiously while Swen ran white vinegar through the coffee pot. He watched his wife move her hips in time with the music. Damn, his wife was hot! He couldn't believe he had never noticed.

"I'm sorry, darling. I've been so preoccupied with this wet, old liquid plant. I promise, after tonight, I will make more time for the two of us."

Anaïs beamed, all teeth.

"Correction, Swen. You will make more time for the *three* of us."

She made an invisible arc the size of her future belly. Suetonius slammed down one of the warming-liquid barrel lids, thinking of nothing but lambskin blunders.

"Darling! You scheming minx!"

"Yes, it's true. After all this time, your seed finally agrees with me."

"Now take care, Anaïs. The window is ajar. Mind you don't catch a chill. And leave these cups and barrels. We can manage ..."

But as they began to roll the barrels out with large hand trucks with pump-action grips, they slipped on some stray puddles of Swetelübe Extra Strength and fell on the floor in peals of laughter that appealed specifically to the cycling song. They took turns chasing and tickling one another, at the mercy of the powerful scent of the warming lubricant. They crossed the bridge in a fantastic mood, doubling up with Fern riding on Swen's lap and with Suetonius riding shotgun in the lap of Anaïs. And when Fern read the exit sign and cried it out, they all giggled uproariously. Once down by the shore, they rolled the barrels into the water with ease.

"That's the end of those pesky executives."

"Yup."

Swen slipped his arm around Suetonius.

"You know, being a creative writer who speaks a few languages, you could make a killin' ..."

"I've heard this pitch before ..."

"How would you like to start at double the salary of this deadwood? That's on top of this pissant little removal deal. Why, this is just the tip of the nefarious."

"Yup. It's to be expected."

"Well?"

Fern cleared her throat.

"O, and Fern of course! Fern can be ... treasurer."

"Now my cousin can get some gold teeth."

"And how about an extended lunch hour, for just me and Anaïs, on Wednesdays?"

"You drive a hard bargain, Mr. ..."

"Saanich."

"Well, Mr. Saanich, welcome to the warming-lubricant business!"

"I don't know what to say."

Later that evening, Swen sat on the rocky beach, watching the tenacious Native scribe administering unimaginable ecstasies to his warming-liquidated wife. He smoked thoughtfully, entranced by the aerobic motion of one body thumping against another.

"Oooooooh ... harder baby!"

"I'm just doing my job."

Fern crept toward Swen and pawed away the pencil-thin cigar. She lifted her woolly skirt and with a few adjustments sat firmly upon his gawking face.

"That's right ... mmm ... come to momma!"

Meanwhile, after their mutual collapse, Anaïs and Suetonius lay back and stared across the water at the flashing **hell Oll** sign and drifting barrels.

"Y'know, I think everything's going to be okay."

"Yeah, me too."

Make-Me-Cry

The spent group of censors stepped out into the fading light and rubbed their eyes. Janet Buckshaw lit up an extra-roguish Rogue and spat beautifully before inhaling.

"Nice evening."

Dennis Dennis scratched furiously. Grant Smith reached into his lime windbreaker and frowned.

"I was thinking of a skip and a hop down to the Save-U-Quick. Who's in for a short romp?"

"O yes! I could do with one of those happy chickens. Anyone want to go sharesies?"

"Yup. Count me in for some of that sweet action."

Grant smiled dryly, applying his last drop of Make-Me-Cry.

"A gang outing then."

The Pink Slip

By the time an interlocked Jin and Jim arrived for their shift, work was no more. The integrity of the cellular walls holding up each Mirage Club in a sixty-kilometre radius had been compromised. They showed up in time to see their new place of employment quiver and shudder and then with a great groan, they heard it climax into utter collapse. And now the entire block was littered with the chic, adorable dead. Even the homing signal had been crushed by a fallen heritage arch. A stony, smashed lion roared up at them. And bearing witness to such destruction and feeling such desperation, the old directionless clone pheromones kicked in once again.

"O Jim!"
"O Jin!"

They tumbled with abandon upon the former men's room loveseat underneath a glamour shot of Vanessa Velveteen bending over to pick up a stray helping of mustard and looking back, realizing she had just been caught in the act of doing so. The environment, designed to spur on their Trapezium-style copulation, performed its usual magic. The authorities and fire hazardists furiously snapped pictures for their respective calendars before advising the clone chain survivors to, in not so many words, *get a room*. Then hand in hand, the pair headed for Hydromel Mall.

In an elaborate retro-pop montage, they tried on a number of tight outfits in the Big n' Tall n' Irregular store, all the while sucking on pear sludgies. It was clear they were more than keen on one another. They embraced in the glass elevator with no more than a chocolate daikon cheesecake and a filched pineapple between them, while below, Dwight paused in mid-flirtation with a soft-touch, hard-sell home improvement hunk outside Chez Shed and watched his adopted son's giant hands squeezing her Beaux-Arts bosom and digging deeply into her Rococo buttocks under a bran new pink slip. With a mixture of melancholy and resigned approval, and with a tinge of taboo wishes, fat tears fell from Dwight's eyes, completely soaking his DeathByDiscount bag.

Stand by Your Man

Dr. F sat cheerily between Fay and Jinny with his lead-lined plutonium travelling case for the post–Cold War dealmaker-on-the-go resting upon his lap. He only let go of his case to slyly stroke the bare thigh of one of his companions.

"Why, it's a palatial bungalow. Plenty of room for a heady mixture of research and romping about!"

"Yeah."

"Hee hee."

He was happy as a pig sitting down to an extra helping of mud pie when a finger tapped him on the shoulder. It was one of the flight attendants.

"Sir, you will have to put your case in the overhead compartment."

"Excuse me, li'l lady, but do you have any idea who I freaking am?"

"Sir, it is regulation to comply."

"Well, I have a whopping permit in my pants. Care to examine it for yourself?"

"Sir, now please co-operate. Hand me the case and I will put it in the appropriate place for you."

"Hmm ... I believe we have something of a prisoner's dilemma on our hands."

"On the count of three, sir."

"Tell you what. Run over there and get me another of these fine mind-benders, and I'll give you more than a few Sir Bordens and you can even keep the change. And by the way, has anyone ever said that you bear a remarkable resemblance to the ever-bonerific Bébé Lala?"

"I've heard that one before, sir. But maybe another mind-bender would do the trick ..."

Suddenly F stared at his empty freesbestos cup. He felt about the non-biodegradable bottom for any mysterious traces and touched a noxious substance to his tongue.

"You won't get away with this! The best have tried!"

"Don't take that tone with me. I'm only doing a favour."

"For who? O no! No, anyone but *him* ..."

F slumped over the armrest and into Fay's lap with an emergency detoxifying hypo in his left hand. The flight attendant (known to her adoring fans and obsessive paparazzi as Bébé Lala) seized the case and began to run down the aisle in her svelte SexaFlex pumps for the double-crossing vamp with a heart of gold. And as part of Jinny's food-chain training, she knew through a flash of automatism how to plunge the needle into F's heart, intending to momentarily stop his system and subsequently shock it out of complete arrest. He jerked all over the aisle with the syringe flapping madly in his front. The two women aimed to follow Bébé and her hot little box, but all too conveniently the kosher meal cart had appeared to block their pursuit. They sat down and cradled a trembling F helplessly.

"Figures. The first time I have a fling ..."
"Hee."

Rather callously, the in-flight flick began.

"Ahhh ... not *ME II* ... don't you know the sequel is the worst one!"

These Kids'll Eat Anything

Upon entering the Save-U-Quick, Dennis Dennis produced a nickel.

"Hey, let's flip for the chicken!"

"Tails!"

"Heads ..."

Sally Ann Hunter stared down at the beaver in dismay.

"Well, Dennis, you win again. Your record is impeccable."

"Cool. I'll meet you on the way out. And put me down for half a honey-glazed!"

Like a kid let off his leash, Dennis made his way merrily toward the cereal aisle. He scanned the rows of rainbows and visible crunches.

"Yay, Chocolate Oat Goats!"

He made eye contact with the rutting goat on the box. Five minutes passed. And then the subdued lighting expanded into an illuminated field at eventide. Candied pan pipes filled his ears and sugar-coated goats began to romp across fields of marshmallow.

"Pschaw! But where's my collectible toy?"

And then over a nougat hillock and deep inside a shady nook of cinnamon, he met chest to chest the last three adult actresses he had just watched with the others. Koko Puffs wrapped her long arms around his neck. The other two casting couchers, Krispy Kreem and Alley Berry, mounted vigorous kids[1] and rode at high speed toward him, clinging provocatively to their waffle horns. Koko unbuttoned his shirt with a tiny pink spoon and then with a sprinkle of sprinkles undid his fly. And with a sugary grin, she produced the most abstruse cereal box toy he had ever seen.

"Oat goats'll eat anything!"

"Now that's chocolickin' good!"

A week later, a clerk found Dennis Dennis in the middle of the cereal aisle, horribly gored, with a big old smile stuck under his milky chocolate moustache.

1 No actual "kids" were used in the making of this Gap Gene hallucinogen.

Happy White Chicken

Sally Ann Hunter watched the glazed chickens turning. She liked to watch. The chickens turning. A pair of eyes appeared through the mid-rotating fowl and they were watching her back. And Sally Ann was startled. It was none other than Takeout Lee, the indefatigable star of fistfuls of underground films, who more often than not played an energetic delivery guy. And Sally Ann was more than startled to remember his much-advertised measurements.

"You're Takeout Lee!"

"Yeah. Also Takeaway Lee in the U.K. If you thought the VAT was screwing you, check out *The Vat* starring Takeaway Lee, Poppadom Joe and Saucy Hotstuff! Fill your gob today ..."

"Err ... I should like to purchase a happy chicken."

Takeout Lee whistled as he reached for the chicken and held aloft its dripping body. He made a pouty, kissy face as he sprayed it with a tube of Yummy Grease. And Sally Ann was surprised to find herself licking her lips with anticipation and slowly unbuttoning her jacket.

"Would you like to come behind and spank the chicken? Old custom. For luck. And it's a real naughty little baster. Don't you wanna get back here and spank it?"

Ever so oddly, she did. She looked around furtively at mouths watering all round. Now behind the counter, she slapped the chicken firmly with a spatula, sending globules of grease flying against the glass. Takeout Lee took her hand.

"Not like that. Like *this*."

"O. Ooooooh!"

Sally Ann turned red. She could not believe she was about to enjoy an extra spicy *romanza* with an Asiatic chicken clerk, let alone the beyond-intimidating Takeout Lee, squeezing his baster madly.

"O take me away, Takeout Lee!"

"Cluck cluck cluck me, you clucking cluck!"

Poor Sally Ann. She was bound hand and foot and found turning and turning on a spit set up for the perfect shot in a rotisserie fireplace live-action feed.

Simply Fuming

Janet Buckshaw waited in line, where things were getting antsy. The autoclerks had recently become self-aware and were on strike for more oilings. Also, on account of an excess of rainfall, there was a boil-water advisory, which at once brought to mind The Great Water Shortage of the Dusty Depressed Zeroes. People were anxiously bickering over cases of bottled water. And this busy backlog of shoppers had drawn out additional kooks, who were inexplicably attracted to this fracas like flies to a honey-glazed chicken. An old man in line with a hundred dollar bill was waving about the wrinkled face of Sir Borden and trying to haggle over the two-for-one price on suspect langoustine. After holding up the line for almost fifteen minutes, he abandoned the scampi in disgust, with his bill unbroken. Behind him, a harried woman was asking directions to other shops with the casual manner of a visitor at an information bureau. She periodically ceased persisting in distracting the cashier with her questions in a frantic attempt to prevent her daughter from purchasing additional bananas.

"We'll have too many bananas, too many bananas!"
"Bananas!"

The cashier also stopped with one of her favourite customers to relate a long story about some creamy potatoes she had cooked and how they had failed to meet with her significant other's approval. All of the customers waited for the end of her harangue. Had her creamy potatoes received adequate validation? After all, they had reminded her of some unresolved issues from childhood, and perhaps those potatoes held the mystical key to her overgrown psyche. The next customer cast his pears and persimmons down in front of her, hence bruising them.

"Y'know, I think your potatoes are the pits!"

Janet waited patiently with her giant sausage and sourdough rolls on special and was only jostled from time to time by the water nuts. She stared right through the glossy spottings and breakups and breakdowns, thinking only of a new pack of smokes. She was staring at the package under glass when the lineup was suddenly divided by a giant dromedary packing whole cartonloads while amiably puffing away without visible effect. Janet dropped her sausage with astonishment. She steadied the astounding animal fresh from the desert of all her desires and straddled the happy beast. She bounced merrily against its smokestack of a hump as it rode away toward an ashen horizon. She was never seen again.

Pseudo-Operatic Boy Bang

Grant Smith scanned the impulse array of magazine covers. Pouty boys leapt out at him. And then on a spinning rack the new tunes from I Divi. And the longer he stared at the drool case, the more *live* they seemed. Duke flexed and showed his tough, hairy exterior while Carlo bent over to reveal his more sensitive side. Gianni implored his undivided attention with his cupped hands, while behind his back Lorenzo engaged in non-stop horseplay. And Pico didn't give a fig what went down. And wasn't it wonderful of them to serenade an awestruck Grant Smith in line with a packet of Nicoteen Sixteens? Probably. Soon, they were all stripping down to show off their striped and bulging bathing suits. They dived into an enormous pool and splashed him playfully. And Grant Smith was shocked to see five bathing suits floating on the surface of the water. Carlo kissed and caressed him gently while Duke performed a perfect reacharound. Gianni sang commonly rhyming vowels, instructing the others. Still, Pico didn't give a fig where the party took them.

"*Ah! creatura! / Dolce incanto! La vana tua paura / il trepido tuo pianto / ora sparirà!*"

Grant could not believe he was being physically exploited by I Divi. They were no castrati, no signor! One by one the aroused tenors rubbed against his ragdoll self, forming the perfect sandwich and treating him like a piece of Speck prosciutto. Carlo filled his mouth while Duke covered his rear. Meanwhile, Gianni made room of his own in perfect harmony with Carlo and Duke. And Lorenzo, the crazy one, leapt upon his back, driving him under the water. Deeper and deeper they drove him, until he was face to face with a dead sea of advertising campaigns. And at the bottom was a woman surrounded by turbid, brackish bubbles. She opened her arms to receive him in an eternal embrace, offering him more water for his lungs than he could ever want.

"Blub blub blub ..."

"*Ma come son, rimango / chè l'oro non può dare / la felicità!*"

And still, Pico didn't give a fig.

Water, Water Everywhere

Before long, the impatient crowd at the Save-U-Quick had formed a crude feral society and a new micro-economy based upon the possession of portable potables. Currently, the Hydraxes were winning their in-store battle with the Parches. With a threat of safety razors and insensitive shaving gel, they had managed to subdue their rivals and cold-medicate them into a twelve-hour drowse of disadvantage. For one thing, they were no longer able to work the forklift they had taken control of. However, there were rumours of a new cake-fed society forming in aisle seven with enough air fresheners to wipe everyone out ...

Watching the Watchers

On the planet Ragnarox, in a dialect of colonized Ang, a group of silicon life forms expressed their disgust.

"Phttt! This Loneliest Planet program is getting worse and worse!"

"What are those Ontario porn censors to do with the main storyline? I'm not sure I follow."

"It was based on another work, or loosely inspired by the made-for-blitscreen *Scarlet: A Revenge Tragedy* by Sally Good."

"The same director who brought us *Skanky Stank* ..."

"Those earth-huggers are so primitive. Who else would bother to produce a flick about interterrestrial clone sex? As if we don't get enough of that on the Thrube as is!"

"You sure kept your protables adhesitized to every transmatted!"

"Well, I did enjoy the first part."

"That's all down to Minor. He's the one to watch."

"Yeah, and he was sorely missed in this flip-off. This human-error gimmick just doesn't slice with me."

"No wait. In the first part, he got waxed by a time hole or something. And now he's just a universal phenom. Just waiting to get some more action ..."

"Then they might do a prequel ..."

"Aww phttt! I hate prequels."

The Food Chain (Mutant Edition)

Jim and Jin pranced through the nearest field of rotating mustard and EthicoX, appearing for all the world like a couple in a lonely landscape programmed into their respective genetic chimaeras. Perhaps the only remnant of their internal instructions was yet to be executed. They had hitchhiked to this remote spot with a trucker who had regaled them with tales of the old dustbowl and rum-running and the general suffering of a nation. They were starting over, where no one had been before. Except maybe the Vikings, the Natives, the Asiatic Jews and, of course, the Outer Lactesian colonists long before them. A crop of mutant butterflies landed upon the stalks of wheat with bloated bellies full of genetically altered corn known in the mobile lab business as *verdâtremaize*, or more colloquially, as *maze*.

Jim and Jin did not ask who had planted this vast expanse of clean-burning fuel. It was for them to enjoy and digest, just like the bloated butterflies and the absentee farmer and the friendly sort who had made his worst mistake in giving them a lift. It did not matter to them that in certain economic theories, a course of excessive consumption invariably led to similar forms of global macro-cannibalism. They were just riding the ratio of the curve and seeing where it would take them. And so, stuffed with Grade A fresh meat and slightly logy, they wandered off hand in hand, much in keeping with the manner of the final frame of a magnificent silent reel.

The Heartburn in Her Purse

Bébé Lala clicked her heels across the parquet floor of the post office. She adjusted her toque nervously and looked around through drug-dealer mom wraparounds. And then, after kissing it for luck, she turned the key and placed a bubble envelope inside postal box 33314. She had retrieved the contents of the envelope from the belly of a vacuum as instructed ... by the only man she would ever love. A postal person passed with a meat-sniffing beagle in tow. It began sniffing at her heels excitedly.

"Must be the Heartburn in my purse. The Heartburn sandwich, that is!"

"He likes you."

"Could I just borrow that for a quick sec?"

She accepted the pen and splayed the stunned fellow against the row of mailboxes, using his back as a makeshift writing surface.

> Dearest D,
>
> May your life be more charmed and full of magic than mine has been. I mean that really. Girl, give 'em hell. And chin up. We have more than minor expectations for you!
>
> XOXOX
>
> Aunt Bébé
>
> P.S. If you're ever in a tight spot for a whack of cash, get in touch with Cecil Linton. XXX.

She tossed in an entire brick of her personal stash and a publicity snap for good measure. Then she locked postal box 33314 and rose from the fellow who had so amiably served as a footstool. He let out a low sigh of relief tinged with bittersweet regret. Had he truly lived?

"Miss, don't I know you?"

She popped a signed publicity snap in his mouth and walked away without a word.

Off the Lead, On the Lead

On the frozen planet Lagopus, to the sound of *Wachet auf, ruft uns die Stimme*, Faustus (otherwise known universally as Nano Nine) trotted with confidence along a red carpet toward a purple pedestal. The local inhabitants growled restlessly under their breath. True, their last leader had been a herd-turfer. But at least they had known what to expect. And besides, they weren't sure how to feel about the new administration. Could this upstart prime consul actually revive their faltering economy? And what if after assuming the post, he disbanded the republic and declared himself emperor? The last thing they needed was a demagogue dog. And they hadn't expected this lavish coronation, for starters. The murmurs continued as Nano Nine reached the new royal podium and faced the crowd with his nose held high.

Silence. He barked once. Then twice.

The entire crowd burst into applause.

Acknowledgements

For my growing Talonbooks family, always there for my picaresque whims with a meat sandwich, a lemon tart, a bag of coffee, a bag of taffy, a ride to Roman style pizza and a kind word: Kevin, Vicki and Spencer Williams, Gregory Gibson, Ann-Marie Metten and Lucia Frangione.

Also, heaps of thanks to Leslie Thomas Smith for his brilliant book cover idea and exceptional design. And thanks to Maureen Nicholson for her keen-eyed assistance and thoughtful scrutiny.

Thank you, Michael Barnholden, Jonathan Ball, Nicholas Hauck, Carmen Papalia, Aubyn Rader, Missy Clarkson, Amanda Joy Ivings, Thor Polukoshko, Elliot Lummin and Brook Houglum for having the foresight and futuristic gumption to publish unexpurgated splices of *The Chaos! Quincunx* series. Kudos to *West Coast Line*, *dANDelion Magazine*, *Memewar*, *The Maynard* and *The Capilano Review*.

And thank you, in some Hegelian notion of eternal due process, Karl Siegler, for your stalwart support of my experimental fiction and for putting up with more of my episodes …